FRIENDS AND LOVERS
IN BLACK AND WHITE

To Linda —
all the best —

Alfred Quoton Kerry
12/1/07

FRIENDS AND LOVERS IN BLACK AND WHITE

a novel

Altomease Rucker Kennedy

iUniverse, Inc.
New York Lincoln Shanghai

Friends and Lovers in Black and White
a novel

iUniverse books may be ordered through booksellers or by contacting:

iUniverse
2021 Pine Lake Road, Suite 100
Lincoln, NE 68512
www.iuniverse.com
1-800-Authors (1-800-288-4677)

This is a work of fiction. All of the characters, names, incidents, organizations, and dialogue in this novel are either the products of the author's imagination or are used fictitiously.

ISBN-13: 978-0-595-41773-5 (pbk)
ISBN-13: 978-0-595-86116-3 (ebk)
ISBN-10: 0-595-41773-6 (pbk)
ISBN-10: 0-595-86116-4 (ebk)

Printed in the United States of America

To the memory of my parents, Henry and Emma Rucker; my husband, Henry; my daughters, Morgan and Alexandra; and my sister, Bonita.

1965 TO 1966

Chapter 1

Jennifer Madison

Do blacks and whites want to be friends? Jennifer sat in the backseat of her parents' Buick as the three drove south to Baltimore and silently contemplated the question. All the way from Detroit she pondered her decision to become one of two black girls in the freshman class at Goucher College. She knew Baltimore wasn't Little Rock, with scores of whites yelling "nigger, go home." But …

Outside the car window she saw a sign that read MASON-DIXON LINE, causing her heart to beat a little faster. "Mom, see that sign?"

Gloria said to her husband, "Ron, look at that. Black folks worked hard to get north of that line, and now here we are driving our baby south of the Mason-Dixon Line." Gloria followed this statement with a guttural sound indicating the family's complexity of emotions.

Ron tightened his grip on the steering wheel. "Times are changing. Black folks don't have to be afraid of that line anymore."

"Maybe not the line, but what it represented: the separation of North and South, free versus slave. Remember those trips down South when we packed fried chicken, deviled eggs, and sweet potato pie? We didn't do that just because we liked fried chicken! We did it because we knew the white-only restaurants wouldn't serve us."

"Of course, I remember," Ron said. "That's what I'm talking about. Times are changing."

Jennifer laughed, attempting to keep the fear and skepticism out of her voice. "Mom, you're living in the past. Slavery's over."

Gloria turned to look at her beautiful eighteen-year-old daughter. Jennifer could see the pride swell in her mother's heart as she gazed at her caramel-colored skin, darker than her mother's, and the high cheekbones inherited from her daddy. Jennifer knew that her mother thought she was smart and hard-working, but she anticipated the warning.

"Sweetheart, you're right. Slavery's over. Nobody's been lynched lately, but racism is *not* dead. Be careful. Watch those white folks. They'll be watching you. They're just waiting for you to mess up."

Ron growled in his deep bass voice, which Jennifer knew was powerful and scary to others; to her, however, it was merely the wonderful sound made by her adoring daddy. "Gloria, please stop trying to scare my baby. It's a new day, and I'm glad to see it."

Gloria shot back, "You know good and well that I'm not trying to scare Jennifer. I'm just trying to prepare her. I want her to be ready for the cold stares from the white girls, who'll look at her like they've never seen a Negro before, or from the professors, who, while attempting to be friendly, will end up being condescending and patronizing. I just want Jennifer to be ready to handle all of the ignorant stuff."

Not wanting to increase her parents' anxiety, Jennifer disguised her apprehension and stifled the scream threatening to emerge from her throat. "I know, Mom. Don't worry. I'll be fine." With her decision to attend Goucher College, Jennifer knew that she had voluntarily entered the civil rights movement as a foot soldier in that new black battalion called "the only black" or "the first black." She felt she was carrying the hopes and dreams of all black people on her shoulders. She surmised that when her white classmates first looked at her, they would see only her black face. She hoped that one day they would see her.

Leslie Cohen

The 1965 white Lincoln Continental with red leather interior was crammed with shoes and boots, sweaters, skirts, bell-bottoms, and jeans representing Leslie's fall wardrobe, which she and her mother, Sue, had painstakingly purchased from Saks Fifth Avenue, Bonwit Teller, and Bloomingdale's.

Leslie removed her sunglasses and placed them on top of her head so that her long blond hair no longer cascaded across her face. "College is going to be so much fun."

"I know you're going to have a great time, and Hopkins Medical School is nearby."

"I'm not going to get sick."

"Who's talking about being sick? I'm talking about med students. Potential husbands."

Leslie sighed, "Oh, Mom." It disappointed her that her mother envisioned her marrying a doctor, whereas she envisioned a career in journalism.

Squinting through her cat-eye sunglasses at the blinding sunlight, Sue said, "Sweetheart, I'm only thinking of your future. Imagine … the wife of a Hopkins doctor."

Leslie grinned at her mother and then said emphatically, "I'm going to be a journalist, not a doctor's wife."

"That's what I meant: the journalist wife of a Jewish Hopkins doctor!"

Paige Wyatt

The black limousine pulled onto the campus. The chauffeur asked, "Miss Paige, where are you living this year?"

From the backseat, Paige's voice reflected her exasperation: "Thomas, how many times have I told you not to call me 'Miss Paige'? It's just Paige. I'm not my mother." She silently vowed that she would never be just some rich man's wife. "You may call my mother 'Mrs. Wyatt,' because she would probably faint if you called her anything else, but I'm just 'Paige.' The world's changing. Everyone's equal. Who cares if my family was one of the four hundred who fit inside of Mrs. Vanderbilt's ballroom? That world is over." Paige understood that her mother was stuck in the fifties, but she flagrantly rebelled against the old-fashioned traditions to which she had been born.

"I'm sorry, Miss Paige." Thomas coughed and then corrected himself. "Paige. Old habits are hard to break."

"Yes, they are. I'm living the same place as last year: Stimson Hall."

This was the third year that Thomas had driven from the Wyatt estate in Greenwich, Connecticut, to Goucher College. In her freshman year, her mother and her mother's maid accompanied her. In her sophomore year, only the maid came to set up Paige's room, as her mother was traveling in France. This year, Thomas was alone, Paige having convinced her mother that it was downright embarrassing having the maid assist her. Thomas pulled the limo onto the circular drive and opened the rear door for Paige. Dressed in ripped jeans and a tie-dyed T-shirt that read STOP THE WAR, Paige led the way to her room, while the elderly chauffeur struggled behind with her Louis Vuitton trunk.

Chapter 2

Jennifer—Leslie—Paige

As Ron turned into the college entrance, a black limo passed him. "I wonder who that belongs to?"

Gloria said, "Some rich white folks."

Jennifer noted the hostile edge to her mother's voice. She wondered, as she stared out the window at the beautiful dogwood trees lining the road to campus, what kind of girl got driven to college in a limo.

Gloria added, "Look at this campus. All of this grass and trees. Boy, white folks been having it good for a long time."

Ron shot his wife a look and said, "Gloria, stop!"

"Stop what?"

Ignoring his wife, Ron asked, "Jennifer, what's the name of the dorm?"

"Stimson Hall, Daddy."

Ron pulled in front of a modern building with a stone, wood, and glass facade and parked behind a white Lincoln Continental.

They proceeded up the steps to the second floor, where they found two paper flowers taped to the door. Underneath the red flower, in bold script, someone had written JENNIFER MADISON; LESLIE COHEN had been written under the yellow flower. Jennifer tapped softly on the slightly ajar door and walked in, her parents following close behind. A girl with long, shapely legs and an older woman were hanging clothes in the closet. The girl turned in response to their entrance. Despite the stifling Baltimore heat, she looked gorgeous. She gulped when she saw Jennifer. Quickly recovering, she smiled broadly and hugged Jennifer. "Great to meet you, roomie. I'm Leslie. We're going to have so much fun!"

Startled by the embrace, Jennifer mumbled, "Yeah. Fun."

Leslie, flashing her radiant smile at Jennifer's parents, turned to the older woman with flaming red hair and introduced her to the newcomers. "This is my mom."

Sue, taking each of them by the hand, said, "Nice to meet you. The girls are going to have so much fun!"

Gloria retracted her hand and nodded. "Fun? Fun is not why they're here. I expect Jennifer to study hard and graduate." Gloria turned to her husband and said, "Ron, let's go back down to the car and get Jennifer's things. Come on, Jennifer." Once they were out of earshot, Gloria whispered to Ron, "Do you believe the color of that woman's hair? I thought I was talking to *I Love Lucy*."

Ron responded in as modulated a tone as his bass voice would permit, "Gloria, she seems nice."

"She had the entire Max Factor line of cosmetics on her face," Gloria sniffed.

"Mom, she was being very kind."

"False eyelashes! My God! We'll see. I like Leslie, though. Pretty. Sweet. Seems nice."

Gloria and Jennifer returned to the room with a desk lamp and typewriter. Ron carried Jennifer's suitcase up the stairs, his forehead covered in sweat. Sue looked at him and said, "It really is hot down here. It's never this hot in New York in September."

Ron put the suitcase down, wiped his brow, agreed that it was hot, and headed back to the car.

Gloria said to Sue, "It's usually not this hot in Detroit in September, either."

"But, I remember two years ago, at the March on Washington, it was so hot, I thought I was going to collapse," Sue said. "I sat down, took off my shoes, and dangled my bare feet in the reflecting pool when Dr. King was speaking."

Pursing her lips, Gloria questioned, "*You* were at the *march*?"

"I organized a group from my synagogue in Scarsdale."

"Ron and I were at the march, too, with a group from our church."

When Gloria returned to the car, she was genuinely smiling. "Ron, that Cohen woman was at the March on Washington. How 'bout that?"

"I told you she seemed nice."

"You're right again, honey. Jennifer will be all right here."

❦   ❦   ❦

After their parents departed, Jennifer and Leslie continued to unpack. As Jennifer placed her high school yearbook on the bookshelf over her desk, Leslie asked to see it.

Jennifer started flipping pages. "That's me with my varsity cheerleading team."

Leslie screamed. "I was a varsity cheerleader!"

"That's me at the National Honor Society induction ceremony." Jennifer was glad to have the opportunity to point this out, as she hoped to undermine any thoughts Leslie might have about how she'd gotten into college.

"I was in the National Honor Society, too."

Pointing to a photo, Jennifer said, "That's my boyfriend. He was the pitcher for the baseball team."

Leslie nudged Jennifer in the side with her elbow. "Cute. Where does he go?"

"Cornell."

"Great school." Leslie jumped up and grabbed her yearbook from her desk. "This is me with the varsity cheerleaders. This is me with the senior class officers. I was vice president. And this is my former boyfriend. He was student council president. We broke up two weeks before prom!" Leslie went to her desk and picked up a framed photograph. "Two weeks. It was awful. But this is my prom picture."

"You look beautiful. Who was your prom date?"

"Thanks. Real sweetheart. Danny Eisenberg. He's just a friend. Danny's a sophomore at Princeton. He saved my life."

The roommates flipped through each other's yearbooks, laughing and telling stories about themselves in high school, with Jennifer noting that there were many similarities between the two schools. Both were large coed public schools, but there were no black students at Leslie's suburban school, whereas Jennifer's school comprised a mix of blacks and whites, two Puerto Ricans, and three Chinese. Looking through Leslie's yearbook, Jennifer assumed that she was probably the first black person Leslie had ever known.

Looking at Jennifer, Leslie said, "We're about the same size. We can borrow each other's clothes. This is going to be so great being roomies!"

Jennifer, with a quizzical expression, said, "You want us to borrow each other's clothes?"

"Of course … that's what roommates do," Leslie said in her high-spirited voice.

Jennifer couldn't wait to tell her grandma that Leslie wanted them to borrow each other's clothes. She knew her grandma would probably retell the story about why she still refused to shop at Bond's Department Store. Jennifer remembered her grandmother's anger and humiliation as she explained that when she first moved to Detroit in the 1930s, Bond's wouldn't let black people try on the clothes. As Jennifer remembered this story, she said, "Of course … that's what roommates do." Jennifer felt grateful for Leslie's offer but hated feeling grateful. She also appreciated that although they were the same height, Leslie had wide white-girl hips and a flat butt while she had a roundly protruding behind, which meant that the same size 6 would not necessarily fit them both. Although they had a lot in common, Jennifer understood that the significant difference, besides the shape of their butts, was that she was black and Leslie was white and this was 1965 in America.

"So, what kind of music do you like?" Jennifer asked, fearing the answer.

"I *love* the Beatles. I was at the *Ed Sullivan Show* when they first came to America."

"You're kidding. You were in the audience?"

"I was right there screaming my head off. Couldn't talk by the time the show was over."

"I saw the show on TV. I love the Motown groups. I also love classical music. I play the violin."

"Classical music? You really like that stuff?"

Jennifer, unsure if she should be insulted, explained, "I played with the Detroit high school symphony orchestra, and we played mostly classical music. Some Broadway show tunes."

Leslie laughed. "My mother will love you. She tried to make me learn an instrument, but I wouldn't do it. Boring. How about the Beach Boys?"

Jennifer winced. "No Beach Boys. Definitely *Gidget* music."

"What's *Gidget* music?"

Jennifer dubbed the music played during those teen beach movies—when all of the white teenagers were wiggling around and surfing, without a black person in sight—as *Gidget* music. She wasn't ready to share this definition, which spoke of more than the sound of the music, with her white roommate just yet, so she merely said, "California surfing music."

"Oh, I get it. The movie *Gidget*." Leslie asked, "How about Johnny Mathis?"

Jennifer happily moaned, "I love Johnny Mathis." She looked at her watch. "It's almost four. We're supposed to meet in the dining room for our first orientation session."

"You're right. I forgot the time. Let's go." Leslie opened the door to their room just as two girls from across the hall opened their door, and she introduced herself.

The girls said a timid hello as they stared at Jennifer. "And this is my roommate, Jennifer Madison."

Jennifer smiled, having noted the slight hint of confusion on their faces when they saw her black one; once again she let it go because they quickly rearranged their expressions to friendly ones.

Oblivious to Jennifer's momentary discomfort, Leslie, with the sound of perpetual joy in her voice, which Jennifer thought could easily become annoying, led them to the orientation session. More girls joined their group along the way, with Leslie continually making introductions.

Upon reaching the dining room, Jennifer methodically scanned the room and saw only white faces.

❦   ❦   ❦

Paige stood at the podium; her long, mousy brown hair was carelessly parted in the middle and hung past her shoulders. Wire-rimmed granny glasses were perched on her small, straight nose. Her face was without makeup, and she wore a black T-shirt with white lettering that read MAKE LOVE, NOT WAR. She was not wearing a bra, as evidenced by the sharp protrusion of her D-cup nipples. The frayed edges of her bell-bottoms dragged the floor. In an unexpectedly sexy yet strident voice, she said, "Welcome, freshmen! Goucher College class of 1969!"

At first, there was silence; then Leslie jumped up, clapping and screaming, "Yeah, class of '69! …'69! …'69!" Leslie waved her arms, encouraging the other girls to join her. The room erupted, and all of the girls started shouting, "'69!" with Leslie leading the chant. When the girls took their seats, Paige began, "It's my pleasure to welcome you to Goucher College and Stimson Hall. Goucher is a place that takes women seriously. This college was founded in 1885 for the sole purpose of educating women at a time when most girls didn't even receive a primary school education. You will be intellectually challenged by the professors and each other. I know that you didn't come to college just to get an MRS degree." Boos rang out. Paige continued, "That's right. You're more than that.

You are the women who will one day lead the world and not merely be some-one's *wife*. But right now, you're here at Stimson Hall, and we're your dorm family. I'm going to outline some of the rules, and then you'll meet your Big Sister, an upperclassman, who throughout your freshman year will be the girl you can go to when you have questions about anything: classes, professors, majors, activities, life"—Paige paused dramatically—"boys!"

Leslie yelled, "Yes, boys!" Others joined in. Jennifer silently wondered if there were any black boys nearby who would ever find her at Goucher College. She assumed the white boys would ignore her or try to make her their black experience. She had already promised her mother that she wouldn't capitulate to such efforts.

❧   ❧   ❧

Paige, assigned as Leslie's Big Sister, looked at Leslie's flawless, lightly tanned skin, long blond hair, and white shorts and smiled slowly as she wondered how she, the class of '67's resident radical hippie, could have been assigned to this Jewish American princess. When Paige shook Leslie's hand, she saw the con-trast between her own chewed nails and Leslie's perfectly manicured pink nails. "Leslie, where are you from?"

"Scarsdale."

Paige pictured the middle-class Jewish suburbs of Westchester County. "Ah, Scarsdale. I'm from Connecticut. Where did you go to school?"

Flashing her brilliant smile, Leslie said, "Scarsdale High. Where did you go?"

"Miss Porter's."

Leslie squealed, "Oh, you went to boarding school! That's where Jackie Kennedy went."

Preferring not to discuss her debutante past, Paige asked, "Do you have any idea about your major?"

Without a moment's hesitation, Leslie said, "English. My plan is to be a journalist."

Now Paige understood why she had been assigned the princess. "I work on the school newspaper. Would you be interested in joining the staff?"

"I was a reporter for my high school paper."

"I'll take you over to the newspaper office and introduce you. If you need anything, anything at all, let me know."

While the other freshmen were meeting their Big Sisters, Jennifer had yet to find hers, so Paige pointed her out. Jennifer approached Madeline Drummond, who briefly looked at her and then purposefully looked away and continued talking. Jennifer waited. Madeline ended her conversation and started to walk away, but Jennifer followed her and introduced herself. Madeline's expression was devoid of warmth. Not easily deterred, Jennifer continued, "I'm from Detroit. Where are you from?"

Madeline sighed audibly. "Grosse Pointe. Guess they put us together because we're from the same state."

Jennifer emitted a nervous laugh and said, "Guess so."

"Well, if you have any questions, give me a call."

Before Jennifer could respond, Madeline walked away. She said, "OK," to Madeline's departing back, concluding that she was either rude or racist. Seeing as Madeline was from a wealthy Detroit suburb, Jennifer assumed she was rude.

Chapter 3

Jennifer

The Freshman Bonfire was held at Donnybrook Park, a meadow dotted with large oak trees on the northern edge of campus between the tennis courts and the stables. Many girls had lost their virginity under a Donnybrook tree. After the dorm meeting, as the freshmen walked toward Donnybrook for the evening's sing-along, Jennifer saw a black face in the crowd and, turning to Leslie, said, "I'll meet you down there."

The black girl saw Jennifer and ran to meet her. They embraced like long-lost relatives. Jennifer introduced herself to Sharon Curtis, a freshman from Atlanta. "You're the first black face, other than my own, my parents', and a janitor's, that I've seen since I got here."

"There's a black senior in my dorm. She's my Big Sister. Really nice. From Philadelphia."

"Lucky you." Jennifer grimaced. "My Big Sister took one look at my black face and said as she was walking away from me, 'Call me if you have any questions.' I don't think she really wants me to call her. It's such a relief to see you. We're supposed to sit with our dorm. See ya later." Jennifer looked around Donnybrook Park and located Leslie and the rest of the Stimson freshmen.

When Jennifer rejoined the Stimson group, Leslie said, "I didn't know you knew anyone on campus."

"I don't."

"I just saw you hug that girl."

With a look of slight embarrassment, as if some secret had been exposed, Jennifer explained, "We just met. Soul sisters."

"Soul sisters?" Leslie looked momentarily confused. "Oh, I get it."

After singing a dozen silly songs, eating hot dogs, hamburgers, brownies, and being taught the revered school song written by the class of 1902, the bonfire ended, and the freshmen wandered back to their dorms.

Jennifer collapsed on her bed and unfolded a paper napkin. Leslie asked, "What's that?"

"A brownie. I love brownies."

Leslie giggled and said, "Me, too. Give me a piece." Jennifer broke the brownie in half and gave it to Leslie, who moaned with pleasure as she popped it into her mouth.

※   ※   ※

At the end of September, Paige coordinated a meeting to recruit volunteers to work in a variety of community programs.

As they walked down the stairs of the dimly lit Kraushaar Auditorium, Jennifer whispered to Sharon, "What are they looking at? They act like they've never seen a black person before." As a result of the surreptitious glances and some outright stares from her classmates, Jennifer felt as if a spotlight was shining on her.

Sharon shrugged and said, "Well, you gotta admit, they haven't seen many of us here."

"I know that there are only eight of us on campus, but I hate being stared at. I'm tired of it!"

"Jen, get over it," Sharon groaned. "They're going to look. You had to know that when you came here. Or you should have known it. At least they're not throwing anything. Hey, and some of these girls are not even thinking about you. You're not on the backside of their minds. That's your own discomfort talking."

Jennifer shot a thankful look at Sharon. "You're right. I feel uncomfortable. I should be thankful for stares. It could be a lot worse."

Leslie called out to Jennifer and Sharon, and motioned for them to come and sit next to her.

Jennifer turned to Sharon. "Wouldn't you know that Miss Blondie would be in the front row? That girl knows she belongs up front."

A white woman in her fifties, a young white man, and a young black man were seated on the stage with Paige.

Leslie whispered to Jennifer, "I was talking to Paige in the newspaper office today. She's amazing. You wouldn't believe how many antiwar marches she's been to."

Jennifer asked, "Has she been to any civil rights marches?"

Leslie shook her head. "Don't know."

Jennifer whispered to Sharon, "I saw that black guy on campus last week with Paige, and he doesn't work on the janitorial crew or in the kitchen."

"He's cute," Sharon whispered back as the room quieted.

"I'm Paige Wyatt, campus coordinator of community programs. I also run the Big Sisters program in East Baltimore, a section of the city with a high concentration of public housing and crime. Our purpose is to act as role models to young girls who've been born into lives that present them with harsh daily challenges. We bring the girls out to campus for picnics, take them on field trips, and just spend time with them. It's about becoming friends"—Paige paused—"becoming sisters. I hope some of you will be interested in participating. I now would like to introduce Eric Crawford."

The tall, lanky black man with a large Afro stood up. He flashed a devilish smile. With his Southern drawl, he said, "Hey, glad to see y'all tonight. I'm the director of the Baltimore Tutorial Project, better known as BTP. It's a tutoring program for inner-city elementary school kids. Baltimore's inner-city schools are overcrowded, not like Goucher with the small classes you guys have out here. My kids need some individual attention. They need encouragement. They're smart, but too many of them think school doesn't matter, that they're nobody. BTP's goal is to let them know that they do matter, that school is important, and that they can do the work if they try. We like the Goucher tutors to come down to the project every Wednesday night. Goucher provides a bus to take you guys back and forth. Do your own thing. Help the kid with reading or arithmetic or any other homework assignment. Hey, we're flexible. My goal is to provide my kids with extra tutoring."

The next speaker was the middle-aged matron in a gray tweed suit and sensible pumps. She requested volunteers to work with the Junior League at the Johns Hopkins Hospital.

Peter Chapin, a VISTA worker, spoke next. He was handsome with long dark-brown curls, heavy eyebrows that almost met in the middle, and a reddish brown beard and mustache that overpowered his ruddy face. He started to speak, at first in a rambling, disjointed manner and then more methodically. His voice was reminiscent of President Kennedy's. Once he started to speak, Jennifer could see pink lips hinting of hidden sensuality, which belied his lean, wiry body. "The VISTA Community Center is a place of refuge for many poor people, adults and children, in East Baltimore. You came here tonight to volunteer. Do you really know why you should volunteer?" Peter stood up abruptly, thrusting his hands into the pockets of his well-worn blue jeans. He paced slowly back and forth and then stopped and turned to face the audience. "I'm going to tell you why. You are sitting out here in the luxurious isolation that Goucher College provides. You leisurely stroll back and forth to class across this lush, green campus with its beautiful trees, and you think all is right with the world. If you never leave this campus, all *is* right with the world—your little world. But let me tell you, there's a bigger world out there and"—Peter paused, glowering at the audience, and then began to speak in staccato fashion—"all is not right with that world. It stinks. It's rotten, and it's not going away. And you cannot tiptoe around it. You can do something about it." Peter lowered his voice, and it became an apologetic whine. "I'm just like you; that's how I know you have the ability to care. Together, we can make a difference. Unlike our parents, who hide in the suburbs and pretend that all is right with America while they sip martinis, we see the despair, inequality, and suffering in our country and around the world. Together, we can make America a better place. I need your help. We can do it together."

The audience applauded enthusiastically, but Jennifer questioned whether her classmates had really been listening. She already knew that all was not right with the world, because she had been born black in America.

Paige stood up, looked at Peter adoringly, and said, "Thanks, Peter. I think you've presented all of us with a real challenge to make America a better place."

Leslie poked Jennifer in the side and said, "They're going out. Look at the way she looks at him!"

"If you're interested in participating in any of these programs," Paige said, "the speakers are available to answer your individual questions, and you can sign up to volunteer. Thank you for coming."

As the meeting ended, Jennifer suggested to Leslie, "I'm going to volunteer for the Big Sisters program. Let's do it together."

"OK," Leslie replied. "It could be fun."

Allison, a freshman from Vermont, who lived down the hall from Leslie and Jennifer, announced, "I'm volunteering for the Junior League project at Hopkins Hospital."

"I bet you think you're going to meet a med student and get your MRS degree," Leslie teased.

Allison's eyes glistened as she said, "Maybe even an intern, or better yet, a resident."

Sharon chimed in, "I'm eventually going to marry a doctor just like my daddy; but in the meantime, I'm signing up for BTP."

"Sharon, I think you're signing up for Eric Crawford," Jennifer commented with an impish grin.

"Exactly. He looks dangerous. My mother would die if she thought I even spoke to anybody like him."

"Can you see him at a Jack and Jill party?" Jennifer asked.

"Of course not," Sharon responded. "Another good reason to sign up."

Leslie asked, "What's Jack and Jill?"

"It's a private social club for black kids."

"Hmm ... I've never heard of it," Leslie admitted. "Are you and Sharon members?"

"Yes."

Looking confused, Leslie questioned, "Why wouldn't Eric be at a Jack and Jill party?"

Not taking the time to explain the black social strata, Jennifer said, "It's *private*." Jennifer then whispered in Sharon's ear so that Leslie couldn't hear her. "Only in 1965 would you see Eric Crawford with his big Afro sitting next to that lady. Just a few years ago, she would have refused to sit next to that Afro. She still won't invite him to dinner ... or us either."

Sharon, who was blessed with flawless chocolate brown skin and a curvaceous body, smiled mischievously at Jennifer. "You're right; but right now, I'm going to introduce myself to Eric."

Jennifer grabbed Sharon's hand and said, "Slow down. He's the first black man you've seen in a couple of weeks who doesn't work in the kitchen or on the janitorial staff. You might be overreacting because of our black man deprivation. He may be our color, but not our kind."

Smiling wickedly, Sharon declared, "I'm going to find out what kind he is." Sharon sauntered over to Eric. He looked up from the table, eyes hesitating at her breasts. His devilish grin reappeared.

"Where do I sign up?" she asked.

Eric stuttered, "Wha ... wha ... what did you say?"

Sharon thrust out her breasts and repeated her question. He slid the sign-up sheet toward her. Several other girls came up to Eric and started asking questions about BTP, so Sharon started to move away, but Eric reached out and touched her hand, motioning to her to stay as he continued to respond to the other students' questions. "Let's go to the Gopher Hole when I'm finished here." The stutter had disappeared. Sharon nodded her agreement and moved away to wait for Eric as more girls signed up for BTP. From the long line of girls waiting to volunteer, BTP appeared to be a popular program, though the main reason was probably that unkempt Afro.

Peter, after answering questions and signing up volunteers, stopped by Eric's table and told him that he could find him at the Gopher Hole. Eric raised his clenched fist in agreement. Peter put his arm around Paige's waist and pulled her to him. He whispered in her ear, "Thanks. You pulled together a good crowd." He then rubbed his hand slowly up and down her back before putting his arm around her shoulder.

"That was a very honest and challenging presentation. I'm sure it made a lot of the girls really think about their lives. It certainly made me think."

"I really didn't know what I was going to say when I first started talking. But I looked out at those faces, and I just had to remind them that the whole world is not as perfect as their Goucher world. I wanted to shake 'em up, to get rid of that complacency. It's 1965. America is changing."

"You're right. You're really passionate about what you do! Intense. I like that."

"I guess you could call it passion." Peter combed his beard with his fingers. "My father called it lunacy. That's when I stopped talking to him."

"I don't talk to my father either."

"Why not?"

"He's an arrogant, selfish SOB who cheated on my mother and thinks his money can buy my love and respect."

Peter squeezed Paige's shoulder as she slid her arm around his waist. "My father's a rich SOB, too."

Paige invited Leslie to join them at the snack bar. Leslie asked Jennifer and Allison to come along. As they headed for the Gopher Hole, Leslie explained as they followed Paige and Peter up the path, "They've been sorta dating since last spring. She met him at an abortion rally. One of the girls on the paper told me that Paige is a descendant of Abigail Adams, the first first lady to live in the White House." Leslie's eyes followed Paige, whose lifeless brown hair drooped over her shoulders, covering the embroidered design across the top of her peasant blouse. Leslie shook her head with dismay as she watched Paige. "You'd never know by looking at Paige that she's old money."

Allison asked, "What do you mean, she's old money?"

"Her family can trace their heritage to the Mayflower. The family has had lots of money for a very long time."

Jennifer said nothing and thought that Paige's family had probably owned some of hers.

The three girls joined Paige and Peter and ordered coffee. Jennifer asked Peter, "What made you decide to become a VISTA worker?"

"That's easy. I was searching for a way to do some good."

Paige interjected, "Peter worked with SNCC, the Student Nonviolent Coordinating Committee in Alabama, before joining VISTA."

Eric and Sharon pulled up chairs and joined them just as Jennifer said, "I'm impressed. Peter, tell me about your time with SNCC."

Between sips of black coffee, he said, "SNCC is doing some really courageous things in the South. Lunch counter sit-ins. I did voter registration. That's where I met Eric. We worked together in Alabama."

"My cousin is a member of SNCC," Sharon offered. "He's working in Georgia, where I'm from."

"My parents are life members of the NAACP," Jennifer added. "My dad always says how important the voter registration movement is. The laws are on the books, but Southern black folks are still frightened, and they have good reason to be. I guess you saw that."

Eric drawled, "I can dig that. We saw that every day. Some black folks wouldn't even let us come into their homes. They were really scared."

Peter nodded in agreement. "The murders of those three civil rights workers in Mississippi only made things worse."

Jennifer shuddered and looked at Peter and Eric. "You guys were risking your lives every day."

Peter said, "We tried not to think about it. We knew the South was a dangerous and scary place. But the work was too important."

"The South offends me," Jennifer explained, without any attempt to hide her anger. "I remember visiting my grandmother in Georgia when I was little and seeing the colored water fountains." Jennifer inquired, "Paige, have you ever been South?"

Paige said, "Oh, yes. My family always goes to Palm Beach between Christmas and New Year's."

Jennifer announced in an exasperated tone, "Paige, Palm Beach is not the South!"

Paige shot back, "Of course it is. Florida's a southern state."

Jennifer explained, "Paige, we were talking about SNCC. We're talking about the small towns and rural areas of such southern states as Georgia, Alabama, and Mississippi, the kind of places where Peter and Eric were doing voter registration—not some wealthy resort area where black people don't live and only a few work."

Paige countered Jennifer's exasperation with condescension. "Oh, I see. Well, if that is your limited definition of the South, then no, I have not been there."

"I didn't think so." Jennifer wanted to like this girl, but she believed she was just one of those phony liberals mouthing words about equality from the sanctity and security of her limo. Jennifer directed her gaze toward Peter. "How did you get involved in SNCC?"

"I was in college, not sure where I was going. My professor at Bowdoin was organizing a group to join the Freedom Riders—you know, white college kids to join black college kids to desegregate buses."

Jennifer said, "Great."

"After I got to Alabama, I stayed and started working on voter registration."

Jennifer turned to Eric, who was talking softly to Sharon. "How about you, Eric? How did you get to Alabama?"

"I was a student at North Carolina A&T. I started participating in lunch counter sit-ins and eventually voter registration."

"I really admire you guys. That's dangerous work." Jennifer admitted, "I don't know if I could have done it. As I watched marches and lunch counter sit-ins on TV, where black folks were being spat at or attacked by dogs or with fire hoses, I was very glad I was watching it all from the safety of my den in Detroit."

Chapter 4

Leslie

The week following the volunteers' meeting, Leslie walked into the room as Jennifer sat at her desk studying. "I got invited!"

Jennifer looked up and asked, "Invited to what?"

Leslie twirled around the room. "The mystery formal at Beta Tau Sig."

"What's Beta Tau Sig?"

Leslie looked at Jennifer as if she were deranged. "What is Beta Tau Sig? Only the best fraternity at Hopkins."

"Sorry. Never heard of it."

"Well, it's the Beta Tau Sig tradition to invite some freshmen girls at the beginning of the year to a party. They invite the girls based on our photo in the freshman book. You know, the pig book. Then they send limousines to pick us up and take us to the party. The guys will be in tails and top hats, and the girls are supposed to wear evening gowns. I've gotta call my mother and have her send my prom dress for the party."

"Sounds like quite a party."

Allison burst into the room. "I got an invitation to Beta Tau Sig!"

Leslie screamed, "Me, too!" and hugged Allison.

Allison stopped jumping up and down and asked Jennifer, "Did you get an invitation?"

"No. I guess the boys of Beta Tau Sig thought I was a real pig." What she really wanted to say was that the white boys of Beta whatchamacallit thought she was a *black* pig.

"Oh, Jennifer. That's ridiculous," Leslie declared. "There is no way anyone could think that you were a pig. No one knows how they make the selections. That's a big secret, but it's supposed to be a great party. I can't wait."

On the Saturday evening of the Beta Tau Sig mystery formal, Jennifer shuttled from room to room helping Leslie and Allison get dressed. As Jennifer zipped Leslie's strapless lavender gown, she said, "Leslie, you look great. I love the dress."

The buzzer rang. Leslie yelled, "I'm not ready. Jennifer, get that for me, please."

Jennifer pressed the buzzer and then ran down the hall to the phone. "Call for Leslie Cohen?"

"The Beta Tau Sig limo has arrived."

Jennifer followed Leslie and Allison to the lobby to get a look at the limo and the Beta Tau Sig frat boys. When they reached the lobby, girls in beautiful floor-length evening gowns were milling around. The front door opened, and two young men grandly entered, dressed in black top hats, white ties and tails, and red-and-white-striped boxers. They shouted, "Beta Tau Sig!" The girls laughed delightedly as they were escorted to the limos.

After the limos pulled away, Jennifer headed over to Sharon's dorm.

"Sharon, did you see the Beta Tau Sigs? Those white boys didn't have on pants!"

"Now we know what the mystery was. No pants!"

"Were you invited to the party?"

Sharon shook her head.

"Me, neither. According to Leslie, Beta Tau Sig is the best fraternity at Hopkins. I bet they don't have any black members."

"And they probably don't want any."

"Maybe." Jennifer paused. "Or they could have some brothers with snow fever who blackballed us."

"Blackballed the black sisters. Hmmm. Coulda happened. Most likely they just don't have any black members."

"The only fraternities I know are Omega Psi Phi, Alpha Phi Alpha, and the Kappas. My Dad's a Q."

Sharon screamed, "So's mine!" Sharon lowered her voice. "The dogs. Woof!"

"My dad does that barking thing, too! Drives my mother crazy."

❦   ❦   ❦

The limos parked in front of the fraternity house, and each girl was escorted from the limo by a frat brother and handed a glass of champagne. The fraternity president approached Leslie. Although he was wearing only boxers, a top hat, and tails, his manner was very dignified. "Leslie, it is my pleasure as president of Beta Tau Sig to welcome you to our fraternity house. You have been selected by the brothers to be Miss Beta Tau Sig for 1965."

Leslie was stunned. "Me?"

The president took Leslie's arm and escorted her to the stage. The band stopped playing when he walked to the microphone with Leslie by his side. "Brothers of Beta Tau Sig and our lovely guests. As president of Beta Tau Sig, I welcome you to our annual mystery formal. This party is a long-standing tradition. Each year, the brothers carefully review the Goucher College freshmen book, affectionately known by one and all as the pig book, and select the most beautiful of all of the freshmen to invite to this elegant evening. Naturally, no *pigs* are invited to Beta Tau Sig." There was loud laughter and a few oinks from the brotherhood. "Gentlemen, please, let me continue. As is our tradition, we honor the most beautiful of all of the beautiful Goucher freshmen with the title of Miss Beta Tau Sig. Miss Beta Tau Sig for 1965 is Leslie Cohen." The frat boys yelled, whistled, and clapped as a fraternity brother appeared and handed a dozen red roses to the president, who presented them to Leslie. She performed her best Miss America wave and beamed her dazzling smile to the entire frat and the assembled lesser beauties. The band started playing very loudly, and the party rocked with a throbbing beat and flowing champagne until 1:00 AM, when the limos arrived to drive the girls, many of whom were falling-down drunk for the first time in their lives, back to campus.

Leslie, followed by a stumbling Allison, walked into the darkened dorm room, where Jennifer was asleep. She flipped on the light and screamed, "I'm Miss Beta Tau Sig for 1965!"

Jennifer, awakened by the scream and the bright light, sat up in her bed. "What?" she said. Then she collapsed onto her pillow.

Leslie waved the roses in front of Jennifer's face. "I'm Miss Beta Tau Sig for 1965!"

"Congratulations, I guess. What's that?" Jennifer mumbled. "And why did you wake me up?"

Allison, slurring her words, announced, "Leslie was selected by the members of Beta Tau Sig as the most beautiful of all of the Goucher freshmen!"

Jennifer said, "My roommate is the most beautiful freshman." She paused dramatically and then asked, "Did they make the selection before or after they got drunk?"

Leslie fell back onto her bed laughing. Allison looked stunned and offended. Jennifer attempted to focus her sleepy eyes on Allison. "I was kidding. Where's your sense of humor? Leslie knows she's beautiful. I know she's beautiful, and now the frat boys of Beta Tau Sig made it official." Jennifer turned over and attempted to go back to sleep but couldn't. She understood one had to be white to be Miss Beta Tau Sig. Placing the pillow over her head, she still couldn't drown out Leslie's and Allison's drunken giggling or the voices in her head, which questioned her decision to become one of Goucher College's first black students.

Chapter 5

Paige

Paige, wearing her MAKE LOVE, NOT WAR T-shirt, without a bra as usual, left stacks of flyers all over campus announcing a peace march in downtown Baltimore. Leslie encountered her at the library placing a flyer on the door. "Hey, Paige, the Big Sisters' trip to the circus was a lot of fun. The little girls loved it. Can you believe that Tawanna, my Little Sister, and LaToya, Jennifer's Little Sister, had never been to a circus before?" Leslie pointed to the flyer. "What's going on?"

"An antiwar march next Friday afternoon protesting the increase in the number of troops in Vietnam. Peter and I are going. Wanna come along?"

"Sure. What should I wear?"

Paige, astounded by the question, said, "Who cares?"

❧   ❧   ❧

"You're not going to wear those to the march, are you?" Jennifer asked as she pointed to Leslie's pink Papagallo flats.

"I was planning on it."

"I think you'd be better off in tennis shoes."

"OK. I asked Paige what to wear, and she said, 'Who cares?'"

Jennifer grimaced. "I can't believe that you asked Paige, the official campus hippie, what to wear to an antiwar march. She probably thought you were crazy."

Paige, Peter, Jennifer, Leslie, and several of Peter's friends joined the march on St. Charles Street. As they approached the square, they could hear chants of "Out of Vietnam now!" and "No more war." They found places on the grass.

The sun was shining, and the aroma of marijuana wafted through the air. Some students were laughing, and others were talking and singing folk songs about peace and love. A priest went to the microphone. "Our young men are dying in the jungles of Vietnam. Each life has value. The question is, why are our young American soldiers being killed in this faraway land? For what? Is it worth their precious lives? I say no! War is not the answer. Now our government is coming after you! That's right, you! More young men are being drafted to fight this unjust war. Are you going to go? I say no to war. We won't go!"

The crowd joined in the chant. "We won't go! We won't go!" Peter jumped to his feet, encouraging all around him to join in. He reached down and took Paige's hand, helping her to her feet. She joined in the chant. "We won't go! We won't go!"

As the chanting reached a fevered pitch, a young man approached the microphone. At first he joined in the chant, and then he reached into his pocket; he held something in his hand and waved it above his head. "It's not enough for us to say that we won't go. In my hand, I hold my draft card that was issued to me, just like every other young American male, when I turned eighteen. This card says that the United States government can draft me at any time and make me go to Vietnam and fight a war I don't believe in." The young man struck a match and lit the draft card. He held the burning card above his head. "I won't go!"

The crowd was initially stunned by the action and then broke into a huge cheer as the card fluttered in ashen pieces to the ground.

When the rally ended, Leslie asked Peter, "What do you think will happen to him for burning his draft card?"

"It's against the law, but probably nothing will happen. It was just a symbolic act."

Paige grabbed Peter's hand. "I hope you won't be drafted."

"I won't." Peter put his arms around her and held her very close. "I'm one of the lucky ones. I've got a medical deferment. Bad hearing."

"I don't want to lose you."

In a voice etched with anger, Peter said, "But what about all of the poor guys who don't have deferments? If the pace of this war keeps up, they're going to have to go. I'm afraid for a lot of the young guys at the center. They're going to get drafted. These young black kids are going to get killed."

Paige asked, "Why do you say that?"

Jennifer spoke up. "The guys at the center aren't in college. So they're getting drafted. They're going to be cannon fodder."

"That's not right," Paige responded.

Peter looked first at Paige and then at Jennifer. "Of course it's unfair. Jennifer's right. College is going to protect the middle class, while the poor kids are going to get drafted. It's just another example of the inequality in our country."

Jennifer added, "And the problem is that there are a disproportionate number of poor black boys."

Paige turned to Jennifer and Leslie. "This stuff is scary. I'm glad I don't have to fight."

Jennifer couldn't resist adding, "And it's not your brother or friend who's going. Everybody you know is in college. Paige, the whole world does not go to college or have medical deferments."

Paige looked blankly at Jennifer and didn't respond as Peter took her hand and asked, "Are you coming back to my place?"

"Yeah. Hey, Leslie, why don't you write an article about the rally for the paper?"

♣   ♣   ♣

After climbing the steps to his attic room, Peter collapsed on the Indian batik coverlet, which was jumbled on top of the bare mattress; he pulled Paige down beside him. She stared at his closed eyes and said, "What are you thinking?"

"I'm thinking that this is a fucked-up world." Peter slid his arms around Paige. "And I'm thinking that I want to make love to you right now." He gently turned her onto her stomach and started slowly massaging her back.

"Scratch my back, puh-leeze."

"Whatever you want."

After they made love, Paige asked softly, "What are you thinking now?"

"I'm thinking that when I make love to you, the world is not as fucked-up as I thought." He led her to the tiny bathroom, which had the smallest shower Paige had ever seen. Peter turned on the water, and the pipes clanked harshly as he held one hand under the shower. "It sounds awful, but the water's hot." He pulled her into the shower and then proceeded to slowly lather her body with soap as he stood behind her and whispered her three favorite words: "I love you."

Chapter 6

Jennifer

On Friday night, when Sharon, Jennifer, Leslie, and Paige entered Peter's row house, music was blaring; the air was thick with cigarette smoke and reeked of marijuana.

Sharon searched the room for Eric while Leslie and Jennifer went to the kitchen for drinks.

"This is a different crowd," Leslie said as she sipped her beer.

Jennifer agreed, "This is definitely not a Hopkins frat party. So far, Miss Beta Tau Sig, people aren't throwing beer on each other or walking around in their boxer shorts."

Leslie laughed, "Well, that's no fun."

Paige joined them and introduced Fred Conaway, a long-haired VISTA worker. Fred took a long drag from his long-necked bottle. "I was just tellin' Paige about the money the city gave us for the center. Now we can stay open every evening. The kids need a place to go at night. They need to get out of those hellhole projects." Fred took another swig. "How can people expect kids to study in places like that? Now, they can study at the center. Hell, they can just find a quiet place. Everyone needs that every now and then."

"You know, most of us don't get that," Jennifer commented. "A whole lot of kids don't have quiet places in their homes to study."

"I always studied in my bedroom," Leslie said.

Paige chimed in, "Me, too. I have this wonderful antique chaise in my bedroom. I spent hours there reading."

Fred explained, "These kids don't have their own bedrooms."

❧   ❧   ❧

They followed Paige upstairs to Peter's room. A few people, including Eric and Sharon, sat around listening to the eerie electronic sounds of Ravi Shankar as incense permeated the air and a joint was passed around.

Peter offered the joint to Leslie, who said, "No thanks. We were just talking to Fred, and he told us about the grant. Congrats!"

Peter held the smoke in his lungs and then finally released it and said, "Thanks."

Leslie turned to Jennifer. "By the way, do you know what Tawanna told me?" She didn't wait for a response. "She said LaToya was disappointed when you were assigned to be her Big Sister." Leslie added hurriedly, "But she says that now LaToya really likes you."

Peter took another hit of the joint, and his facial expression did not lose its Zen-like placidity. Jennifer asked, "Do you know why she was disappointed?" She silently hoped that Leslie wasn't going to say what she thought she was going to say.

Leslie said, "Yes, I do. You're not going to like this. She wanted a white girl to be her Big Sister."

She'd said it. Jennifer blinked to fight the angry tears that welled in her eyes and then looked at Eric and Sharon, who shook their heads sadly. Jennifer said disgustedly, "She never said anything to me, but I'm not surprised."

Leslie looked aghast. "You're not? I was shocked. I thought she'd prefer having a black Big Sister."

Jennifer sighed. "Poor LaToya! She must have wondered how, out of all the Big Sisters from Goucher, she got the only black one."

Eric groaned. "What a bitch. I remember that same shit when Peter and I were in Alabama. Lot of them old black folks would rather have Peter talk to them about voter registration than me." Eric went into his Uncle Tom routine. "Dat white boy knows what he talkin' 'bout. Sho do."

Jennifer didn't laugh. She hated it when Eric did that Uncle Tom bit, but she also knew he was telling the truth.

Jennifer directed her comments to Paige. "Paige, you run this program. These poor little girls know how to play the system already. They want a white Big Sister because they think they'll get a lot of presents out of it. Look at some of the Big Sisters. Every time they get together with their Little Sisters, they bring them some worthless trinket." Jennifer felt simultaneously humiliated and enraged. "I've been meaning to say this for a while, Paige. I think the Big Sisters program has lost its focus. Supposedly, the program was about these little girls receiving some personal attention from an older person. Guidance. Counseling. That's what you said back in the fall at the volunteers' meeting. What it's turned into is a bunch of Miss Anns descending on these poor little black girls with worthless trinkets. They're not developing warm friendships. They're just reinforcing the role of the dominant and powerful white woman."

Despite Paige's granny glasses, Jennifer could see the flash of anger in her eyes. She responded angrily, "That's not true."

"Paige, come on. You've seen it. You do it yourself. You're always handing out presents. *Noblesse oblige*, I guess you'd call it. Some of these Big Sisters spend the entire visit allowing these little black girls to comb their hair. It's pathetic."

Leslie interjected, "You know, Paige, it is true. I've seen it."

Jennifer continued, "Paige, you've come up with some very good field trips. Most of these girls would never have gone to the theater or walked on a college campus but for Big Sisters. But without the trips, the only thing some of these little girls get is the feel of white people's long, straight hair and a growing hatred of their own short, nappy hair."

Peter, who had been silent throughout this discourse, spoke. "It's really important that the little girls get more than trinkets and an occasional field trip. This is about people getting to know other people. Breaking down barriers. That's what's going to make the world a better place. What are you going to do about it, Paige?"

Paige looked flustered. "I'll just have to arrange more field trips."

Jennifer, shaking her head in frustration, said, "That's not good enough. You need to talk to the Big Sisters about their attitude."

Peter placed his arm around Paige's shoulder. "Jennifer's right. Why don't you try a sensitivity session? Many of the girls have never spoken to a black person before. They're probably not aware of how their actions can be perceived."

"Peter, you're right," Paige admitted. "I'm going to hold some sensitivity training."

"Paige, did you say Peter was right?" Jennifer inquired.

"Yes, Peter's right."

"Excuse me." Jennifer stood up and headed for the door. "I'm out of here." Sharon and Eric got up and followed her out of the room. As they descended the narrow staircase, Jennifer said over her shoulder to Sharon, "Do you believe her? Paige only accepted what I said when Peter agreed with me. She needed a white man to tell her how to treat black children. Wouldn't accept it from me."

Eric said, without any hint of a stutter, "Jennifer, calm down. I know what you're talking about. It's that 'white man's validation' thing again. You know, the first night I met you guys, as I was sitting on that stage, I was thinking how much I hated coming out to Goucher to ask for volunteers, because those self-proclaimed white liberals descend on my program like Miss Ann, the benevolent mistress of the plantation."

Eric's comment, delivered with his Southern drawl, made Jennifer and Sharon burst into laughter.

"I'm not kidding," Eric said. "You know just what I'm talking 'bout. It just happened. Paige couldn't or wouldn't hear you. But when Peter, *the white man*, spoke, dat's it! Done."

Chapter 7

Leslie

The following Friday afternoon, Jennifer walked into the room and found Leslie getting dressed. "Where are you going?"

Leslie continued to search through her closet. "I'm going to Sabbath dinner at my college mother's house. Mrs. Gottlieb is picking me up in ten minutes."

Jennifer flopped on her bed. "That's really nice to be able to get out of here and have dinner in a real home rather than another cafeteria meal. How'd you meet her?"

"Hillel, the Jewish students' group, set it up. Not that I keep kosher or anything, but it's nice to have a Sabbath dinner every once in a while. Reminds me of home." As Leslie rushed out of the door, she asked, "What are you doing tonight?"

Jennifer fell back on the bed. "Studying and wishing I was at home eating my mother's banana pudding." Leslie closed the door, and Jennifer stared at the ceiling. Feelings of isolation and loneliness engulfed her, but she fought the feelings. Instead, she got up, organized her notebooks in preparation for studying after dinner, and then headed to the cafeteria. As soon as she opened the door, she encountered Allison in the hall. "Going to dinner?"

Allison responded, "Yes."

"Let's go."

❧   ❧   ❧

Mrs. Gottlieb, seated behind the wheel of her black Cadillac Sedan DeVille, said, "Darling, you look absolutely gorgeous."

Although Leslie had known since childhood that she was beautiful, she still loved and thrived on the compliments.

"I knew you would," Mrs. Gottlieb continued, "because you always do. That's why I didn't bother to tell you that I arranged a little date for you."

Leslie's response betrayed her apprehension. "A date?"

Mrs. Gottlieb negotiated the Cadillac onto the beltway. "I knew you would be surprised. And such a pretty girl like you, you probably would say, 'Don't do it.' That's why I didn't tell you. But you'll like him."

Older women were always trying to set her up with their sons, grandsons, or nephews. She clearly didn't need assistance in this department, but the sons, grandsons, and nephews did, and she was the chosen one.

Mrs. Gottlieb turned into her driveway and pointed to the house next door. "The young fellow I want you to meet is my neighbor's nephew. Wonderful people."

"I'm sure he's very nice." She envisioned another Jewish boy staring at his feet, embarrassed that he needed to be fixed up.

They entered the house, and within minutes the doorbell rang. "I'd like you to meet my Goucher daughter, Leslie Cohen. This is Dr. and Mrs. Rosenthal, and this is their nephew, Joel." Mrs. Gottlieb paused so she could observe Leslie's reaction. "Joel goes to Hopkins."

Joel looked at Leslie and made no attempt to disguise the joy on his face. "Leslie, it's great to meet you." Leslie smiled politely.

Mrs. Rosenthal asked, "Goucher daughter? What's that about?"

Mrs. Gottlieb explained as she led the group to the dining room, "My rabbi set up the program to give the Jewish girls at Goucher a place to go during Passover if they couldn't get home to their families and any time they needed a good Jewish home to go to." She put her arm around Leslie and gave her a little squeeze. "And I got this sweetheart." Mrs. Gottlieb pointed to a chair. "Leslie, sweetheart, you sit here next to Joel."

After prayers, Dr. Rosenthal asked Mr. Gottlieb, "Saul, did you hear that the Colts are going to trade that quarterback they paid a fortune for just last year?"

Before Saul could finish chewing and answer, Mrs. Rosenthal said, "Who cares about football. I want to know all about Leslie. Sweetheart, where are you from?"

"Scarsdale."

"Do you know the Bermans? Neil and Susan Berman."

"I don't think so. My parents may know them."

Mrs. Rosenthal nodded. "I'm sure they do. Neil has a huge ob-gyn practice in Scarsdale." Without catching a breath, Mrs. Rosenthal looked at her nephew and said, "Joel is premed at Hopkins. Joel is from—"

"Aunt Esther," Joel interrupted, "I can speak for myself. Leslie, I'm from Pittsburgh."

Leslie turned toward Joel, and as she looked at him, she knew her mother would like him: attractive though not handsome; medium height; thick, dark brown hair; studying to be a doctor. She could hear her mother say, "What's not to like?" Oh, but the nose! She guessed he didn't get a nose job for his bar mitzvah. "What year are you?"

"Junior."

Leslie tried to keep her eyes off his nose. "Have you thought about where you want to go to med school?" She couldn't believe that question had come out of her mouth. It was like her mother was speaking instead of her.

"Clearly Hopkins is on my list, but I'm open."

Mrs. Gottlieb added, "Dr. Rosenthal went to Hopkins."

Mrs. Rosenthal explained, "That's how I ended up in Baltimore. Married a Hopkins doctor. That's how we know the Bermans. Dr. Berman went to Hopkins. Leslie, tell us more about you and college. Do you have a roommate?"

"Yes, I do."

Mrs. Rosenthal asked, "Is she Jewish?"

"No, she's black."

"Black?" Aunt Esther screeched. "I didn't know that there were any Negroes at Goucher."

Joel rolled his eyes and sat back in his chair. "Aunt Esther, we don't call them Negroes anymore. The word is *black*." Joel flashed a quick apologetic smile at Leslie.

Mr. Gottlieb huffed, "We used to call them colored. I can't keep up with all of these names."

"Whatever you call her, I understand from Leslie that she's very nice," Mrs. Gottlieb added. "But Leslie, you didn't mention that she's black."

"Her name is Jennifer Madison. She's from Detroit." Leslie, for a reason she couldn't explain, felt compelled to add, "Very smart. Really nice."

Dr. Rosenthal asked, "How many Negro, excuse me, black girls are at Goucher?"

As Leslie answered, "I don't know," she wondered why she didn't and whether not knowing meant something. She was sure Jennifer knew.

Dr. Rosenthal turned to his nephew. "How about Hopkins? How many black students?"

"I have no idea, but very few." He then turned to Leslie and said, "I'd rather talk about Leslie. Leslie, what do you want to major in?"

The discussion had made Leslie inexplicably uncomfortable. She was relieved when Joel changed the subject. "English. I want to be a reporter."

Mrs. Rosenthal said, "That's nice. Joel, cousin Mort's son is a reporter."

"Aunt Esther, I don't know cousin Mort or his son."

"You young people just don't keep up with the family like you should." She shook her head, and Mrs. Gottlieb nodded in agreement. "I'll call cousin Mort for his son's number. Maybe you'd like to talk with him about being a reporter, Leslie?"

When she heard her name, Leslie snapped back into the conversation and stopped trying to count the number of black students. "Of course. That's very nice of you, Mrs. Rosenthal." Aunt Esther smiled broadly at Leslie, who returned the smile and noticed Mrs. Rosenthal's nicotine-stained teeth for the first time.

Mrs. Gottlieb asked Leslie to assist her in the kitchen. As soon as the door to the dining room swung closed, Mrs. Gottlieb asked, "What do you think? I picked a good one, huh?"

Leslie reached over and gave her a quick peck on the cheek. "My mother thanks you."

"That's what I thought. Jewish, doctor. Perfect."

When they finished dessert, Mrs. Gottlieb looked at Joel imploringly. "Joel, would you mind driving Leslie back to Goucher for me?"

Joel looked first at this aunt, winked at her, and then said to Mrs. Gottlieb, "Glad to."

As Joel drove Leslie back to campus, he explained that he hadn't wanted to come to dinner, because his aunt was always trying to fix him up; he described some of her previous efforts, which had been disastrous. Leslie listened, laughing softly at the right moments; she shifted her gaze to the window, however, because Joel's nose kind of turned her off.

Jennifer was in bed reading when Leslie returned. "How was dinner?"

"Mrs. Gottlieb arranged a blind date for me, her next-door neighbor's nephew, Joel. Premed at Hopkins. He asked me out for tomorrow, but I already have a date, so we're going to the movies on Sunday."

Jennifer moaned, "I'm so jealous. You don't even need any help meeting guys, and yet you're getting blind dates while I have no dates at all."

"What can I say? People love me."

"And you're blond and gorgeous!"

"Oh! Roomie, you're such a sweetheart."

Jennifer added, "Sweetheart? No, I'm envious!" She returned to her book, thinking that if she'd gone to Howard, she'd probably have gone out with someone just like her father tonight. She asked herself what she was doing at this college. She'd already lost count of how many times she'd asked herself the same question.

As Leslie got undressed, she intentionally kept her voice nonchalant when she asked, "How many black girls are at Goucher?"

Looking up from her book, Jennifer said, "Eight."

"That's all?"

"That's all. Why did you ask?"

As Leslie stared into the mirror and removed her makeup, she responded, "Just wondering."

Chapter 8

Paige

Paige was seated in the Gopher Hole with members of the Peace Initiative Committee. "We really need to plan something for campus."

The senior seated next to Paige asked, "What do you suggest?"

"I've been thinking of borrowing a concept from Martin Luther King—a quiet vigil. You know, we would just stand and be silent."

"Well, if we're silent, how would anyone know what we were protesting?" Leslie asked.

Paige suppressed her frustration at Leslie's naïveté. "Signs. Banners. We'll make posters that say PEACE NOW, STOP BOMBING VIETNAM, NO MORE AGENT ORANGE."

"I think we'd get a lot more attention with noise," Leslie suggested.

"Everyone does noise. This would be different. Provocative. Silence often speaks volumes."

A student asked, "Where?"

Paige smiled triumphantly and pointed out of the window. "Right there. In the courtyard. I can see it now. Everyone walks through here around noon checking their mailboxes. We'd all stand silently as they passed by. We'd say nothing." Paige stopped speaking as the idea germinated. "I know. We'll have our heads bowed as in prayer. Our signs will speak for us."

Leslie thought about it as the students engaged in side conversations and then announced, "Paige, I like it."

Warming to her plan, Paige added, "I'll contact the chaplain and arrange to have the chapel bell toll at noon to signal the start of the vigil and again at one o'clock to signal the end."

On the following Friday at noon, twenty girls, with heads bowed, kept silent vigil in the courtyard. Some students walked by and barely glanced at the demonstration; others stopped, looked briefly, and then moved on; and others stopped and joined the ranks of the demonstration.

Jennifer's Russian literature class ended at 12:20 PM. After class, she approached the professor. "Dr. Rokowsky, I'd like to schedule an appointment with you to discuss my paper topic."

Professor Rokowsky looked at her watch. "Now's good."

"Well, thank you, but I was planning on participating in the peace vigil now. It started at noon. I didn't want to miss class, but I thought I would go over now. Do you have any other time later today?"

"What vigil?"

"The Peace Initiative is holding a silent vigil right now in the courtyard to protest the escalation of the war."

"That's a wonderful idea. I'll go over with you, and we can talk about your paper afterward."

Jennifer, accompanied by Professor Rokowsky, walked to the courtyard; she spotted Leslie, walked over to her, and stood by her side, while the professor stood next to her. When some students saw Professor Rokowsky, with her Russian cape draped dramatically around her shoulders, they stopped and joined the protest. Professor Rokowsky spotted two of her colleagues and motioned to them, and they also joined the demonstration.

The courtyard, normally boisterous during this time of day, became a sea of silence. At one o'clock the chapel bell rang, indicating the end of the vigil. Professor Rokowsky broke the silence in a strong contralto by singing the first verse of "We Shall Overcome." Paige, surprised by the unexpected singing, timidly joined in, as did the others. When the song was over, the group quietly dispersed.

Professor Rokowsky turned to Jennifer. "Ready to talk about your paper?" She sat down on the bench. "Have a seat. It's a beautiful day. Let's talk here." As Jennifer sat down, Paige approached them.

"Dr. Rokowsky, thank you for attending the vigil. I appreciate your support."

"You're welcome. I have to thank Jennifer. She told me about it."

"Thanks for bringing Professor Rokowsky."

Jennifer mumbled, "Sure," certain that Paige's thank-you was insincere.

Paige turned back to Professor Rokowsky. "Why did you start singing 'We Shall Overcome'? That's a civil rights song."

"You can't pigeonhole life. This was an antiwar rally—a peace vigil. That song is about peace as well. It's about peace within our country and everywhere."

Paige pondered the answer and said, "You're right—peace here in America and in Vietnam."

The photographer from the college newspaper captured the scene, and Paige appeared on the front page with head bowed and a banner behind her head that said PEACE NOW.

1966 TO 1967

Chapter 9

Jennifer

Even as a sophomore, Jennifer still liked the college food. Goucher was on the "A" food plan, whereas the all-male Johns Hopkins University, which used the same food service, was on the "C" plan. When feeding boys, quantity was more important than quality.

Under the "A" food plan, there were special Italian nights, when the cafeteria was transformed into an Italian restaurant. Oktoberfest featured a German meal. In the fall, there was a Texas-style barbecue, where a pig was cooked over an open pit in the courtyard between Mary Fisher and Heubeck Halls. The black cooks wore oversize white aprons and large chef's hats, their dark faces glistening with sweat in the early fall sunshine. The black cooks made sure to give each black student an extra helping of ribs.

At the monthly Black Students Association meeting the following week, after announcing the Black Art Exhibit at neighboring Morgan State College, Brenda, the group president, asked if there were any other items for discussion.

Unsure if she should raise her concern, Jennifer asked, "Was I the only one offended by the black cooks in those oversize aprons and hats last week?"

"They did look ridiculous, but that barbecue was good!" one of the juniors said.

"The barbecue was delicious," Jennifer persisted, "but what about the cooks?"

"Jennifer, that's what cooks wear at a barbecue like that," Brenda said, seeming a little perturbed. "You're only upset because all the cooks are black and all of the students, except the eight of us, are not."

"You're right. I may be overreacting to the fact that all of the service people on this campus are black. I probably should just be glad that those black folks have jobs."

"That's the truth," Sharon said.

Jennifer, still feeling compelled to address her discomfort, suggested, "What about a soul food night? They've done Italian and German. How about a black night? The school should honor our black heritage."

There were murmurs of agreement from the rest of the group.

"I'll organize it," Jennifer said. "What should we demand?"

"Fried chicken, ham, candied sweet potatoes, potato salad," some of the girls answered.

Jennifer added, "If we're going to do soul food, we have to have rice, gravy, collard greens, hot sauce, and corn bread."

Then Brenda, who was from a small town in North Carolina, shouted, "Chitlins! We've got to have chitlins!"

Taken aback by Brenda's suggestion, Jennifer said, "I don't know about chitlins. I've never eaten chitlins."

"You're kidding! Never eaten chitlins? What kind of black person are you?" Brenda asked with an astonished look.

Jennifer thought, *The kind who doesn't eat chitlins. Where is it written that, to be black, one has to eat chitlins?* To Brenda, though, she responded more kindly. "My mother refuses to serve chitlins in our house. She dislikes the odor."

Brenda laughed but repeated her position. "Your mother is too ciditty for me. If we're going to do this, we've *got* to have chitlins." There were mumbles of agreement from the others.

Visions of her mother stormed Jennifer's brain. "Brenda, my mother says, and I quote, 'You know, you have to wash those nasty things three times to get them clean.' I'm not confident that the cooks will wash the chitlins the requisite three times."

This time, the entire group burst into laughter.

Brenda, emphasizing her North Carolina accent, which to Jennifer signaled her growing disdain for this discussion and a challenge to the Northerners, said, "Y'all too ciditty for me. I'm from the country. We've got to have chitlins if we're going to do this."

The fact that Brenda had said "ciditty" twice, the second time with that downright nasty North Carolina accent, was a warning that Jennifer understood. Deciding that she didn't wish to battle the group's increasingly hostile president over the issue of chitlins or no chitlins, she acquiesced. "You're right. You guys have convinced me. Chitlins are authentic soul food. I'm not cooking them or smelling them, so it's not my problem. Chitlins should be on the menu. But I bet the food service won't go for it. What'll we do if they refuse our demand?"

"A sit-in, of course," was the enthusiastic response.

"Come on, girls. This is not exactly a segregated lunch counter at a five-and-ten-cent store," Brenda said without using her exaggerated North Carolina accent, which suggested to Jennifer that she had calmed down.

"You're right, but we're doing this soul food dinner to make a point," Jennifer said. "Brenda, you were the one who said we had to have chitlins. We want them to do soul food to honor our black traditions."

"I love chitlins but chitlins are not exactly an honored black tradition," Sharon explained.

Jennifer, warming to her new position, said, "Now that I think about it, they are. Brenda's right. Chitlins are a symbol of our slave legacy: how blacks made do with nothing at all and persevered. We've *got* to have chitlins."

"Everyone agree on the chitlins?" Brenda asked.

The group said yes.

Brenda turned to Jennifer, once again using her North Carolina accent. "OK, Miss Ciditty, do it."

Jennifer, recognizing the challenge in Brenda's voice, said, "Done." She returned to her dorm and contacted the food service with the proposal.

Three days later, the food service manager telephoned Jennifer. "We can do your soul food dinner next week."

"Really?" Jennifer was stunned and somewhat disappointed. There would be no need for a sit-in.

"The only problem is we won't be able to do the chitterlings." Jennifer was amused by the white manager's pronunciation of "chitterlings," with three syllables, rather than the use of the black vernacular.

With a tone that Jennifer hoped sounded militant, she asked, "Why can't you do the chitlins?"

"We're just not equipped to do chitterlings. We'll do the rest of the menu but not the chitterlings."

Jennifer, reclaiming the simmering anger that had caused her to suggest a soul food dinner, declared, "Oh no, we must have the chitlins! I'll have to discuss this with the Black Students Association if we don't have the chitlins." She said "Black Student Association" as if it were some powerful organization and not merely eight black college girls; she smiled at her audacity.

The manager said, "Well, I'll see what we can do."

Later in the afternoon, as Jennifer walked into Van Meter Hall, she saw Brenda. "We may have to do a sit-in. They say they can't do chitlins."

Brenda put her hand on her hip and laughed. "Miss Ciditty, I can guarantee you one thing. I will never participate in a sit-in about some chitlins."

"I'm so glad you said that. Neither will I. My parents would kill me if I did some silly stuff like that."

"There are real issues out here. Let's not waste our time on stupid stuff like chitlins."

The next day the manager called Jennifer and said the chitterlings were on the menu, alleviating the need for the sit-in that none of them really wanted to have.

❦   ❦   ❦

Soul Food Night was a great success. Several white girls declared their love for the chitterlings, which the sisters repeatedly explained was pronounced "chitlins."

Eric, joining Sharon for dinner, announced to Jennifer and Leslie, "These chitlins are almost as good as my mama's."

Leslie looked at the chitlins and then at Jennifer. "You don't have any."

"That's right. I don't. Chitlins are hog intestines."

Leslie said, "I think I'll pass."

Eric eventually smacked his lips and leaned back in his chair. "That was some kind of good. I've got niggeritus."

Leslie blanched and then looked at Jennifer to see if she would react. Jennifer refused to react and kept eating the potato salad.

Brenda stopped by their table. "Jennifer, great job. Everyone is loving the food." She paused and grinned. "Including the chitlins."

"I just told 'em that the chitlins were almost as good as my mama's." Eric patted his stomach and added, "I've got niggeritus."

Oh, Jesus, he said it again, Jennifer silently lamented.

Laughing and hitting Eric on the back, Brenda said, "Eric, me too. Niggeritus! Chitlins can do that."

Leslie asked in a timid voice, "Eric, what's niggeritus?"

Eric released a whooping laugh that drew the attention of the entire dining room. "Niggeritus?"

Sharon poked Eric in his side and said, "Lower your voice."

"I'm sorry, Sha … Sharon. I'm … I'm … I'm sorry." Eric's nervous stutter, combined with the laughter he was now trying to suppress, prevented him from answering Leslie.

Jennifer looked disapprovingly at Sharon and then at Eric. At this point, Brenda was also bent over laughing loudly. "Leslie, all it means is that the person is very full from overeating and they're now sleepy. It's a colloquial expression in the black community."

Leslie still looked confused and slightly uncomfortable but just said, "Oh."

Eric and Brenda continued to laugh while Sharon looked embarrassed, and Jennifer couldn't believe that she had just defined *niggeritus*.

Chapter 10

Leslie

Leslie lay on the lawn behind Mary Fisher Hall enjoying the sun before her next class. A woman from the dean's office approached her. "Excuse me. We're taking pictures for a new college catalog. May the photographer take your picture?"

Leslie looked up at the two people standing above her blocking the sun. "Sure. What do you want me to do?"

The photographer said, "Just lie there, and I'll take a few shots."

"OK." Leslie closed her eyes and continued enjoying the sun on her face.

"Got it. Would you mind walking for us so I can get some shots of you with the campus in the background?"

Leslie grabbed her books. "I have a class in fifteen minutes, so I'll walk toward Van Meter."

The photographer hoisted his camera. "We'll follow you."

As Leslie approached the chapel, John, who played fullback on the Hopkins football team, was walking toward her. He smiled; she nodded but kept walking. The photographer called out, "Hey, wait. This would make a great photo." The photographer turned to John. "May I take your picture for a Goucher catalog?"

John grunted, "Sure."

The photographer positioned them so that the Hopkins athletic jacket was clearly visible. After several shots, the photographer yelled, "Got it."

The following day, the photographer said to Leslie, "The camera loves you. Have you ever thought of doing any modeling?"

Leslie looked down at the photographs. "Not really."

"Well, you should. I'm doing a fashion layout, and you'd be great."

❈   ❈   ❈

Leslie and five professional models were photographed in front of Kraush-aar Auditorium, in Donnybrook Park, and by the stables. The pictures appeared in the *Baltimore Sun.*

❈   ❈   ❈

Jennifer picked up the newspaper from Leslie's bed. "Instead of being a reporter, you may have found another career. People will be interviewing you."

Leslie shook her head. "No. Too frivolous. Here, these are the shots that they may use in the college catalog."

Jennifer looked carefully at the photographs of Leslie at various places on campus. "Leslie Cohen, the face of Goucher College."

Chapter 11

Paige

For Christmas break, Paige joined her mother at their Palm Beach home.

Mrs. Wyatt said over lunch by the infinity pool, "Oh, honey, I'm so glad you decided to come. Can you believe this is your last Christmas vacation before you graduate? What are you going to do?"

Paige speared a shrimp from her seafood salad and popped it in her mouth. Her sunglasses hid her confusion and anxiety. "I'm not sure yet."

"Would you like to travel for a while? When I graduated from college, your grandparents sent me to visit Aunt Louise in Italy. The two of us traveled all over Italy and France for three months."

Loving the feel of the warm sun on her face, Paige teased, "I think I'll pass on traveling with Aunt Louise for three months."

"Don't be silly," Mrs. Wyatt scolded her daughter. "Aunt Louise is eighty-five years old. She's not traveling very much anymore. Why do you tease me all the time? You know I didn't mean that."

Paige looked at her mother. "Because I love you so very much."

"I love you, too, honey." Mrs. Wyatt shifted her chair a little to the right to avoid the sun. "But most of the time, I don't know if you're teasing or you're serious."

"Most of the time, I don't know either."

"You could travel through Europe on your own, if you like. Or with a friend. Maybe South America. I love Brazil. You really liked Rio when we went to carnival a few years ago."

"Is this my father's suggestion?"

"If it was his idea, I know you'd refuse," Mrs. Wyatt admitted. "No, it's not his; its mine. I'm sure he would support the idea, though."

"Mother"—Paige fought to keep her tone neutral, because she didn't wish to upset her—"I don't care what he'll support or not support."

"I know that, honey. What about graduate school? A job?"

"I just don't know what I'm going to do. Right now, all I want to do is soak up some sun for a few days." She closed her eyes and enjoyed the way the sun felt on her skin. What she was trying to figure out was if she really was in love with Peter. Unwilling to share her quandary, she merely said, "It was awfully cold in Baltimore when I left."

Mrs. Wyatt gazed out at the calm turquoise ocean. "Well, that won't be a problem here. But don't get too much sun. It's bad for your skin."

Chapter 12

Jennifer

At one o'clock, Jennifer, Sharon, and Yvonne met in the lobby of Stimson Hall to wait for the shuttle into Baltimore. The shuttle driver reeked of old sweat and was missing one of his upper front teeth. Jennifer whispered to Sharon, once they had taken their seats in the back of the bus to distance them from the funk, "My grandmother always said, 'If you see a snaggletooth man, you're going to have bad luck.' I hope he's not going to ruin my weekend."

❦   ❦   ❦

The girls checked into the New Haven Holiday Inn and were handed a flyer announcing, "The Brothers of Harvard University Request the Pleasure of Your Company at a Get-Down Boogie, Suite 700, 9 until."

Jennifer and Sharon waited until eleven to go to the Harvard party, knowing that it would start on colored people's time. The heavy rhythm of Sly and the Family Stone welcomed them into the hot and musty suite.

Jennifer said to Sharon, "My hair is definitely going back. Thank God I brought my hot comb. Did I ever tell you about Leslie and the hot comb?"

Shocked, Sharon asked, "Leslie used your hot comb?"

"No. Leslie didn't know what a hot comb was. I used the hot comb when Leslie wasn't in the room. When she returned, she asked me, 'What's that smell?' I said, 'What smell?'"

"You didn't?"

Jennifer leaned closer to Sharon so she could be heard over the loud music. "At the time, I really didn't know what she was talking about. Anyway, a couple of weeks later, she was lying on her bed reading *The Second Sex*, that book by

Simone de Beauvoir that she just loves, and I was using the hot comb. She said, scrunching up her nose, 'There's that weird smell again. What are you doing?' Well, I immediately got my back up. I said, 'princess.'"

Sharon shook her head. "No, you did not say, 'princess'!"

"You're right. I didn't say, 'princess,' but I thought it." Jennifer moved aside to let a brother walk by. "Then I explained to her that I was straightening my hair and that the smell was a combination of my hair, oil, and the heat from the hot comb. I told her that I didn't appreciate it when she said it was a weird smell."

"What did Leslie say then?"

"You know Leslie. She apologized immediately. She didn't mean any harm. Leslie just had never smelled the burning aroma of frying hair."

Laughing, Sharon said, "You mean the aroma that every little black girl learns from birth?"

"You got it."

As Jennifer and Sharon stood in the darkened suite sipping grape Kool-Aid spiked with grain alcohol, two boys came over and asked each of them to dance.

As Jennifer danced, she could see Paul, a friend from home who had been in her Jack and Jill chapter. Paul had always been an arrogant snob. After he was accepted at Harvard, he became unbearable. But he could introduce her to other Harvard guys. Her dance partner was not a finey and couldn't even dance. *How did this happen?* She wondered. Only really handsome brothers could get away with not knowing how to dance. When the record ended, she thanked her partner and then made her way through the crowded room to Paul.

When Paul saw her, his arrogant expression melted into a warm smile. "My home girl. You're looking good, mama!"

"Paul, I am *not* your mama."

Paul lifted his hands in surrender. "OK, Jennifer."

"Don't give me that ghetto crap. How's school? Are you still premed?"

"No, premed kicked my butt. I've switched to sociology. My plan is still to go to medical school. I've got the basic science courses, but I decided ..." The noise of the room drowned out the rest of the sentence. Someone was screaming, "There's a party over here!"

Jennifer saw Sharon and motioned her over. "Paul's an old friend of mine from home. Junior at *Harvard*." With a wicked grin, Jennifer added, "Paul is going to be a *doctor*." Sharon's attention was piqued.

"My father's a doctor," Sharon said. "What specialty are you interested in?"

Paul looked right at Sharon's breasts and said, "I don't know yet."

Jennifer announced, "Why don't you two dance? Sharon, let me warn you, Paul does the Detroit Bop! And not very well."

Paul said, "Call me out, Jennifer." Paul extended his hand to Sharon. "Would you like to dance?" Before Sharon could respond, Paul wound his arms tightly around her. He was glad the record was slow; it gave him an excuse to press against this beautiful girl.

Jennifer headed for the spiked Kool-Aid. Without saying a word, a guy appeared, grabbed her hand, and started dancing. He held her very close. In order to stop this stranger from squeezing her to death, Jennifer pulled her head back, arched her back, and tried to make conversation. "Where do you go to school?"

"Brown."

"I have a friend there. Do you know Larry Brewer?"

"Yeah." He pulled her closer.

"Is Larry here?"

"Nah."

Jennifer thought this guy was not much on conversation, but she continued. It was the only way to keep him from nuzzling her neck. Besides, his face was sweaty, and his breath smelled of cigarettes and McDonald's French fries.

Jennifer pushed away again. "Where are you from?"

He grunted, "Watts."

The way in which he had proudly grunted "Watts" indicated to Jennifer that it was time to move on. Her mother's voice resonated in her head: "You can take some niggers out of the ghetto, but you cannot take the ghetto out of some niggers." Here she was at Yale University, a bastion of the Ivy League, wrapped in a sweaty embrace with a monosyllabic brother from Watts, albeit a student at Brown. "Excuse me. Ladies' room."

The party went on until three in the morning. As the party ended, Paul asked Sharon to go to his room to talk. She refused.

Jennifer was lying on the bed when Sharon returned to their hotel room. "What do you think of Paul?"

"He asked me to go to his room"—Sharon paused and rolled her eyes toward the ceiling—"to talk."

"Talk? Right!"

"Exactly. He's got potential written all over him. Harvard, premed, good-looking. So, I let my Southern Jack-and-Jill nice-girl training stop me from jumping on him. He'll wait. He's a Jack-and-Jill nice boy with home training."

On Saturday morning, Jennifer and Sharon walked over to the teach-in. The mood of the crowd was intense, which contrasted with last night's gregarious partying. Today was about the business of the black revolution. There was a large poster of H. Rap Brown; on it, in bold letters, was his quote, "Black power is going to get your mama."

This morning, in this brightly lit lecture hall, with the sun filtering through the arched leaded glass Gothic windows, Jennifer noticed that all of the boys had Afros of varying lengths. Many wore dashikis. Some of the girls had Afros, too.

As Jennifer surveyed the room, she saw what she determined was the handsomest boy she had ever seen. On stage, he said, "Good morning, brothers and sisters. I'm David Walker, president of the Yale University Afro-American Association. On behalf of all the brothers at Yale, I welcome you to Spook Weekend, where together we will plot our strategy to continue the black revolution. As W. E. B. DuBois said, we are 'the talented tenth' and have a responsibility to all black people to focus our energy and intellect toward the creation of a better world for black people and all mankind."

The crowd erupted. They were on their feet, shouting, clapping, and raising clenched fists in a thunderous response before heading to the various workshops.

Sharon selected "Afro-American History, A Required Course of Study." Yvonne and her Yalie boyfriend went to the "Black Student Recruitment" workshop. The workshop entitled "Guerrilla Warfare versus Civil Disobedience" led by a Guatemalan student from Yale attracted Jennifer, but she decided to attend the workshop "The Ivy League as Slave Owner." Jennifer found a seat in between a heavyset boy wearing a green army jacket and a tough-looking brown-skinned girl with a short, tight Afro, dark brown lips, and hoop earrings dangling to her shoulders.

The workshop leader explained, "The Association of Black Collegians at Princeton—we call ourselves ABC—learned that Princeton has significant financial investments in the racist state of South Africa. These investments help to perpetuate the apartheid system. ABC demanded that the university divest itself of its financial investment in that racist country. Some American companies have already stepped forward and refused to do business with South Africa until the country ends apartheid. ABC is demanding that Princeton do the same." Many in the workshop clapped and shouted their support. "We want other campuses to support this cause."

Several in the crowd yelled, "Right on! I dig it!"

The dangling-hoops sister stood up. "I hear you, brother. But why are we talking about South Africa when right here in the good old USA American companies are subjecting our black brothers and sisters to discrimination? The capitalist system is being used to control and exploit downtrodden folk right here at home. These companies pay us less than they pay the white workers for the same work. Sometimes, they won't even hire black folks at all. Before we worry about Africa, we better talk about protecting our black folk right here in the community."

Someone yelled agreement from across the room. The debate, which had begun in measured, reasoned tones, now turned into boisterous argument. A dashiki-clad brother jumped up. "That's the problem with black folks. We've forgotten where we came from—Africa."

The sister was shouted down, and a vote was taken to support Princeton's antiapartheid teach-in.

Several girls walked out in protest. As the meeting was breaking up, Jennifer said to the girl with the hoop earrings, "I agree with you. It's important that we deal with the problems right here at home."

The girl, who was taller than Jennifer, slowly looked her up and down; with her dark brown lips firmly set in a snarl, she replied, "Why didn't you say something during the debate? I know why: you were too busy trying to look cute with that long hair." The girl abruptly turned her back and stalked out of the room, leaving Jennifer speechless. She encountered Sharon after the workshop. "How was your workshop?"

"We have got to get a Black history course on campus. How was yours?"

"This sister just attacked me for having long hair."

"What was that about?"

"I told her I agreed with her position, and she accused me of not saying anything because"—Jennifer lowered her voice to a growl—"'I'm too busy trying to look cute with that long hair.'"

"Ugly."

"We talk about black sisterhood, brotherhood, black is beautiful, but there's still lots of stupid stuff that keeps black folks apart: hair, skin color, size of nose. We've got to move beyond that stuff. You shoulda heard her!"

"Takes time."

Jennifer said, "Tell you the truth, this problem is not going to be solved until black men really start believing that black women are beautiful. As long as black men still buy into that Madison Avenue version of beauty—the thin, blond, white woman—we're going to have a problem, and sisters like that one are going to be angry and mean."

Sharon moaned, "It's always a man issue, isn't it?"

Jennifer grinned. "Not always. Sometimes it's money. I wish we weren't so angry all the time."

Saturday night's party was held in a stately Gothic building. The deejay blasted the latest record by the O'Jays. Jennifer joined a group who continued the earlier debate over investment in South Africa, and a boy touched Jennifer's elbow. "I saw you at the 'Ivy League as Slave Owner' workshop this afternoon. I'm Phillip Jackson."

She extended her hand. "Jennifer Madison."

Phillip said, "That debate deteriorated into a black-man-versus-black-woman fight."

"It did."

"That was a bad trip that sister put on you. Personally, I like your long hair."

"Well, thanks. Sisters are really hard on each other sometimes."

"But that's what Spook Weekend is all about: ending those feelings, destroying self-hate, developing a coalition where we are all brothers and sisters." Phillip then added with a big smile, "And a good time."

"You're right. A good time."

"So, let's dance."

❦   ❦   ❦

On the bus back to Goucher, Sharon excitedly told Jennifer that Paul had invited her to Harvard the next weekend. "What about Phillip?"

"Seems nice. Goes to Princeton." Jennifer leaned across the aisle and touched Yvonne's arm, as she had started to fall asleep. "What do you know about David Walker?"

Yvonne was slow to respond as she transitioned from drowsiness to alertness. "David Walker. Smart. From New York. Dad's a lawyer. Talks black. Sleeps white."

Jennifer groaned, "Oh no, not another brother who talks black and sleeps white."

Yvonne sighed, "Afraid so."

Jennifer persisted, although it was clear that Yvonne wanted to fall asleep. "Does he go out with that sister he was dancing with?"

"Nah. She's just a friend. A cover. David knew he couldn't invite his white girlfriend to Spook Weekend. The sisters would have rioted."

"Who's the white girlfriend?"

"Nancy somebody. Goes to Vassar. The brothers joke that she's blacker than David. Always making the black power sign with her fist. Good night, ladies. Wake me when we get to Baltimore."

Chapter 13

Paige

As Paige and Peter strolled in Donnybrook Park in early May, he stared in wonder at the majestic towering oak trees and the scattering of lavender wildflowers. "I love the natural beauty of this place, the silence that's only interrupted by the sounds of the birds and the soft breeze through the trees. It's tranquillity. I guess that's what I'm looking for. Yet, I spend my time in the chaos of the inner city, where the constant clanging sounds of trash trucks combine with police sirens. I'd like to bring some tranquillity there."

Reaching down to pick a wildflower, Paige mused, "I've always loved this part of the campus, too. But, I don't need the tranquillity. In my life, tranquillity has been bought and paid for. I want some action. I want to be a part of this chaos."

"So, what are you going to do?"

She mockingly said, "I'm going to graduate."

"Cut that out. You sound like my father. I don't think he'll ever forgive me for dropping out of college. Actually, it's not the dropping out that bothered him so much. He doesn't understand my choices. Freedom rides. Voter registration. The center. He'd be happier if I'd taken a year off to hike through Europe. That he could get. Helping black and poor people. Trying to change the status quo." Peter shook his head as he reached for Paige's hand. "He doesn't understand that."

"Is that why you do it? Because it pisses your father off?"

Peter stepped back and thought for a moment. "No. Well, maybe."

"I love upsetting my father." Paige wrapped her arms around Peter's neck. "I hope it matters to you that I really admire what you do."

"Did you invite your father to graduation?"

"I don't want to, but I'm sure my mother is going to make me. I'm surprised that she doesn't hate him. He left her after fifteen years of marriage for another woman after cheating on her. I hate him."

"But I'm sure he loves you."

"I don't think he knows how to love."

They walked silently across the meadow. "Paige, I know how to love. When I'm with you, things feel right. I'm not so fed up with life. Marry me."

"Marry you?" Paige gasped. "Where did that come from?"

"Let's get married right here in Donnybrook Park."

Paige stopped walking and grabbed Peter's hands. "I don't believe in marriage."

Squeezing her hands, he said, "But Paige, I want to belong to you. You are my one good thing in this crazy world."

"Peter, we don't need marriage to belong to each other. Marriage makes people very angry and sad. I watched as my parents got divorced. I want you to be with me as long as you want to be there. When we don't want it any longer, we can just walk away and not destroy each other in the process."

Peter brought her hands to his lips and kissed them. As he stared into her gray eyes, he said, "I need you with me."

"Let's live together."

❧   ❧   ❧

Paige telephoned her mother. "Peter and I have decided to live together. I'm going to move in with him after graduation."

Mrs. Wyatt asked, "Honey, are you getting married?"

"No, I just told you," Paige said tersely; she immediately regretted her tone but didn't apologize. "We're going to live together. He asked me to marry him, and I said no. You know why I don't want to get married."

The sound of maternal patience and tolerance was clearly heard by Paige when her mother said, "Ever since your father and I divorced, you've been saying that you never want to get married. You shouldn't give up on marriage and happiness just because your father and I were divorced."

"Mother, we are *not* getting married."

Mrs. Wyatt sighed. "Paige, I spoke with your father last week. Apparently you haven't invited him to graduation. Do that."

"I knew you'd say that. You're way too kind."

"He's entitled to be at your graduation."

Paige acquiesced. "I don't want to fight with you. I'm in love. I'm happy." She used the insolent tone she normally reserved for her father. "By the way, marriage does not guarantee happiness. I think you of all people should have figured that out by now."

"Stop it," her mother snapped.

"I'm sorry. It's just that I'm happy right now, and I want you to be happy for me. Having him at graduation is going to upset me. I'm sure he'll hate Peter. He'll probably claim he's too busy to come anyway—some big deal he'll have to handle. That's his style."

❦   ❦   ❦

Following the ceremony, the graduates and their families and friends gathered for a reception in the College Center Courtyard. Paige, still wearing her graduation robe, located her mother and Peter in the crowd. Mrs. Wyatt hugged and kissed her daughter. "Darling, I'm so proud of you." She then turned to Peter. "Peter, I wanted to say this when Paige was with us. I'm sure you know that I would prefer that you and Paige get married, but Paige is a woman who's been making her own decisions for quite some time despite what I or anyone else tells her. So, please know that I wish only happiness for you two."

Peter gave Mrs. Wyatt a peck on the cheek. "Thanks. I'd like us to get married, too." Peter shrugged his shoulders and looked from Paige to her mother.

Mrs. Wyatt saw her ex-husband in the crowd. Paige followed her mother's glance and saw her father in a dark blue Brooks Brothers' pin-striped suit, pushing his way through the crowd. Mrs. Wyatt said, with little movement of her lips, "Here he comes."

Mr. Wyatt, accompanied by his third wife, approached the three of them and attempted to kiss Paige. She recoiled. He said, "Congratulations, Paige. No honors?"

Paige didn't respond, causing her mother to jump in. "John"—Mrs. Wyatt quickly turned to her ex-husband's wife—"Lilly, I'd like you to meet Paige's friend, Peter."

Peter, wearing ripped jeans and a STOP THE WAR T-shirt under his boarding school blazer, shook her father's hand.

Paige could tell by her father's tight-lipped expression that he disliked Peter. In their brief Christmas telephone call, Mr. Wyatt had spent most of the conversation ranting about how he hated all of these young men with long hair who were fleeing to Canada to avoid serving their country. Paige took Peter's hand and announced to her father, "Peter and I are getting married."

Mr. Wyatt roared, "What? You can't marry this man. I don't know anything about him. I forbid it."

Paige looked directly into her father's steely gray eyes, which she'd inherited, and said, "I don't care what you think."

The veins in Mr. Wyatt's forehead bulged. "I will not pay for this hippie life."

Paige responded patiently, "Nobody asked you."

Lilly grabbed his arm and said, "Calm down, John."

Mr. Wyatt snatched his arm away from her. "Stay out of this, Lilly."

Paige immediately shouted, "That's right. Stay out of this, Lilly."

Peter stood silently watching the father-daughter battle. Paige's mother hissed, "Stop it. Everyone just stop it. You're making a scene."

As Leslie and Jennifer approached Paige's family, Leslie said to Jennifer, "They don't exactly look like the happy family. I love that pink Chanel suit Paige's stepmother is wearing. Looks great on her."

Jennifer said, "I don't think you should say that in front of Paige right now. Maybe we shouldn't say anything to them at all. It looks kind of unpleasant over there."

Leslie said, "I think Paige needs us right now to break up this little family gathering. I won't mention the suit. I'm surprised Paige let them come at all. She hates her stepmother."

Jennifer whispered, "The stepmother looks like she's about thirty. No wonder she hates her."

Leslie and Jennifer reached them, and Leslie cheerfully said, "Paige, congratulations!"

Paige's mother, appearing relieved to see them, introduced them.

With a dour expression on his face, Mr. Wyatt said, "Nice to meet you." He then turned to his daughter. "Paige, we'll talk later."

Paige responded, "No need."

Mr. Wyatt abruptly turned his back and walked away from the group. His wife followed him as she chirped, "Nice meeting all of you."

Peter pulled Paige aside. "What was that about? Did you change your mind? Are we getting married?"

"Of course not. I just wanted to piss him off."

1967 TO 1968

Chapter 14

Jennifer

Leslie announced, "Danny has invited me to Princeton for the weekend!"

"Danny who?" Jennifer asked.

Leslie lifted her prom picture from the desk and waved it in front of Jennifer's face. "My prom date."

"Is he asking you out?"

"No. Just friends. He's like a brother to me. Have you forgotten that I'm dating Joel again?"

"If you're dating Joel again, why are you going to Princeton to visit Danny?"

Leslie groaned, "Because, I'm only kinda sorta dating Joel again. And, Danny invited me. So, I'm going. Besides, I've never been to Princeton. Here we are juniors, and neither one of us has dated anyone from Princeton yet. That's reason enough to go. And Danny says all of the eating clubs are having big parties this weekend. Wanna go?"

Jennifer hesitated. "I don't know. Remember that guy, Phillip, I met at Spook Weekend last year? He goes to Princeton. He never called me."

"So what? You didn't really like him, anyway. Besides, he's not the only black guy at Princeton. Danny said that there were lots of black guys at Princeton. It'll be fun."

"Lots of black guys? I'll definitely go."

Leslie saw a notice on the Ride Board and arranged to ride to Princeton with Susan Chin, who lived in Stimson. Leslie sat in the front seat of Susan's Volkswagen convertible, and Jennifer and Allison crammed into the tiny backseat.

As Susan drove, she explained, "I go to Princeton every weekend. Anytime you want a ride, just let me know. My boyfriend, Barry, is a member of Colonial. Where are you girls going?"

Leslie answered for them. "We're going to Tower. My friend from home invited me up and told me to bring some friends."

As she drove, Susan explained that she was from San Francisco and had met Barry through a friend from home.

Leslie asked, "Where's Barry from?"

"Philadelphia. I love his name. It's so old Philadelphia: Barton Winston Pennington IV."

Allison sniffed, "The fourth? That's Main Line Philadelphia, all right."

Susan drove onto Prospect Avenue and parked the car in front of Colonial, where Barry was waiting. He was of medium build and wore wrinkled madras plaid pants, a white oxford shirt, and topsiders without socks.

Leslie announced, "He's cute."

Barry opened the car door, leaned in, and gave Susan a quick kiss.

They grabbed their luggage and headed down Prospect to Tower. As they passed the stately eating club mansions, Jennifer remembered what she'd heard about the clubs and said, "I don't think Four wants me to drop by Colonial."

Leslie asked, "What do you mean 'Four'?"

"Barry! I don't think Barton Winston Pennington IV is ready for a black girl at Colonial. Did you see those white columns? The place looks absolutely antebellum."

Leslie asked, "You think so?"

Allison was silent.

Jennifer said emphatically, "I think so. Did you notice the way he didn't look at me?"

Leslie said, "Jennifer! Stop being paranoid."

Leslie, Jennifer, and Allison walked in to Tower, and Leslie stopped the first boy she saw. "Do you know Danny Eisenberg?"

The guy yelled out, "Tell Eisenberg to get his ass down here," and then disappeared. Danny looked over the banister, saw Leslie, and bounded down the stairs two at a time. Jennifer thought he was better-looking and thinner than he appeared in the prom picture. Danny grabbed Leslie in a bear hug. "Leslie, you look terrific. Glad you could make it."

"Thanks for the invite. Danny, this is Jennifer, my roommate whom you've heard so much about, and my good friend, Allison."

Danny kissed each girl on the cheek and then stood back and made an exaggerated show of looking them up and down. "Pretty girls are always welcome at Tower." The three of them followed Danny through the club, stopping periodically as he yelled quick introductions and then headed to his room to change for the party. As they walked back over to Tower, Allison casually took Danny's arm. Leslie shot Jennifer a quizzical look. Jennifer whispered, "She said she was going to have him in bed *tonight*."

Leslie said with mock pride, "That's our girl! The little slut!" She watched Allison giggle in response to something Danny said and then nuzzle his neck. Leslie said to Jennifer, "Not to worry—Danny can handle her."

Tower was jammed. All along Prospect, the music blared out of the eating clubs onto the street. The sound of the Who mixed with that of Jimi Hendrix until they were virtually indistinguishable.

Danny and Allison disappeared into the crowd, while Leslie and Jennifer went to the taproom for beers. A boy Danny had introduced earlier in the day came over to Leslie. He ran his fingers through his shaggy hair, pushing it out of his eyes, and asked Leslie to dance. Leslie held her beer above her head as she and Matt made their way to the dance floor.

Jennifer sipped her beer and watched the dancers; what she saw confirmed her belief that white people had no rhythm. No one asked her to dance or approached her in any way. Periodically, she would see a guy look her way. If he saw her glance at him, he'd abruptly turn away, avoiding eye contact. To have a reason for moving across the room, Jennifer put her half-full cup of beer down and headed over to the keg to get another.

Flushed from dancing, Leslie came over. "How're you doing?"

Between clenched teeth, Jennifer hissed, "Where are all those lots of black guys you promised me?"

Leslie made a little pouty face. "I don't know. Does it matter?"

Jennifer smiled weakly. "Does it matter?" Her smile disappeared as she snarled, "Of course it matters!"

Matt grabbed Leslie and pulled her back onto the dance floor as she yelled over the throbbing sound of an electric guitar, "Just have a good time."

Just then, a pimple-faced boy approached Jennifer. Obviously already drunk, he said, "Dance?"

Jennifer followed him to the dance floor, where he began twirling in circles and bouncing up and down as if he were chopping wood and doing the polka. Suddenly he yelled, "Yeah! Get down!" Jennifer watched him in disbelief as she struggled to maintain some semblance of rhythm. Out of the corner of her eye, she saw a good-looking guy with dark brown hair and a thick mustache with flecks of red; he wore a black turtleneck that accentuated his broad shoulders and flat abs, and he was dancing on beat. The record finally stopped. Jennifer attempted to thank her drunken partner, but he staggered away before she could do so.

Once again Jennifer was standing alone and watching the party go on around her; then a tall black guy entered the room, and her plummeting mood lifted. He was Jack-and-Jill fine. On closer scrutiny, Jennifer could see that he wasn't alone. He was accompanied by a short blond girl, whose arm was draped around his waist. Jennifer added him to her snow fever list. Her mood again descended as she felt the anxiety and then depression of being the only black girl at this party. The good dancer was walking toward her. She was struck by his beautiful blue eyes. "Would you like to dance?" Blue Eyes asked.

As a Sam and Dave record played, they started hand dancing. He pushed her into a turn, neither one missing a beat. Jennifer shouted, "You're good."

"So are you." She could feel the others watching them, believing that some were admiring their dance moves while others were staring because a white boy was dancing with a black girl.

Without saying a word, Blue Eyes gently put his arm around Jennifer's waist and took her hand, and they swayed slowly to the music. He pulled his head back to look at her face. "Where do you go?"

"Goucher."

"Been to Princeton before?"

"First time."

The record ended, and they held on to each other just a fraction of a second after the music stopped. Blue Eyes loosened his embrace but did not fully let go. "I'm Steven Greenberg."

"Jennifer Madison."

As the slow strains of the next song began, Steven placed Jennifer's hands around his neck and wrapped his arms around her waist so that they were dancing face to face. She looked up into his blue eyes, wanting to say something, but her tummy quivered, and she felt nervously shy. Instead, she placed her head against his cheek, followed his lead, and thought, *Thank you, Jesus, for this slow song.*

The record ended. Steven whispered into her ear, "How about a beer?"

"Honestly, no, I hate the stuff. Any soda around here?"

"Sure, there's a soda machine in the basement. Follow me." Steven took her hand and headed toward the basement steps. The touch of his hand on hers made her tummy quiver again. She also asked herself if she should be following this blue-eyed white boy to some unknown basement. It was hard to ponder these thoughts while the sounds of a screeching electric guitar assaulted her ears and the din of drunken voices surrounded her. While crossing the dance floor, Jennifer waved to Leslie, who returned the wave and silently mouthed, "Who's that?" and then did a thumbs-up.

Facing the red light on the soda machine, Steven said, "I guess you're not the only one in this madhouse who wanted a soda. Why don't we walk over to Chancellor Green? We'll get you a soda over there, and I can show you the campus."

On the way out of Tower, Jennifer found Leslie, introduced Steven, and explained that they were going over to Chancellor Green. Leslie quickly pulled Jennifer aside. "He's cute. Now, go have a good time!"

The chilly night air greeted them as they headed down Prospect toward the center of the campus. Steven began his tour. "That's Cannon Club." A girl was sitting astride the Revolutionary War-era cannon, riding it as if it were a bucking bronco, while people stood around yelling and throwing beer on her and each other.

Jennifer stepped quickly to the side to avoid being splashed by flying beer. "What's that?"

Steven grinned. "That, unfortunately, is what my many drunken classmates define as a good time."

"They're so drunk that they're not going to remember whether they had a good time or not."

"Often, that's the point." Steven pointed to a building with a reflecting pool. "That's the Woodrow Wilson School." They walked some more. "That's Firestone Library, and this way is Chancellor Green."

Once they entered Chancellor Green, Steven asked, "Would you rather have some hot chocolate or coffee?"

"Hot chocolate sounds perfect."

Steven went to the counter, warmly greeting Mrs. Kendall, the grandmotherly woman who was a legend at Chancellor Green because she had worked the night shift there for over twenty years. He ordered hot chocolate and joined Jennifer in a booth against the wall.

They sipped the hot chocolate and chatted, discovering that they were both juniors and both government majors who were planning to go to law school.

Jennifer sipped her hot chocolate and surreptitiously stole looks at his blue eyes. She wondered whether she found his eyes so special just because she wasn't used to looking at a man with blue eyes or whether she was mesmerized by his *Seventeen* magazine version of handsome.

"I'd like to get into civil rights law," Jennifer said. "NAACP Legal Defense Fund. Stuff like that."

"My dad has a friend who worked with Thurgood Marshall on the *Brown v. Board of Education* case."

"Really? I wonder if they had any idea how important that case would be."

"Umm, good question." Steven placed his hand on top of hers.

She stiffened but didn't move her hand or his. "What area of law interests you?"

"Litigation."

"I bet you watched every episode of *Perry Mason!*"

Steven intertwined their fingers. "You got it. He never lost a case."

Steven returned to the counter for refills, and Mrs. Kendall requested that he play "Rhapsody in Blue."

Steven took the two cups of hot chocolate over to the booth. "I've had a request from my only fan."

Jennifer reached for the proffered mug. "I heard. I'd love to hear you play."

Steven went over to the piano, and the strains of Gershwin's "Rhapsody in Blue" filled the room. Midway through the piece, Jennifer joined Steven on the piano bench so she could see his hands move across the black and white keys. As he worked the pedal, his thigh pressed against hers. She didn't outwardly react but enjoyed the touch of his body. When he concluded, Mrs. Kendall clapped, and Jennifer joined in.

She leaned against him, resting her head on his shoulder. "That was great! Play something else."

Mrs. Kendall, still behind the counter, said, "Ain't he wonderful?"

"You're absolutely right. He's wonderful," Jennifer agreed.

Steven stood and gave Mrs. Kendall a slight bow. "Mrs. Kendall, meet Jennifer."

"Nice to meet you honey," Mrs. Kendall said. "Now, Steven, play that fancy one I like."

"'Fur Elise'?"

She scowled. "I'm too old to remember the name. You know the one."

Steven started to play the first few notes of "Für Elise" and stood up to see if it was the piece Mrs. Kendall wanted to hear.

She yelled from behind the counter, "That's the one!"

He sat back down and continued to play "Für Elise," launched into Henry Mancini's "Pink Panther," and ended with "Moon River."

"You're out of sight," Jennifer said. "When did you start playing?"

"Seven and continued off and on with lessons through high school."

"Thanks for the concert."

After saying good night to Mrs. Kendall, they walked out into the frigid night. This time, Steven pulled up the collar of his navy pea coat and then put his arm around Jennifer as they walked slowly, huddled close together against the cold. As they entered Blair Arch, Steven stopped. "Let's stay out of this wind for a minute." He turned to Jennifer and looked into her eyes. Her heart started to beat faster, anticipating his kiss. She wanted him to kiss her, yet she was socialized to believe that she shouldn't want this white boy to kiss her. While she pondered her conflicting feelings, he kissed her gently on her lips. During the kiss, she wondered how she could ever have not wanted him to kiss her. He kissed her again. This time, she was certain she didn't want him to stop kissing her.

Chapter 15

Leslie

Leslie was dressing when Allison knocked and asked, "Where are you and Joel going tonight?"

"Morris Mechanic Theater."

"Nice!" Allison picked up the prom photo of Leslie and Danny, looked at it, and then placed it back on the desk without comment. Leslie noticed but said nothing, as she knew that Danny had never asked Allison out after that first Princeton weekend. Allison never discussed it, and neither did she. Allison asked, "How long have you two been going out?"

"That's kind of hard to calculate. I met him freshman year. Remember?" As she applied blue eye shadow, she said, "We went out a couple of times, but then he got all weird. Studied all the time. We dated off and on last year. But, I was also dating Scott."

Allison interrupted Leslie's rambling response. "You were dating Jonah and Paul and Ezra. Shall I go on?"

"OK, you're right. I had a lot of dates sophomore year. But, I've been seeing a lot of Joel this year. Since he started Hopkins Med School, he's calmer. It's like he saw his future." Leslie adjusted the pitch of her voice to imitate the sound of a hospital intercom. "'Calling Dr. Joel Eisenberg. Dr. Eisenberg, you're needed in the ER.' He started to relax and have some fun. Nice guy."

Jennifer walked in just as Leslie said "nice guy." "That's it? Nice guy? Doesn't sound passionate to me."

"Passionate is not always a requirement," Leslie sniffed as she put on her pearl necklace.

Allison groaned in response, and Jennifer asked, "Have big plans tonight?"

Leslie laughed. "Cut it out. We're going to a play."

"And what happens after the play?" Jennifer winked at her teasingly.

The buzzer sounded, indicating that Joel was in the lobby. "Who knows?"

After the play, Joel took Leslie to the house he shared with two other Hopkins med students.

"Where are your roommates tonight?"

"Those two guys study more than I do. They're probably at the library."

Joel handed her a glass of wine. "I know I was kind of a mess until I actually got into med school. I'm glad you didn't completely give up on me."

Leslie's smile turned to light laughter. "Don't be silly. I understand. You were really stressed out. I know how much you wanted to get into Hopkins Med School."

Joel rubbed his hands across his face. "My whole family woulda been disappointed."

"I know the pressure you were under," Leslie said sympathetically. "My son, the doctor—every Jewish mother's mantra."

Joel finished his wine and put the glass on the table. He took Leslie's wineglass from her hand and placed it on the table beside his, extended his hand to Leslie, and led her up the stairs to his bedroom. Joel didn't turn on the lights but closed the door behind them and embraced her. "I've wanted to make love to you from the moment I saw you standing in Mrs. Gottlieb's living room. I couldn't believe it—an extraordinarily beautiful blind date arranged by Aunt Esther!"

"Ah, that's sweet."

Joel gently pressed her lips open with his tongue as they staggered back onto his bed, and his hands explored her body. He rolled on top of her, entered her, and then fell asleep. Leslie stared at the ceiling, then at his nose, and then back at the ceiling. Eventually she watched him awaken in a panic. "What time is it?"

"One. I didn't sign out, so we've got to go." She stood up, adjusting her clothes, and added, "Now!"

The following morning, Leslie slept late, missing breakfast.

Jennifer asked, "Big night, huh?"

Leslie sighed, "Late night."

"How was the play?"

"A little too depressing. I was more in the mood for a musical—you know, a little singing, a little dancing. Instead it was two and a half hours of strident conversation."

"Even with my student discount, I think I'll pass on that one. How's Joel?"

"Joel is a very *nice* guy," Leslie sighed. "But …"

"But what?"

"Uh, I don't know. We'll see."

"You seem kinda weird. Are you OK?"

Leslie sighed again, stretched, and then fell back on the bed. "I'm OK. No big deal."

Needling her roommate, Jennifer said, "Ah, come on. Tell me."

Staring at the ceiling, Leslie recalled how she had stared at Joel's ceiling last night and confessed, "I've really tried to like him. I think the only thing I like about him are his credentials."

"What are you talking about? Credentials?"

"Going to be a doctor." Leslie stuck her index finger up. "Not bad looking." She stuck another finger up. "Jewish." She raised her third finger. "On the surface, he sounds like a match for me, but I don't feel it."

"Keep looking."

"Like I ever stopped!"

Chapter 16

Paige

Paige was awakened by the sound of the refrigerator door closing. She called out to Peter, but he didn't respond. She turned over and went back to sleep for another hour. When she awakened, she walked into the kitchen and found her favorite coffee cup sitting on the counter next to a note: "Things to do. Love you, Peter."

She tossed the note in the trash and got dressed. Later in the day she telephoned Peter at the center, but he wasn't there. He returned to the apartment around midnight after she had gone to sleep. She awakened when he eased into bed. "Where were you all day?"

He kissed her. "Tired. Good night."

In the morning, Paige handed Peter the *Baltimore New Press*, as he drank his coffee by the one window that admitted morning light into their apartment. "Peter, look at the front-page article about the draft card burning. Some people got arrested. According to this, it got violent."

"I don't need to read it. I was there."

Paige was surprised. "I didn't know you were at the rally."

"Yeah. In fact, I helped organize it."

With a scolding tone, Paige said, "You didn't tell me anything about that."

Peter placed his mug on the table and stood up next to her. "I know. I thought it was better for you if I didn't."

"What do you mean better for me?" Paige asked petulantly.

Paige could hear the serious and almost sad tone in his voice and see it in his face. "I knew people would get arrested. I didn't want you to worry."

"I'm not a child who needs protecting."

"No, you're not, are you? My mistake." Peter got more coffee. "JoJo got his draft notice yesterday."

"Who's JoJo?"

Peter took another sip of his coffee. "JoJo's the guy who works on cars at the garage near the center. Dropped out of school at sixteen. Real love for engines. I just knew his draft notice would come soon."

"Is he going to go?"

Peter, his voice rising sharply, said, "Of course he's going to go. What are his alternatives? Doesn't have any. In fact, he said his mother's happy. She thinks the army will make a man out of him. I think the army will make him a dead man."

Paige rattled by the anger in Peter's voice, merely said, "Sad."

With his bowed head in his hands, Peter said, "That's just one of the many sad stories I deal with every day at the center. I know I'm helping some kids, but it's not enough. I need to see more results."

"You're making a difference. Because of the center, a lot of kids have a safe place to go after school. Tyrone never would have gotten that basketball scholarship without you. You convinced that coach to take a chance on him despite his juvenile record. You're the one who suggested I do the profiles on the kids in the newspaper. See how happy they are when they see their name and picture in the newspaper? You should be proud of what you do."

"I am. It's just not enough."

Paige looked at Peter quizzically. "What's enough for you?"

"I wish I knew the answer to that. I look around, and I see so much that's wrong." Peter flipped through the paper. "Not enough."

Chapter 17

Jennifer

As Susan pulled up to Colonial, Jennifer could see Barry talking with Steven. With Susan and Barry watching, Steven kissed her gently on the lips. "It's great to see you."

Barry grabbed Susan's luggage and headed into Colonial with a mere wave of his hand.

🍁　　　🍁　　　🍁

Princeton's Tigertones closed the performance in Alexander Hall with songs from *West Side Story*. As Jennifer listened to the music, the urban Romeo and Juliet story suddenly spoke to her. She realized, as Steven placed his hand on her back to lead her out of the auditorium that she was embarking on her own version of the story. She saw Susan and Barry and waved to Susan, who rushed over. "That was fun, wasn't it? We're headed to Nassau Street to get something to eat. Join us."

Before Steven or Jennifer could respond, Barry interjected, "I'm sure they have their own plans."

Susan said, "Oh, come on. You guys are hungry."

Barry repeated, "Susan"—he paused for a moment, and his eyes darted from Susan to Jennifer and Steven—"I'm sure they have their own plans."

Jennifer quickly said, "Another time."

As Jennifer and Steven headed toward Tower, he asked, "Why didn't you want to go and eat with them? It was fine with me."

"No reason." She suspected that Barry didn't like her because she was black, but she didn't want to talk with Steven about that.

Steven put his arm around her waist and said, "Fine with me. I prefer having you all to myself."

❦   ❦   ❦

Jennifer rode up to Princeton with Susan the following weekend, and they chatted like best friends all the way. When they reached Colonial, Steven and Barry were waiting for them. Steven explained, "I was just telling Barry about the party Tower is having tonight: Tower-A-Go-Go. There will be a deejay from New York, complete with go-go dancers in cages. Should be fun. Come by."

Susan did a little shimmy of her narrow hips and said, "We'll be there!"

Barry said, "We'll try to stop by."

As Jennifer and Steven walked down Prospect, she said, "I don't think they'll come."

"Why?"

Jennifer retorted, "Barry said they'd try, and he runs that show."

Steven shrugged his shoulder, oblivious to Jennifer's real concerns. "No big deal."

Around midnight, Jennifer was shocked to see Barry and Susan arrive at Tower. Barry brusquely shoved his way through the crowd until they were next to Steven and Jennifer on the crowded dance floor. Steven yelled, "Glad you could make it."

Susan said, "Me too," as she did a frantic shimmy and Barry shuffled his feet while staring at the floor.

Steven pulled Jennifer into his arms and whispered, "We need to give Barry and Susan some dance lessons."

Jennifer laughed knowingly. "They're hopeless. And besides he's so drunk he can barely stand up, let alone dance."

The deejay pumped up the volume, and the sound reverberated, drowning out all conversation. Barry yelled, "Switch!" Jennifer was unsure of what she'd heard, given the din of the music, but she understood when Barry roughly jerked her hand and continued his spastic shuffle and Steven started dancing with Susan. As Jennifer looked at Barry drunkenly shuffling back and forth, she lost the beat. She closed her eyes in an attempt to regain her rhythm. She opened her eyes, saw Barry's red face, and thought that he had to get blurry-eyed drunk in order to dance with her. When the next record started, Steven yelled, "Switch!" and rescued her.

As the deejay packed up his equipment, Barry, holding a beer in one hand and rocking back and forth in a determined effort not to fall down, mumbled to Steven and Jennifer, "Great party. I danced my ass off!"

Inwardly laughing at Barry's assessment of his dancing, Jennifer said, "Barry, I think you were truly inspired by those go-go dancers."

Barry threw his head back, almost losing his balance, and howled, "No shit!" Regaining his balance, he added, "Hey, Susan and I are going into the city tomorrow. Greenwich Village. Wanna come?"

Steven said, "Sure." Jennifer wanted to protest but decided against it, because she really liked Susan.

The quartet got to Greenwich Village in the afternoon and blended into the chaotic scene of street vendors, speed chess players, long-haired hippies, elderly white women accompanied by their Jamaican health aides, chanting Hare Krishnas, Midwestern tourists searching for Jack Kerouac, and street musicians of varying degrees of talent. They wandered up and down the streets, going in and out of shops, watching the hordes of people, and being stared at by the Midwestern tourists. A middle-aged white woman actually pointed at the four of them, forcing Jennifer to acknowledge that two young white men, a Chinese girl, and a black girl were not a group routinely seen on the streets of America. They passed a flower vendor, and Jennifer stopped. "Look at these flowers. They're beautiful. Especially those roses. I've never seen roses that color."

Steven asked the vendor, "How much for the roses?"

Jennifer said, "Don't buy them. They'll die by the time we get back to campus."

"You're right." Steven smiled at the vendor and said, "Sorry. Not this time."

Steven suggested, "How about some jazz?" and led the group to a club a few blocks away. When they entered, the bartender said, "Hey, Steven, my man. Haven't seen you in a while."

Steven replied, "Hi, Mack. These are my friends, Barry and Susan." He put his arm around Jennifer's shoulders and pulled her to him, "And this is Jennifer!"

Mack said, "Hey, good to meet ya. Steven, you want to sit in? Herbie's over there."

Barry asked Steven, "What's he talking about?"

Mack said, "Steven, your friends don't know." Mack pointed at Steven. "This guy plays a mean piano."

Barry said, "Go for it. I'll take care of the girls." Barry gallantly put one arm around Susan and his other arm around Jennifer and ushered them to the table.

Steven sat down at the piano and joined in.

After Steven played for several minutes, Barry said, "He's good."

Jennifer agreed, "He really is terrific."

When Steven finished the set, Barry, Susan, and Jennifer were on their feet, clapping. Steven joined them at the table, and Jennifer embraced him. Steven kissed her on the lips for a very long time and then said, "Thanks."

❧   ❧   ❧

As Susan and Jennifer drove back to Goucher on Sunday evening, Susan said, "Steven really likes you."

"Think so?"

"Oh, come on, Jennifer. I saw that long, romantic kiss he gave you last night." Susan, needling her, continued, "He wasn't just saying he was glad you enjoyed hearing him play the piano."

Jennifer leaned comfortably back in the passenger's seat. "I think he likes me. And I like him. He's really cute. Kind. Smart." She stopped her musings and looked at Susan. "It's obvious to me that you and Barry are very much in love."

Jennifer watched Susan's expression evolve into a contented smile as she stared ahead at the New Jersey Turnpike. "You're right. I'm in love. Barry's wonderful. When I think of the rest of my life, I see Barry there by my side."

"I don't have any experience with being in love, but I think that's exactly what you're supposed to feel. Have you met Barry's parents?"

Susan shook her head no, but the smile did not leave her face.

"Hmm, I'm surprised, seeing as they live nearby." Jennifer wondered what Barry's mother thought of Susan.

Chapter 18

Leslie

On Sunday night, when Jennifer returned from Princeton, Leslie, wrapped in her pink velour robe, was sitting on the floor of the hallway and talking with Allison. Leslie asked, "How was your weekend?"

Jennifer smiled broadly, stepped over Leslie's and Allison's legs, which were blocking her path, and said, "Great" as she entered their room.

Leslie said, "Good for you. Come out here and join the pity party. We're discussing whether I should break up with Joel or not."

Jennifer stuck her head out the door. "What?"

Allison said, "That's right. We need you. Come out here and talk some sense into her."

Jennifer left her suitcase in the middle of the floor, came out into the hall, and sat down next to Leslie. "What happened?"

Allison spoke up. "So far, all I can tell is nothing happened."

Leslie whined, "Don't say it like that. So far, I haven't given you a reason. That doesn't mean nothing happened."

Jennifer got up, removed her knee-high leather boots, and sat down again on the floor next to Leslie. "Wait a minute. You two have been talking for a while, so you've got to let me catch up. What did I miss? Fill me in."

Leslie leaned back against the wall. "That's it. Nothing happened. I didn't see Joel today, because he studied all day."

Allison blurted out, "Leslie, he's a Hopkins med student. He has to study."

"I know that. I study, too. In fact, I finished the first draft of my sociology paper today. Pretty good, too. Joel's a very nice guy ..." Leslie's voice trailed off.

Jennifer said, "This is very simple. You just don't feel it. There's no click. You want to like him because of his résumé: Hopkins med student, the future doctor, your mother would get her Jewish doctor son-in-law, your college mother introduced you to him, she likes him, and on and on. We've had this discussion before. But do *you* like him?"

Allison and Jennifer stared at Leslie. Leslie looked down at the floor and did not meet their gaze. Allison asked, "Does he turn you on?"

Leslie blushed and screamed, "Allison! Really!"

"Really what?" Allison questioned. "You know exactly what I mean!"

Jennifer said, "Come on, Leslie. What are you thinking?"

"I'm thinking there's absolutely nothing really wrong with Joel—but for the nose. He's just not the guy for me. All right, already! He doesn't turn me on! How do you tell someone that? It's so much easier to break up with someone when they do something awful. I may have to pick a fight with him."

Allison said, "That's not right. But then if he's boring in bed, he's got to go!"

Leslie agreed, "You're right. I'll just have to tell him. Not the sex part. I don't want to hurt his feelings."

Jennifer asked, "When are you going to do it? Aren't you going with him to his aunt and uncle's anniversary dinner this Saturday?"

"Crap. You're right. I can't do it this week. It's a sit-down dinner dance at a hotel. Aunt Esther would have to rearrange the tables."

Allison noted, "That would be too embarrassing for Joel. His aunt and uncle and Mrs. Gottlieb would be asking him what happened right there at the party."

"Can't do it this week." Jennifer stood up and headed into the room. "Be your usual kind self."

Leslie frowned, "Seeing as I can't break up with him this week, maybe he'll do something to give me a *reason* for breaking up."

Leslie looked pleadingly at Allison, who shook her head and said, "Not going to happen."

Chapter 19

Paige

Paige came to the community center to meet Peter for dinner. When she entered his office, he was slumped over his desk. "What's the matter?" Peter didn't move. "Talk to me. What is it?"

He sat up and stared blankly at Paige. "He didn't even make it out of basic training."

Paige started messaging his shoulders gently. "Who didn't make it?"

"JoJo. He died in basic training at Fort Bragg. He didn't even get to Vietnam. He died while being trained to die in Vietnam."

"I'm so sorry. It's very sad to lose a friend."

"You don't get it. There's too much sadness out there. I've got to do something. This war has got to end. Our country's unfairness has got to end."

"What are you going to do?"

"I don't feel like eating. Go get yourself something to eat. I've got some paperwork to do here. I'll see you later."

She moved toward the door and looked back, wishing she could do or say something comforting. "Take some time to deal with this. It's such an unnecessary death. You need to be alone."

Paige stopped by the deli down the street from their apartment, bought an Italian sub, and went home. She nibbled at the sandwich as she made a few phone calls to confirm some quotes for her article about the deplorable living conditions in public housing. By midnight, Peter had not come home. In the morning, as she made coffee, she found the note: "Dear Paige, remember I love you. But I must go and do something to end the unfairness in the world. Love, Peter."

Paige reread the note and wondered where he was going, when he was coming back, and what he was going to do. She quickly got dressed and went to the center. She met Eric at the front door, and he handed her a note: "Eric, I've got to go. Take care of the center. Always your friend, Peter."

Paige looked at Eric after reading the note. "What does it mean?"

Eric shook his head. "I have no idea. He never said anything to me about leaving."

Paige stared into Peter's empty office. "He never said anything to me either. He knew he was always free to go. That's the way it was between us."

❧   ❧   ❧

Paige continued to work at the newspaper and waited for Peter to contact her. She wanted to understand what had made him leave and what he was doing. For several weeks, neither she nor Eric heard from Peter. Finally, Peter called her at the newspaper. "I'm not coming back. I'm not good for you now. Move on with your life."

Paige cried into the phone, "I love you. You love me. What are you talking about? Where are you?"

"It's best for you that you don't know where I am. Remember that I love you. But move on to a life without me. I'm not what you need."

Chapter 20

Jennifer

On the plane to Detroit for Christmas break, Jennifer contemplated when, what, and how she was going to tell her parents that Steven was white. Now, as the plane was touching down on the wet runway, she was losing her nerve.

The Madison's Tudor-style home was in a quiet neighborhood of large single-family homes, each with a manicured lawn and a two-car garage. Upon entering the house, Mrs. Madison would pick up any bits of litter that might be found on the sidewalk or lawn—abandoned bus transfers, cigarette butts, a plastic top from a McDonald's soft drink cup—and immediately rebuke the thoughtless person who had dropped it in her yard. Gloria had a personal vendetta against McDonald's and held the restaurant personally responsible for half of the litter in Detroit. As she drove through the Detroit slums, she'd say, "Look at that trash on the ground. Those lazy women are just sitting there collecting welfare checks and having babies. They could at least pick up the garbage. Look at those nappy-headed children. Those women sit on their fat butts all day and won't even comb their children's hair. It's absolutely a disgrace. It's people like that who hold the entire race back."

Jennifer would respond to her mother's periodic rants by saying, "Mother, poor neighborhoods are neglected by the city government, and consequently the city doesn't schedule sufficient garbage collection in these areas."

Her mother would then look at her with a resigned expression. "Sweetie, that garbage is nowhere near a garbage can. These people just throw the stuff out the window. They don't care. When's the last time you dropped paper on the ground and didn't pick it up?" There would be a short, dramatic pause, and then her mother would scream, "Never!"

The first morning at home, Jennifer and her mother sat at the kitchen table eating homemade blueberry muffins, drinking coffee, and catching up on Detroit and family gossip. After sipping black coffee, Mrs. Madison asked, "Well, Jen how's school?"

"School's good. I'm working on a paper for my archaeology class. I went to the Princeton-Yale game with Steven."

"Tell me about Steven. You've been seeing a lot of him, haven't you?"

She took a deep breath and was about to speak but opted to take another sip of coffee. Still stalling for time, she said, "I'm going to get some butter." She got up and opened the refrigerator, hoping her normally talkative mother would launch into another subject. Instead, Mrs. Madison quietly waited for Jennifer to return to the table. "Steven's a junior at Princeton. Poli-sci major."

"Where's he from?"

"Long Island."

"Hmm. What's his last name?"

"Greenberg?"

Mrs. Madison eyes widened. "Greenberg? Is he white?"

"He's Jewish." Jennifer started chattering to fill in the gaps as her mother digested the whiteness. "He has dark brown hair and a thick mustache. Blue eyes."

Placing her cup in the dishwasher, she asked, "Who's Leslie dating now?"

"She finally broke up with Joel. No one special at the moment."

"Are you still thinking about law school?"

"Absolutely. Steven wants to go to law school, too. His father's a lawyer."

Mrs. Madison finished her muffin and didn't comment.

When Mr. Madison returned home that evening from work, his wife met him at the door. "Ron, that boy Jennifer is dating at Princeton is white!"

"Gloria, she's only *dating* the boy."

"I know she's a sensible girl, but this sounds serious to me."

"If it's serious, we'll know. How serious can it be?" He chuckled and patted his wife's hand. "She's home one day, and she goes out with her high school boyfriend. Relax."

The telephone rang, and Mrs. Madison answered.

The male voice said, "May I speak with Jennifer, please?"

"I'm sorry, but Jennifer has gone out for the evening. May I take a message?"

"Mrs. Madison?"

"Yes?"

"Hello, how are you? I'm Steven Greenberg, a friend of Jennifer's."

Mrs. Madison asked, "Who?"

"My name is Steven Greenberg. I go to Princeton. I'm a friend of Jennifer's."

Mrs. Madison spoke in the voice she reserved for business and formal occasions, or, as her husband always teasingly called it, her "proper" voice. "And your name is again?"

"Steven Greenberg."

"Fine. Steven Greenberg." She repeated the name as if she were trying to remember. "I'll tell Jennifer you called."

Steven interrupted Mrs. Madison as she was saying good-bye. "Mrs. Madison, please tell Jennifer I'll call her tomorrow. It was nice chatting with you. I hope you and Mr. Madison have a happy holiday."

She walked into the den, where her husband was sitting in his recliner and laughing at Redd Foxx's antics on *Sanford and Son.*

"Ron, guess who was on the phone?" Before he could guess, she said, "That white boy I was just telling you about. Actually, he was very polite and pleasant. I didn't let on that I knew who he was, though. I didn't want to give him that satisfaction."

Ron didn't respond. He kept his eyes glued to the TV. His wife stood above him, waiting for his reaction. He finally said, "Gloria, this is the sixties. Don't you remember how our hearts filled up when Martin Luther King delivered his dream speech? That dream was for a day when people would be judged by the content of their character and not the color of their skin. I admit that it's not my preference that Jennifer marries a white man, but my bottom line is that I want her to marry a man who loves and respects her and who makes her happy."

Gloria said, "Jennifer can't be happy with a white man. America won't let her."

"You mean *you* won't let her."

"Go watch Redd Foxx!" his wife snapped.

Ron stared at the TV, but he stopped laughing.

When Jennifer came in later, her mother said, "Steven Greenberg called."

Jennifer's face and voice reflected her excitement. "Really? What did he say?" She then panicked at the thought that Steven had spoken with her mother.

"I told him you were out for the evening. Let's get to the mall early in the morning and finish our Christmas shopping."

In the morning, Jennifer and her mother drove to the mall in bumper-to-bumper traffic on snow-covered streets. After listening to Nat King Cole sing "The Christmas Song," the radio newscaster said, "The Detroit police have just arrested a suspect for the murder and robbery of the gas station attendant last Saturday night."

Mrs. Madison said, "God, I hope he's not black."

Jennifer asked, "Who's not black?"

"The guy the police just arrested. Some people think all criminals are black."

After battling crowds in the mall, they headed home. Just as they entered the house, the phone was ringing. Jennifer grabbed it and answered in a breathless voice.

"Hello, may I speak with Jennifer, please?"

"Steven!"

"Hey! How are you?"

"Fine, how are you?"

"Missing you."

She didn't feel comfortable responding to Steven's comment with her mother standing nearby. "Steven, hold on. I'm going to change phones." Jennifer turned to her mother and said, "I'm going to take this upstairs." Still wearing her coat, she yanked off her boots, ran barefoot up to her bedroom, and grabbed the receiver while yelling, "Mother, I've got it. You can hang up now." She waited to hear the phone click. "I'm so glad you called."

"I told your mother that I would call back today."

"She didn't mention it."

"Hold on. My mother wants to say hello."

Mrs. Greenberg got on the telephone, "Jennifer? Hello. How are you?"

"Fine, Mrs. Greenberg. Thank you."

"I won't hold you, but I wanted to wish you and your family a happy holiday. I've heard so much about you from Steven. I look forward to meeting you. Well, give your family my regards. Here's Steven."

Steven got back on the line.

"Steven, that was very nice of your mom. What have you told her about me?" She thought that what she really wanted to know was what his mother thought about her son dating a black girl. She wondered if his mother was one of the new liberals who liked the idea of her son having a black experience she could chat about at cocktail parties.

"Everything … well, not quite everything."

"You mean you didn't tell her I'm black."

"I told her that. I didn't tell her what soft and luscious lips you have and how I love to nuzzle your ear when we dance."

She wondered if this was his sly way of saying she had big lips. She dismissed the thought and said, "Steven, you're crazy."

"Yes, I'm crazy about you. By the way, seeing as you brought it up, did you tell your parents that I'm Jewish? When I called, your mother acted as if she didn't know who I was."

"Yes, I told my mother."

"What did she say?"

"Nothing."

"What did your father say?"

"I assume my mother told him. She tells him everything, but he didn't say anything to me."

"I hear something in your voice that I can't figure out. I wish I could see your face."

Glad that he couldn't see her face or read her mind, which was questioning what they'd started, she merely said, "We'll talk about this later. Are you going skiing?" The conversation switched to Steven's ski trip to Vermont.

Chapter 21

Leslie

The word spread quickly across Hopkins campus that Leslie was no longer dating Joel. She turned down lots of dates, but when the current president of Beta Tau Sig, whom she'd known since freshman year when she was Miss Beta Tau Sig, called and invited her to the fraternity's luau, she accepted.

The fraternity house was decorated with fake palm trees, tiki torches, seashells, and sand on the dance floor. Each girl was given a lei of orchids. Piña coladas were served in hollowed-out pineapples. The frat boys quickly tired of the sweet piña coladas and switched to drinking beer out of the pineapples.

By midnight, Leslie's date was drunk. She got a ride back to school with a girl from her dorm.

Allison was in the hall playing cards when Leslie returned. "How was the party?"

"I'm back early. That should tell you something. My date got so drunk that he couldn't stand up and then proceeded to throw up. He didn't quite make it to the bathroom—disgusting. After that, I left. Joel never got drunk like that. Maybe I shouldn't have broken up with him."

"Having second thoughts?"

"Momentarily. I'll feel better in the morning. Love isn't rational. That's the problem with it."

Chapter 22

Paige

Leslie met Paige at the Gopher Hole. "I'm so glad you called. I haven't seen you in forever. Any news about Peter?"

Looking wan, Paige said, "No, he hasn't contacted me again. Eric hasn't heard from him either. I came out because I wanted to tell you that I'm moving."

"Where?"

Paige looked around wistfully at the student center and remembered the many times she and Peter had sat here. "California. I've been accepted in a writing program at Stanford."

"Excellent school."

"I'm thrilled I got in. Most of all, I need a change of scene. I think California will do me good. I can't just stay here waiting for Peter to come back. He's not coming back. I'm going to do what he said: go on with my life without him."

"When I first met you two, I knew you were very much in love. I'm so sorry that it's turned out this way. Love is supposed to make you happy, not sad."

Paige's eyes darted around the room and then looked longingly out at the courtyard. "Remember the peace vigil with Professor Rokowsky singing?"

"Yeah."

"She sang 'We Shall Overcome.' I asked her why she started singing that song for an antiwar demonstration. It wasn't a civil rights march. I didn't get it. She told me that the song was about peace for everyone, that Vietnam and civil rights were all connected. I didn't really get it even after she explained it to me. I pretended I did, but I didn't—just like I really didn't get Peter. He wanted to marry me. He said that I was the one thing that made him feel that the world wasn't completely fucked-up. Maybe I should have married him." Paige stood up and smiled wistfully. "Peter's love made me happy. Unfortunately, it was not forever love. I kind of knew that. I secretly wanted forever love, even though I never admitted it to myself. I don't think I really believe in forever love."

Leslie stood up and embraced her. "We all want forever love."

"I'm still not sure. Forever probably isn't for me."

"What if Peter comes back?"

Paige concentrated on dangling her keys around her finger before she spoke. "Life is full of what-ifs."

Chapter 23

Jennifer

Jennifer spotted Susan walking from the library and caught up with her in front of the chapel. "I've been looking forward to seeing Simon and Garfunkel for weeks. But since Dr. King's assassination, I really don't want to do anything. I just feel sad all of the time."

Susan said dryly, "Me, too. This is a horrible time. I'm not going to Princeton this weekend."

Jennifer was incredulous. "You're not going? You and Barry have been dying to see Simon and Garfunkel."

All of a sudden, Susan started to cry. Silently, the tears rolled from her eyes down her porcelain cheeks. Jennifer put her arm around Susan. "What's the matter?" Jennifer dragged Susan over to the Japanese cherry tree, which was in full bloom, and they sat down on the grass. Just as they sat, a Frisbee landed at their feet, so they moved to the other side of the tree.

"Tell me what's wrong!"

As other students strolled by on their way to class, totally oblivious to Susan's obvious misery, she spoke in a tiny voice. "I broke up with Barry. I've dated him for almost two years. We're both seniors. I thought he loved me. He doesn't want to marry me. He told me so last night."

Jennifer took Susan's hands in hers. "I'm so sorry."

Choking back the tears, Susan continued, "Well, he didn't actually say it, but he's making plans for after graduation, which he's made clear don't include me. I thought he would ask me to marry him. But he hasn't, and for the first time, I know he never will."

"How do you know that? Just because he hasn't asked you yet doesn't mean he won't. He may be planning to do it on graduation day when your family's here—make it really special."

Susan's face was now covered with tears, but her eyes, although red and sad, were alert. "I've given this a lot of thought. You helped me figure it out."

"Me?" Jennifer gasped. "What did I do?"

"We've spent a lot of time talking when we were driving back and forth to Princeton. You asked me once if I had met Barry's parents."

"Did I?"

"Yes. At the time, I didn't think anything about it. But I started to think about it. I even suggested to Barry that we go visit his parents. He made some excuse. Said his parents were in Europe. He's never brought it up again, and neither have I. He didn't want me to meet his parents, because he wasn't in love with me. I'm Chinese. I know the importance of family. And so does Barry."

Jennifer looked at Susan's sad face and said, "I'm really sorry it didn't turn out the way you wanted."

She found another ride to Princeton and was silent during the three-hour trip. Although the other passengers were friendly, it just felt wrong to Jennifer that she wasn't riding with Susan.

Jennifer and Steven entered Dillon Gym for the Simon and Garfunkel concert, taking seats on the main floor. As was her habit, she looked around to see if any black people were present; there were none on the main floor, although she could see a couple of black guys seated in the bleachers. When the lights darkened, Art Garfunkel's voice enraptured Jennifer, and she briefly forgot her lone-black-person status. When the duo sang "Bridge Over Troubled Waters," Steven put his arm around her and held her close. As they exited the crowded gym, Jennifer heard a vaguely familiar voice yell, "Who's that fine sistah with the blow hair?"

Within seconds, the owner of the voice was standing next to Steven, saying, "Hey, Steve, great concert."

Steven replied, "Yeah, it was. Phillip, meet my girlfriend, Jennifer Madison."

Jennifer now understood why the voice was familiar. She greeted Phillip and explained to Steven that she had met Phillip at Yale's Spook Weekend.

Steven said, "What's Spook Weekend?"

"I'll tell you later."

Phillip said, "That's right. How are you?"

"Fine."

He grinned wickedly, "You certainly are!"

❧   ❧   ❧

The following Tuesday night, Jennifer received a phone call. "Hey, fine thang. How are you?" It was Phillip. "The Black Students Association is having a party this weekend. Come."

Surprised by the call, she suspected Phillip was more interested in pulling her from Steven than he was in her. She told him that she would let him know.

❧   ❧   ❧

Steven called and asked, "Jen, what time are you arriving on Friday?"

"I'm not coming to see you this weekend."

"Why not? What's going on?"

"Susan and Barry breaking up has made me think about us. I don't think we should see each other anymore."

Steven yelled into the phone, "What are you talking about? What do they have to do with us? I'm sorry they broke up, but that's them; that's not us."

Jennifer took a deep breath. "I think they broke up because they were about to graduate and reenter the real world. Their relationship was part of the ivory tower college world."

"What are you talking about? What ivory tower?"

Recent events, combined with Phillip's call, forced her to confront feelings that she had sublimated. "The real world doesn't accept mixed-race couples. The real world kills Martin Luther King. The real world riots and burns everything in sight because of anger and grief. You know when you go to a wedding, there's usually that part in the ceremony when the minister, priest, or rabbi asks all the guests to support the new marriage? Then the guests smile and murmur their support. Barry understands that nobody will do that for Susan and him. And nobody is going to do it for us."

"Jennifer, we don't need anybody if we have each other."

"Steven, that's a romantic notion, right out of the movies. This is real life. Do you see these riots? Detroit has gone crazy. I can't do it now. It's too hard."

Steven begged, "Jennifer, don't give up on us. We're better than all of that. We're different."

"Steven, have you read *The Souls of Black Folks*?"

"No."

"It's by W. E. B. DuBois. In it, he explains that the problem of the twentieth century is the color line. I'm not ready to cross it."

"What are you talking about? What color line?"

"That's just it. You don't know about the color line, and I don't want to have to teach you. Do you realize that the Supreme Court only recently outlawed a Virginia law stating that blacks and whites couldn't get married?"

Steven paused and said, "I read about the case."

"I can't do it. I'm not strong enough. It's too hard. The time isn't right yet." Jennifer returned to her room, put on a Johnny Mathis album, and stared at the ceiling while she lay on her bed.

Leslie walked in and saw her staring at the ceiling. "What is it? You're listening to Johnny Mathis."

"I broke up with Steven."

"Why? What did he do?"

"Steven didn't do anything."

Leslie sat on her bed. "Oh no. Steven hasn't turned into Joel, has he?"

That comment made Jennifer laugh, although she felt like crying. "No! You know Susan and Barry broke up?"

"Yeah. So?"

"I think they broke up because Barry won't cross the color line, and neither will I."

"You broke up with Steven because he's white? You're discriminating against him? You?"

"Hey, black people can be racist too!" Jennifer shamefully admitted. "I'm not discriminating. I'm protecting myself. I know the time is going to come for me and Steven, just like it came for Susan and Barry, when our relationship is going to have to work outside the confines of the college campus, and the country and my mother are not ready yet. Have you been watching the news? Have you seen the rioting? Detroit's on fire. Now's not the time."

On Saturday night, Jennifer attended the Princeton Black Students Association party with Phillip. "Girl, you look good. I liked your blow hair, and I like the Afro. What made you get an Afro?"

Jennifer responded, "Sign of the times."

"Hey, I remember when we met at Spook Weekend, that sister called you out because of your blow hair."

"I remember, too. I wonder what she would say about me now."

On Sunday afternoon, as Phillip walked Jennifer to meet her ride, they passed Steven walking alone near Blair Arch. Phillip spoke to Steven, who nodded and kept walking. Then Steven stopped suddenly and turned around. "Jennifer?"

"Hi, Steven," she said in a timid voice. She had anticipated and feared this encounter all weekend.

Steven stared at her. "I didn't recognize you."

She placed her hand on her bushy hair. "It's my hair."

Steven said, "Afro," and walked away.

1968 TO 1969

Chapter 24

Leslie

Bloomingdale's required the girls on the Summer College Board sales staff to wear something from the winter collection, which they were pushing for their back-to-school promotion. So, in the middle of July, Leslie was wearing a black leather vest, wool pleated miniskirt, and long-sleeved white blouse with black patterned tights.

Leslie got into her mother's silver Lincoln Mark IV and headed for the Scarsdale Country Club, singing along to the Beach Boys' "Good Vibrations." She smiled as she recalled the time during their freshman year when Jennifer labeled the Beach Boys *Gidget* music. Eventually, Jennifer had explained that her dislike for *Gidget* music was caused by her feelings of exclusion. There were no black people in any of those beach movies. Until Jennifer mentioned it, she'd never noticed.

Leslie walked through the ornate, red-carpeted lobby to the second floor, followed the familiar cackle, and found her mother playing mah-jongg with the cackling Mrs. Feinstein and several other ladies.

Leslie flashed her perfect-daughter smile for the benefit of her mother's friends.

Mrs. Feinstein asked, "Leslie, how do you stay so thin? You look like a stick."

"Watch what I eat. And how is your daughter Rachel? Did she go to Canyon Ranch again this summer?" Leslie knew Mrs. Feinstein's daughter had switched from childhood fat camps to spas, an adult version of the fat camp, and Mrs. Feinstein knew she knew. That ended that conversation. Acknowledging her mother's chastising look while knowing that when they got home they would laugh and trade funny Feinstein stories, she said, "Mom, I'll wait for you on the patio."

She pushed up the sleeves of her shirt and unbuttoned her vest, took a seat on the enclosed, air-conditioned porch overlooking the pool, and ordered lemonade. She could see that someone was swimming laps. The guy didn't come up for air. Leslie started to count laps—one, two, three … ten—and he was swimming when she sat down. Finally, he got out of the pool. Leslie thought, *Golden hunk.* She couldn't see his face, because he was rubbing his head vigorously with the yellow club towel, but she could see the body, which was darkly tanned. He had long, strong legs and sinewy arms, and the muscles in his back were taut; she could see them flex as he dried his hair. She hoped that he wouldn't turn around and destroy what was a spectacular male specimen. As the golden hunk turned and walked toward the patio, he got better-looking the closer he got. With sun-streaked blond hair, he was almost too handsome. His eyes were hidden behind mirrored aviator sunglasses.

The hunk walked to the bar and ordered lemonade. As he waited for his drink, he turned around, leaned against the bar, and scanned the patio. Although he was still wearing the sunglasses, Leslie knew he was looking at her. She returned the look but didn't smile. She quickly finished her lemonade and motioned to the bartender for another.

The hunk raised his glass in a kind of salute. Leslie started to raise her glass but decided she'd play hard-to-get. From the look of this guy, it was only natural to fall at his feet and beg for his attention, so she tried to hold out a few minutes before she did the inevitable. Instead she lowered her eyes as if she hadn't noticed the gesture. Then she decided that she was too old to be coy; besides it wasn't her style. She hadn't been coy since junior high school when she still had braces. She graced him with her dazzling smile.

The hunk took the lemonade from the bartender and brought it to Leslie.

This time, she raised her glass and made a toast. "To the Scarsdale Country Club's lemonade."

Without removing his mirrored sunglasses, he said, "I'm Jason Abrams."

"Leslie Cohen."

"You know, I only recently discovered the lemonade here. I was a Coke man myself."

"Oh really? I've loved the lemonade here since I was a kid. Do you belong to the club?"

"My parents do. I haven't been here too often. I've seldom spent summers at home."

"I was wondering because I've never seen you before."

Jason removed his sunglasses. "I am normally not rude—and this question, I'm sure, will appear that way—but why are you dressed like that? I'm sitting here half naked, and you're dressed for Dartmouth's Winter Carnival."

The way he said "naked" made Leslie immediately horny. She wondered whether it was obvious to him that she had been staring at his chest. She thought that it probably was. "I work at Bloomies. The store makes us wear the winter clothes on the sales floor." Just then her mother appeared.

Mrs. Cohen turned to Jason and said, in her sexiest voice, "Hello, I'm Sue Cohen."

Jason stood. "Nice to meet you, Mrs. Cohen. I'm Jason Abrams."

Sue waved her hands, indicating that Jason should sit down. "Where do you live?"

"Merrydale Drive."

Sue smiled. "Lovely street. Where are you in school?"

"A senior at Yale."

Sue continued, "Your major?"

"Economics."

Sue's smile broadened. "Excellent. What do you plan to do?"

"I'm hoping to be drafted by the NFL."

Leslie could see her mother's smile freeze and knew that she didn't like that answer.

Through the frozen smile, Sue asked, "What's the NFL?" Leslie started to answer, but Sue, with a flick of her hand, silenced her.

Jason laughed. "I guess you don't follow football. The NFL is the National Football League. I'm a quarterback."

Sue didn't let the smile leave her face as she said, "My husband loves football. You should stop by. He'd love to talk to you about football."

Leslie stood up in an attempt to end her mother's questions. "I'm sure Jason is too busy to stop by and talk football with Daddy."

"I love talking football," Jason said, rising to stand next to Leslie. "Why don't I stop by and take you to dinner, and then I can spend a little time talking football with your dad?"

Sue chimed in, "That sounds like a wonderful idea, doesn't it, Leslie?"

Leslie's look silenced her mother. She then turned to Jason. "My mother doesn't usually make dates for me. I'm actually capable of doing that myself."

Grinning, Jason said, "Of course, but I'm sure your mother is like mine and makes all of her husband's dates."

Sue's sexy voice returned when she said, "You're absolutely right, Jason."

Jason gave Sue a broad conspiratorial smile. "How about dinner tomorrow, if that's good for Leslie and Mr. Cohen?"

Before Leslie could respond, Sue said, "That's perfect for Milton."

Leslie shrugged. "Well, I guess that makes it good for me, too."

"Leslie, darling, I'll meet you in the car."

Leslie gave Jason her address, and they agreed on plans. When she got to the car, her mother was sitting in the driver's seat with the air-conditioning blasting. In a feigned nonchalant voice, Sue said, "He seems nice."

Leslie stared at her, and Sue stared back; then they both burst into giggles. "He's fabulous. I've got to call Jennifer immediately!"

Upon entering the house, Leslie raced to her bedroom, stripped out of the hot clothes, fell across her bed, and dialed Jennifer's home in Detroit.

"Hi, Mrs. Madison. It's Leslie. How are you?"

"Fine, sweetheart. How's your mom?"

"Great."

"Give her my regards. I'll get Jennifer." Mrs. Madison went to the bottom of the stairs and yelled, "Jennifer, phone. It's Leslie."

Jennifer picked up the phone in her room. Without even waiting for so much as a hello, Leslie said, "I've met the one."

Chapter 25

Paige

Paige loved her sunny garden apartment in Palo Alto. In the afternoons, she sat out on her patio and drank wine as she wrote stories for her creative writing class at Stanford.

She looked up from the typewriter when her next-door neighbor came out on his adjoining patio. "Hey, David. How's the future Clarence Darrow?"

"You mean the future Thurgood Marshall."

Paige laughed. "That's what I meant."

"Good." David explained, "I'm taking this course from Professor Stein called Individual Rights and Liberties. He's Jill's dad. It's about civil rights cases. Today, William Foster was a guest lecturer. The guy's brilliant—probably one of the only black partners at a major Wall Street law firm. He and Stein worked together in the Civil Rights Division at the Justice Department under Bobby Kennedy. Am I talking too much?" he asked and then went on. "It was great—probably the best day I've ever had in law school. How about you? What are you working on?"

Paige sighed. "My day hasn't been as good as yours. The assignment is to write a story about a childhood experience."

He waited for her to continue.

"This one's about my favorite rocking chair."

"What about the rocking chair?"

Paige stood up and stretched. "That's just it. I can't think of anything to say. I really liked the rocking chair. Want a glass of wine?" As they sipped the wine, she asked, "Don't you just love California? The weather just makes me feel happy."

David sipped his wine. "Me too. That's why I decided on Stanford. After four freezing years at Yale, I wanted sunshine. And best of all, it doesn't matter that the heater in my MG doesn't work."

Paige agreed, "Me, too. I wanted sunshine. I also needed to get away from the East Coast. Far away." Mentioning the East Coast made her think of Peter. She still felt an ache each time she thought of him. When she glanced back at David, he was staring at her.

"So what happened back East?"

Paige sighed again. "Long story. I'll give you the short version. In love. Living together. Great guy. He disappeared. I needed a change of scene. California."

"For a creative writing major, that's a very short version."

"I guess it is. How about you and Jill? Do you two have a future?"

"Hey, we started talking about your childhood rocking chair, not my love life."

Paige got up and refilled her wineglass, started to take a sip, and then stopped. "Sorry. I was thinking about mine."

Chapter 26

Jennifer

"It went down this morning. I'm calling from inside Nassau Hall." Phillip's eyes scanned the mahogany-paneled room where Princeton's Board of Trustees met.

As soon as Phillip said Nassau Hall, Jennifer recalled the time Steven took her picture next to the stone tigers outside the historic building. Remembering the moment briefly brought a smile to her face, but it was quickly replaced by a frown. She'd pushed Steven away, but in Phillip she had found a kindred spirit. "The takeover?"

"Yeah, we negotiated with the president until midnight and got nowhere. He said Princeton would not even consider withdrawing its investments from South Africa. Hold on." Phillip yelled out to his classmates. "Hey, don't touch that painting. That thing's priceless." He turned back to the phone and continued. "Sorry 'bout that. Anyway, in that aggravating way of smug liberals, he gave us some long song and dance about how Princeton was actually helping the black people of South Africa by providing jobs. He said it was preferable for American corporations to stay in South Africa and use their influence to end the apartheid system and provide education and training and other stuff for its black employees. Hold on." Phillip yelled again. "Guys, get off that table. We're not here to destroy this place!"

"What's going on?"

"Some of the guys are kinda rowdy. Then he played what he had the audacity to think was his trump card. He said—now get this—he said the South African investments were highly profitable for Princeton. Are you listening? He said that the profits allow Princeton to provide scholarships. Now, I've got to give it to him; he didn't go so far as to say 'to poor niggers like you,' but he implied it. Can you believe that shit?"

"You're kidding."

"Kid you not, so at seven this morning, the brothers entered the building and secured it. You know, the Continental Congress met in this building. They love this place. We've been inside over twelve hours now."

Jennifer was shocked. "Did you take hostages?"

With a menacing laugh, Phillip said, "Nah."

"What's happening now?"

"Not much. Kind of a stalemate. We made a statement this morning listing our demands. The president responded by saying Princeton University wouldn't tolerate vigilante tactics." Phillip raised his hand to signal that he would be off the phone shortly. "Hey, I've got to go; the brothers want me for a caucus."

"Be careful. Don't do any crazy stuff."

"Don't worry. By the way, your boy Greenberg and some other white boys are holding a support demonstration outside the building. They wanted to come in and join us, but the brothers voted against it. I told you the guy was OK. Later."

A couple of hours later, Phillip called again. "Everything's crazy. Princeton called in the state troopers."

"You've got to get out of there, now," Jennifer pleaded.

His voice sounded manic. "We will. I've just drafted a statement, which we're going to read to the press, and then we'll leave. I want your comments. You know what pisses me off the most? We've kept this thing peaceful. Some of those crazy, long-haired white boys outside tried to burn a stuffed Princeton tiger in effigy on the lawn outside Nassau Hall. Once again, your boy, Steven, came through. He put out the fire."

Jennifer sensed Phillip's frustration. "What does the statement say?"

She could hear him take a deep breath before he started to read. "You've got some common sense. It needs more work, but basically it says, 'We're leaving the building peacefully and voluntarily because the university has elected to focus on our actions rather than our reasons for being here. We abhor the apartheid practices in South Africa and Princeton's participation in it.' You know the rhetoric. Remember? We were talking about this same subject when we first met at Yale's Spook Weekend."

Reflecting on all that had happened since then, she sadly said, "I remember."

Chapter 27

Leslie

Leslie put almost ten thousand miles on the red Triumph convertible her parents gave her for her twenty-first birthday driving back and forth between Goucher and Yale her senior year.

Jason was already a favorite of *Sports Illustrated*, so the Harvard-Yale game, a rivalry spanning generations, was getting lots of press coverage. Leslie drove to Yale for the game and, against all rules, spent the night with Jason in the dorm. They lay in his twin bed staring into the darkness. Leslie asked quietly, "Are you nervous?"

Jason hesitated and then replied, "No, not nervous—excited. I've got a good shot at the pros, but this game will clinch it. This game could make me a star."

"You are a star."

"To you and Dad."

"Wrong," Leslie said shrilly. "You can't tell me you don't hear all those people screaming your name, especially the girls. They're sitting there with their dates, and they're going on and on about how wonderful you are. I see the way girls look at you. I smile to myself and think, *Sorry, girls. He's mine.*"

Jason whispered into her ear. "Are you president of my fan club?"

"Yeah, though I'd prefer to be the only member."

"You're the only member as far as I'm concerned."

Jason rolled on top of Leslie, covering her slender body with his own. He tenderly ran his fingers through her hair and rubbed it against his cheek. She knew he loved the feel of her body, the smell of her, and especially the sounds of her slow and then rapid breathing as she reached her climax. She loved the feel of his strong hands on her body. She knew she loved him, but she was unsure if Jason was ready for such a declaration.

❧   ❧   ❧

Saturday afternoon was very cold. Leslie could see Jason blowing into his cupped hands and rubbing them together in a futile attempt to keep them warm. At halftime, Yale was losing 7–0. Leslie knew that Jason's dreams of going pro were slipping through his numb fingers. She sat glumly in the stands beside his parents and pulled her blanket tightly around her.

In the fourth quarter, Yale scored a touchdown but missed the extra point. The score was 7–6. With less than fifteen seconds on the clock, Yale still had time to score. The question was whether they would go for another running play or whether Jason would throw. Jason dutifully called time-out and went over to the sidelines to discuss the play with the coach.

"What do you wanna do?" Jason asked.

The coach barked, "Running play."

"Coach, I can do it."

The coach glared at Jason as the other players gathered around. "Your passing has been off all day. Running play." Jason stalked back on the field and called a quick huddle. The ball was snapped; he dropped back into the pocket, faked a handoff to the fullback, and then threw a long, spiraling pass, avoiding a blocker. He stood back and waited. Moments ticked by as Jason watched the football spiral through the air. Finally, after what felt like a lifetime to Jason and only a second to Leslie, the ball, thrown for fifteen yards, was caught in the end zone. Yale won.

It was pandemonium. Leslie, standing from the moment the team got into formation, dropped her blanket and jumped into the air. She was no longer the least bit cold.

Jason's father yelled to no one in particular, "That's my son! He's going pro!"

Leslie hugged Mr. and Mrs. Abrams and screamed, "He did it!" Suddenly she started to shiver. In one instant she was excitedly screaming; in the next she knew that this one completed pass had sealed Jason's fate and possibly hers.

❧   ❧   ❧

Leslie and Jennifer sat on their beds watching the news. When Walter Cronkite said, "And that's the way it is," Jennifer got up and switched off the television, picked up an art history book, and started to read. Leslie continued to lie on her bed and stare at the mobile hanging from the ceiling.

This was their fourth year as roommates, and the decoration in their dorm room had evolved with each passing year. Leslie currently had a passion for mobiles. Their taste in music still differed. However, Jason had introduced Leslie and Jennifer to the music of Bob Dylan. Although Jennifer disliked Dylan's gravelly voice, she was captivated by his lyrics.

Leslie got up from her bed and put on a Johnny Mathis album.

Jennifer looked up from her book. "Uh-oh. You're playing a Johnny Mathis album. What's the love problem?"

"I don't have a love problem."

Jennifer explained, "You look a little weird, and we always play Johnny Mathis when we are falling in or out of love—not when we are in love. So what's going on?"

Laughing, Leslie said, "Oh, you think you know me so well."

"After four years of being roommates, I think I do. So, what's going on?"

Leslie asked, "When did you have your period?"

"My period?"

"Yes, your period. When did you have it?"

Jennifer thought for a moment and said, "Couple of weeks ago. Why?"

Leslie winced, "I think I'm a little late."

"How late?"

"Well, if you had your period two weeks ago and we normally have it about the same time, it could be a couple of weeks."

Jennifer looked at Leslie as she lay on her bed staring at the motionless mobile above her head and asked in a very matter-of-fact voice, "Leslie, you and I are both very careful people. You know whether or not you're late. Are you pregnant?"

Leslie held back tears and said, "My period is eight days late."

"Oh, shit."

Leslie started to cry.

"Go to a doctor and find out," Jennifer said pragmatically.

Leslie sat up on her bed and wiped the tears from her face with both hands. "If I'm pregnant, which I sincerely hope I'm not, I guess I'll have an abortion. It's weird, though. We've always talked very cavalierly about abortion—how we'd get one without a second thought—but the reality of it is pretty scary. No, that's not the right word. It's sad."

"Look, this is all premature. You're just eight days late. Don't go getting all angst-ridden on me!"

"But I have to think about it."

"Would you marry Jason and have the baby?"

"Jason has not asked me to marry him. Remember? And I certainly wouldn't want to get a proposal that way. Besides, I don't want to be a mother. That's a hell of a way to begin a marriage."

Jennifer got up from her bed and moved to the foot of Leslie's bed. "Don't be scared. I'll help you through this. I'll go to the doctor with you. I'll make the appointment. Whatever you need me to do, I'll do it." Tears continued to stream down Leslie's face as Jennifer held back her own. "Are you going to tell Jason?"

"I don't want him to feel trapped. I need for him to choose me. He could have any girl he wants. Just think what it's going to be like when he goes pro! For my sanity, I need to know that he wants me, and I'll never know that if I force him to marry me, which, like a nice Jewish boy from Scarsdale, he'd do."

"Jason loves you. He'd want to help you make this decision. You should tell him."

The tears were replaced with a determined look. "No, I don't think I'll tell him. This is my decision." Leslie's face softened into a little-girl smile. "Besides, I don't want one of those quickie weddings. I want the temple to be packed with all of our friends and family and me in a magnificent wedding gown and you in pink. I insist you wear pink. I love you in that color. I always envisioned my maid of honor in one of those big bridesmaids' hats, but you don't wear hats anymore since you got the Afro. Well ..."

Jennifer interjected, "For you, I'll wear one of those big hats."

Leslie moaned. "What are we doing planning a wedding? I may be pregnant!"

"Leslie, Jason loves you. You may decide on an abortion anyway, but you should talk it over with him. That's what it means to be a couple. You rely on each other."

Leslie's voice was adamant. "No, I've made up my mind. I'm having an abortion, and he'll never know. You better not tell him, either. Don't tell anyone."

Jennifer promised, "I won't tell. You know you can count on me. First thing in the morning, I'll call and get you a doctor's appointment. Off campus. Don't want anyone gossiping. I'll go with you."

Leslie continued to stare up at the mobile. "Thanks, roomie."

❦   ❦   ❦

Two days later Leslie strolled into the dining room and cut into the cafeteria line in front of Jennifer. She was smiling when she whispered, "Cancel that appointment. It came."

Chapter 28

Paige

Paige heard the knock at the door and resented the interruption, because the words were finally flowing. Without getting up, she yelled, "Who is it?"

A gruff voice said, "Miss Wyatt? This is the FBI."

Paige got up, looked through the peephole, and saw a man in a baggy dark suit. She opened the door just a crack. "Yes?"

The man flashed an identification badge embossed with the gold shield of the FBI. "May I come in?"

As Paige allowed the agent to enter, she asked, "What do you want?"

The agent asked, "May I sit down?"

Paige said, "I'm sorry. Of course you may sit. But I still don't know why you're here."

The FBI agent casually surveyed her apartment and then explained. "The FBI is interested in Peter Chapin. I'd like to ask you a few questions about him. When did you last see him?"

Paige could hardly catch her breath when she heard Peter's name. "Why is the FBI interested in Peter?"

The agent didn't answer but merely repeated his question. "When did you last see Peter Chapin?"

Paige challenged, "Why should I talk to you when you won't tell me anything? Am I being charged with something?"

In responding to her question, Paige could hear the FBI agent's tone become even more authoritarian, which further angered her. "Miss, you are not being charged with anything. I merely want to know when you last saw Peter Chapin."

"I haven't seen Peter since I moved to California. The last time I saw him was about a year ago when I was living in Baltimore."

The agent asked, "Do you know where he is?"

Paige shook her head. "I wish I did, but I don't."

"Has he contacted you in any way? A letter? Card? Message from a friend?" Paige went to her desk. She returned and handed a birthday card to the agent. "He sent me this. There was no return address on the envelope."

The agent looked at the card. "Do you still have the envelope?"

Paige shook her head.

"Miss Wyatt, would you mind if I took this card with me? I'll return it, but I'd like to run some tests first."

"Sir, before I give you this card, you've got to tell me what's going on. Why is the FBI interested in Peter? Has he done something? I've worried about him for the past year. Is he in danger?"

"Miss Wyatt, we know that you used to live with Chapin. He's involved with an antiwar group we believe has set fires in several army recruiting stations." The agent reached into his pocket. "This is my card. If you should hear from him, please contact me. Encourage him to turn himself in."

Paige took the business card. "I don't know what you're talking about. That's not the Peter I knew," she said, though she knew her voice didn't sound all that convincing. She prayed he was all right and knew that she would never call this J. Edgar Hoover lackey if Peter contacted her. "Take the birthday card. This is all crazy."

Chapter 29

Jennifer

Jennifer peered into the little window on her post office box and could see that she had some mail. She said a quick silent prayer before opening it. She turned the dial. The mailbox snapped open. There was a fat envelope from Harvard Law School. Jennifer walked over to Leslie, who was reading a letter as she stood in front of her mailbox. Jennifer showed her the envelope. Leslie gasped, "Open it."

Jennifer grimaced. "I think I want to wait until I get back to the room. If it's bad news, I don't want to humiliate myself in public."

"Don't be silly. It's a fat envelope. Everyone knows fat envelopes mean you're in. Open it."

Jennifer ripped open the envelope, saw the word *congratulations*, and screamed, "I'm in!"

Leslie hugged her and joined in the screaming. "Congrats! You're in! You're in!"

"I've got to call my parents. I'll see you later." She ran all the way from the post office to Stimson. Jennifer screamed into the phone, "Mom, I got into Harvard!"

"Oh, baby, I'm so proud of you. You worked hard. Daddy's not home yet. I won't tell him. I'll let you tell him yourself."

"Thanks, Mom. I'll call back this evening. I'm so happy."

"Sweetie, I'm happy for you. Love you."

After dinner, Jennifer called home. The phone rang. Normally her mother would answer, but instead she heard her father's annoyed tone. Jennifer smiled upon hearing his voice, knowing how much he hated to answer the phone. She screamed, "Daddy, I got into Harvard!"

Ron yelled, "Jennifer … oh, sweetie … congratulations! Gloria, Gloria, pick up the phone. Jennifer was accepted at Harvard."

Gloria picked up the extension in the kitchen. "I know, Ron. That's why I wanted you to answer the phone."

"You knew and didn't tell me?"

Jennifer said, "Daddy, Mom wanted you to hear the good news from me."

"Baby, we're so proud of you. A Harvard lawyer. We've come a long way." Jennifer could hear the joy and happiness in her parents' voices. She also knew that with each accomplishment they looked back in awe at how far they had come.

❧   ❧   ❧

The following week, Allison stopped Jennifer as she was coming out of Van Meter Hall. "Jennifer, can I talk with you?"

Jennifer's face had displayed a perpetual smile ever since she'd received her acceptance letter. "Sure. What's up?"

Allison appeared unusually reticent and nervous. "Let's go get a soda at the Gopher Hole. We can talk there."

The two girls walked through the courtyard. Jennifer, noting that the pink rhododendrons were in full bloom, said, "I hope the blossoms last until graduation. My mother loves rhododendrons. We have a garden in my backyard with rhododendrons, azaleas, lots of roses, and a whole bunch of stuff I don't know the names of, but my mother does."

Allison selected the booth in the back. Jennifer preferred to sit near the windows in the sun, but she followed Allison to the back booth. "What's up, Allison? You look strange. Something the matter?"

Allison was obviously troubled when she spoke. "Jennifer, I really don't know how to tell you this. After all, we've been friends for our entire time in college, lived in the same dorm, studied together, partied together—everything." Allison paused, searching for the right words to continue. Jennifer said nothing. "Jennifer, it's about my wedding. You know that Mason and I are going to have a small wedding and reception at my parents' home." Allison faltered again.

"Of course, I know about the wedding. You and Leslie have talked nonstop about weddings ever since December when Jason put that three-carat rock from Tiffany's on her finger."

Allison stared into her Tab, shook the ice that was melting in the glass, and then went on. "If it was up to Mason and me, we'd love to have you attend the wedding. But Mason's parents just aren't used to"—she breathed heavily—"black people. So, I can't invite you to the wedding. I hope you understand."

Jennifer looked at Allison and saw relief fill her face when she uttered in a soft monotone, "I understand." Jennifer's heart started to pound. An uncontrollable feeling of nausea engulfed her. Beads of perspiration popped out on her upper lip.

Allison heard the words "I understand" and started to get up, assuming the discussion was over. Then she added, "By the way, I'd appreciate it if you didn't mention this to the other girls."

Jennifer, still seated, said sternly, "Sit."

Allison immediately sat down.

"I told you I understood, but I don't believe you understand what I meant by that." Jennifer spoke very slowly. "I'm going to explain it to you. I understand that you and Mason are just as racist as Mason's Mississippi parents. I have known you since we were freshmen. We have lived in the same dorm, eaten the same food, gone to the same classes and the same parties. For you to sit here and tell me I cannot take a seat in your parents' home while you repeat your wedding vows because I am black is unacceptable. It's an insult, and I will not tolerate it. I will not accept your bigotry. I will not help you to feel better by condoning and excusing your racism—and please understand me, I'm saying *your* racism, not your in-laws' … yours!"

Allison cried, "But, Jennifer, it's not my fault, and it's not Mason's. It's his parents."

Jennifer got up to leave. "Allison, it is your fault. You could take a stand here, but instead you want me to just accept the insult. Well, I won't. Racism continues to exist because people are too polite to talk about it. But I will talk about it. I'm going to tell everyone we know that you're just as much a racist as your Mississippi in-laws."

Jennifer walked up the hill to the dorm alone. Last week's smile had disappeared. She felt hurt, angry, sad, stupid, and disappointed. When she walked into the room, Leslie, seeing her angry expression, asked jokingly, "What's the matter with you? Did Harvard decide they'd made a mistake?"

"No, Harvard didn't make a mistake. I made one." Jennifer explained her discussion with Allison.

Leslie shook her head. "I can't believe she did that. Oh, Jennifer, I'm so sorry."

"College brings different people together for a short time, but then we all grow up and go back home where we belong."

Leslie raged, "That's not true!"

Jennifer smiled gratefully at Leslie. "What I said doesn't apply to you."

"Thanks. Wait until I see Allison." She then stormed out of the room; she saw Allison entering her room and marched in behind her, leaving the door open. Allison attempted to close it, but Leslie stopped her and screamed, "Don't you close it. I want everyone to hear what I have to say. I'm disgusted with you, and I'm disappointed, too. That probably hurts most of all—to discover that your friends are not who you believe them to be, to find out that they are people you could never like or respect. I had no idea you felt this way."

Allison interrupted, "Leslie, I feel terrible about this. You know if it were left up to me, Jennifer would be at the wedding, but I have to think of Mason's parents. After all, they're going to be my family, and I have to get along with them. Leslie, I need *you* to understand."

Leslie said contemptuously, "I do understand, and I also know that it is up to you, and until people like you learn that, this world's a sorry place. What you're doing is saying to Jennifer that although she's been your friend, just because of the color of her skin, she can't sit in the same room with your white mother-in-law. What do you think she'd do, burn the place down? Can't you see how twisted your thinking is? I feel sorry for you."

Leslie turned abruptly and headed for the door; then she called out over her shoulder without turning around, "I'll tell my mother not to expect you and Mason at my wedding, because you have just been uninvited, and Jason and I will not be at yours. Think of it as a boycott." She slammed the door.

Leslie returned to the room and found Jennifer stretched out across the bed staring at the mobile of ugly bridesmaid dresses she had created during Leslie's endless search for the perfect pink bridesmaid's dress. "I just told Allison that her racism disgusted me. I also told her that Jason and I were *not* coming to her wedding and that she could consider it a *boycott!*"

Jennifer turned to Leslie with a quizzical expression. "Did you say 'boycott'?"

"I certainly did."

Jennifer chuckled. "A boycott. I like that. Thanks."

Chapter 30

Leslie

Just after the sun set, the wedding ceremony began. The gentle aroma of roses filled the candlelit synagogue. The chuppah was completely covered in a blanket of hundreds of baby pink tea roses, pale white lilies of the valley, and dark-green English ivy. Attached to the end of each row was a garland of baby pink and white roses intertwined with pink satin ribbon.

Jennifer, as maid of honor, was radiant in a silk organza dress of the exact same shade of pink as the roses, and, as Leslie had always envisioned, Jennifer wore a broad-brimmed hat to match the pink of the gown. The hat had looked ridiculous perched on top of her Afro, so she'd straightened her hair. Leslie's mother was pleased. As much as she adored Jennifer, she was not ready for the maid of honor at her only daughter's wedding of the century to have an Afro. Paige and the other five bridesmaids had identical dresses but in a slightly darker shade of pink. Mrs. Cohen wore a floor-length pale pink evening gown by Pauline Trigere, and Jason's mother's gown had a bolero-style jacket of dusty rose by Galanos. Leslie was resplendent in a sophisticated off-white gown created by Priscilla of Boston of silk taffeta and Chantilly beaded lace with a long train.

Jennifer and Paige adjusted Leslie's veil as they waited to begin the procession. Paige said, "My mother would love this wedding—not the synagogue part but all of the rest of it."

Leslie commented, "She wanted you to marry Peter."

"I'm not sure she wanted me to marry Peter. She just wanted me to get married."

Jennifer asked, "Did Peter really want to marry *you*?"

"Yes," Paige answered. "I said no. Marriage isn't for me. But it's perfect for Leslie."

Jennifer turned away from Paige and smiled at Leslie. "Marriage to Jason is especially perfect for Leslie."

Despite it being her wedding day, a day that should have been all about her, Leslie reached out and took Paige's hand. "Any more news yet on Peter? Have you heard anything?"

Sadly, shaking her head, Paige said, "No, I have no idea where he is."

"I'm sorry," Leslie whispered. "I hope he's all right."

Sue Cohen came over and readjusted her daughter's veil. "Darling, you look beautiful."

Leslie walked down the aisle between her father and mother. Despite the veil, everyone could clearly see her beaming smile.

Jason stood under the chuppah with the rabbi and watched Leslie as she walked down the aisle. His broad smile mirrored hers. Everyone in the temple could tell that he felt great pride in becoming Leslie's husband. When the rabbi announced that they were husband and wife and the glass was placed at his feet, he smashed it with the heel of his shoe as the crowd smiled at them and each other in agreement that this was a perfect match.

When Leslie and Jason entered the Scarsdale Country Club ballroom, the twelve-piece band played the theme from *Romeo and Juliet*, with the bandleader announcing, "Ladies and gentlemen, I am pleased to introduce Mr. and Mrs. Jason Abrams. Don't they make a golden couple?" The guests roared, "Mazel tov."

At the reception, each round table was covered with a pink damask tablecloth with a huge centerpiece of white orchids and roses of several shades of pink, which completely obscured the people seated on the opposite side of the table. Throughout the extravagant seven-course meal, guests were jumping up and hugging and kissing each other.

After dancing with his mother and Leslie's mother, Jason asked Jennifer to dance. Jason did a stiff two-step while his Uncle Bernard was twirling Leslie around the dance floor.

Jason asked, "When does law school start?"

"Tuesday after Labor Day."

"Excited?"

"Very. A little scared, too." Jennifer looked at her roommate as she danced with Uncle Bernard. "Leslie looks gorgeous. You two are a perfect match!"

Jason laughed. "You mean a match made in Scarsdale."

Jennifer laughed but then said with a serious look, "Make her happy, Jason. She loves you very much."

Jason looked admiringly at Leslie, who was now dancing with her ten-year-old cousin, Seth. Seth had cut in on Uncle Bernard, who was now doing a frantic shimmy with Golden Door denizen Rachel Feinstein; silver sequins flew everywhere, because Rachel had not lost as much weight as she'd hoped. Jason's face switched from its usual affable expression to a serious look Jennifer had never seen before on him. "Jennifer, I'm going to try. I'll do the very best I can."

The band broke into the hora. The best man and one of the ushers brought chairs to the center, and Jason and Leslie sat and were lifted by Jason's buddies into the air as the pace of the hora quickened and the ballroom filled with dancers swirling around them.

1969 TO 1970

Chapter 31

Paige

David came up the walk, wearing tennis whites and carrying three tennis rackets and his evidence textbook. He stopped at Paige's patio. "What are you working on this time?"

Paige sat hunched over her typewriter. "We're supposed to write about love."

"That's a big topic. What about love?"

"I'm working on a master's in creative writing, remember? I'm supposed to create." She stood up in frustration. "But nothing's coming. I tried writing something about the wedding I was in this summer. My friend Leslie got married, and I was a bridesmaid. The pink dress did nothing for me. It should be enshrined in the Hall of Ugly Bridesmaids' Dresses. But Leslie's happy. The assignment's not coming together."

David sat down and placed his tennis rackets and law book on the table next to Paige's typewriter. "You were in love. Write about that. You gave me the short version a while ago. You lived together. He left. You moved to California. Fill in the blanks. Why did you love him? Why did he leave? How did you feel when he left?"

"Well, thank you very much," Paige said sarcastically. "You're just full of questions."

David laughed. "I'm going to be a lawyer. I'm full of questions, and I've already learned that there is seldom one answer to a question. So tell me about the guy you lived with. Sometimes if you say it out loud first, then you can write it down."

"OK. His name is Peter Chapin. Peter dropped out of Bowdoin to go South and work in the civil rights movement. He was a Freedom Rider and then did voter registration."

David said, "I'm impressed. I already like the guy."

"Peter's unique. After his work with SNCC, he went to Baltimore and worked in a community center. That's when I met him. We met at a rally to legalize abortion. He got involved in the antiwar movement. He got really frustrated with the escalation of the war. I think he's doing antiwar activities now, but I'm not sure. I haven't heard from him."

"Did you love him?"

Paige didn't answer immediately. "I thought I did. I loved being with him. How about you? Are you in love with Jill? She's Professor Stein's daughter. Is that how you met her?"

David held up both hands. "You're the one who has to write something about love, not me."

"Answer the question."

"Hey, I already told you that questions don't always have an answer. I met Jill because I worked for her dad as a legal research assistant. I like her, but I'm not planning our future at the moment. My future is still too uncertain. I know I'm going back to New York after graduation. I'm applying to law firms there. That's all that's on my mind at the moment. That's the short version of my story. Tell me more about Peter."

"When I was with Peter, I didn't want to get married. He wanted to. It was me who insisted that we live together. I'm not sure if I believe in forever love. Or marriage. I knew then that I wasn't ready for it. I think I also knew Peter wasn't ready, although he said he was."

"Married? Marriage is not on my mind. Did you really think about getting married?"

"No, I really didn't. My parents divorced when I was a kid. It was really ugly. Marriage isn't for me. I didn't really take Peter's offer seriously. The fifties are over. People don't have to get married anymore."

David said, "My folks are happily married. I think I want that eventually. First, I've got to find the right lady and the right time."

"The right person. Is that all it takes?" Paige asked.

"No, it takes a lot more than that."

Paige stood up and did a ballet stretch. "You're right. But what else?"

"I don't know. And I don't have to write about it. You do."

"Thanks for reminding me."

Chapter 32

Jennifer

Jennifer walked up the steps to Harvard Law School and entered the lecture hall for her first law school class. She took a seat, scanned the room, and spotted the only other black woman in the room. After class, Jennifer went over and introduced herself.

"Hi. I'm Jennifer Madison."

The girl grunted, "Hey."

"What's your name?"

"Barbara Jean Gresham. Call me BJ. Barbara Jean is way too country."

"OK, BJ, where are you from?"

"Chicago."

"My part of the country. I'm from Detroit. Went to Goucher. Where did you go for undergrad?"

A smile had yet to surface on BJ's face when she tonelessly said, "Wellesley."

As soon as BJ said "Wellesley," Jennifer recognized her as the girl who made the comment at the Spook Weekend antiapartheid workshop about her long hair. Instinct told her not to remind BJ of their prior meeting. "Are you taking constitutional law this semester?"

"No."

"I have Professor Diamond. I hear he's supposed to be really good."

"Good for you." BJ abruptly grabbed her books and stalked out of the classroom, leaving Jennifer standing alone. As Jennifer watched her walk away, she thought that BJ was still as angry and mean as before.

In late October the class discussion turned to the issue of corporate civic responsibility. That day, the professor decided it was Jennifer's turn to be his Socratic method victim.

"Ms. Madison, what's the holding in *Consolidated Casualty v. Neighbors, Inc.*?"

Jennifer started to explain the decision, but before she could finish, the professor interrupted. "Ms. Madison, was the lower court trying to dictate corporate policy?"

Once again, Jennifer began a response only to be cut off by the professor. "Ms. Madison, why should a corporation care about community issues?"

This series of back-and-forth questions and responses between the professor and Jennifer continued for about twenty minutes. Finally, the professor said, "Thank you, Ms. Madison," and Jennifer took her seat. She felt exhilarated yet exhausted. Throughout the twenty-minute grilling she could feel the heat rising in her body. When she took her seat, she took a quick and furtive glance at her underarms to make sure there were no obvious pit stains to betray her nervousness.

After class, as Jennifer passed the professor's podium, some students had surrounded him and were asking him follow-up questions, but he made a point to say, "Good job, Ms. Madison."

BJ followed Jennifer out of the classroom and walked up beside her. This was the first time BJ had spoken to her since the first day of school. "You did a good job in there today. You handled yourself. I liked your comments."

Jennifer said, "Thanks," as she started to walk in step with BJ. "I don't think you remember me, but a couple of years ago at Spook Weekend, I remember you making similar comments at a workshop."

BJ looked confused. "Spook Weekend?"

Jennifer ventured on. "Spook Weekend at Yale. There was a workshop on Princeton's investments in South Africa. I attempted to congratulate you on your comments then, but you dismissed me with some comment about my long hair."

BJ chuckled derisively. "Well, I was younger and meaner then. Hey, are you in a study group?"

"Yeah."

"I'm not. Got room for one more?"

"Sure."

Chapter 33

Leslie

Leslie browsed through Saks Fifth Avenue. She was about to leave the store and then decided that she wanted to try on that black cocktail dress after all. She headed back to the elevator and got off on the third floor. She took the black dress off the rack and headed to the dressing room. The cut was perfect for her wide hips, and she loved the deep V neckline, which showed off her cleavage. Leslie emerged from the dressing room and handed the dress to the salesclerk. "I'll take it. I really don't need another black cocktail dress, but I want it." She handed her credit card to the clerk.

The clerk looked at the card. "Mrs. Abrams! I thought I recognized you. Washington is certainly excited about your husband."

Leslie smiled. "Well, Jason is very happy about playing for the Redskins."

The clerk handed Leslie the shopping bag. This time, she made it to the parking lot without more shopping, got into her Jaguar convertible, and drove to her Georgetown town house. Leslie walked into the marbled foyer and headed upstairs to the bedroom to put the dress away. She picked up the fabric swatches from her bedside table and looked at them in the afternoon light. She still wasn't sure which she preferred for the bedroom draperies. She'd ask her mother's opinion this weekend. Within minutes, the front door opened, and Jason yelled, "Leslie, are you here, babe?"

She ran to the top of the staircase. "How was practice?"

Jason took the steps two at a time. "Practice went OK. Should be a good game on Sunday. When are our parents coming?"

"Saturday afternoon. I made reservations for them at the Four Seasons."

"Good. I'm going to shower before we meet the Kleins for dinner."

"Where are we going?"

"Rive Gauche on the corner of M Street."

"Good. I like that restaurant. We can walk."

Jason started removing his clothes and dropped them on the floor as he headed for the shower. Leslie followed him, picking up the discarded clothes and tossing them into the hamper. She could hear the shower running and assumed Jason was in the shower. Suddenly, he was standing behind her with his arms around her waist and kissing her neck. "I love you, babe," he said.

Leslie leaned back into his arms. "I love you more."

Jason pulled her to the bed and removed her clothes as they slid under the soft comforter. They lay in the spoon position with Jason hugging Leslie very tightly. He whispered into her ear. "Life does not get any better than this. Beautiful wife whom I love and who loves me back—a wife who actually likes me, and I like her. And I'm the starting quarterback for the Redskins." He laughed lightly. "I'm happy. How about you?"

Leslie turned over to face him, remembering how she dreamed of this day. "You're right. We have it all."

Jason smothered her lips. After a long kiss, his hands roamed her body. He moaned, "Show me how much you love me."

Chapter 34

Paige

When David got home, he knocked on Paige's door to see how her interview with *San Francisco* magazine had gone. He heard muffled sounds from inside. She didn't answer the door, but he could hear crying. He knocked again. "Paige, its David. Open up."

Paige fumbled with the lock; finally, she got the door open. Her face was ashen, and her eyes were bloodshot and swollen. Her hair was a tangled mess.

"What's the matter?"

She shook her head, unable to speak. She pointed to the television set. David heard the newscaster announce, "There has been a shootout between the People's Liberation Army and the New York City police. The FBI has been searching for several members of this underground group for over a year. This organization is allegedly responsible for the hijacking and robbery of a Brinks truck in Queens and the murder of the driver, as well as the bombing of the Statue of Liberty. Three members of the group were found today in a Bronx tenement; shots were fired from inside, the police stormed the apartment, and the three people inside were killed. The dead are Antonio Lopez, Robert Wells, and Peter Chapin, the alleged gunman in the Brinks truck murder."

Photos of each of the dead men were shown. David turned off the television and sat beside Paige on the sofa, where she was huddled in the fetal position. He put his arms around her. "I'm sorry."

She continued to sob and nestled into David's arms. "Please hold me."

"I will."

David sat with his arms around Paige for a long time without speaking. Finally, Paige began to chant, "Peter's dead. Peter's dead." Eventually she cried and, through her sobs, said, "David, Peter was gentle and loving. He cared deeply for the world. He loved me. What happened? How did this happen?"

David continued to hold Paige in his arms and stroke her cheek. It was warm and covered with tears. Her body shook as she sobbed. She looked into David's eyes and then begged him to kiss her. "Please, David, hold me, love me, please, please ..."

David held her tighter as Paige stared unseeingly into David's eyes and then thrust her tongue into his mouth, sucking harder and harder on his lips.

David pulled back.

"David, don't think. I can't. Please."

"Paige, I'm sorry. I'm not Peter."

"Yes, you are."

She attempted to remove his jeans, but David refused to cooperate. Paige studied his face. She was reading his mind. "I know you don't want me, David, but I need you tonight."

"No, you don't need me. What you want is Peter, and he's dead. Is there someone I can call?"

Paige shook her head. The phone rang. David got up and answered it. A panicked voice said, "Who is this?"

"I'm David Walker, Paige's next-door neighbor."

"I'm so glad she's not alone. This is her mother. Has she heard the news?"

"Yes, she has. I'll get her." David handed the phone to Paige.

Paige listened as her mother said, "Darling, I'm so sorry. I just heard the news about Peter on TV. I think you should fly home immediately."

Paige mumbled, "No, I can't."

"Well, I'll come out there."

"No, Mother, that's not necessary. I'll be fine. I'm starting a new job next week." Paige let the phone drop as she fell back onto the sofa and started crying again.

David picked up the phone. "Mrs. Wyatt, are you still there?"

"Yes, I'm here."

"Don't worry. I'll stay with Paige tonight. I won't leave her alone."

Mrs. Wyatt said, "Thank you. I'll be there tomorrow."

David hung up the phone, picked Paige up, and carried her to the bedroom. He laid her down on the bed and pulled the sheet over her. He returned to the living room, where he could hear her sobs. Finally, the sobbing stopped. She fell asleep. Around midnight, she awakened and found David asleep on her sofa. "You can go home now. I'll be fine. It was just such a shock. I hadn't heard from him. None of our friends had. I knew it was probably something bad when the FBI came, but I never thought this. Not this. Go home. I'll be fine. Thanks for being here."

1970 TO 1971

Chapter 35

Jennifer

Jennifer admired Leslie's beautifully decorated home. The style was both sophisticated and homey. She could overhear Jason talking with Leslie on the telephone.

"Hey, babe. Jennifer's here. I thought you'd be here by now." Jason yelled from the kitchen, "Jennifer. It's Leslie on the phone. She wants to speak with you."

Jennifer took the phone from Jason, and Leslie said, "I'm still in New York. My client wants to meet again in the morning, so I won't be back in DC until tomorrow afternoon. Sorry to miss your first night in DC. Just make yourself at home. Your room's ready. I even bought that Chloe soap you like so much. I've started using it too. Smells great."

"I'm sure you're convincing somebody to spend far more money than they had planned to on advertising."

Leslie laughed. "You know I am."

Jennifer handed the telephone to Jason and heard him say, "Love you, babe." He walked into the garden room, where Jennifer was looking out of the window at the fountain on the patio. "What do you want to do for dinner? We'd planned for the three of us to go out, show you some of DC. Still want to go?"

"Sure."

Jennifer debated what to wear. If Leslie had been here, she wouldn't have had to decide. Leslie would have selected something for her or given her something of hers to wear. She decided on a red cotton knit sundress and strappy high-heeled sandals.

Jason and Jennifer walked to Jour Et Nuit, a French restaurant in George-town. The maître d' greeted Jason warmly and escorted them to Jason's favorite table on the second floor. As they walked through the candlelit dining room and up the circular staircase, Jason waved to several people he knew and acknowledged those who obviously recognized the Washington Redskins' star quarterback.

Jennifer was conscious of the admiring attention Jason received from the other diners, especially women. She respected the gracious manner in which he handled the attention. As always, Jason was quick with a wink to a pretty girl.

The wine steward poured some wine into Jason's glass. He took a sip and nodded his approval; the steward then filled their glasses, and Jason offered a toast: "Welcome to Washington." They clicked glasses, and Jason looked around the restaurant. "I bet these good people are wondering if we're having an affair. They're thinking, *She's such a beautiful girl, that lucky devil.* And they're right." He paused for a few seconds, and Jennifer blushed. "You are a beautiful girl. I've always loved the color of your skin. You've got that golden brown color white people spend all summer trying to perfect." Jason reached over, took her hand, and whispered, "A little gossip never hurts. There's no such thing as bad publicity. Ask my wife."

Jennifer laughed and quickly withdrew her hand.

After a meal of chicken Marsala and mango sorbet for dessert, they walked back from the restaurant, Jennifer stepping gingerly on the cobblestone side-walk. When they reached the house, she headed up to the guest room, but Jason stopped her.

"Don't go up yet. How about a cognac?"

"No thanks. I've already had too much to drink."

"Cognac doesn't count as drinking." Jason poured himself a drink.

"For me, it does. I think I'll just go to bed."

Jason sipped his cognac. "You know, DC is a town that loves gossip. Tomor-row, the gossip will be that Jason Abrams, the quarterback for the Washington Redskins, was seen in a Georgetown restaurant last evening, having an inti-mate dinner for two with a beautiful unidentified woman. Might even make one of the columns."

"Oh, really?"

Jason continued, "Just think if they knew that same beautiful woman was staying at my house."

"Now that would fuel the gossip, until they found out I was Leslie's roommate for four years and therefore more used to living with her than you. Jason, I'm going to bed."

Jason kissed her gently on the cheek as he'd done many times before. He then kissed her hard on the mouth. She tried to pull away, but he held her. She stepped on the top of his foot with the heel of her sandal as she'd learned to do in her self-defense class. "Don't do that!" Jennifer yelled nastily.

"Oh, come on. Don't tell me you didn't feel anything."

She wanted to slap that self-assured grin off his handsome face. "Cut it out! What the hell do you think you're doing?"

"You're a beautiful and desirable woman."

She put one hand on her hip and, with the other hand, jabbed her finger in his lasciviously grinning face. "I am *not* a desirable woman. I'm your wife's friend. Don't fuck it up." Jennifer turned and walked deliberately toward the steps. "Let's forget this ever happened."

Jason, looking truly dejected, said softly, "I'm sorry. It never happened. Drunk. I was drunk."

Jennifer went up to the guest room, locked the door, and changed into jeans and a T-shirt, not wanting to be in pajamas alone with Jason in the house. That night, she lay on the bed, afraid to fall asleep. Although Leslie had graciously offered her their guest room for the summer, she knew that she couldn't stay here now.

Jennifer called Leslie the following afternoon. "Hi. Thanks for the offer, but I'm going to share an apartment with Sharon's friend Lisa. Turns out her roommate's away this summer after all."

Leslie said, "That'll be fun: two single girls sharing an apartment. It will be sorta like when we were roommates in college."

"Exactly. Lisa's going to show me the singles scene. You know, I'm still searching for the one."

For the next couple of weeks, Jennifer avoided Leslie's calls, claiming to be too busy working to get together. Finally, Leslie insisted. "Come with me and Jason to a big party. One of Jason's Redskins teammates is giving it." She laughed. "Plenty of men!"

It was a typical DC summer day, hot and humid. Jennifer, Leslie, and Jason drove out to the DC suburb of Potomac, a community of large old estates replete with stables full of championship horses and modern-day mansions with swimming pools and tennis courts. The party was at a six-bedroom, all-glass split-level with swimming pool, steam room, and indoor and outdoor hot tubs. There were a couple of people in the pool and another hundred mill-ing around inside and outside of the house when they arrived. The road lead-ing to the house was jammed with every luxury car imaginable: Jaguars, Corvettes, Mercedes, even a gold Rolls Royce, which belonged to the wife of a Redskins defensive end. She was a runway model and also did print work for *Vogue* and *Harper's Bazaar*.

The smoke from the barbecue grill billowed into the clear blue sky and car-ried the rich aroma of sizzling spareribs throughout the area.

With his arms around the waists of both Leslie and Jennifer, Jason gallantly squired them through the crowd toward the bar located in the yellow-and-white-striped tent behind the house. At Jason's initial touch, Jennifer gave him a look that she knew he would understand to mean, "Don't fuck with me!" Leslie paused occasionally to greet friends and introduce Jennifer. After they'd each secured a drink to fortify them for what promised to be a wild afternoon, Leslie started her running commentary on various people in the crowd. "That guy in the white pants over there is a local sports announcer. The guy he's talk-ing to, with his shirt off, is a lawyer. Represents several of the players. The other guy is a very rich surgeon. Just loves to hang around jocks. I believe he did some knee surgery for someone on the team recently. The gorgeous six-foot brunette is his wife. She's a highly respected criminal defense lawyer. Over there, those three huge guys are linebackers for the Skins. Wild men! You can be sure they'll do something obscene before the afternoon is over. The big red-head will take a leak wherever he is."

Jennifer scowled. "You're kidding."

"I'm not kidding. I saw him do it at a charity football game for disabled children. The Redskins' management won't let him attend charity events any-more. He reminds me of that gross pig at Hopkins. What was his name? I think he was a Beta Tau Sig. He always peed on somebody."

"You mean Big John?"

"Yeah, that's the one."

Jennifer laughed. "As I recall, Big John adored you."

"Don't remind me." Leslie continued her commentary. "Oh, now these two are interesting. The older woman in the red bikini—nice suit … I saw it at Saks last week—she's married to one of the trainers, and she makes it her personal business to sexually initiate young players to the big-time world of sports. I guess you could call her a trainer of sorts, too."

"Mmmm."

"The other one is married to a player. He's a great guy, very low-key; she has ambitions to be the hostess with the mostest, basically a little Southern twit. Actually, she's a pretty good cook."

Jennifer interrupted Leslie's monologue and pointed to two black men sitting in deck chairs by the pool. "Who are they?"

"Sorry, kid. Married. Nice guys. Both play for the Redskins."

"Damn, the good ones are always married."

"Not all the good ones. Follow me."

Jennifer followed Leslie as she wove her way through a crowd of men toward a rather innocuous-looking brown-skinned man in horn-rimmed glasses. He certainly didn't look like a football player.

Leslie said, "Jerry, I'd like you to meet my dear friend and college roommate, Jennifer Madison. Jerry plays for the Redskins. Jennifer's in DC for the summer working at the Justice Department. I wanted to introduce you two because I know you dream of going to law school when you finish with football."

Leslie then excused herself, as adeptly as her mother, the Jewish matchmaker, would have done.

Jerry was just under six feet with broad shoulders and a narrow waist. Jennifer looked at him. "I know a little something about football. You're obviously not a linebacker."

Jerry laughed. "Yeah, you're right. I'm a pass receiver."

"Well, then, you're the one Jason is supposed to throw the ball to."

"That's me! Jason's quite a player."

Jennifer smiled. "So Leslie tells me. My former roommate is not really objective when it comes to Jason, so if you say so, I'll believe it."

"Jason's really a good guy. You know, with all of the coverage he's gotten from the national press, not just here in DC, you'd expect him to be a really arrogant SOB, but he's not."

"I'm glad to hear that."

"Jason told me about you. You go to Harvard, right?"

"That's right."

"Harvard. I'm impressed."

"Don't be. Harvard's kicking my butt."

At the other end of the pool, guys were yelling, laughing, and pushing each other good-naturedly. Jennifer could see Jason and a large, dark chocolate man, who was wearing a maroon banlon shirt and matching pants with maroon patent leather shoes, laughing and shadowboxing. Suddenly, Jason fell into the pool. Everyone gathered around laughing, waiting to see him get out, drenched and humbled. They could see his body floating at the bottom of the pool. Leslie started screaming. The guy who'd playfully pushed Jason into the pool removed his maroon patent leather shoes and dove in to rescue him.

The boisterous, partying crowd grew silent. Jennifer ran to Leslie's side and put her arm around her as Jason's limp body was brought to the surface and laid on the deck. The surgeon Leslie had pointed out earlier kneeled over him and started to administer mouth-to-mouth resuscitation as Jason's rescuer stood dripping wet above them. As the doctor placed his lips over Jason's, Jason quickly turned his head to the side and yelled, "I don't kiss on the first date." The crowd, which had been hushed at the presence of presumed death, broke into relieved, hysterical laughter as Jason got to his feet. "Bobby, you almost killed me!"

At the sound of Jason's voice, Leslie relaxed her viselike grip on Jennifer and yelled, "You jerk! You scared me to death."

His rescuer grabbed him in a bear hug. Jason screamed, "Bobby, now you *are* killing me! Let go of me!" He then turned to Jennifer. "I'd like you to meet Bobby Jones, my assassin."

"Bobby, you should have killed the jerk," Leslie said.

Laughing, Bobby said, "Maybe next time."

Bobby Jones was a first-round draft pick from the University of Kansas. He was huge, all bulging muscles and large, prominent lips; he was ruggedly handsome and every bit the ignorant jock. But for football, he wouldn't have attended college. At best, if he'd gotten lucky, he would have worked as a service station attendant and fixed cars in the alley behind the public housing project where he grew up in Baltimore.

Jennifer was immediately drawn to this virile beast of a man, especially to the sudden tenderness he displayed when he thought that Jason had drowned and then the good humor he displayed when he realized that it was all just a silly joke.

Bobby boomed, "Jason, my man, how come you know a fine sistah like this?"

"My wife and Jennifer were roommates at Goucher College. You probably know it, being from Baltimore."

Bobby laughed menacingly. "Sure, I heard of it. It was that fancy college for little rich white girls where my aunt was a cleaning lady." He turned to Jennifer. "What were you doing there, sistah?"

Jennifer bristled at the question but responded good-naturedly. "Obviously, it wasn't just for rich little white girls."

Leslie said, "Jennifer, I'm starving. Let's get something to eat. See you later, Bobby."

But Jennifer turned to Bobby. "Have you eaten?"

"Nah."

"Join us."

"I can dig that. Let me get out of these wet clothes."

Leslie shot Jennifer a warning look and said, "Roomie, that one is a wild man."

Jennifer laughed. "I can tell."

Bobby returned and joined Jennifer and Leslie by the pool. His plate was piled high with greasy barbecue ribs, potato salad, and baked beans. He sucked the ribs cleaned and tossed a bone into the swimming pool.

Leslie was appalled. "Don't do that."

Bobby smacked his lips and threw another bone into the pool. "Don't do what?" He then tossed a bone onto Leslie's lap.

Leslie jumped up, shrieking, "Are you crazy?" Leslie stalked away in search of a bathroom to remove the stain.

Jennifer said to Bobby, "You really shouldn't have done that."

Bobby said, "I scare the shit out of her. I like messing with her."

Jennifer shook her head. "You're bad. Leslie's a wonderful person. Please, don't mess with her. She doesn't understand messing with."

Bobby scowled and then grinned sheepishly. "All right. You asked me nicely, so I'll stop. You live in DC?"

"No, I'm working in DC just for the summer at the Justice Department. I'm in law school."

"A lady lawyer. That's nice. I don't need a lawyer at the moment, but could I call you anyway?"

"Absolutely."

Leslie reappeared. "Jennifer, are you ready? Jason and I are getting ready to go." Leslie added while glancing imperiously at Bobby, "I've had enough of this party."

Bobby looked at Leslie, which made her look away, and then at Jennifer. "Don't leave now. I'll drive you home."

"OK, Leslie, go ahead. Bobby'll drop me off."

Leslie looked concerned and asked, "You sure you'll be all right?"

Jennifer kissed Leslie on the cheek and whispered in her ear, "I'm a big girl, roomie. I'll be fine."

    ❁   ❁   ❁

Jennifer and Bobby drove back into the city in his black Corvette. He raced along the two-lane country road at eighty miles per hour despite a thirty-five-mile-per-hour speed limit. He handled the car expertly, and Jennifer was surprisingly unafraid. She enjoyed the speed.

Bobby was silent all the way into the city. When they passed the Washington Monument and the Lincoln Memorial, he said, "Let me show you the best view in all DC."

"This is quite spectacular right here, but if you can beat this, I'm for it."

Bobby drove to southwest Washington. He slowed down on Fourth Street as three teenage boys slowly pimp-walked across the middle of the street. One of the boys shouted, "Nice ride, man."

Bobby pumped his fist to acknowledge the boy's compliment. "Thanks, brother." He pulled into the underground parking garage of his apartment building and took the elevator to his penthouse. Without turning on any lights, he walked over to the sliding glass doors and opened them, inviting her to join him on the balcony. Although it was late at night, the air remained sticky hot. As she stood on the balcony, her skin felt clammy. A single drop of sweat trickled between her breasts.

From Bobby's balcony, Jennifer could see the Kennedy Center, the Japanese cherry trees at the Tidal Basin, and in the distance the twinkling lights of the Virginia skyline.

They retreated into the air-conditioned apartment. Bobby flicked a switch, and the mellow sounds of an old Temptations record filled the sparsely furnished space. In the living room, a complex stereo system with gigantic Bose speakers was set up near a red velvet Mediterranean sofa, which appeared to have been purchased at a cheap warehouse furniture store. "I bet you were one of those little yella girls when a bad dude like me asked you to dance, you'd look at him like he killed your mama or somethin'."

Jennifer laughed and responded with mock righteous indignation, "I did not."

"Yeah, you did."

"Why don't you ask me to dance now and see what I'd do?"

Bobby moved slowly toward Jennifer and extended his hand. "Dance?"

Jennifer slipped her arms around his waist and nestled her head in his chest. They swayed gently to the music as Bobby's thigh pressed between her legs. The persistent rhythmical movement of his thigh between her legs was soothing and exciting.

Bobby whispered in her ear, "They call her coffee because she grinds so fine."

Laughing, Jennifer said, "I didn't grind when I was a teenager. Now I know what I was missing."

Bobby looked shocked. "You didn't grind? Everybody grinds."

"Nice girls didn't."

"Well, I guess in the slums of East Baltimore, I didn't know any nice girls, because everybody did." The pressure of his thigh caused pleasant sensations throughout her body. She could feel his hardness pressing against her. By the time he reached down to kiss her lips, her body was crying out for him. Together, they walked into the bedroom. Despite Bobby's thick, rough fingers, he gently slipped the spaghetti straps off her shoulders, bowed his head slowly, and kissed and licked the tops of her shoulders. Jennifer sighed with pleasure. She continued to enjoy the feel of his hands as he rubbed up and down her arms and kissed her shoulders. His tongue moved across her shoulders and, this time, up the side of her neck. Instead of more soft moans, Jennifer abruptly stepped away from Bobby and broke out in a peal of laughter.

Bobby looked confused. "What's the matter?"

Jennifer, still giggling, said, "I'm sorry. I'm really ticklish on my neck."

"OK, OK, no more neck kisses for you." Bobby turned her around and unzipped her dress, which fell to the floor, exposing her black lace strapless bra and bikini panties. He stood behind her, reached his hand under her bra, caressed her breast, and asked, "Does this tickle?"

Jennifer leaned against him and moaned, "No."

Bobby removed the black lace bra and dropped it on the floor. He covered each breast with his hands and slowly massaged them, and then he rolled her nipples between his thumb and forefinger. Just when she felt that she could no longer stand because she was weak from the sensations, Bobby turned her around so that she faced him; then, with his hands firmly around her waist, supporting her, he began to suck her engorged nipples. She wrapped her arms around him, holding on so she would not collapse to the floor. He then gently eased his hand between her legs, firmly pressing the silky lace that separated her body from the touch of his rough hand. Moments later, Jennifer cried out in complete satisfaction. Bobby lifted her and placed her on the black satin sheet, which was cool, in stark contrast to her warm body.

As Jennifer lay there, enjoying the sensation that had enveloped her, Bobby stood at the foot of the bed, fully clothed, staring down at her. "You're really beautiful."

Jennifer stared up at him, still breathing hard from the sensations that had overtaken her. "I don't believe that just happened. I'm lying here naked—well, almost naked—and you didn't even take off your clothes."

"I wanted to pleasure you."

"Well, you accomplished that. Come here. Join me."

Bobby stood at the foot of the bed, removed his clothes, and then crawled onto the bed beside her. They lay there for a long time not moving, with Jennifer's head resting on his shoulder as Bobby gently stroked her face with his rough fingertips and stared at their reflections in the mirrored ceiling above the bed: Bobby was muscular and very dark; Jennifer, slender and very light in comparison to the rich chocolate darkness of Bobby's skin. As he stared at their reflection, Bobby said, "I like the color of your skin."

❧   ❧   ❧

On Saturday evening, after buying hard-shell crabs at the wharf, they sat on Bobby's balcony eating crabs and listening to the two-album set of the *History of Motown*.

Bobby said, "When I was growing up in the projects in East Baltimore, somebody would have a transistor radio, and we'd stand around on the playground for hours just listening to that radio. A couple of the block boys could really croon, and they'd stand around harmonizing. We'd all sing, but I wasn't as good as Junior Robertson. That nigger could sing. It's too bad; he's in prison. That boy could sing better than Smokey Robinson. Shit, you should have heard Junior singing 'Ooo Baby Baby.'"

"I loved 'Ooo Baby Baby.' Why is Junior in jail?"

"Robbery—I think he might have shot someone during a robbery. I think that's what Aunt Gladys told me."

"That's awful."

"Yeah, it is. Nigger didn't have nothin'. I could be in jail now, too, if it wasn't for football. My brother spent a couple of years in the joint. He's out now. Trying to get it together. Coach liked me. Kept me straight. If it wasn't for him, I'd never have gone to college. I'd never heard of the University of Kansas, but he arranged it, and here I am today."

Jennifer asked as offhandedly as she could, "What did your brother do?"

To Jennifer's consternation, Bobby remarked casually, "UUV."

"Unauthorized use of a motor vehicle? He stole cars?"

"Yeah, UUV, selling drugs, shoplifting, little stuff."

Jennifer cracked open another crab and realized that what Bobby referred to as "little stuff" were serious felony offenses and therefore not "little stuff" to her.

Bobby continued, "Hey, I meant to tell you. I told my Aunt Gladys you went to Goucher, and she remembered you."

"Did she?"

"Yeah, she said you were nice to her, that you didn't have your ass on your shoulders."

Remembering her discomfort with the fact that most of the campus service staff were black, she said, "I'm glad to hear that. Some of the white girls were so disrespectful to the workers."

Bobby scowled. "Who you tellin'? I know just what you talkin' 'bout. Aunt Gladys would come home sometimes and talk about how she wanted to slap some of those girls, but she knew if she did, she would get fired, and she needed that job."

"I understand."

The doorbell rang, and Bobby answered it. "Hey, man, come on in. I've been waiting for you. Jennifer, this is my man, Fast Eddie. I buy my weed from my man here. Good dude. Handles only the best Colombian dope."

Fast Eddie chimed in, "That's right. Only the best for you, Bobby. The Skins going to the Super Bowl this year, right, man?"

"If it's up to me, you know we will." The two men slapped five. "'Cuse me, man, while I get my checkbook. I ain't got no cash on me."

Bobby disappeared into the bedroom, and Jennifer followed him. Keeping her voice low, she said, "You can't write a check to this guy to buy dope."

Bobby looked confused as he continued searching for his checkbook. "Why not? I ain't got no cash on me."

She wanted to scream, but she lowered her voice and spoke very slowly and precisely. "Bobby, dope is illegal. If you write a check to this guy, the police could trace him to you. It's bad enough that you let him come to the apartment. Don't be stupid. You could get arrested."

Bobby dismissed Jennifer's remarks and proceeded to write the check.

"You're a celebrity. You know the cops are always busting football players on drug charges. Don't make it so easy for them. I'm just saying, don't be stupid and make it easy for them."

"Who you calling stupid?"

She saw the angry look on his face, but she felt he was more hurt than angry. "I didn't mean to call you stupid. I'm just saying you're leaving a trail of evidence that could get you arrested. Fast Eddie is a dealer. The cops probably know it and they're checking him out. A check from you to this guy would lead them right to you. Be careful."

Bobby reluctantly agreed. He walked out into the living room, where Eddie was admiring the stereo equipment. "Bobby, you got a nice box here."

"Thanks, man. I can't find my checkbook right now, so I'm going to have to check you later."

"No problem, my man. For you, you can owe me." Fast Eddie left a plastic sandwich bag full of marijuana with Bobby and left.

Bobby turned to Jennifer. "Well, counselor, you satisfied?"

"Sort of."

"You want a hit?"

"No, thanks."

As he placed the plastic bag under the sofa cushion, he said, "Illegal. Huh, counselor?"

"That's right."

Chapter 36

Leslie

Leslie met Jennifer for lunch in Georgetown Saturday afternoon. "It was fun having you in DC this summer. But we didn't spend as much time together as I'd wanted. Bobby monopolized all your time."

Jennifer glanced at the menu. "I know. I did spend lots of time with him. In fact, he's taking me out tonight for a farewell dinner."

"When I took you to that party, I didn't intend for you to meet Bobby. I thought you'd like Jerry. I think he's more your type."

"It just clicked with Bobby. Maybe, one day, I'll be happily married like you, but right now I'm just trying to get through law school and grab some good times where I can."

"Remember, when you do get married, I'm going to be the matron of honor."

Jennifer placed her menu on the table and leaned back in her chair. "Leslie, when I finally get married, if I ever do—"

Leslie interrupted, "Of course you're going to get married."

"Well, we shall see. But if I do, you will definitely be my matron of honor."

"Good. I'm glad that's settled." Leslie looked around the restaurant and then out the window at the people walking along M Street. "You know, I really like it here in DC. Jason's doing well, it's easy to get to New York to see my parents, I love our house, and I like my job. This is the nation's capital, but it really is a football town. It's really working for us."

As Jennifer listened to Leslie describe how happy she was, the memory of Jason's advances at the beginning of the summer forced her to say a quick, silent prayer for Leslie's continued happiness.

❧   ❧   ❧

Saturday evening, Jennifer and Bobby had dinner at a famous French restaurant in Virginia that she'd heard about during the summer. Normally, reservations had to be made two weeks in advance, but Bobby had the Redskins PR
person get the reservation for him that morning.

The high-speed drive through the winding roads of the Virginia countryside in Bobby's Corvette was exhilarating and dangerous, and she loved it. As
they were seated at a table that looked out onto the rose garden, Bobby said,
"I'm going to miss you."

"I'm going to miss you, too." Jennifer's response was automatic, but once
the words were said, she realized that they were true. She knew that they had
little in common, but he had been just what she needed during this summer
break from law school.

Bobby ordered the prime rib, rare, and Jennifer had the trout almondine.
Throughout dinner they reminisced about all of the wonderful meals they'd
enjoyed. As they waited for the chocolate soufflé, Bobby said, "You know, I
can't get away during the season to come to see you very much, but would you
come down here? I'd send you a plane ticket."

"I'd love to. Of course, I'm not always going to be able to get away
either—studying and my job, you understand. Our schedules are probably
going to conflict in the fall."

Bobby nodded. "We'll work it out."

Before the soufflé arrived, Jennifer got up to go to the ladies' room. As she
crossed the dimly lit restaurant, she saw Jason in one of the side rooms. She
started to walk in his direction, until she realized that the young woman seated
across from him was not Leslie. Jennifer immediately changed directions,
quickened her pace, and fled before he could see her.

When Jennifer returned to the table, the waiter was presenting the chocolate
soufflé. Bobby tasted the rich dessert. "Hey, this is good. I should order
another one of these."

"Don't. I want to get out of here."

Bobby looked hurt. "I thought you liked this place."

"I do. I just saw Jason having dinner with a woman, and it's not Leslie. I
don't want him to see us."

"You think my boy's cheatin' on your friend?"

"Looks like that to me."

Chapter 37

Paige

Paige regretted giving up her sunny garden apartment in Palo Alto, but after accepting the job at *San Francisco* magazine, it was too inconvenient, so she opted to move into the city. Her new apartment was perched on a hillside with a magnificent view of the Golden Gate Bridge and Sausalito on clear days. On a cloudy day, she had to remind herself that Sausalito really existed.

Memories of Peter's death haunted her. She admitted to herself that she'd longed for him when he disappeared. Now that he was dead, she would always love the idea of him.

San Francisco magazine was more than just a sophisticated local publication. It contained its share of features on local restaurants, theater, nightclubs, popular places to live, and local celebrities, but it also contained some tough, in-depth investigative reporting. After Paige did a few successful fluff pieces like the one on the hot tub craze, she approached the editor with an idea. She cornered Charlie in his office as he was putting the fourth packet of sugar into his morning coffee. "Charlie, I'd like to do an article on lesbians. The focus is always on gay men, but there's a less visible gay female group out there, too."

Charlie slurped his coffee, which spilled onto his wrinkled white shirt. "I like it. Do it."

Paige telephoned a reporter she'd worked with in Baltimore. "Quincy, I'm doing an article on gay women. Could you introduce me to someone who'd be willing to talk with me?"

"Sure. Gretchen would be perfect. We've been friends since our high school days in Seattle. Of course, I didn't know she was gay when we were in high school. Heck, I didn't know I was gay in high school. Correction: I knew, but I didn't tell anybody. She's an architect. Restores Victorian houses."

When Paige and Gretchen met for lunch the next day, Gretchen said, "Quincy told me that you're not gay."

"No, I'm not. That's why I need some guidance."

Gretchen looked a little wary. "Guidance?"

"I went to a women's college, so I'm surprised that I don't know any lesbians. But I don't."

Gretchen smiled and countered, "You don't *think* you know any lesbians. You probably do."

After thinking for a moment, Paige said, "You're probably right. And that's the point of my story. Lesbians are invisible. What's your life like? Do you tell people? What does your family think? Does it affect your work? How have you been discriminated against? I have lots of questions."

Over the next few weeks, Paige accompanied Gretchen to dinners, parties, and meetings with gay women. They attended a church in the Mission District where gay couples could have marriage-like ceremonies. The minister, Reverend Simonds, arranged for Paige to attend a gay marriage ceremony.

In a few weeks Paige and Gretchen became virtually inseparable. Each was convinced that the other was the only person in the world who truly understood her likes and dislikes, her passions, quirks, and obsessions, her fantasies and sense of the absurd. In a very short time, Paige and Gretchen became lovers.

The article was a sensitive and poignant portrayal of gay women. Paige's article told a story of triumph, happiness, and inner tranquillity.

As usual, the *San Francisco* magazine newsroom was hectic and noisy, but the buzz level rose perceptively, causing Paige to look up from her typewriter. Charlie was walking through the newsroom with Mark Elliott, a TV news reporter, who reported from exotic locations around the world. The guy seemed to specialize in revolutions. If there was a civil war anyplace in the world or if a handful of peasants and soldiers were even entertaining passing thoughts of revolution, Elliott was there. He'd started his career with the wire services with Charlie but was tapped by TV. With his ruggedly handsome good looks and a cleft in his chin, he was perfect for TV. His appearance offended no one, and according to the ratings, he charmed millions of viewers.

As they approached Paige's desk, the contrast in the appearance of Mark and Charlie was comical. As usual, Charlie was dressed in a coffee-stained, rumpled white shirt—sleeves rolled up, exposing hairy arms—and wrinkled trousers buckled below his beer belly. Mark wore an expertly tailored tweed jacket, dark plaid shirt opened to show a single gold chain around his neck, jeans that were faded from wear but had perfect creases, and the obligatory Burberry raincoat. Even on television in the middle of some godforsaken war-torn area, Elliott always managed to look perfectly groomed.

Charlie introduced Mark, explaining that he would be in town for just a short while before going to South America on assignment. Paige, without smiling, rose from her typewriter and firmly shook his hand.

"I read your article on gay women. Excellent."

Before Paige could respond, Mark said, "How about lunch?"

Assuming that the invitation was to both of them, Paige said, "Sure. Lunch sounds good."

Mark turned to Charlie, patted him on the belly, and said, "Charlie, you should have a yogurt at your desk."

Once they sat down in the restaurant, Mark said, "I hadn't intended to invite you to lunch. I was just going to stop by your desk, congratulate you on the piece, and keep going. But once I saw your gray eyes, I changed my mind."

Paige smiled. "I'm glad you did."

"I invited you to lunch because you have two things I admire besides beautiful eyes: talent and independence."

She could feel herself blushing when she said, "Thanks, but how did you determine that?"

"Read your article." Flashing a guilty smile, he added, "Charlie told me. How about dinner tonight?"

"We haven't finished lunch."

"So what? I'm only here for a little while, and I already know that I want to see more of you."

That evening, Paige and Mark took the ferry over to Sausalito. They stood on the open deck and watched the snow-white seagulls follow the ferry in perfect formation across the bay, occasionally swooping down into the water for fish and then soaring back into formation behind the ferry. At a seafood restaurant, Mark regaled her with stories of Vietnam. His cool, intelligent, almost scholarly, television persona reflected none of his rich sense of humor, hearty laugh, or sensuality. Paige told him about her research on lesbians. They swapped newspaper stories and soon were confessing their life stories. She told him about Peter, whom Mark had read about. He was fascinated by Paige's description of Peter and their relationship. Mark told Paige about Lynn, the woman he'd lived with for two years.

After dinner, they strolled along the steep and winding sidewalks of Sausalito, going in and out of shops and art galleries, and then they stopped for coffee at the hotel near the ferry landing. The ferry ride back across the bay was freezing cold. He opened up his Burberry coat and pulled her gently toward him so that the coat surrounded her. She leaned against him and savored the smell of his cologne.

Mark kissed her and then whispered in her ear, "I want you." They returned to Paige's apartment. She held Mark's hand and led him directly to her bedroom. The smell of lavender potpourri perfumed the air. Paige lit a candle by her bed, and Mark wrapped her in his arms. In between kisses, they released each other only to remove the clothing that was separating them and then collapsed on the bed, where they made love until Paige couldn't remember having ever been happy before.

Paige did not return any of Gretchen's calls for several days, as she was completely engaged in falling in love with Mark. Just as Paige and Mark were leaving her office for lunch, Gretchen entered the office reception area. Shocked to see her standing there, Paige made the introductions and explained that they were on their way to lunch. Mark insisted that Gretchen join them, and she agreed.

"I feel like having a luxurious lunch, some place a world away from a war zone," Mark said. "Let's go to the Hyatt at the Embarcadero and eat at the revolving restaurant. Fun?"

The two women nodded their silent agreement.

During lunch, Mark kept them laughing with stories about the inevitable mix-ups he'd encountered while traveling in war-torn countries, the various places he'd slept in that had been infested by exotic vermin, and his acquired taste for foreign cuisine. When Mark left them at the restaurant to keep an appointment, the previous lighthearted mood quickly evaporated.

"He's your lover, isn't he?" Gretchen asked in a voice steeped in pain and anger.

"That's none of your business."

Gretchen looked wounded by Paige's response. She asked pathetically, "How can you say that?"

"Because it's true. I never promised you anything. We made love. It was enjoyable, but that's all it was."

Gretchen ended the conversation. "I accept that it's over. I even accept that it never really was. But I don't accept the way you handled it. You treated me as if I was invisible, as if my feelings didn't count. That's where we started. Remember? Gay women are invisible." Gretchen rose and walked away. Paige didn't watch her leave. Instead, she got the attention of the waiter and ordered another gin and tonic. She said to the waiter, "Extra lime, please."

❦   ❦   ❦

That evening, as Mark and Paige lay in bed looking out at the faraway lights of Sausalito, Mark broke the silence. "I've never been in a love triangle before where the man and the woman are fighting for the love of the other woman."

Paige responded tersely, "You're not in that kind of triangle now. I don't know what you're talking about."

"I'm talking about Gretchen."

"What about her?"

Mark turned on his side so he could look directly at Paige before speaking. He said tenderly, "I can tell that you two were lovers."

Paige abruptly sat up. The patterned Miramekko sheet that had been covering her body fell exposing her nakedness. She screamed, "Lovers? What the hell ever gave you that idea?"

He sat up, caressed the curve of her cheek, and allowed his hands to slowly descend, gently caressing her shoulders and the roundness of her breasts. He said, matter-of-factly, "I've known you were lovers since the moment I met you in the newsroom. Of course, I couldn't have known it was Gretchen, but I knew it was a woman."

"That's crap. I know why you're saying this: just because of the article."

Mark slowly shook his head. "No, not because of the article. There was something in the very essence of you. I sense it's a tenderness that you can only share with a woman—a closeness, a vulnerability that you refuse to show men for some reason."

"What are you saying?"

"I'm saying that I'm trying to evoke that same vulnerability in you. I'm saying I love you. I'm also saying that I understand your relationship with Gretchen. I'm just trying to replace her. At first, I thought it was Peter who haunted us, but that's what you wanted me to think. It's Gretchen. Or maybe it's not Gretchen. Whatever it is, I want you now. Marry me."

As Paige listened to Mark, she realized that he was saying just what she wanted him to say. She wanted him, and not merely as a warm body for temporary comfort; she wanted to belong to him.

Paige called her mother in Palm Beach. "I'm getting married."

"Paige, what are you talking about? Who are you going to marry?"

"His name is Mark Elliott. He's a TV correspondent."

"I've seen him on TV. I didn't know you knew him. When did you meet him?"

"Two weeks ago."

Mrs. Wyatt did not respond.

"Mother, are you there?"

"I'm here." She took a deep breath and then shrieked, "Two weeks ago! Paige, what are you doing? This sounds crazy."

"Mother, I'm in love. I want to marry him. He wants to marry me." Paige could hear her mother's labored breathing. "Say something."

"Darling, all I've ever wanted for you is for you to be happy. But this sounds dangerously impetuous. I thought you didn't believe in marriage."

Hurt that her mother didn't automatically embrace her decision and embarrassed by her prior stance on marriage, she felt compelled to explain. "He makes me feel that I'm supposed to be with him. I feel connected to him. I can't explain it."

"You don't have to explain it to me. But be sure you understand what you're doing." There was a long pause. Her mother broke the silence. "So, can I start planning a wedding? I love weddings. I've had plans for yours ever since you were ten. Should we have the wedding in Palm Beach or New York?"

"Mother, the wedding is planned. We're getting married in two days. Mark is leaving on assignment in South America, and I'm going with him."

"Darling, are you sure? This seems so fast."

"We would've gotten married tomorrow, but we're giving you and Mark's dad a day to get out here. We want you both at the wedding. Reverend Simonds is going to perform the ceremony. He's the minister I met during my research on the lesbian article. I love him. He's the perfect person to do it."

"Paige, I'll be there. I love you, sweetheart." Mrs. Wyatt held her breath and then asked another question. "May I invite your father?"

The reference to her father momentarily dampened her spirits. "Absolutely not. Don't even tell him."

"I understand. I thought that would be your reaction. I wish you didn't feel that way. I'll be there tomorrow."

On Wednesday afternoon, one day before Mark was scheduled to leave for Rio, he and Paige were married in a ceremony conducted by Reverend Simonds in the sanctuary of his Mission District church and attended only by Paige's mother, Mark's father, David, and Charlie. After the ceremony, they all had dinner at the St. Francis Hotel; Mrs. Wyatt had quickly arranged the reception, which included a three-tiered white chocolate wedding cake, a photographer, and a penthouse bridal suite, with red rose petals on the bed and Dom Perignon champagne on the nightstand.

Chapter 38

Jennifer

Law school was just no fun. There were a few weirdoes who loved it, but most students saw it as a necessary and painful means to a hopefully satisfying and lucrative end. Bobby called her regularly, and the last weekend in October, Jennifer flew to DC for the Washington Redskins-Dallas Cowboys game. On the flight, she read the *Washington Post*'s sport section and learned that the Redskins and the Cowboys were old rivals, so the fans, the team, and especially Bobby, who was quoted in the article, were especially hyped about the game.

Bobby picked Jennifer up at National Airport and drove directly to his apartment. With no preliminary conversation, they made love. Later, Jennifer slid out from under the black satin sheets.

Bobby asked, "Where are you going?"

"To get my robe."

"Wait." He reached under the bed, pulled out a red fox jacket, and threw it at her. "Here. Put this on."

Jennifer screamed with surprise. She put the jacket on and paraded around the room to Bobby's admiring catcalls and whistles.

"Bobby, I love it." As she paraded around the bedroom in the jacket, she wondered how she'd explain it to her mother. There was no explanation her mother would understand, so her mother would never see this coat.

"Just a little something to keep my little mama warm at the game."

Jennifer cringed at the phrase "little mama" but smiled and patted the soft fur of the red fox jacket.

❦   ❦   ❦

On Sunday afternoon during the second quarter, the Redskins were trailing the Cowboys 7–3. The defense had played tough and held the Cowboys to just one touchdown, but the Redskins' offense couldn't seem to get the ball in the end zone. Jason was sacked. Leslie screamed when Jason hit the ground. "Oh my God. Look at him. He's getting up so slowly. That's not like him."

"Do you think he's seriously hurt?" Jennifer asked.

"I don't know. But Jason is always aware of the crowd." When Jason slowly rose to his feet, the crowd cheered. In response, Jason pumped his fist in the air, indicating he was OK. The crowd cheered louder. Leslie relaxed. "He's OK. Look at him. He was playing the crowd. Milking them for sympathy. By the way, I love that jacket. It's marvelous."

In a sassy voice, Jennifer said, "Bobby gave it to me to keep me warm at the game."

Over the roar of the crowd, Leslie asked, "What's with you and Bobby? He's not your type, roomie. What was that quote from your mother? 'If you don't want to marry a garbageman, don't go out with him.' Remember that?"

"I remember. I hope you're not suggesting Bobby is a garbageman," Jennifer responded self-righteously.

"You know what I mean. He's just not the kind of man you were looking for during college. He's not marriage material. Your mother will hate him. Why risk getting involved?"

"We're not talking marriage. He's fun."

"You mean he's good in bed."

"That, too!"

The Redskins got off to a miserable start in the third quarter. Jason was intercepted on the fifteen-yard line.

Bobby stormed over to the offensive coach, who was diagramming plays with Jason. "Motherfucker, give me the fucking ball. I can score." He turned to Jason and then spit on the ground. "This cocksucker has been throwing interceptions all damn day. Give me the damn football."

The coach barked, "Calm down, Jones. You'll get your shot." Bobby stalked away and sat on the bench. The television cameras zoomed in on him. He ignored them.

On second down, Jason attempted a long pass, which the receiver dropped. With twenty seconds to go in the fourth quarter, Jason called a time-out and went to the sidelines to discuss the play with the coach. The entire stadium was on its feet. The roar of the crowd was deafening.

The coach said, "Jones, this is your shot. Don't blow it or it's your ass."

Bobby growled, "Look. Just give me the ball, and tell those motherfuckers up front to block just a teeny-weeny bit." His sarcasm twisted his face into a menacing scowl.

The Redskins ran onto the field. The crowd grew quiet, anticipating what would probably be the last play of the game. Jason rolled out and handed off to Bobby; the first hole opened up perfectly. Bobby dashed through, broke one tackle, and shook off another. The crowd, already on its feet, screamed louder with each successive yard. As he ran, Bobby could hear the sounds from the fans, but he could also distinguish the sounds of approaching cleats and the grunts and moans as he broke tackles and ran for twenty-five yards to score the winning touchdown. This time, when the TV camera zoomed in on him, Bobby waved and yelled, "Hi, Mom."

❦   ❦   ❦

A couple of weeks after the Dallas game, Bobby flew to Cambridge to visit Jennifer for the first time. She was nervous, as she assumed that the law school ambience was bound to bring out all of Bobby's prejudices against intellectuals. They strolled through Harvard Yard. Bobby looked handsome in the cashmere jacket and overcoat Jennifer had selected for him. Because of Jennifer, he no longer wore Thom McAnn shoes and dressed more conservatively than he had when they first met. Jennifer flinched at the memory of the maroon polyester trousers, matching banlon shirt, and maroon patent leather shoes.

"Bobby, I've got a class at two that I can't miss. Why don't you wait for me at my room, and I'll see you a little after three, OK?"

"Can I go to class with you? I've never been inside a law school."

"You want to?"

"I asked, didn't I?"

They walked over to Langdell Hall. Just as they began to climb the steps, BJ appeared, out of breath. As usual, she was late for her class. Jennifer stopped her and introduced her to Bobby.

BJ wheezed, "Hi, Bobby. Nice to meet you. Heard about you from Jennifer. My little brother is a big fan of yours."

Bobby nodded, put his arm around Jennifer, and continued walking up the steps, leaving BJ alone on the lower step. Jennifer stumbled as a result of the unexpected pressure on her back. Disengaging herself from Bobby's arm, she stopped and said more emphatically, "Bobby. This is my *friend*, BJ."

Bobby mumbled, "Hey."

BJ stopped cold on the steps and muttered under her breath, "Muthafucka."

As Bobby and Jennifer entered the classroom, a couple of the guys recognized Bobby right away, and before class started, they came over and told him what big fans they were. Even the professor recognized Bobby, welcomed him to the class, and made a bad joke about being an armchair quarterback. All of the students were obligated to chuckle politely, but Bobby laughed heartily, obviously enjoying being the center of attention.

After class, as they left the lecture hall and walked back across campus to Jennifer's room, she attacked. "Why did you treat my friend like that?"

"What you talkin' 'bout?"

"BJ. You ignored her like she didn't exist!"

"That ugly bitch? She a friend of yours?"

"How dare you call my friend an ugly bitch!"

"I didn't do nothin' to da girl."

"That's just it. You treated her as if she didn't exist. You refused to look at her. That's insulting. People want to be acknowledged. You love it when fans recognize you!"

Bobby mumbled, "No big deal. I didn't mean nothin'."

On Monday evening, BJ knocked on Jennifer's door. "J, you in there?"

Jennifer yelled through the closed door. "Yeah, come on in." She was propped up in the only comfortable chair in her room, reading.

"What are you reading?"

"Antitrust. Need a break. Sit down. I've been meaning to talk with you."

"About what?"

"Bobby. I wanted to apologize for his rude behavior."

BJ waved her hand dismissively in the air. "No problem. Just another brother who can't stand dark-skinned sisters with short hair. We bring 'em down."

"Oh, BJ. There you go again with that skin color and hair crap. That's not the explanation for every encounter between black people or even between black people and white people. Bobby's just crude sometimes. No manners. But really, he's a gentle, caring soul."

"Cut the heart-of-gold routine, J. The brother has a big dick and cash in his pockets, and that's why you're dating him."

"I can't believe you said that to me. You don't know Bobby, and I thought you had come to know me better than that."

"Look!" BJ sat down on Jennifer's bed and leaned comfortably against the wall. "Yes, you do believe I said it. J, you're a nice, middle-class yella girl from Detroit, with long hair and a mama and daddy who love you and each other, and you're slumming. Hey, I bet your parents even had a wedding with a white wedding dress and bridesmaids, and you've been looking at the picture dreaming of your own wedding since you were nine years old. Am I right?"

Jennifer was surprised by the accuracy of BJ's portrait. "Yes, my parents do love me and each other, and yes, they had a wedding. So what?"

BJ continued. "If I didn't know you, I'd hate you for it, but I know you're a good sister. So, I don't. Besides, I'm just jealous. I wish I had all of that. I don't know where my daddy is. If he called me, I would only curse him out. Who needs that? As for Bobby, it's OK to do a little slumming. I can't help myself; I've always called a spade a spade. Hey, I was one of the hundreds of little dark-skinned girls in the projects with short braids and too many barrettes in our hair. I hated little girls like you, with two long braids and another dangling over to the side with crisp white satin ribbons tied neatly at the ends."

Jennifer laughed. "How did you know that?"

BJ growled, "J, give me a break. I can just look at you and tell. I now know that the amount of grease in a black woman's hair directly correlates to her socioeconomic class. My hair wasn't long enough to tie a ribbon on it. We were the little girls who lived next door to black bucks like Bobby, and he hated himself and hated us for living in the projects. So, once he got out, the buck refused to look back, and when, by chance, he's forced to take a look at us, he just gets angry. He's too stupid to know where that anger comes from, but it bubbles up each time he sees one of us. I'm surprised a nigger like him doesn't have an incurable case of snow fever and isn't dating every white girl he can find."

"Now you're against interracial dating," Jennifer groaned.

"I didn't say that. I'm against every decent brother dating some ugly white woman and not leaving any black men for me."

"Why does the white woman have to be ugly?"

BJ retorted, "There is no such thing as a pretty white woman. That's an oxymoron!"

Jennifer screamed, "BJ, I don't believe you. You're angry with all white people, all black men, and most black women, especially if they have long hair. When are you going to stop being so angry?"

BJ closed her eyes as she rested her head against the wall. She opened them and looked directly at Jennifer. "Not yet. The times aren't right yet. Remember, they killed Reverend King. I guess I'm still a field nigger. Your folks obviously worked in the big house."

Jennifer laughed. "You're a field nigger, all right. Summa cum laude graduate of Wellesley and a Harvard Law student."

Smirking, BJ said, "I'm talking about my past, my childhood, my family. The past is hard to overcome. I'm trying, but I have no illusions that it's difficult." She stood up, stretched her arms over her head, and then plopped back onto the bed. "I'm glad to be here at Harvard. I love this law school stuff. I can't wait to get out there and practice law. But there are others, right here at Harvard and certainly out there in America, who still don't think I belong here. I don't look the part. I'll show 'em."

Jennifer gazed at her friend with admiration. "I know you will."

"We will." BJ continued, "Back to this man issue. I want a man to love *me*. Where's mine? I want to be loved and cherished, too. Instead, my good brothers are rejecting his sisters for white girls. You don't see a whole bunch of white men dating black women, do you?" Before Jennifer could answer, BJ said, "No, you do not. So, what happens? The good brothers go white, the bad brothers go to jail, and a whole bunch of sisters are left to fend for themselves. Sad. So, until we have some equal opportunity in dating … hey, I like that. Equal Opportunity Dating. EOD. That's it. Equal Opportunity Dating, meaning as many white boys dating sisters as there are brothers dating Missy Ann. Counsel, until we have some EOD, my position remains the same."

"I dated a white guy in college."

BJ snorted, "What happened? He dump you when his mother found out?"

Jennifer shook her head. "No, his mother knew I was black. I broke up with him just because he was white. I knew that eventually the relationship was going to be difficult. I didn't want to work so hard for love. Love should be easy."

BJ snorted again, "Girl, you are fooling yourself. Love is not easy. Black or white."

"Have you ever dated a white guy?"

A frown crossed BJ's face. "No white guy has ever asked me out. They've asked me for my class notes, but never out."

"Would you date a white guy?"

"I don't know. Probably not. I've known lots of folks with snow fever. Hey, do you remember David Walker?"

"No. Who's David Walker?"

"Spook Weekend. Yale." BJ laughed and then added, "That weekend that you unfairly accused me of being nasty to you."

Jennifer countered, "You *were* nasty to me."

"OK. Coulda been. Probably was. Anyway, David Walker was the president of Yale's Afro-Am Society, the black student group."

Jennifer leaned back in her chair, threw her head back, smiling at the memory, and then said, "Yes. Yes. Yes. Now, I remember. He was fine, fine, fine."

BJ's frown was replaced with a smile. "David was fine, but he had snow fever. He dated some sisters, and he was always very nice to me. Good dancer. Good guy."

"Where's he now?"

"Last I heard, Stanford Law School."

Jennifer laughed. "Snow fever is not a terminal illness. Brothers can recover. Hopefully."

BJ laughed as well. "Some of them. Hey, I'm going to run. Don't worry about the Bobby thing. I understand him, probably much better than you do. J, be careful. That bad attitude of his can be dangerous. That black buck was in the projects too long. He may never recover." BJ got up from the bed and straightened out Jennifer's bedspread. "See ya."

Jennifer tried to return to reading the antitrust cases, but BJ's comments about Bobby kept running through her mind. She also remembered her mother saying, "You can take some niggers out of the ghetto, but you can't take the ghetto out of some niggers." The telephone rang, breaking this disturbing thought. It was Leslie. "Did I catch you at a bad time?"

"No, just studying, as usual. I could use some pleasant conversation."

"I'm not sure if this qualifies as pleasant conversation. Have you talked with Bobby lately?"

"He was up here last week."

Leslie feigned surprise. "Oh?"

"What is it? You obviously called to tell me something. Say it, already."

Leslie hesitated. "Well, this is hard for me to tell you. You're my friend, and I want to protect you."

"From what?"

Leslie blurted it out. "A woman filed a paternity suit against Bobby. She says he's the father of her one-month-old son."

Jennifer screamed into the phone, "What?"

Leslie sighed and then struggled to continue. "I debated telling you this, but even Jason agreed that you should know, and I wasn't sure that bastard would tell you himself."

"Wait a minute. I know you don't like Bobby—"

Leslie cut her off. "I like Bobby. As long as he's running up and down a football field, I like him just fine. I just don't like him *for you.*"

Jennifer, regaining her composure, turned into the lawyer she was studying to become. "Fine. So far all that's happened is some woman has filed a lawsuit. Big deal. Filing a lawsuit certainly doesn't mean he's guilty."

Leslie countered, "However, roomie, Bobby has already admitted to the press that he's the father. The sportswriters here in DC are having a good time with the story. Apparently, when she had the baby, welfare paid for the delivery. The press is playing up the angle that this rich football player's baby's delivery was paid for by welfare."

There was silence. Jennifer wasn't prepared for Leslie's last comments. "I don't know what to say."

"What are you going to do?"

"What am I supposed to do? I don't know. Maybe nothing. Thanks for telling me."

On Friday afternoon, Jennifer flew to DC. Bobby picked her up at the airport, never mentioning the paternity suit or the baby. Jennifer waited. Finally, after dinner in Georgetown, they went to Bobby's apartment. "Jennifer, baby, there's somethin' you should know."

"What is it?"

"Some bitch has filed a lawsuit against me for child support. Dat's all."

Jennifer was appalled by his cavalier manner. "What do you mean 'that's all'? Are you the father?"

Bobby shrugged his shoulders. "Probably."

"Probably? Are you going to pay?"

"Yeah. It's not a lot of money."

"What are you saying? You're going to pay some woman child support for a baby that you say is 'probably' yours. Don't you know?"

"All right, Jennifer. Don't give me that lawyer shit. The baby's mine. I know it; so I'll pay her off, and that's all there is to it. It ain't got nothing to do with you, so stay out of it. I just told you because you'd read it in the papers, that's all, or that bitch Leslie would tell ya."

Jennifer attempted to maintain her composure. "Are you going to marry the mother of your child? Do you love her?"

"I'm not going to marry the bitch. She knows that. I never promised her that. It was just bloomer puddin'."

Jennifer continued to control the anger that was building inside of her. She spoke slowly and deliberately. "Bloomer puddin'? What are you talking about?"

"Sex. You really are a bougie yella girl. Don't even know what bloomer puddin' is."

"No, I don't know what bloomer puddin' is. I do know that you just called the mother of your child a bitch. Do you realize that?"

"I said it, didn't I? Look, baby, this ain't got nothin' to do with you and me and what we've got. I love you, baby. You're the one. You've got to know dat. Look, I'll pay her off. No big deal. I got the money. I gave Linda some money for her kid."

Jennifer was stunned. "Who's Linda? What kid?"

Bobby confessed. "My last year in college, this girl, her name's Linda, claimed I knocked her up. I promised to help her with the boy, and I do. It's no big deal."

"Are you telling me you have a son who must be, what, about five years old?"

"Yeah. He's five."

"Do you see him?"

"Nah, I told you. I send her a little money for the kid, and she don't hassle me."

Jennifer, who up to this point had been pacing back and forth across Bobby's living room, stopped pacing and sat down on the sofa, which was still the only furniture in the room. With disgust dripping from each syllable, she slowly said, "I do not believe you. You have probably brought two children, two sons, into this world, and you've made no attempt to be a father to either of them. Bobby, have you forgotten what it was like to grow up without the love and guidance of a father?"

"I ain't forgotten shit."

"Well, why are you doing the same thing to your sons? How can you?"

"Jennifer, leave it alone. It ain't your business."

"Don't give me that smart-ass shit. I'm disgusted by your irresponsible attitude. You go around making babies with women you don't care anything about, and now you're willing to walk away from the whole thing, after throwing a little money at it, and pretend that nothing happened and that it has nothing to do with us. It has everything to do with us. Black men, for a lot reasons, haven't been fathers to their children. We need fathers, and for you to ignore your responsibility is criminal. You're a jock. Every time the TV camera focuses on one of you after you've done something spectacular, what do you do? You wave to the camera and say, 'Hi, Mom.' Nobody ever says, 'Hi, Dad.' You notice that? You know why that is? Because dad hasn't been there. Mom has sweated it out all by herself, and so her son waves to her. I'd like to see the day a black kid yells, 'Hi, Dad,' but if it's left up to men like you, that day will never come. This whole thing confirms that you're a confused, selfish man with feelings for no one but yourself."

With a suddenness that Jennifer couldn't imagine, Bobby slapped her across the face, and she fell to the floor, her face stinging, tears filling her eyes. No words came out of her mouth, just muffled sobs. She tried to catch her breath but couldn't. Quickly, Bobby dropped to the floor, holding her, begging her forgiveness. "Jennifer, baby, I'm sorry. I didn't mean it. Forgive me, baby, forgive me." He pleaded with her, but she couldn't speak. She just stared at him with fear and repulsion.

Bobby continued to plead, "Baby, I'm sorry. I didn't mean it. I love you. Forgive me."

Jennifer got to her feet. She gathered her belongings as Bobby followed her, pleading for her forgiveness. She opened the door and started down the hallway.

Bobby stood in the hallway cursing and screaming as she walked toward the elevator. "Get out of here, you hainty yellow bitch."

As she waited for the elevator, she could hear his apartment door slam. She took the elevator to the lobby, refusing to look at her reflection in the mirrored elevator wall. Even she didn't want to see the humiliation that must have been apparent on her face. She was embarrassed to confront her own bad judgment. As she rode to the lobby, she gathered as much dignity as she could muster, and then, lugging her suitcase, she walked to the building's entrance. She took a cab to Leslie's house, vowing that she would never be this stupid again.

Chapter 39

Leslie

When the cab pulled up in front of Leslie's house, Jennifer was relieved to see lights on throughout the house. Leslie answered the doorbell. Seeing Jennifer's tear-stained face, Leslie hugged her and led her into the living room.

After they settled on the sofa, Jennifer, no longer crying, said, "You were right. Bobby wasn't the right man for me."

"What happened?"

"He admitted the child was his, and then he told me about another one! He's five years old."

Leslie gasped, "Another child?"

"Yes, he got some girl pregnant his last year in college. May I have a glass of water? Crying makes me thirsty."

Leslie jumped up and ran to the kitchen and returned with the water. Jennifer took a few gulps and then said, looking down at the floor to avoid seeing the pity she anticipated would be Leslie's reaction when she confessed, "He hit me."

Leslie screamed, "What? Oh my God. That bastard! Are you OK?" She moved closer and started searching her face for bruises. "Did you call the police? Do you want me to call the police?"

Jennifer wearily shook her head. "No, don't call the police. Can you imagine what kind of spectacle that would be? The press is already covering the baby story. I don't want my parents reading about it. They would be so disappointed in me. Your parents, too. Let it go."

"Are you sure? That animal shouldn't be allowed to get away with this."

"You're right. But I don't want to get involved in all the mess. The best thing to do is forget this ever happened."

Leslie stood up and headed for the kitchen. "Well, you've come to the right place. I have just what you need to make you feel all better. I just happened to have some cream cheese brownies and vanilla ice cream."

Despite her anger and humiliation, Jennifer managed to laugh. "That's exactly what I need."

Jennifer followed Leslie into the kitchen. "Is Jason here?"

As Leslie placed a scoop of vanilla ice cream on top of each brownie, she said bitterly, "No, he's out at some sports banquet being the star quarterback." She slid the brownie over to Jennifer. "All of these jocks are crazy."

"What did Jason say about the baby scandal?"

Leslie savored the sweet taste of the brownie. "He said that it's not a big deal. A lot of the players have illegitimate kids. They just do a better job than Bobby in keeping it quiet." Leslie took another bite. "Welcome to the world of big-time sports."

Chapter 40

Paige

Paige quit her job with *San Francisco* magazine and flew to Rio with Mark. Holding hands on the flight, Mark commented, "You can probably do some freelance work for Charlie while we're traveling around."

Paige leaned her head on Mark's shoulder. "I talked with him about it."

"Are you going to do it?"

When Mark asked the question, she realized that the two of them hadn't discussed what she would do, although she knew that she would write. "Traveling with you should give me lots to write about."

On the way from the Rio airport, Paige pointed to a hotel. "My mother and I stayed in that hotel."

"I didn't know that you'd ever been to Rio before."

"Mother and I came down for carnival when I was about fifteen, maybe sixteen. It was amazing. I'd never seen anything like that before. It makes Mardi Gras look tame." Paige laughed sheepishly. "I met some kids and spent the night on the beach. Mother was hysterical. She was really ready to kill me that time."

"There's a lot I don't know about you."

"We have the rest of our lives to talk about it and make new memories."

Upon their arrival at their hotel, the porter placed the suitcases in the room; Mark tipped him, shut the door, and pulled Paige in for a passionate kiss. They spent the next twelve hours in bed making love.

The following day, while Mark interviewed some government officials, Paige wandered around Rio gathering material for possible articles. They spent the next day soaking up the sun on Ipanema Beach. The following day, Mark left Rio to follow up on a story for what was supposed to be three days but turned into ten. Upon his return, they spent the entire day in bed, but when Paige awakened the next morning, Mark was getting dressed and explained he'd be gone for a few days.

Upon Mark's return from yet another undisclosed location, Paige complained, "I haven't written anything in two months. I don't know what to write."

"Rio is a fascinating city. Do a travel piece. Charlie could probably use a good travel piece for *San Francisco*. Do an article on surfing. Visit the churches. The architecture is fascinating."

Paige whined, "I don't want to write about beaches or churches. I want to do something more serious."

Mark suggested, "How about the schools? Many kids here don't go to school at all."

Paige perked up. "I kinda like that." She wrapped her arms around Mark's neck. "I miss being with you. You're never here."

She heard the exhilaration in his voice when he said, "That's the nature of my job. I've got to travel on a moment's notice. I never know where a story lead will take me."

Paige completed an article on the poor conditions of the Rio schools and the children who didn't attend school at all. Charlie turned it down for *San Francisco*. After receiving rejections from several magazines, she sold it to an American Catholic education journal.

Within six months of their arrival in Rio, Paige and Mark's passion for each other was as inflamed as the first day they met, but the marriage became impossible. Neither of them could define what it was they expected. Whatever it was, what they had was not working.

As they sat on the balcony of the small apartment they'd sublet from another journalist, Mark said, "I'm flying to New York next week."

Paige perked up. "Great. I would love a few days in New York."

"I think they're going to offer me a spot in the Washington Bureau."

Paige jumped up. "Washington Bureau? The White House? Mark, that's fabulous."

He shook his head. "I'm going to talk with them. If they offer it, I'm going to turn it down."

"Why would you do that?" she asked angrily. "We need to talk about this!"

"It's not the kind of story I want to cover right now. I like what I'm doing. I like the third world issues."

"Oh, come on. Think about it. Washington would be good for both of us. You know how stymied I've felt for the past few months. My career has basically stopped."

Mark replied with a noncommittal, "We'll see."

The week in New York was a passionate rekindling of their love. They walked in Central Park, went to the theater, had delicious meals, and gloried in being together and in love. The network offered Mark the assignment to the Washington Bureau. Without consulting Paige, he turned it down.

They were back in Rio only three weeks when another offer came. Mark walked in and saw Paige's luggage sitting in the living room. He called out, "Where are you going?"

Paige emerged from the bedroom with her coat in her hand. "I've been offered a position with *Superwoman* magazine in New York."

"Never heard of it."

"It's a new women's magazine." She didn't put her coat down, indicating that she didn't have a lot of time for this discussion. "Emphasis on today's liberated women. Fashion. Articles on careers, love, life."

"You didn't tell me anything about it."

"It was my decision." She added, "Just like turning down the Washington Bureau was yours."

"Does this mean you're going to live in New York?"

"Yes."

"What about us?"

"We'll live in separate places where we can both work, and we'll get together. It'll be like a hot, raunchy affair."

❦   ❦   ❦

After six months in New York, Paige filed for divorce.

1975 TO 1976

Chapter 41

Jennifer

On Friday afternoon in early spring, Jennifer strolled down Wall Street in search of a place to eat lunch. It had been two years since she graduated from Harvard and accepted the position with the Wall Street firm of Webster, Symington, and Meredith. As she walked pass a construction site, a worker made an elaborate gesture of tipping his hard hat. Her graceful, purposeful stride, long hair draping softly around her high cheekbones, evoked respectful compliments rather than obscene catcalls. She smiled, acknowledging the hard hat's greeting, but never altered her stride.

She stopped at La Croissant for lunch. As Jennifer read the menu, she glanced out the window just as a ruggedly handsome white guy in his late twenties with blondish hair and an angular, square-jawed face walked by. He carried his suit jacket slung over his shoulder. As he walked away, she admired the way his tight-muscled butt looked in his trousers.

The waiter arrived, and Jennifer quickly took another look at the menu, as that perfect butt had distracted her. "I'll have roast beef on a croissant with lettuce and herbed mayonnaise."

She nibbled at her sandwich and continued to gaze out of the window at passers-by. A white woman in her early thirties walked by holding the arm of a short, rotund white man. The woman was elegantly dressed in an ivory ultra suede suit. Under the jacket she wore a silk blouse of the exact shade of ivory as her suit, with the blouse unbuttoned to reveal a lot more cleavage than was respectable for afternoon. The outfit was classy yet trashy. She speculated that the man must have a lot of money or power, or both, to compensate for being so fat and ugly. She wondered what it would be like to make love to a fat man.

She checked the time; she had a two-thirty meeting with Bill Foster, the only black partner at the firm. She idolized him; unfortunately, he was married. She often hoped that he would belch or pick his nose so she could take him down from the pedestal she had put him on. Instead, with each encounter, her respect and admiration for him grew. She continued to gaze out of the window. She saw a white man in his late thirties, carrying a briefcase; he walked past the window with a black woman of about the same age, who was also carrying a briefcase. By the way they walked, it was obvious to Jennifer that this was a business relationship. The man was walking on the inside, and the woman was on the curbside of the sidewalk. Anger welled up in Jennifer's chest. She questioned why, when white men walked with black female business associates, they all of a sudden lost their gallantry and walked on the inside. *If it's a white girl*, she thought, *they'd be by the curb. Just as Sojourner Truth said, ain't I a woman?* Jennifer continued to look out of the window. Approaching was the handsomest black man she'd seen in ages: he was about six feet tall, with dark caramel skin, a medium build, and a black mustache, wearing a navy blue Pierre Cardin pin-striped suit, a sky blue shirt with white collar, and French cuffs. He was with two white men, who were dressed in conservative business suits. He exuded sophisticated confidence combined with a little bit of a block-boy swagger.

Jennifer left the restaurant and entered the gray marble and dark mahogany wood-paneled lobby of her building, taking the third bank of express elevators to her office on the thirty-fourth floor. She entered the reception area, an eclectic combination of antique furniture, Oriental rugs, and modern paintings, and took a quick glance at the wall where the names of the partners and, in much smaller print, the associates were listed in gold leaf. Seeing her name gave her a lot of pleasure, despite the tiny print.

Jennifer went into her office and immediately took a call. A female voice said, "Ms. Madison, Mr. Pendleton is calling. Please hold on." In a moment, Roger Pendleton was on the line. He was one of the younger partners at the firm, a compulsive overachiever, on his way up and working hard to get there, as was his wife. He was a nice man, however, not a piranha like some others, including his wife.

"Hi, Jennifer. How are you coming on your draft of the Jameson construction case?" Without waiting for a reply, he continued, "I'm leaving the office in a few minutes. Joining the family for the weekend at our house in the Hamptons. I'd like to see your draft on Monday when I return. Can you make that?"

She knew that although the request had been formulated as a question, it was not. In a pleasant way, Pendleton was saying, "I want your draft on my desk Monday morning regardless of what you have to do to get it there. Although I'm going to the Hamptons for the weekend, you, lowly associate, should work all weekend so that draft will be ready for me upon my return." Jennifer said, "Sure. I'll have a draft for you on Monday."

At two thirty, Jennifer took the spiral staircase to Foster's office, where Lucinda Williams, the only black secretary at the firm, greeted her warmly.

Gesturing toward the door, Jennifer asked, "Is he ready for me?"

"Not quite. He's still on the phone. Any plans for the weekend?"

"I've gotta work on Saturday to finish a memo for Pendleton. I just saw a fabulous BMIS while I was at lunch."

"What's a BMIS?"

"Black man in a suit."

Lucinda laughed louder than she had intended. "Never heard that before." She laughed again. "BMIS. I'll have to remember that one."

Bill Foster was a powerfully built, dark-skinned man in his fifties. He'd played football at Dartmouth and still worked out regularly. For a black man born to sharecropper parents in rural Honea Path, South Carolina, to become a partner in a major law firm was an extraordinary achievement. But Bill Foster was not arrogant or cocky. His elegance and grace allowed him to move comfortably in the divergent worlds he inhabited. At a cocktail party in a fashionable Park Avenue penthouse, he could casually remark that he'd picked cotton as a child without having the comment sound like a self-deprecating up-from-slavery routine; rather, it was merely a statement of fact.

Foster was seated in an oversize black leather swivel chair behind a mahogany desk. On the wall behind his desk hung his Harvard law degree, while on other walls were photographs of Foster with Martin Luther King, Jr., Gloria Steinem, Bobby Kennedy, Hubert Humphrey, Jackie Robinson, Walter Cronkite, and dozens of other familiar faces. There were plaques and citations from various organizations including the NAACP, the ACLU, and the United Nations. On his desk were a picture of his wife, Carol, their children, and his mother at his summer house on Martha's Vineyard and a smaller silver-framed photo of Carol taken the year they were married.

"I've got a new project."

"I'm relieved to hear you say 'a new project.' I was afraid you weren't happy with the memo I wrote on that government contract problem last week."

"Not at all. The memo was right on point. This is a pro bono case. My old friend, Larry Neal, brought it to me. He's the director of a community program in Harlem. He'd like us to act as legal advisers to a group of domestic workers he's trying to organize into a union. Interested?"

"Sounds like a really good idea."

"Mabel Johnson is president of the group. Give her a call. Because it's pro bono, you're limited to five hours a week of your billing time on it." Foster stood up, signaling that the meeting was over. "Have a good weekend. Carol and I are going to the theater. She says the play got great reviews. I don't even know what it is."

Jennifer returned to her office and called Mabel Johnson. A teenage boy answered the telephone. "My mom's not here. Won't be home until after six." Jennifer then called Leslie, and from the sound of her voice, she could tell that something was wrong.

Leslie spoke softly. "Oh, Jennifer, I don't know where to start. I'm swamped with this ad campaign for the new soap, but all I can think about is having a baby. I don't think we ever will."

Jennifer said gently, "It just takes a little time. You're going to be a wonderful mother."

"Don't you remember how faithful I always was about taking the pill? Turns out all those pills were a waste of money."

"You're destined to have two perfect children. You owe that to the world."

Leslie laughed and then sighed. "I had one of those dreams again last night—you know, the one where I'm standing in some public place. This time it was party at the French embassy. I look down, and I'm naked below the waist. I then start rushing around trying to find someplace to hide before anyone sees me. I always wake up before I can find a place to hide. My therapist says it's anxiety."

"Leslie, your doctor told you that you and Jason are perfectly healthy. Your period just came, right?"

"Right. Anxiety. I've got to relax. I remember the first time I had the dream. It was the night before Jason's last game against Harvard. I knew that game was crucial to his going pro. I had the dream, not the French embassy part, of course. That time I think it was a football stadium. Appropriate, huh?"

"Very. Hey, you'll be interested in this. Bill just assigned me a pro bono project to set up a domestic workers' union."

Leslie said flatly, "Sounds interesting. Roomie, I gotta go."

Jennifer called Mabel Johnson and arranged to meet her Saturday morning and then headed home. Even though it was after seven o'clock on Friday night, many associates were still in their offices working and might be there several more hours. She walked from the subway to her Manhattan apartment, ever mindful of avoiding the dog poop.

When Jennifer arrived at the office, Mabel Johnson was waiting patiently for her. Momentarily panicked that she was late, Jennifer started to apologize, but Mabel cut her off. "I'm a little early. Got a ride with a neighbor, so I didn't have to take those dangerous subways from the Bronx." Her large hands were rough and cracked. Her black crepe dress was shiny from wear and stretched tightly across her ample bosom. She carried a large beige purse with artificial flowers on the front encased in clear plastic. Her mixed-gray hair was a mass of short curls.

Jennifer asked, "Mrs. Johnson, why do you want a union?"

"I've been doin' day work since I was fifteen. Left school in the ninth grade. Now, I'm fifty-eight. It was honest work, and I was able to support my family, but I'm starting to think about quitting. Can't work like this forever. But I don't have any Social Security. You see, I asked my people to pay me in cash. I've never paid into Social Security. Well, sometimes I did when I had the night job cleaning up at dat Wall Street building. They took out Social Security. By da time dey took it out, I didn't have nothin' left. Now I knows that was a mistake. And lots of folks done just like I did. We all in the same boat."

"I suppose you don't have health insurance?"

"You right. Dat's another problem. Don't have any. Never had sick leave either. If I didn't work, didn't get paid."

They discussed strategy, and then Jennifer walked Mabel to the lobby. She looked around at the grandeur of the surroundings and remarked, "You know, when I worked on Wall Street, there were no colored lawyers at all. Proud of ya. I bet your parents are really proud of you, too."

Chapter 42

Leslie

Leslie sat in the waiting room of Dr. Carter's office, an infertility expert, at Georgetown Hospital, flipping through a magazine, unable to focus on even the photographs. She purposely didn't pick *Parents* magazine, thinking it might be bad luck. The receptionist said, "Mrs. Abrams, you may go in now."

She heard her name and was embarrassed that the other people sitting in the waiting room had heard it. She imagined that they recognized her. She didn't want them to know that she couldn't have a baby. By the time she was seated across from Dr. Carter, it occurred to her that all of the people in the waiting room were just like her. They couldn't have babies either.

Dr. Carter asked, "Mrs. Abrams, how long have you been trying to conceive?"

She was taken aback by the question; she had just met this man, and he was asking her very personal questions. Then some rational thought returned, and she answered, "Two years."

"I'm going to examine you, and then we'll do a series of tests. Your husband will also have to be examined."

"Dr. Carter, how long will all of this take? When will I find out what the problem is?"

"Mrs. Abrams, there may not be any problem. To many of my couples, I say, 'Just relax and it'll happen.' I know no one likes that answer. Let's do a few preliminary tests first, and then I can give you a better idea."

After two hours of examinations and tests, Leslie went home. She stripped off all of her clothes, got into the tub, and just sat there, staring at nothing. She got out of the tub, climbed into bed, pulled the comforter over her head, and went to sleep. When Jason came in, he found her in bed staring at the ceiling.

"What did Dr. Carter say?"

Leslie attempted to sit up, but she felt weak. She mumbled, "They did a bunch of tests, examined me. It'll probably take a week to get the results."

Jason rubbed her back. "How do you feel? Did the tests hurt?"

Leslie grumbled, "Some of them hurt like hell."

Continuing to massage her back, Jason said, "Told you to let me go with you."

"It still would have hurt like hell if you had been there."

"But I could have held your hand."

"You've got to go and be tested, too. The doctor's number is on the desk."

Jason got up and walked over to the desk. Jason laughed. "My cousin told me about this. He said they give you some girlie magazines in order to get a specimen. I think I'll bring my own magazines. Better yet, you should come with me and be my inspiration."

Leslie moaned, "Jason, that's not funny."

"I'm kidding. I want to have a child just like you do. It'll happen. You're supposed to do the world a favor and be the mother of beautiful babies."

Leslie pulled the comforter over her head again and moaned.

Chapter 43

Paige

The head of each *Superwoman* department was seated around the glass conference table in Paige's office, discussing plans for the next issue, when her secretary stuck her head in to tell Paige that Leslie was on the phone. "Quiet, everyone. Let me take this." She walked over to her desk. "Leslie, are you in New York?"

"No, but I'm coming up. Let's have lunch while I'm in the city." They agreed to meet, and Paige returned to her meeting.

The following week, when Leslie arrived at Paige's office, her secretary explained that Paige was running late and asked her to have their lunch delivered to the office. Paige entered wearing a Chanel suit. The two exchanged hugs, and Leslie said, "Love the suit. Reminds me of the one your father's wife was wearing at your college graduation. *You* were wearing jeans under your graduation robe."

Removing the jacket and tossing it on the sofa, Paige said, "Don't remind me. You mean his ex-wife. Lilly's gone. She's been replaced by Monique, wife number four. And, I still love jeans. Designer jeans, of course. We did a feature on jeans a few months ago. So, how are you?"

The two ate at the conference table in Paige's office and caught up on each other's lives. Paige showed her the mock-up of the next issue while apologizing for having lunch in the office because of her overbooked schedule. Leslie explained that she was in New York for some business meetings and Jason's dad's birthday party.

Paige said, "I can't remember the last time I saw Jason."

Leslie laughed. "I can barely remember the last time *I* saw him."

"Just look at the cover of *Sports Illustrated*. He's probably on it. By the way, Mark's in New York this week. If Jason's coming, why don't the four of us have dinner? Jason and Mark have never met."

"Are you two a couple again?"

Paige shouted, "Absolutely not! We're friends who made a mistake and got married. We should have just been satisfied being lovers."

"As I recalled, you married him after knowing him for two weeks."

"Thanks a lot for reminding me of that, too. What is it with you? Are you my grim memory bank?" Paige waved her hands dismissively. "I'm kidding. Besides, it was a great two weeks! I admit it. I can be reckless and impetuous. Dinner tomorrow night with Mark and Jason?"

The two couples met for dinner at Twenty-One. Paige introduced the two men, and Jason greeted Paige with, "And it's Superwoman, herself. Hey, Paige."

Paige said, "Hey yourself, Mr. Quarterback."

Mark said to Jason, "I keep reading about you breaking records. You had a great season last year."

"We did all right. No Super Bowl ring, though. Mark, I feel like I know you. I was watching you on TV even before you married Paige."

Mark responded, "Same here," and then turned to Leslie. "What brings you to New York?"

Leslie said, "I had some meetings with an ad agency. My firm picked up several contracts in the last year. We're really growing."

Jason chimed in, "I'm sure some people think I'm just married to a beautiful woman. They're wrong." He put his arm around Leslie. "I've got my own superwoman. Her company's doing great."

Leslie smiled. "Thanks to you. I know some of my clients came to me because of Jason."

"But they stayed because of you," Jason added. "Mark, what are you doing in New York? I saw you on TV a couple of weeks ago, and you were in Nigeria."

"We shot lots of film while I was in Nigeria. So, I'm here editing it for a news special and adding some narration."

Paige asked Mark, "How long are you going to be here?"

"Until you kick me out of your apartment."

"I'm serious. How long are you going to be in New York? You can continue to stay in my apartment as long as you like, but I'm leaving for Milan next week. Fashion shows."

Mark looked surprised. "I didn't know you were going to Milan."

"Neither did I until this afternoon. Just decided. Feel free to stay in the apartment as long as you like."

All of them saw the dejected look on Mark's face. "I don't want to stay if you won't be there."

Paige laughed. "Don't be silly. Make yourself at home. Far better than a hotel. You stay in too many hotels. Do you even have an apartment someplace anymore?"

Mark looked at the menu and then back at Paige. "As a matter of fact, I have most of my stuff at my dad's. I use his address as my permanent address. I spend so much time traveling that I gave up my apartment. I was rarely there. Guess playing house with you is over for now. What's everyone going to have?"

Jason looked at the menu. "Prime rib's great here. I'm going to have that."

Leslie asked, "When did you have the prime rib here?"

Jason thought for a moment. "I can't remember when, but I know it was good."

❧   ❧   ❧

When Paige and Mark returned to her apartment, she said, "I really want you to stay. I'll be back in three days. I like knowing that you'll be here when I get back."

Mark took her hand and led her to the bedroom. "You've got a deal."

Chapter 44

Jennifer

Jennifer picked up the phone to hear Judson Miller, one of the partners, burst into a tirade. "I'm fed up with fighting with Garrison. I need those documents now! Give Garrison a call, and make arrangements to review the documents in his office in Chicago."

Appreciating that Miller's anger was not directed at her but at their opponents' delaying tactics, she said calmly, "When would you like me to go?"

Miller growled, "Yesterday!" He chuckled lightheartedly. "Seeing as that's impossible, arrange something for early next week, preferably Tuesday. That's the day the client said he would be available to go over the documents with you."

It was almost five o'clock on Friday, but she was sure Garrison would still be in his office, since it was only four o'clock in Chicago. A lawyer like Garrison probably never left his office. Jennifer placed the call, quickly explaining her request. She reminded herself that this guy probably thought the legal profession was rapidly going downhill because of the admission of women. She wondered how he'd react if he also knew she was black. She hung up without saying good-bye, and Garrison hung up without waiting for her response.

The Monday evening flight from New York to Chicago was filled with exhausted businessmen. As always, she scanned the gate area to see if any interesting men might be on board. She'd always thought that being tightly squeezed into a coach seat for a couple of hours next to the right person had the potential to spark a wonderful relationship. Unfortunately, from the looks of the old white men in baggy, wrinkled suits, she realized that this was not going to be such a flight.

In the morning she met her client, Jonathan Carlisle, and together they went to Garrison's office. Jennifer, with Carlisle standing slightly behind her, approached the receptionist's desk. Before Jennifer could say anything, the receptionist, an attractive woman in her late thirties, turned to Carlisle and asked, "Good morning, sir. May I help you?"

Jennifer, seeing that the receptionist had ignored her in order to speak to the white man first, removed the business smile from her face. "I'm Ms. Madison. We have a nine o'clock appointment with Michael Garrison."

Upon hearing Jennifer's voice, the receptionist turned to look at her and said, "I'll buzz his office." She dialed. "Miss Madison is here to see Mr. Garrison." With a pleasant smile on her face, she said, "His secretary will be right out."

Jennifer refrained from explaining to the receptionist that it was "Ms." and not "Miss" and fantasized about slapping that phony smile off her face.

Garrison's secretary escorted Jennifer and Carlisle to a conference room filled with stacks of documents. After about half an hour, the door to the conference room opened, and a tall light-brown-skinned man entered.

"Ms. Madison?" He extended his hand to Jennifer. "I'm Michael Garrison."

It had never occurred to her that Garrison was black. She'd envisioned an elderly white man. And he wasn't wearing a wedding ring.

Around lunchtime, Garrison returned to the conference room. "If you like, I can suggest several nearby places for lunch."

"Mr. Carlisle's trying to make a six o'clock plane, so we're going to work through lunch. It would be helpful, though, if you could suggest a place that could deliver a couple of sandwiches."

"My secretary will take care of it. If you need anything else, please let me know."

Jennifer smiled at Garrison. "I certainly will!"

Carlisle left at four, despite several documents that remained to be reviewed; so, Jennifer methodically continued the process of determining which documents would be important to the development of the case. At five, Garrison came into the conference room. "Done? Any concerns regarding documents?"

"No. I'm finished."

"Good. Now we can stop acting as opposing counsel." He leaned against the wall. "I saw the shock on your face when I introduced myself. I was just as surprised to see you."

They both laughed. Jennifer asked, "Do you realize I thought you were some mean bastard who thought women brought the profession down? I was kind of looking forward to this jerk I envisioned finding out I was black, too."

"At least you made a judgment about a person without first considering their race."

Jennifer shook her head. "No, I didn't. You sounded white on the telephone. But, even if I'd known you were black, you were still difficult!"

"OK, is all forgiven?"

Jennifer thought, *A finey like you … of course.* She said, "Yes. Tell me about yourself. Are you from Chicago?"

"No … St. Louis."

"My mother was raised in St. Louis. Do you know my uncle, George Parker? He's principal of Westside High School."

"Good teacher. Very nice man. The black population in America is so small that if we talk to each other long enough, we're always bound to know some of the same people."

Jennifer clarified, "You mean the *educated* population is small. We all know each other." Having noted that this finey wasn't wearing a wedding band, she asked, "How did you come to settle in Chicago?"

"My ex-wife is from Chicago, and she wanted to be near her family."

"How long have you been divorced?"

"Five years."

She liked that answer but was compelled to ask the next question. "Any children?"

"Two."

Wrong answer, she thought. "How old?"

"My son's twelve, and my daughter's ten."

"Ah! Well, let me pack up. I'm going to take these documents with me." As Garrison escorted her to the reception area, she regretted that he was a BMIS that someone else had gotten to first.

Chapter 45

Leslie

Leslie jumped out of the taxi and rushed into the restaurant. Danny was seated at the bar waiting for her. "I'm sorry I'm late. The appointment took a lot longer than I thought it would."

Danny looked at Leslie's flustered expression. "Calm down. No problem. I always have time for you. Let's get a table." Danny motioned to the maître d' that he was ready, and they were escorted to a table by the fountain.

Leslie attempted to place her briefcase under the table, but she kept kicking it. Danny said, "Let me take that." He picked up the briefcase and placed it next to his feet. "Now relax. Take a deep breath."

Leslie shook her head sadly. "Do I look as upset as I feel?"

"You're as beautiful as always."

Leslie smiled gratefully. "Tell me your news first. Did Gail sign the divorce papers?"

"Yes, finally. I had to give her the house in Florida and our apartment. I kept the house in the Hamptons. I think she may actually move to Florida. I hope not. That would make seeing the kids more difficult."

Leslie inquired, "What about custody?"

"She'll have custody. I'll pay all of the bills, but they'll live with her."

"Are you OK with that?"

"Yeah, Gail's a great mother. And I'll see the kids regularly, and so will my folks. Gail hates me, but she still loves Mom and Dad. Enough about my divorce. What did you think of Sherry? I hear she's the best infertility doctor in New York."

Having finally calmed down, she said, "Danny, thanks so much for getting me in to see her so quickly. She loves you."

"I've made lots of money for her and her husband."

"When I called, her receptionist said I wouldn't be able to see her for another three months! I couldn't wait that long. Of course, when you called, she worked me in immediately. Given the difficulty of getting an appointment with her—I mean, without your assistance—I think no one is able to have babies the old-fashioned way anymore."

Danny laughed. "Not my ex-wife. Our kids are just thirteen months apart."

"Lucky Gail. Jason and I have been trying for two years, and nothing's happened. Anyway, she ran a bunch of tests and promises to call me with the results next week. Thanks again for setting it up. I wanted a second opinion. Jason's satisfied with Dr. Carter, who says everything is fine and it'll happen. That's not good enough for me. I'm sure there must be something wrong, and I want it fixed."

"Leslie, there may be nothing wrong with either of you."

"Well, I want another doctor to tell me that. Thanks again for setting it up so quickly. You're such a good friend to me." Leslie reached over and took Danny's hand. "You've been helping me since high school. Because of you, I got to look like the cool girl with a prom date from Princeton rather than the girl who broke up with her boyfriend two weeks before prom."

"You know, when I was moving out, Gail made a point of giving me our prom picture."

"You're kidding."

"Nope."

"Why would she do that?"

"Who knows?"

While looking at the menu, Leslie said, "I think my copy of that picture is at my parents' house. Thanks again for doing this favor for me. It means a lot to me." She rose from her chair, leaned over the table, and kissed Danny on the cheek. Retaking her seat, she said, "I'm going to try to help some old friends out, too. I'm setting up a lunch between Jennifer and Paige."

Danny put his menu aside. "I saw Paige at a charity event a few months ago. She's quite the powerful editor these days."

"Yes, she is. Did you talk with her?"

Danny shook his head. "No. I don't really know Paige. The only time I met her was when she was a bridesmaid at your wedding. Of course, I know Jennifer." The waiter approached, and they ordered; then Danny asked, "Why do you have to set it up? Aren't they friends?"

"Paige and Jennifer never really got along when we were in college."

"I remember that they were both bridesmaids at your wedding."

"Yeah. They're both friends of mine but not really friends with each other."

"Why not?"

Leslie thought about that. "I'm not really sure. They seemed to get on each other's nerves. Just didn't click. Anyway, I'm arranging for the two of them to get together. Jennifer has this pro bono client that's trying to set up a union for domestic workers. I think it's a great idea. I thought maybe Paige's magazine could help in some way."

Danny offered, "Doesn't sound like a *Superwoman* article to me."

"I know Paige wants to do some different things with the magazine. We'll see."

"How's Jennifer?"

"Good. Working hard at the firm."

"I remember she dated Steven Greenberg for a while when we were in college. I think she met him that weekend you came up to Princeton."

"She did. And that same weekend, you had that one-night thing with Allison. Remember?"

Danny smiled broadly. "I remember. It wasn't a one-night thing."

"It wasn't? I didn't know that."

"It was a two-night thing. You guys stayed Friday and Saturday nights."

"Same thing. You never called her after that."

After lunch, Danny's driver was waiting outside the restaurant. As they approached the car, Danny asked, "Where can I drop you?"

"Kennedy Airport?"

The driver opened the door, and Leslie and Danny got in. Danny said, "Chuck, take me back to the office and then drive Mrs. Abrams to Kennedy."

The driver said, "Yes, sir."

Chapter 46

Paige

Paige was hunched in the backseat of the taxi. "Christina, tell me again why I have to go and see this designer in his studio. You're the fashion editor. That's your job."

Christina repeated the same speech she had given Paige back in the office. "Paige, I think this designer is really exciting. He's young, brash, different. I think the magazine should do something spectacular with him. That's why I want you to meet him. You're going to be blown away, and then you'll agree to my idea for a fabulous spread featuring him and his work."

"What's so special about him?"

"It's hard to put in words," Christina said. "That's why I insisted you come with me."

"OK. This better not be a waste of my time."

"You're going to be very glad you came." Christina said a silent prayer that she was right. She was not looking forward to dealing with a disappointed Paige. "That's Donald. Isn't he cute?" She pointed at a guy whose black hair was pulled tightly into a ponytail that fell to his waist. He stood outside of his building smoking a skinny brown cigarette when their taxi pulled up.

Paige looked out the window. "I don't care if he's cute or not. Show me the clothes."

Donald greeted Christina with an air kiss and then extended his hand to Paige as Christina made the introduction. "Ms. Wyatt, I'm so glad you could come see my work."

Paige extracted her hand from his firm grip and said, "Show me what you've got."

Donald led the way up the stairs into his workroom, where two six-foot-tall models waited. "Ms. Wyatt, please have a seat over there."

"No, thanks. Let me see your racks. I'll decide what I want to see on the models." Paige brusquely went through the racks, quickly making her selections. "Show me these. Now, I'll sit."

Donald gave the selections to the models and walked over to Paige. "Coffee?"

Paige said, "No, thanks."

Christina, trying to lighten the moment, said, "Donald, I'd love some."

Donald disappeared behind a screen and reappeared with an earthenware mug of almond-flavored coffee. When he handed Christina the mug, Paige noted the tattoo on his hand and asked, "What's that?"

Donald laughed and said, "A drunken mistake."

Paige said, "I don't like drunks."

"Neither do I," Donald said. "Learned my lesson the hard way."

The two models paraded in front of Paige. She said nothing. Donald signaled to them to quickly change. Christina started to comment on the designs, but one quick look from Paige silenced her. The two models returned. Paige said, "Turn around, and walk slowly back across the room."

Paige stood up. "I've seen enough. I like it. Very exciting." She thought that Donald was handsome in a unique way. She decided he had a marketable face.

Donald stood and extended his tattooed hand to Paige. "Thanks."

Grabbing his hand so that she could have a closer look at the tattoo, Paige said, "You're good. And I like that mistake on your hand. It should be your trademark. Christina, work it into the spread."

Chapter 47

Jennifer

When Jennifer telephoned, Leslie immediately started to apologize. "I'm sorry that I was so down the last time we talked. My period had just come. You know, each month I get all excited about the prospect of getting pregnant; then my period comes, and I just crash."

"I'm sorry. I'm convinced you'll be pregnant very soon. It's meant to be."

"I hope so. In fact, I was in New York just for the day. Sorry I missed you. When I called your office, they said you'd be in depositions all day out of the office. Anyway, Danny set up an appointment for me with the best infertility doctor in New York."

"Danny Eisenberg?"

"Yes. I'm waiting on the results. Anyway, enough about me. I am not completely out of it. You mentioned that housekeepers' union thing. I think you ought to call Paige; maybe her magazine will do an article about the union."

Jennifer hesitated. "I don't know. I haven't seen Paige since I've been in New York. She's your friend, not mine. I just can't call her up and ask for a favor."

"So, I'll call her. Trust me. She'll be glad to help."

"Are you sure? You two have always been close, but Paige and I always seemed to rub each other the wrong way in college."

"That was college. Forget that. I'll set it up."

A week later, Jennifer approached the maître d' at Chez Alain's, a French restaurant frequented by the media crowd. "The reservation is for Paige Wyatt."

The dapper gentleman with a mane of glowing snow-white hair looked at Jennifer approvingly and said, "Ah yes. Ms. Wyatt is not here yet, but I'll show you to her table."

Jennifer noted the pointed reference to "her table" and followed the elderly gentleman to a table in the far corner of the restaurant, which provided an excellent view of the other patrons, allowed the diner to be seen, and yet was private enough for business or intimate conversation. Within moments of being seated, Jennifer saw Paige give the maître d' a quick, affectionate peck on both cheeks. "Jean Paul, good to see you."

"Ms. Wyatt, your guest has arrived, and I escorted her to your table."

"Thank you, Jean Paul." Paige strode confidently across the restaurant, nodding to acknowledge those patrons she recognized or those who recognized her and stopping briefly to kiss an elderly woman.

"Jennifer, love, it's so good to see you. It's been a very long time." Paige bent down and blew a kiss into the air beside each of Jennifer's cheeks.

Paige was no longer the hippie with stringy mousy brown hair that Jennifer remembered. She was elegantly dressed in an off-white Chanel dress; she wore gold chains around her neck, a simple gold-and-diamond Rolex watch on her left wrist, and several gold bracelets on the right, and she was carrying a Louis Vuitton purse. Paige's hair was now a rich, lustrous chestnut brown that fell in magnificent soft waves to her shoulders. The wire-rimmed granny glasses were gone, revealing steely gray eyes. She was stunning, obviously the personification of the superwoman her magazine portrayed: the elegantly dressed, confident, professional, femme fatale.

Paige quickly sized up Jennifer: expensive, tailored navy blue suit, burgundy silk blouse, simple gold earrings, antique pin on her lapel, poised, confident, and self-assured, just as Paige expected.

Momentarily, each was unsure of how to successfully bridge the intervening years and experiences.

Jennifer began, as it was on her behalf that Leslie had set up this luncheon. "Paige, when I see you, I automatically think of Peter. I was really sad when he died. Such a tragedy. I'm so sorry. I really liked and respected Peter."

Paige sipped her wine, contemplated the statement, and then looked directly into Jennifer's eyes. "Thank you. I'll always miss Peter. He was a very special man. It was inevitable. I can see that now." She stopped, pictured Peter's face, and smiled. "I know a lot more things now than I knew when we were in college. I'm sure you do, too."

Jennifer responded sincerely, without the sarcasm that had tinged many of her college interactions with Paige. "You're right. I do."

"There's really something to be said for being older and wiser. Now, tell me about this organization and what I can do."

Jennifer launched into an explanation of the domestic workers' union as they ate lunch. Paige asked insightful and sensitive questions, which impressed Jennifer. After an hour of discussing the reasons and plans for the union, Paige responded, "I like it. I'm going to have *Superwoman* do a campaign. Really champion the idea."

Jennifer leaned back in her chair. "Paige, that's wonderful."

Paige raised her wineglass in a toast. "To the domestic workers' union." After they clicked glasses, Paige said, "Now, be honest. You only came to this lunch because Leslie set it up. You didn't really think I would be interested in helping, did you?"

Lowering her head slightly to hide her embarrassed smirk, Jennifer said, "You're right. I didn't. Leslie insisted, and I went along to humor her. She's been running my life, or trying to, since college. I just didn't think it was a sexy enough topic for your magazine. It's not glamorous. Domestic workers aren't exactly your demographic."

Paige nodded her head thoughtfully. She countered, "When I took over as editor of *Superwoman*, one of the things I wanted to do was expand its format and address some of the harder, more controversial issues. I think we've started to do that. I didn't want the magazine to be just another slick Madison Avenue publication for upper-middle-class professional women, and I know you're thinking, *white women*."

Jennifer sat back in her chair and this time didn't attempt to hide her smirk. "White women. That's exactly what I was thinking."

"I don't want the magazine to be just for white women. I want it to be for all working women with different kinds of jobs."

"I admire you for taking that position." Jennifer looked at her watch. "I'm going to have to get back to the office." She laughed and added, "I'm a working woman! I enjoyed lunch. We'll have to do it again soon."

"Absolutely. I'd like that. Thursday, the magazine is hosting a party at the Palomino Gallery in the Village. Please come."

They exchanged air kisses, and Jennifer said, "I'd loved to."

Upon returning to the office, Jennifer telephoned Leslie. "I just had lunch with Paige."

"Was she interested?"

"Very interested. You didn't prepare me for the new Paige. She's gorgeous. Where did that hippie go?"

"She's an important New York editor now and looks the part. Remember, Paige's mother has actually been on the Best Dressed list. I told you when we were freshmen that Paige was old money."

"I forgot. That's what I've been trying to explain to you for years. Paige, because of her old money, could go through her radical hippie period and then return to her sophisticated New York persona when she got good and ready, and no one says a thing. A phase. I do some weird stuff, and no one will ever let me live it down. Never give me another chance. Thanks for setting up the lunch."

On Thursday evening, Jennifer climbed the stairs to the Palomino Gallery. She was totally unprepared for the explosion of bright light she encountered upon reaching the top of the staircase. Jennifer grabbed a glass of champagne off of a silver tray and strolled through the gallery looking at the photographs and the diverse collection of people: stockbrokers, dancers, journalists, lawyers, musicians, the unemployed, socialites, hustlers, and, of course, a few artists. The noise level reached a hysterical, fevered pitch as old friends and new acquaintances attempted to conduct conversations. Jennifer was surprised to find that the cigarette smoke was not very thick.

The photography, all black-and-white, was displayed throughout the gallery, suspended from the ceiling by thin, transparent wire.

"What do you think of the photographs?" The deep, resonant voice came unexpectedly from someone standing behind Jennifer. When she turned, she discovered that the voice belonged to the BMIS she'd seen walking past the window only a few weeks ago. She said nothing, but a smile slowly stretched across her face.

"I have a feeling you're not enamored with this exhibit, right?" he asked.

Jennifer grinned sheepishly as her heart started beating very fast. He was strikingly good-looking. It made her nervous and excited just to look at him. She attempted to control her glee but not the smile. "You're right. I'm not."

"I agree with you. This stuff is too avant-garde for me. I'm David Walker."

Jennifer blurted, "I know who you are."

He was taken aback by her response. "Uh, you do?" Without missing a beat he added, "I know I'd like to know who you are."

Jennifer extended her hand. "Jennifer Madison. You were president of Yale's Afro-Am Association, right?"

"That was a while ago, but you're right."

"Well, I remember seeing you at Yale's Spook Weekend when I was in college. That was sometime in '66, '67. We didn't actually meet, so don't feel embarrassed that you don't remember. I was very impressed with your speech."

"Thanks. Those were good times, weren't they?"

"The best."

David added, "Those were the days when black was beautiful."

"It still is; we just don't talk about it as much." She thought that he was definitely black and beautiful.

"I'd like to think so. I'd like to think that black people truly believe in their innate self-worth. Unfortunately, the times are such that many black folks are merely struggling to stay alive. What do you do to stay alive?"

"Lawyer with Webster, Symington, and Meredith."

"Excellent firm. Bill Foster's a partner there."

"That's right. He makes me so proud."

"I heard Foster speak when I was in law school. Powerful speaker. Brilliant. He's a good man."

Jennifer asked, "So, you're a lawyer, too?"

David laughed. "Yes, isn't everybody these days? As I was saying, I was most impressed because he didn't disappoint me. He was a legend, and he lived up to his reputation."

A waiter stopped and offered them some melon balls wrapped in prosciutto. They each took two. As the waiter turned away, David quickly grabbed two more, saying, "I don't know about you, but I go to cocktail parties hoping to scrounge enough hors d'oeuvres to make a meal. Usually, I'm disappointed. Would you like to get out of here and get some real food?"

"Love it."

Just as David and Jennifer were attempting to make their way through the crowd to the door, Paige saw David. "David, I'm glad you came. Haven't seen you in ages."

"Hi. Paige, I'd like you to meet Jennifer Madison."

Paige laughed. "Jennifer! So glad you came." Paige kissed the air on either side of Jennifer's face.

Jennifer said, "Paige. You look stunning." Paige was wearing a black silk caftan split in the front so that a lot of thigh was exposed.

Surprised, David asked, "You two know each other?"

Paige explained, "Jennifer and I went to college together. But I didn't know you two knew each other."

"We just met," Jennifer explained.

"Well, that's great! Jennifer, David was my next-door neighbor when I was at Stanford, a good and invaluable friend." Paige turned to David, and they exchanged fleeting smiles. There was a look in Paige's eyes, which clearly was not intended for Jennifer. Noting the look, Jennifer hoped that it didn't mean Paige had slept with this man.

"Paige, I'm going to take Jennifer to dinner. See you later." He grabbed Jennifer's arm and ushered her to the door. Jennifer yelled back over her shoulder, "Paige, I'll call you." By then Paige was surrounded by two young men, one of whom had a black ponytail that fell to his waist.

David suggested Delhi Café, an Indian restaurant on Bleeker Street. They each glanced at the menu and, without consulting each other, ordered curried lamb. "David, tell me about your practice."

"I'm with Bullock and Chase."

"They have offices all over the world."

"Almost. We have offices in London, San Francisco, DC, Paris, Geneva, Rome, Tokyo, and, of course, New York. I clerked in the San Francisco office when I was in law school."

"What kinds of things do you do?"

"Basically international trade—helping clients to develop international markets for their products. How about you? Do you get to work with Bill Foster?"

"Yes, I do. I do mostly real estate development transactions, and I do some litigation. I'm working with Bill on some government contracting matters, and he recently gave me a pro bono project that Paige is helping me with. I'm helping to organize a union for domestic workers. Paige is going to run an article in *Superwoman* on the group."

"That's great. Where are you from?"

"Detroit. How about you?"

"Right here. When I was born, my parents lived in Harlem, but they moved out to Long Island when I was in elementary school. My grandparents still live in a brownstone in Harlem. They've been in that same house for over fifty years. I love that house. I'll have to take you up there. You'd like my grandparents."

"I'm sure I would."

"And they'd like you. I can hear Granddad now." David lowered his voice. "'David, that's a pretty little girl you got there. Bring her over here so I can get a good look at her. Yep, she sure is pretty.'"

"Is that your grandfather talking or you?"

"I inherited my eye for beauty from my grandfather."

"I see. Your father is also a lawyer, right?"

David looked surprised. "Yes, how did you know that?"

"I told you. I remember you from Yale's Spook Weekend."

"It's a shame we didn't meet. I've obviously wasted a lot of time not know-ing you, but I'm going to try to make up for that."

The remark pleased Jennifer, but she decided to ignore it. "What kind of practice does your father have?"

"Oh, general practice. He does everything: wills, divorces, criminal defense, real estate, represents some small businesses. He represents the Greater Abys-sinian Baptist Church," David added proudly.

"That's Adam Clayton Powell's church in Harlem, isn't it?"

"Yes."

"I went there once when I was a little girl on Easter Sunday. The choir was powerful."

"Are you Baptist?"

"Yes."

"Me, too. Well, I haven't actually been to church in quite a while, to my mother's consternation. Do you like gospel music? Spirituals?"

"Love 'em."

"Me, too. My parents still go to Greater Abyssinian occasionally. Would you like to go?"

"Yes, I would." Jennifer listed in her head all of the places David suggested they go. She wondered if he meant any of this or if he was just talking to hear himself.

David asked the taxi driver to wait while he walked Jennifer to her apart-ment. She unlocked the door and stepped inside. David remained standing in the hall and didn't follow her. She started to invite him in, but she'd heard him ask the taxi to wait, so she didn't.

David said, "I'm going to have to call Paige and thank her for insisting that I attend another one of her magazine parties. I've turned her down the last cou-ple of times. I can take only so much of the chic literary snob types. But I got to meet you this time."

"I'll have to call and thank her, too."

Without any attempt to kiss her, David said, "Good night" and headed for the elevator.

Chapter 48

Leslie

Early Thursday evening, Leslie entered her darkened town house. When she opened the door, the mail was scattered on the floor. She picked it up and started sorting through the envelopes. A letter from the District of Columbia Government was addressed to her and to Jason. She opened the envelope and found a notice that a parking ticket remained unpaid. The parking ticket was for Jason's Ferrari, which she never drove. She glanced at the ticket for illegal parking in front of a Capitol Hill address. She tossed the ticket onto Jason's pile of mail and headed for her bedroom to change out of the suit she'd worn since seven that morning when she'd met a client for a breakfast meeting. It was now seven in the evening. She was exhausted.

About an hour later, the telephone rang. Jason said, "Hey, babe. How was your day?"

Leslie sighed, "Long and exhausting."

Jason said, "You sound tired."

"Very."

"Babe, why don't you turn in early. Don't wait for me. I've got a charity event—you know, give a trophy to some kid. I have no idea how long the program will be. Don't wait up."

"Don't worry. I won't. I feel like I could sleep for twenty-four hours."

Leslie warmed up a bowl of chicken noodle soup and ate it as she nibbled on a few whole-grain crackers. She then went upstairs to bed and decided to telephone her mother.

"And how's Jason?" her mother asked.

"Fine. He's making an appearance at a charity event tonight."

"That's nice. Why didn't you go?"

Leslie thought for a moment. "Hmm, I don't know. He didn't tell me about it. He's asked to do so many of these appearances that I guess he just asks me for the really big ones."

"That's sweet of him. Jason is a wonderful guy."

Leslie smiled. "Yes, he is. Mom, I'm going to turn in. Love you."

Leslie fell asleep immediately. Around midnight, she awakened. Jason wasn't home yet. She walked down to the kitchen to get something to eat. As she rummaged in the refrigerator, her eyes rested on the parking ticket. She picked it up and once again noted the address: Capitol Hill. She wondered what Jason had been doing on Capitol Hill. She was no longer sleepy. She rushed upstairs, threw on some clothes, jumped into her car, and headed for the Capitol Hill address on the parking ticket. She found the address and saw a car that looked just like Jason's Ferrari. She slowed her car and checked the license plate. It was Jason's car, and it was parked in front of the address on the parking ticket. She circled the block and pulled into a parking space several houses away. Within five minutes the front door to the address on the ticket opened, and Jason came out of the door. A woman with short, dark hair waved as Jason walked to his car, got in, and drove away.

Leslie watched until his car disappeared around the corner. She then started her car and drove aimlessly around Capitol Hill; she passed the Capitol, drove down Constitution Avenue past the Smithsonian museums, and then headed for the Washington Monument, sobbing all the while. She eventually headed down Pennsylvania Avenue toward Georgetown. When she arrived home and walked into the kitchen, Jason was drinking a glass of milk and flipping through the mail on the kitchen counter. Leslie entered the kitchen, startling Jason. "I thought you were upstairs asleep."

Having wiped her tears before entering the house so there would be no evidence that she had been crying, she said without any emotion, "No, I'm just coming in."

Jason walked over and started to kiss her, but Leslie walked away, avoiding his kiss. Jason asked, "Where have you been?"

"Out."

"Out where?"

She didn't answer; instead she asked, "How was the charity event?"

"Fine. The usual folk. Redskins got some good publicity. Trying to make the community love us. You know the drill."

"Yes, I think I do. Oh, here's the rest of your mail." She reached into a pocket of her jacket and pulled out the parking ticket.

Jason looked at it. "What's this? Damn, did I get another parking ticket? I think these guys just stand by meters waiting for the last minute to be up, and then they smack me with a ticket."

Continuing to stifle her tears, Leslie said, "There aren't any meters at that address."

He took a gulp of milk. "Really?"

"Yes, and you know that, because I just saw you come out of that address half an hour ago."

Still holding the glass of milk in his hand, his eyes narrowed slightly, and then he asked, "What are you talking about?"

"Jason, don't do this. I saw you."

Jason walked over and put his arms around Leslie. "Babe, what did you see?"

Leslie screamed, "I saw you walk out of a woman's house half an hour ago—a house, given this parking ticket, you've obviously been to before."

He attempted to put his arms around her, but she pushed him away. "Leslie, I love *you*. You're my *wife*. Yes, I was at that house. The house belongs to the Redskins PR person who arranged for me to do this charity event tonight. I gave her a ride home. Her car wouldn't start. That's it."

"Why were you at her house the other time?"

"Stopped by to pick up some info on an event. It was raining; that's probably why I didn't see the ticket. Probably blew off. Her block has a time when you can't park because of rush hour. I was probably there during rush hour." Jason looked down at the ticket. "See? 'Rush hour violation.' I parked anyway, ran in, started talking, and got a ticket. That's it."

This time, Leslie let Jason embrace her. She wanted to believe him. She settled into his arms and loved the feel of him holding her.

Chapter 49

Paige

Paige adored her secretary, partly because she was amused by the incongruity of her presence. Mrs. Callahan was a grandmother, slightly plump, who attended Mass daily and was devoted to and protective of Paige. Mrs. Callahan was also a symbol of Paige's ongoing battle with her father, because she'd hired her away from her father's brokerage firm by doubling her salary. Mrs. Callahan buzzed, "Mark's on the line."

Paige quickly picked up the line, eager to talk with him. "Where are you? Timbuktu?"

Mark laughed. "No. I was in Timbuktu last week."

"You're kidding."

"Yes, I'm kidding. Right now, I'm two blocks from your office. How about lunch?"

Paige's voice turned from miserable to apologetic as she explained that she had a meeting in half an hour and couldn't get away from the office.

"Why don't I pick up a couple of sandwiches and come over to your office so we can have a quick lunch?"

Paige protested. "Mark, you don't have to go to that trouble. We can have dinner tonight, though."

"Are you kidding? It won't be any trouble. I'd just like to see you even if it's just for a few minutes."

Paige, distracted by the photography editor, who had stuck his head into her office, said, "OK. I really only have a few minutes, but I'm hungry."

Mark bought two turkey sandwiches on wheat bread with mayonnaise and headed to Paige's office.

Mrs. Callahan greeted him warmly. "What exotic locations have you been to lately?"

"Just returned from Cambodia. I brought Paige a sandwich."

"Go right in. You know the way."

When Mark entered Paige's office, he held up a small brown paper bag and said, "Lunch."

Paige leaned back in her swivel chair. "What've you got?"

"Turkey sandwiches …" He paused dramatically, walked around the desk, swiveled Paige's chair so that she was facing him, kissed her passionately on the lips, and then whispered, "And me!"

All thoughts of the page layout disappeared as soon as Mark pulled her to a standing position and then put both of his hands under her skirt and started massaging her butt as he kissed her neck. Within seconds, Mark's hand was reaching for Paige's red bikini panties and yanking them to the floor. He unbuttoned her blouse and buried his head in her breasts. His tongue pushed aside her red lace bra and searched out her nipple, which instantly became hard at his touch. Paige glanced furtively toward the door.

"Locked it when I came in."

Mark slid to the floor, pulling Paige on top of him onto the Oriental rug, and they made love on the floor behind her desk. Mark helped Paige to her feet, straightened her skirt, and rebuttoned her blouse. He said very seriously, as if he were speaking to a small child, "I let you have dessert first; now I insist you eat your lunch."

He handed Paige a turkey sandwich and took one for himself. "Eat fast," he said. "You have a meeting in ten minutes."

After finishing half of her sandwich, she announced, "That's the best lunch I have ever had."

Mark gave her his famous half smile. "I'm out of here," he said. "Dinner, tonight." He unlocked the door and left the office. Two men and a woman were seated in the reception area. The woman whispered to the man seated on the sofa next to her, "That's Mark Elliott."

Chapter 50

Jennifer

On Friday morning Jennifer's mood vacillated from cheerful exhilaration to irascible depression. David hadn't asked her to go out. She made up her mind that if he didn't call in a couple of days, she'd call him, but she preferred that he'd call her first. Just as she was about to leave for lunch, he called.

"This blues group I really liked when I was in law school is at Odetta's tonight. The lead singer does a great James Brown imitation. Would you like to go?"

The irascible depression evolved into glee as she said, "Yes!"

❦   ❦   ❦

Jennifer made a mad dash through Bloomingdale's at lunch for something sexy to wear, but nothing caught her eye. She decided to wear her favorite black cashmere sweater with her skintight Gloria Vanderbilt jeans, which accentuated her round behind and black leather high-heeled boots.

Odetta's was crowded when they arrived. When the singer began a slow blues song, David asked her to dance. As they danced, she thought that there was something wonderfully protective about him. As she swayed in his arms, she questioned why she wanted protection. David's hand pressed more firmly against her back, and then his fingers danced along her waist. He bent his head so that his lips grazed her ear. As they danced, she knew that she was falling hard. She couldn't stop herself, and she didn't want to.

They took a cab from Odetta's to Jennifer's apartment. This time, David didn't ask the driver to wait. When Jennifer unlocked the door to her apartment, he politely waited for her to ask him in.

"Come on in. It's Friday. No early-morning rush to the office. How about a drink?"

He asked for a beer. "Sorry, no beer. How about some red wine?" She handed him the wine, and they settled on her sofa. He raised his wineglass in a toast. "To us. We're from the same place and time."

Jennifer sipped her wine. "The same place and time. It's uncanny. We've known each other two days, but it feels like so much longer. I do have a jump on you. I remember you from college, the fiery and dynamic president of Yale's Afro-Am Association."

"Yale! Great times. We spent days talking about the revolution and that devil white man and the capitalist, imperialist society." David laughed. "We had those white people so scared. Remember that *Newsweek* cover with some brother at Cornell with a bandolier of bullets across his chest during a protest?"

"Outrageous. What was the protest about?" Jennifer asked.

"I don't remember. Black history courses? Or the lack thereof?"

"Don't you remember how black students would get up in sociology class and tell all the awestruck white kids about the black experience?"

"Absolutely. Each black student became the embodiment of blackness. And, of course, we were all poor, to hear us tell it. At least, we all claimed to have come from the ghetto. In fact, what you had at Yale were a bunch of basically middle-class black kids mouthing off."

Jennifer laughed at the memories. "But white America put us all in the ghetto. So, some of us played the role."

"You have to admit that there existed a cohesiveness among black people that's missing today. Everybody was your brother or sister." David thrust his fist into the air. "Power to the people. When I was at Yale, there was tension in the air that was always on the verge of exploding. It was hot. Black power. Vietnam."

Jennifer got up, searched through a pile of old records, and put one on the stereo. "Remember this?" The sound of the Last Poets' "The Revolution Will Not Be Televised" filled the room.

David laughed until tears came into his eyes. "Remember it? Are you kidding? I was the one who called a special meeting of the Afro-Am Association just to play this record."

"You're kidding."

"This was radical stuff. It was the blueprint for the black power revolution set to music."

They listened to the album, each remembering a past time and place; their recollections were very similar, although they had been at different colleges. Each wondered what their lives would have been like if they had met then, but neither articulated the question.

They each had kept the conversation light and teasing as they reminisced about college when they first returned to the apartment. But now they were silent. As they sat on the sofa listening to the soundtrack from *A Man and A Woman*, Jennifer realized that she felt comfortable. This was exactly where she was supposed to be. She knew she wanted him to hold her, to become a part of her. She saw herself in him. Their desire for each other had built all evening with every touch, look, and sound. David leaned forward so that he was within inches of Jennifer's face. He put both hands on her cheeks and continued to look at her and smiled. There was no stark contrast but a warm blending of tones. He placed his lips on hers, and she responded. She wanted him to make love to her right then, but she didn't want this to be casual disco sex. Somehow she knew that she wanted their first time to be memorable. As if reading her thoughts, he got up. "Jennifer, this was great. I'm going to go now. Going to the office in the morning, but can we meet for lunch around one o'clock?"

She didn't want him to leave. She already knew that she never wanted this man to leave her side. At this moment, all she wanted to do was drag him into her bedroom and watch their reflection in her antique rococo mirror as they made love. She knew that as soon as he walked out of her apartment, she would ache inside until she saw him again. She swallowed these feelings and said, "I'll be at my office in the morning too. Lunch sounds great."

"How about Thorn's in the Village? I'll meet you there at one o'clock."

For the next three weeks, Jennifer and David went to the theater, the movies, and the Museum of Modern Art. They went to the Village, wandering in and out of shops and listening to music; to the Apollo in Harlem, dancing; to Greater Abyssinian on Sunday morning, where they sat next to his grandparents; and then to his grandparents' Harlem brownstone to have Sunday dinner after service. They roller-skated and cycled through Central Park and were genuinely happy about being together and falling in love.

David called her first thing in the morning at her office just to say hello. After calling twice in one morning, he admitted that he'd never done that before with anyone and said, "I've made reservations at the Rainbow Room for tomorrow night."

"The Rainbow Room. What's the occasion? Did you complete that trade deal?"

"No, I didn't. Still working on the revisions. I've never been to the Rainbow Room, but I hear it's really special, and I want to go there with you."

"I've never been there either."

"Perfect—so it will be the first time for both of us."

When David arrived at Jennifer's apartment Friday night, wearing a charcoal gray Pierre Cardin suit and white shirt with French cuffs and gold cuff links, she thought she had never seen a handsomer man.

They proceeded through the art deco lobby to the skyscraper's elevators, which took them to the top of the building. Two elderly couples joined them on the elevator, exited first, and headed to the restaurant. David and Jennifer could overhear them as they explained that they were celebrating their fortieth wedding anniversaries.

When David approached the hostess, he said, "It's not our fortieth wedding anniversary, but it is a very special evening." They followed the hostess to a table by the window.

As Jennifer took her seat, she turned to David. "This view is magical. Now I see why everyone says the Rainbow Room is so amazing."

After a dinner of oysters Rockefeller, Caesar salad, lamb chops, and key lime pie, they returned to David's apartment.

"Stay right there," David said. He disappeared up the spiral stairs to his loft bedroom. When he returned downstairs, he took Jennifer in his arms and stared into her eyes without speaking. He finally said, "I'm crazy about you." They embraced, glorying in the closeness of their bodies. David pulled away and whispered, "Follow me." He led Jennifer up the spiral stairs, at which point she saw that the loft was softly illuminated by the light of thirty flickering candles.

She gasped. "David, it's beautiful."

"You're beautiful." They made love for the first time. He took his time to savor each part of her body. As they lay side by side, David whispered, "I've wanted to make love to you from the moment you turned around at the Palomino Gallery." Jennifer didn't respond. She merely wiggled closer to him, luxuriating in the touch of his body.

Chapter 51

Paige

Paige telephoned Jennifer's office. "My ex-husband, Mark, is in town. I'd love it if you and David would join us for dinner."

Jennifer said, "Sounds great."

"David tells me that you two have been seeing a lot of each other."

She wanted to gush and say how absolutely crazy she was about David, but because she was talking to Paige, whom she was still trying to figure out, she replied with a noncommittal, "Did he?"

"Jennifer, David is one of my dearest friends. He was at my wedding! He's a great guy. I think you two could be good together."

Still unwilling to share her intimate thoughts with Paige, she said, "We've been having fun." She was amused by the irony that David was such a good friend of Paige, someone she hadn't liked in college. As she listened to Paige, she realized that she and Paige had changed for the better.

Quickly shifting into her editor persona, Paige continued. "The reporter I assigned to the story loves you, and she of course loves Mabel. *I love Mabel.* Jennifer, the domestic workers' series is going to be groundbreaking. Thanks for bringing it to me."

"I guess we really should thank Leslie."

"Well, I'll thank Leslie, too. Jennifer, it's been good working with you on this. We're going to have some fun with this and do something revolutionary. I'll see you at dinner."

❦   ❦   ❦

Jennifer and David entered the restaurant, the maître d' escorted them to the table where Paige and Mark were seated.

Mark stood as they approached the table. The two men hugged and patted each other on the back. David said, "It's been a while. Man, it's good to see you."

"David, always good to see you." Mark flashed his half smile at Jennifer, a smile that caused women across America to swoon as they watched him on TV. "And this is Jennifer. Pleasure to meet you."

Refusing to swoon in the presence of the TV star, Jennifer firmly shook Mark's hand. "Great to meet you. I've enjoyed watching you on TV."

Paige greeted Jennifer with her trademark air kisses on each cheek and said, "Looking at him on TV, America would never have expected him to be married to a crazy girl like me."

The half smile disappeared. "Cut it out, Paige," Mark said. "You're not a crazy girl. Different, but not crazy."

"Gee, thanks. 'Different, but not crazy.' I'll take that. Besides, I forgot that you are no longer married to me. That would make more sense to America."

David, shaking his head, said to Jennifer, "Ignore them. They do this all the time. They can't remember if they're married or not, so I surely can't."

Mark asked, "Jennifer, do you know that David was one of the four guests at our wedding?"

Jennifer nodded. "Yes, David told me the story. Quite a whirlwind romance."

"Seeing as we are divorced, whirlwind romances are obviously not a good thing," Paige added.

Mark, ignoring Paige's sarcastic remark, said, "Jennifer, Paige told me about the domestic workers' union. Good idea. I did a report a couple of years ago about all the workers who are outside of the Social Security system. I think it's great that you're helping them organize. How did you get involved?"

Jennifer explained, "Bill Foster, a partner at my firm, assigned it to me as a pro bono assignment. I loved the idea immediately."

Mark nodded. "Bill Foster is a terrific guy. I've never met him, but I've heard about him. In fact, David, I remember you told me that you met him when you were at Stanford Law School."

"That's right. That was back in the day when Paige and I were next-door neighbors, drinking wine on the patio and enjoying the California sunshine."

Mark turned to Paige. "I think it's great that *Superwoman* is going to do a series. Paige, good story."

Paige glowed. "Thanks, Mark. I think it's the kind of story that will really make a difference."

Paige's response to Mark's compliment reminded Jennifer of the time in college when Paige accepted her suggestion regarding the Big Sister program only after Peter agreed with her: white man's validation. She pushed the negative memory out of her mind, recognizing that was the past and both she and Paige had grown up a lot since then. Instead she said, "I admit, I didn't think *Superwoman* would be interested. After all, a lot of the women who read the magazine can do all the things they do because another woman is at home cleaning their house and taking care of their children. While they're making lots of money, they're paying these domestic workers a pittance. But as Mabel admitted, she quit jobs when the employer tried to take out for Social Security. It was very shortsighted of her, but that's not surprising for people who make very little money." As she spoke, Jennifer thought that this time Paige didn't need a white man's validation to do the right thing.

Mark agreed, "Jennifer, you're absolutely right. These workers who are outside of the Social Security system have kept this economy going. I interviewed a lot of day laborers—you know, the guys who stand on the corner early in the morning trying to join a crew to do some painting or yard work. Those guys only wanted to be paid in cash."

"You're right, Mark," David added. "That's a whole other group of workers outside of the economy. Those guys don't even get counted when the unemployment statistics are done, because they are outside the system." David raised his glass in a toast. "Here's to Jennifer and Paige: pioneering women, who are making a real difference."

Chapter 52

Leslie

Leslie was sitting in the kitchen, drinking a cup of herbal tea and reading the *Washington Post*, when Jason entered. He walked over, lowered the newspaper, and kissed her. "Good morning, babe."

"Morning." Leslie immediately returned to reading the newspaper.

Jason lowered the newspaper again, and Leslie said angrily, "What is it?"

"Testy this morning, are we?"

"I am not testy!"

"You sound testy."

"Jason, what do you want?"

Jason attempted to kiss her again, but Leslie moved her head to the side to avoid his kiss. Jason said, "That does it! I'm taking you to St. Thomas right now, and we will make love all day and make a baby. How about it?"

Leslie didn't want to smile, but she couldn't help herself. "Jason, that's sweet. But I've got things to do. I can't go to St. Thomas."

"Oh, yes, you can. We're going to St. Thomas, and we're going to make a baby! That'll put a smile on your face."

Jason picked Leslie up from the kitchen chair, threw her over his shoulder, and carried her upstairs. "Start packing. There's a noon flight, and we're going to be on it."

Leslie started to protest. Jason held up his hand, and then he put his fingers in his ears. "No, I don't want to hear it. I can't hear you." With fingers still in his ears, he wiggled his other fingers and stuck out his tongue. "The doctors told us to relax. That's what we're going to do: three-day marathon of making love in St. Thomas. Guaranteed baby making."

❧   ❧   ❧

The flight attendant came down the aisle and smiled broadly at Jason. He nodded but didn't speak. Leslie was bent over placing her briefcase under the seat and didn't see the exchange between Jason and the flight attendant. She came down the aisle again and stopped at Jason's seat in the first-class cabin. She flashed a beguiling smile. "Sir, may I get you anything?" This time, Leslie noticed her. Jason looked up and said, "My wife usually likes a pillow." Jason turned toward Leslie. "Babe, do you want a pillow?"

Leslie looked at Jason, searching his face for any betrayal of interest in the beautiful flight attendant. She could see nothing. All she could see was a look of genuine concern for her. She said, "Yes, that would be nice."

Jason turned back to the flight attendant. "Would you please get a pillow for my wife?"

The flight attendant smiled at Leslie and Jason and said, "Certainly. I'll be right back." She returned with the pillow and handed it to Jason.

Jason said, "Thank you," and immediately placed the pillow behind Leslie's neck. "That good?"

"Yes. Thanks."

For three glorious days, Jason graciously avoided all of those who recognized him and attempted to engage him in conversation. Instead he concentrated on spending every moment alone with Leslie. Most of the moments were spent in bed making love, not just trying to make a baby.

Jason called out from the chaise on the balcony, "Leslie, come out here. See the sunset. It's amazing."

Leslie joined him on the balcony wearing a gold bikini and white lace floor-length cover-up. "Ah, that is beautiful." Jason grabbed her hands and pulled her onto his lap. She leaned back against him, and silently they watched the setting sun.

Jason whispered in her ear, "Let's make a baby right now."

"Jason, on the balcony? Are you crazy? People could see us."

"So what?" He slid her bikini bottoms off, and in an instant, he was inside of her. They clung to each other. Jason gasped, "These swimmers are bound to hit the mark."

She laughed, punching him in the chest. "I love you."

Chapter 53

Jennifer

Bill and Carol Foster's apartment was on Park Avenue. They had often debated moving to Long Island or Connecticut, but they liked the vitality and convenience of living in the city. Carol's passion for flowers and a garden was fulfilled by frequent trips to their summer home on Martha's Vineyard.

Tonight, the Fosters were entertaining a few good friends at a dinner party. Bill had invited Jennifer and said, "Bring a date. As a matter of fact, bring this new guy I've been hearing so much about."

Jennifer was shocked. "You? What have you heard?"

"Don't be so surprised. I hear the gossip, too." He grinned. "Lucinda told me."

"I'll bring him. You're going to like him. He reminds me of you."

Besides Jennifer and David, the guests included Oscar and Juanita Brewer and Willie Johnson and his wife, Claudia. Oscar, a doctor, was an old friend of Bill's from South Carolina. He and Bill had attended the same segregated elementary school in Honea Path, but Oscar's father, also a doctor, had sent him to live with his sister in Philadelphia for high school to avoid the segregated high school. Oscar and Bill stayed in touch, and Oscar was best man at Bill and Carol's wedding. Willie was a lawyer, and Claudia was a social worker; they, along with the Fosters, had been involved in many civil rights causes over the years.

Bill offered David a drink and insisted that he call him Bill. David overcame his discomfort at calling this great man by his first name. He softly said, "Bill," swallowed, and then said, "I heard you speak when I was in law school at Stanford."

Bill had an uncanny ability to remember names and faces. "Of course. I remember you now. My friend, Sidney Stein, introduced us. You were his research assistant. Have you seen Sid lately? He called a couple of weeks ago when he and his daughter were in town. I missed him."

David answered, "I was able to catch up with them." Jennifer walked up at this point and, overhearing them, inquired, "Who are you two talking about?"

Bill offered, "Sidney Stein. He's an old friend of mine. I didn't see him when he was in town a couple of weeks ago, but David did."

Jennifer looked at David. "You didn't mention it."

David shrugged and asked Bill his opinion on the Supreme Court's recent decision on busing. Jennifer was intrigued as to why David had so quickly dropped the subject of Sidney Stein.

The Foster's oval mahogany dining table was set with Baccarat crystal and antique Minton china, which twinkled in the warm glow of candlelight. Carol had prepared roasted duck with orange sauce.

After they were seated in the dining room, Willie asked, "Bill, what's the status of the appointment?"

Claudia added brightly, "Congratulations, Bill. I think it's just marvelous!"

"Thank you, Claudia, but wait a minute. Right now, it's just talk. Several people have approached me about being attorney general, but nothing's final. No one really knows if the attorney general is going to step down."

"Would you be interested?" David asked.

Bill grew serious before responding to David's question. "Very interested. I love the law, and being attorney general of the United States would be a great honor."

Carol said, "Bill would make a terrific attorney general. There's no doubt about it."

Bill smiled at his wife across the table. By the way he gazed at her, Jennifer surmised that there was a long history of love and support there. Carol was elegantly beautiful. She was no longer the pretty young girl captured in that photograph on Bill's desk. She was a woman who Jennifer understood had stood devotedly by Bill's side over the last thirty years.

"Thanks, honey."

Carol protested, "Don't thank me. It's the truth."

David added, "You'd have support all across the country. Sidney said so a couple of weeks ago."

Bill cautioned, "Well, folks, I appreciate all of your kind words; however, you and I know it's not that simple. Any time a black person is appointed for anything in this country, the dynamics are different for blacks than for whites. The first black attorney general! I'm certain there are elements out there—I can't identify them for you now, but believe me, they're out there—who don't want to see me appointed attorney general of the United States of America. You've got to remember my background in civil rights. I'm a known liberal with black skin. America has come a long way, just in my lifetime, but I assure you it hasn't come far enough. If I get this appointment, it'll be after intense gamesmanship. But I've been playing the game a long time." Everyone laughed knowingly. "I've even learned a few of them; so rest assured, I'm going to play."

Oscar said, "Amen to that!"

"So am I." Carol stood. "On that note, how about some coffee and dessert in the living room?"

Jennifer jumped up from the table. "Let me help you, Carol." Once in the kitchen, Carol grabbed both of Jennifer's hands. "I like him. David's a good man. He's right for you."

Jennifer grinned. "You really think so?"

As Carol removed the bread pudding from the oven, she said, "He loves you."

"Carol, he hasn't said that, and neither have I, but I know I love him."

"Well, tell him," Carol ordered.

"No, not just yet. I don't want to scare him off. He needs time. We're very much alike."

"Let me tell you from my own experience, Jennifer. When you find a man that's special—like David and, of course, my Bill—you hold on to him. It's going to be a battle, because you and I both know there are a lot of black men out there not worth having. The white man has kicked them in the teeth so hard and so often that they're no longer any good to themselves, never mind a woman. On top of that, too many of the good ones marry white. It appears that there is a direct correlation between education and snow fever. So when you find a good one, you cherish him and do what's necessary to keep him."

"I understand."

"Good, honey." Carol shot Jennifer a look out of the corner of her eyes. "Watch your back at all times. Remember I told you that."

When Jennifer and Carol returned to the living room, Bill said, "Jennifer, I was just telling everyone about what a great job you've done on the domestic workers' union. Juanita just mentioned that she saw the article on Mabel Johnson in *Superwoman*."

Jennifer explained, "My college roommate was Leslie Abrams. I'm sure you've heard of her husband, Jason Abrams. He plays for the Washington Redskins."

Both Willie and Oscar said, "Sure."

"Leslie suggested I call an old friend of ours, Paige Wyatt, who happens to be the editor of *Superwoman*, to get some media coverage for the union. The magazine is also underwriting the organization of the union and a cross-country speaking tour for Mabel."

Juanita said sarcastically, "I'm a little surprised to hear that *Superwoman* is doing all that. I read the magazine, but it has only recently acknowledged that there were black women in this world. They only portrayed some skinny, thirty-year-old white chicks with briefcases."

Jennifer giggled and turned to David. "She just described Paige."

David looked at Jennifer. "That's mean."

"No, it isn't." Jennifer explained to Juanita, "Paige and I went to college together. I knew her, but I never really liked her, so I was reluctant to take the idea to her, but my roommate encouraged me."

Willie interrupted, "Is Jason Abrams married to a black woman?"

"No, my college roommate is white."

Willie nodded. "That makes sense. I figure I would have heard if he was married to a sister."

Willie's wife poked her husband in the side with her elbow. "If that star quarterback was married to a sister, *Ebony* would have had them on the cover of the magazine by now. That would have been big news: a black woman getting a rich, handsome white man to marry her."

Jennifer joined the group's knowing laughter and then continued, "I told Paige just what you're telling me. She wants to broaden the readership. Bill, you're going to like this. Leslie's arranged for Mabel to be on the *Phil Donahue Show*. How about that?"

Bill roared, "Fantastic!"

After the dinner party, Jennifer and David went to his apartment. As Jennifer unbuttoned David's shirt, she murmured, "You didn't tell me that Professor Stein was in town."

"I forgot."

"His daughter, Jill, was with him, wasn't she?"

David walked to his closet to hang up his jacket. "Yeah."

"Why didn't you introduce me to them? Why didn't you even mention that you had seen them?

David put his arms around Jennifer. "No reason."

With David's arms around her, Jennifer felt warm and secure, but she continued, trying to explain her feelings. "I'm more concerned because Jill's white. Jill symbolizes the threat all white women represent for black women. We resent them for luring away our good black men, and we resent you for betraying us this way."

David rubbed his eyes as he attempted to curb his temper. "It's not betrayal."

"I think it is."

David laughed. "You're wrong. It's merely a new choice." He grabbed Jennifer and started tickling her. "I'm an equal opportunity lover. My girlfriend in kindergarten was Chinese. I took Candace, who is black, to my high school prom."

"Stop tickling me. Stop it. I can't talk." Jennifer wrestled away from David's embrace. "But it's a choice black women don't get to make. I don't get to be an equal opportunity lover. Puh-leeze!"

He tickled her. "That's me!"

❦   ❦   ❦

When Jennifer opened her eyes, David was propped up on one elbow, staring at her. He put his fingers to her lips, and she kissed each one. He pulled her into his arms, and they snuggled beneath the warm comforter. As she lay in his arms, last night's discussion was put away, although not forgotten.

David pulled her closer to him. "We had that huge, delicious dinner last night, and yet I'm starving. Hungry? Why don't you lie here, and I'll run to the store."

David got out of bed and walked naked over to the closet. Jennifer watched as he pulled on a pair of jeans and an old Yale rugby shirt. She thought he looked good naked and wearing a three-piece suit or ripped jeans.

David slipped his bare feet into a pair of Gucci loafers, walked back over to the bed, and sat on the edge. "Don't want you to move. I'll be right back, and then I'll fix you the best mushroom omelet you've ever had." As he talked, his hands roamed under the covers, seeking out the warmth of Jennifer's naked body.

Within fifteen minutes, he was back with a chilled bottle of champagne, a dozen eggs, and mushrooms. "Come down here and talk to me as I cook. I just read in the *National Enquirer* that a lady with no legs gave birth in Australia to a baby that weighed twenty-two pounds. How about that?"

As Jennifer came down the spiral steps from the loft, she said, "I should have figured you for a closet reader of the *National Enquirer*."

"I'm not a closet case. I read it in the checkout line; I deliberately pick the long line so I can read in depth."

"Did you also check out the centerfold in *Jet*?"

"Nah, didn't have to. I've got a subscription."

When Jennifer reached the kitchen wearing David's black velour bathrobe, he hugged her and searched under the robe to caress her naked body.

"Here, sit on this stool where I can look at you."

"You've got a deal."

They ate the omelet, drank the entire bottle of champagne, crawled back in bed, and spent the rest of Sunday dozing, reading the *New York Times*, and making love.

❦   ❦   ❦

Two weeks later, Jennifer was in Bill's office discussing a contract matter. Bill threw the contract on his desk. "The inevitable shit has hit the fan."

Surprised by Bill's language, but taking his lead, Jennifer asked, "What shit?"

"The district attorney is investigating a Harlem program I represented a few years ago that got some money from the city; he's looking for financial irregularities."

Jennifer asked, "Am I being paranoid, or is the timing of this investigation awfully fortuitous?"

"Young lady, you got it."

"This stinks."

Bill shook his head slowly. "I have a feeling it hasn't even begun to stink. Before they're finished, it'll smell worse than garbage cans in Harlem on a hot July day."

❦   ❦   ❦

Later that evening, Jennifer said to David, "I'm so angry. I want to punch the first white person I see."

David said jokingly, "That devil white man again, huh? What did he do this time?"

Ignoring the joke, Jennifer explained the district attorney's investigation of Bill. "One would think that when a black person has attained Bill's position in life, he wouldn't have to take as much shit. As long as we're imprisoned in our black skins, we're subject to the crap. I've told you how I've heard those white boys at the firm, lowly associates, challenging Bill or criticizing some work he's done. They would never say such things about a white partner in Bill's position. But these young, know-nothing white punks have the audacity to question him. He's a partner in a Wall Street firm, and they're two minutes out of law school, and yet they think they can criticize him."

"I know." David got up and started to pace. "I have to deal with the shit every day, too. It's funny that when I go to Paris on business, though, I feel less on guard than when I'm in New York. In Paris, I don't feel my clients are constantly judging me first as a black man and automatically assuming I must be incompetent. I get to be a lawyer first in Paris, and I love it. All we can do is never give them any excuse. We always have to be better than they are. Bill will beat this thing, because he's the best and he's tough. Come here. Let me hold you."

The telephone rang. Jennifer reluctantly removed herself from David's embrace and answered. It was her father; he explained that he was coming to New York for a business seminar. "Can I take my little girl out to dinner?"

"Oh, Daddy, yes, and you can meet David."

"I'd like to meet David."

"Daddy, you'll like him. See you Thursday." Jennifer hung up the phone and turned to David. "My dad's going to be in town on Thursday. He wants to take us out to dinner. I can't wait for you to meet him!"

"What day did you say, Jennifer?"

"Thursday."

"I'm sorry. I can't make it."

"Why not?"

David stammered, "I … I've got to meet with a client."

Jennifer did not want to believe what she was hearing. "David, this is my father I want you to meet. It's only for dinner. Can't you arrange something?"

"No, I wish I could. I'll try, but the meeting's already set."

❦   ❦   ❦

Around midnight, David called, waking Jennifer. "How was your dinner with your dad?"

Although Jennifer had enjoyed dinner with her father, her anger that David hadn't joined them caused her to answer curtly, "Fine."

"I'm really sorry I missed him. Maybe next time." David did not wait for a response. "Grant Wilson is giving a party at his apartment tomorrow night. Want to go? Not cocktails. A real party!"

❦   ❦   ❦

When they arrived at Grant's, his apartment was packed with people, who were talking loudly and occasionally guffawing, dancing, eating, and profiling. Grant was a lawyer, so there were lots of lawyers present as well as doctors, stockbrokers, a professional basketball player who'd been Grant's college roommate, and a general assortment of the young, black, and beautiful single set.

David slapped five with Grant. "My main man. How goes it?"

Grant, with his arm around the waist of an absolutely gorgeous woman who looked like she could have been a model, responded, "Hey, it's a happening!"

David, with his arm around Jennifer, said to Grant, "You remember Jennifer."

Grant grinned. "Of course … looking lovely as ever."

Jennifer and David got drinks and joined a group that was vigorously debating the quality of the chitlins at the new soul food restaurant, Chitlins and Champagne.

"Even my grandmama would approve," the basketball player said.

"Are the owners black?" another man asked.

"With chitlins and greens like that? Of course!" Grant shouted.

The man warned, "Hey, you know, they could have the sister back in the kitchen and the white man behind the cash register."

"Not this time," the basketball player assured them.

David and Jennifer made their way onto the balcony and stood looking out at the New York skyline and then looked back at the crowd in the apartment.

Jennifer asked, "Do you notice anything weird about this party?"

"What do you mean 'weird'?"

"There's a room full of successful, professional people, and they're all black. There's not a white face in the crowd."

David asked, "What's weird about that?"

"Nothing really. All of these people work with white people all day. I assume they have some white friends, but when it's time to party, really party, there are no white faces."

"This is a party," David explained, as if that clarified everything. "We don't want to have to work this party. We do that all day long."

Jennifer turned to David. "Can you imagine Paige at this party?"

David laughed. "I don't think so. I'm probably the only black person that Paige knows."

"That's not true. Paige knows me. She knows a lot of black people. She knows all kinds of different people. Don't you remember that motley assortment of folk at the Palomino Gallery, the night we met? Those were Paige's people. You may be her only black *friend*. That's the difference. Knowing someone and being friends with someone are two different things."

Chapter 54

Jennifer, Leslie, and Paige

When Jennifer arrived at the French restaurant for lunch, Leslie and Paige were seated and already engaged in animated conversation. Paige looked up as Jennifer strolled toward the table. She got up and air-kissed Jennifer on both cheeks. "Jennifer, I love that suit."

Leslie rose and hugged her. "Hey, roomie. That is a great suit. Who's?"

Jennifer said, "Anne Klein, on sale."

"Good for you. I love a sale," Leslie said as she giggled.

Jennifer smiled. "I know."

Upon sitting down, Jennifer looked at her two glamorous friends. "Do you realize that this is the first time in a few years that the three of us have been together?"

Leslie chimed in. "The last time all three of us were together was at my wedding."

"That *was* a beautiful wedding," Jennifer said. "I even straightened my Afro for that wedding."

Paige agreed, "It was a great wedding. And thanks to Leslie, we're together again celebrating. The magazine has gotten more positive mail on the article on Mabel Johnson and the domestic workers' union than any other story the magazine has ever run."

Leslie said, "I knew it could be important."

Jennifer added, "I'm certainly glad of the positive response. Mabel's elated."

Paige sipped Perrier water and announced, "I hate to be a typical magazine editor, but my sales are up 10 percent this month. That's the biggest monthly percentage increase in the history of the magazine."

Jennifer commented soberly, "It's clearly a result of attracting a new and different readership than *Superwoman* has had in the past. See, black women do read."

Paige turned to Jennifer and said, "Jennifer, cut the sarcasm. You're absolutely right. It's just the way the magazine should go, and it's what I wanted to happen when I took over. So, thanks to you two, we've broken new ground."

Jennifer laughed. "OK, I was being sarcastic. Come on. But some people still don't believe black people read."

Leslie raised her wineglass. Her red fingernails were perfectly manicured as always, and her three-carat diamond engagement ring, accompanied by a diamond wedding band, sparkled brilliantly. "May I propose a toast? To Goucher College, the place that brought us together."

The three women delicately clicked their wineglasses.

Leslie continued, "College was lots of fun."

"It was the first time I was far away from the safe cocoon my parents provided in Detroit," Jennifer admitted. "At eighteen I wanted to go every place, learn new things, meet new people."

"You met new people, all right; you met us, and now here we are. And the three of us are probably different from some of our classmates, because college was not merely an isolated interlude for us." Paige, thinking about all of the experiences in her life, said, "We didn't return to the insular lives of our childhood. The three of us have expanded our horizons to include people, places, and ideas that were not a part of our childhood realities. That's what I want the magazine to do. We've turned political and social theory into real life. Here we are, three women—one born white Anglo-Saxon Protestant, one born black, and one born Jewish. As children in the fifties and early sixties, our lives didn't intersect. But they did in college, and they do now."

Jennifer nodded in agreement. She felt a real kinship and affection for these two women. But she had to burst Paige's bubble. "What you say about the three of us is true. We have stepped beyond the confines of our race, class, and religious backgrounds, but America hasn't caught up with us yet. Look around. I'm the only black person in this restaurant."

Leslie countered, "Jennifer, you're so cynical. Always have been. But you're right. I didn't even notice that you were the only black person here."

"Neither did I," Paige said. She took a quick look around. "They don't even have black help in this place."

Jennifer sighed, "I always notice. In fact, I'll let you in on a black secret. If there's one other black person in a room, even though we don't know each other, we kind of nod to each other to acknowledge the other's presence, which says, 'It's OK. I'm here too.'"

Paige's face reflected her complete befuddlement. "You've got to be kidding."

"I kid you not. But sometimes, I'll attempt to secretly nod to the other lone black person in the room, and that person will quickly look away. It breaks my heart when that happens, because I know that one *likes* being the only black person in the room, and instead of acknowledging camaraderie, they're resentful that I'm there. They like being the *only*. I guess it makes them feel *special*."

Leslie said, "I've seen the racism. I'll never forget that incident in college when Allison told you she couldn't invite you to her wedding."

"I'll never forget that one. That hurt." Jennifer grimaced at the memory. "But, Leslie, you were terrific. Remember, you told her that you were boycotting her wedding."

Paige laughed, looking at Leslie. "Did you actually say 'boycott'?"

With pride in her voice, Leslie said, "I certainly did."

"Good for you."

Jennifer then asked, "Have you seen Allison?"

Leslie shook her head. "No, I haven't, but she had the nerve to call me and ask if Jason could get her Super Bowl tickets. Can you believe it? Well, I told her absolutely not and reminded her why." Leslie leaped to a new topic. "I can't wait to meet David. He sounds wonderful, and he must be, because both of you think so."

Smiling broadly, Jennifer said, "He is wonderful, and you will find out for yourself tonight. I'm sorry Jason couldn't come to New York with you, because I'd love to get his opinion." Jennifer teased, "Not that I really care what you guys think."

Leslie groaned. "That's for sure. I will not remind you of that Bobby Jones episode. Told you over and over that man was not for you, but you wouldn't listen. You found out on your own."

Jennifer said begrudgingly, "I could never understand why you gave me such a hard time about Bobby." She lowered her voice and whispered, "After all, he was terrific in bed."

Leslie rolled her eyes and said, "You told me."

"Tell me," Paige exclaimed. "There's nothing I like better to hear about than good sex; however, I prefer to have it rather than hear about it."

They raised their glasses in a toast. "Hear! Hear!" they said, and then Leslie continued, "Bobby was just not right for Jennifer."

"How can good sex not be right for someone?" Paige questioned with a look of utter astonishment on her face.

Leslie snapped, "Shut up, Paige. There's more to a relationship than sex, and you know that. Jennifer met him because Jason and I took her to a party given by one of his Redskins teammates. I can't remember who it was, but he had a great house."

Jennifer sighed, "That was a great house: lots of glass, big swimming pool."

"Anyway," Leslie continued explaining to Paige, "I planned on introducing Jennifer to this really nice player who had dreams of going to law school. Instead, Jennifer goes for the muscle-bound ignorant brute. They had nothing in common." Leslie turned to Jennifer. "Didn't your mother always say, 'If you don't want to marry a garbageman, don't go out with one'? Well, Bobby was a garbageman."

Jennifer said accusingly, "Now, you admit it. You thought he was a garbage-man." She stopped her teasing tone. "Is that why you only dated Jewish boys in college? You were making sure that you would marry a Jewish man?"

Leslie dabbed her mouth with the linen napkin before speaking. "I guess so."

"I thought so. It's always been my preference to marry a black man, some-one like my dad. But obviously I don't always follow my mother's advice, nor have I always kept my eye on marriage as an ultimate goal, as you can tell from some of my past relationships. But my mother will love David. Every black mother would."

Paige added, "Every black, white, Chinese, and Indian mother would."

Jennifer turned to Paige. "Wrong. That's what I was saying earlier, Paige. We're not there yet. Maybe one day, but not yet. You may look beyond race, but others don't." Jennifer's sad expression switched back to a broad smile when she said, "Leslie, remember how your mother reacted when she first met Jason? I predict a similar scene."

Leslie flashed her brilliant smile. "That good, huh?"

"That good. My mother will see him and immediately start planning the wedding and the baby shower."

Paige turned to Leslie. "Speaking of babies, are you still trying to get preg-nant?"

Leslie became sober and said in a resigned voice, "Yes, but I don't think it will ever happen."

Jennifer reached out and touched Leslie's hand and said soothingly, "It'll happen. Don't worry."

Leslie said, "I hope so. I've seen two specialists, and they each say nothing is wrong with us. That I should just relax."

Paige sat back in her chair, threw her hair back from her face, and announced, "I'm going to have a baby."

There was shocked silence at the table. Initially, Leslie was speechless, and then she said, "You're not married; you're not even dating anyone special. Paige, you used to hate babies. What are you talking about?"

Paige explained, "I've just decided I'd like to have a baby, and I'm going to have one."

Jennifer said, "You've got to explain this."

"I'm talking about being a single parent. I have lived with someone and been married; neither relationship worked out, and I don't predict I'll ever get married again. I don't want to be a wife. I'm obviously not good at it, but I would like to be a mother."

Leslie asked cattily, "What makes you think you'll be good at being a mother?"

"I feel it. I'd like to share my life with a child. I have lots to give, and no one to give it to."

"Have you thought of adopting?" Jennifer asked.

"Yes, but I would prefer to have a child. I want to experience giving birth. That's got to be a high."

Jennifer, using her best cross-examination techniques, started to pepper Paige with a series of questions: "Who'll be the father? Will the man have any say in this? Are you going to be artificially inseminated? Doesn't a child need a father? Is this fair to the child? Is this fair to the father?"

"Whoa! Back off, Jennifer!" Paige hissed. "You're a lawyer all right. I'm not on the witness stand here."

"I'm sorry. It's hard to turn off the lawyer in me."

"I've given it a lot of thought. I'm going to select a man who's handsome and intelligent, with no genetic problems, and make a baby. Very simple."

Jennifer shook her head. "So you're not going to be artificially inseminated?"

"I didn't say that." Paige smiled mysteriously. "I don't know yet."

Leslie spoke up. "I think a child needs two parents, and what about the concept of sharing a child with a man you love? What about that?"

"There will be no sharing. I don't need a man for financial support or nurturing."

"Not you, but what about the baby?" Leslie asked.

Jennifer said, "I guess I'm just old-fashioned and not liberated, because I'd prefer to share a child with a man I loved and who loved me. What I really want is to entrust my heart, body, and spirit to a man whom I love and who loves me back and know that he will always be in my corner and keep me safe."

Leslie reached out and took Jennifer's hand. "That's exactly what I've always wanted too."

Paige folded her napkin and placed it on the table. "Well, Leslie, you already have it, and Jennifer is about to have it. Me, I don't have it, and I don't think I ever will. I'm not sure I even want that. So, I'll do what I have to do." Paige pushed her chair away from the table, reached down for her Gucci purse, and then stood. "This has been a great lunch. Sorry, I have to run. I'm always going in too many different directions at the same time. But then, that's me. I love it. You two stay and catch up. My treat. They already know to put this on my tab."

Leslie said, "Paige, you don't have to do that."

Paige proceeded to send air kisses first to Jennifer and then to Leslie. "Don't be silly. It's my pleasure. I'm sorry I won't be able to join you guys tonight, but I have a business event. Anyway, I already know David and adore him. Leslie, you'll love him."

❦   ❦   ❦

That evening, Jennifer and David met Leslie for dinner at the Top of the Sixes. To Jennifer's surprise, Leslie was accompanied by Danny Eisenberg. "Danny, this is a surprise. I haven't seen you in ages," Jennifer said as Danny pecked her on the cheek.

"It has been a long time."

"Leslie, Danny, this is David."

Leslie kissed David on the cheek. "David, I'm so glad to meet you."

Danny shook hands with David. "Nice to meet you."

David responded, "Danny, nice to meet you, and Leslie, I've really been looking forward to meeting you. I've heard a lot about you and your husband from Jennifer. Sorry he couldn't make it. Your husband's a great quarterback."

Leslie smiled demurely and said, "That's what the newspapers say."

Jennifer explained, "Danny and Leslie are old friends." She chuckled and then added, "He took her to her senior prom when she broke up with her boyfriend two weeks before prom."

Leslie smiled. "Yes, Danny and I have been friends forever." Leslie turned to Danny and asked, "What's good here?"

Danny glanced at the menu. "You love lamb, and it's really good here."

Jennifer said, "I love lamb, too. I think I'll have that."

The food was excellent and the conversation stimulating. Danny, with his expanding waistline and thinning hair, appeared to still be a genuinely nice guy even though he'd become quite a legendary trader on Wall Street.

David asked Leslie, as he cut into his steak, "Should I feel guilty about this red meat? What's Jason's training diet like?"

Leslie smiled. "Hey, who knows? David, Jennifer tells me you're fluent in French."

"Yes, I am."

Leslie said, "I love France. Danny rented a house in the South of France last year."

David, still attempting to talk football, responded, "South of France is great. Love it. Leslie, I was wondering, what kind of training regimen does Jason have during the off-season?"

Leslie laughed. "David, I don't keep up with all of that football stuff. All I know is that I want dessert. Who's going to have dessert?"

"Leslie, you're amazing," Jennifer said. "You can still eat dessert and look fabulous."

"She is amazing," Danny added as he smiled at Leslie.

❀   ❀   ❀

The next morning, Leslie called Jennifer. "I think I should wear periwinkle blue. I look great in that color."

"Where are you going to wear blue?"

Giggling, she screamed, "At your wedding, of course, when I'm matron of honor. Jennifer, I *love* him. David is wonderful. What can I say? He's the one for you."

"I'm glad you liked him."

"How could I not like him? You two have so much in common. You two belong together."

"That's just what I said when I met Jason for the first time, and you two got married."

"Yeah, well, I've got to run. I just wanted to tell you how much I like David. You're absolutely glowing. There's only one thing that can make you glow like that."

"He is good for me. Now I just have to convince him I'm good for him." Taking a deep breath, she said, "Do you have a minute?"

Hearing the shift in Jennifer's voice, Leslie reluctantly said, "Yeah?"

"We're old friends, so I'm going to just put it out there. What's going on between you and Danny?"

Leslie became irritated. "What do you mean by that?"

"Don't get angry. We both know each other's good and bad sides, so just hold on. I think something's going on with you and Danny. Do you want to talk about it?"

"Now, you just wait a minute …"

"I'm sorry. Obviously, I'm out of line. I'm sorry I said anything. I just thought you might want to talk."

Leslie's anger disappeared as suddenly as it had appeared. "That's OK. I'm going back to DC today."

Chapter 55

Jennifer

Webster, Symington, and Meredith's Christmas party was a professional obligation. Given the negative coverage that Bill had been getting in the newspapers about his indictment and the gossip that was naturally circulating in the office, Carol Foster wasn't looking forward to this year's Christmas party. If she and Bill stayed away, they would only play into the hands of the gossipmongers. So, she bought an exquisitely sexy dress for the party, had her hair done, got a facial and a manicure, and put a determined smile on her face.

As they were leaving their apartment, Bill said, "Darling, you look wonderful. You're more beautiful than the day we married, and that's hard to beat. I'll always love you."

Carol beamed. Bill always knew exactly how and when to bolster her confidence and make her feel that all was right with the world. He wrapped her sable coat around her shoulders as she took a last look at herself in the mirror. The diamond-and-emerald earrings Bill had given her for their anniversary sparkled. For a fifty-eight-year-old woman, who still had her slender figure after three children, she was pleased at her reflection. Her biggest problem was those errant gray hairs that mysteriously appeared on her chin in the middle of the night and greeted her when she looked in the mirror each morning. She kept tweezers by the magnifying mirror, just to pluck these single gray intruders.

Carol, like Bill, had an excellent memory for names and faces. Although she didn't see many of the other partners' wives except at these firm functions, she always remembered their names, their children's names and schools, and some other little tidbit about them, such as where they vacationed, who played bridge, who played tennis, or who was on which charity boards. As a result, everyone at Webster, Symington and Meredith thought she was a tremendous asset to Bill.

The party was in full swing when they arrived. Carol walked over to Emma Symington, the elegant and gracious wife of the son of the Symington of the firm name. Emma was talking with Paula Pendleton, the wife of one of the younger partners, who was aggressively attempting to further her husband's career. Paula leaned forward conspiratorially. "Carol, I've been so concerned about you with all of this mess about the indictment. I've been meaning to call you, but you know how it is. Busy, busy. This mess is just terrible."

Just then, Jennifer waved to Carol from across the room, and Carol, relieved to have something to divert her attention from Paula, waved back. Paula noticed and said, "As if you don't have enough problems!"

"What do you mean, Paula?" Carol asked.

Paula feigned embarrassment. "Oh dear, I do talk too much. It was nothing."

David hadn't accompanied Jennifer to the Christmas party, as he was out of town on business, so she had come to the party alone. When she'd found out David couldn't come, she decided against wearing the red cocktail dress she'd bought for the party. It was far too provocative and sexy to wear when she didn't have a date. So, she'd opted for a nonthreatening black velvet suit.

Jennifer was talking to Bill's secretary when Carol approached them. In a curt voice, Carol said, without bothering to speak or even acknowledge Lucinda, "Jennifer, I'd like to speak with you, now!" She abruptly turned and headed for the hallway. Jennifer, perplexed by Carol's rude manner, immediately followed her out. When they reached the hall, Carol hissed between clenched teeth, "I'm warning you. Leave my husband alone. I gave you some advice before. I told you that when you have a special man, fight for him. Bill is special to me. He's my life, and I'm not going to have you take him from me. You're pretty and young, but he's mine, and you're not going to take him. You can try, young lady, but you'll have a fight on your hands. I'm an old bitch who has fought tougher bitches than you … and won."

Speechless, Jennifer couldn't believe the venom in Carol's voice nor what she was saying or why. She pleaded, "Carol, no, no. You're wrong. I don't know where you got this idea, but I am not having an affair with Bill. I'd never do that. I don't know why you have such an idea, but it's not true."

Carol, unmoved by Jennifer's plea, said only, "Someone told me."

"Oh my God, Carol, it's not true. Do you see what's happening? Someone is using you and me to undermine Bill. Some filthy person has told you this just to destroy your love and respect for your husband just when he needs you most. There's no question that I admire and adore your husband, but he's *your* husband. I respect that."

Bill's secretary, having watched this scene, put her arms around Carol, who was rigid with rage; she said calmly, "Carol, believe her. Jennifer isn't having an affair with Bill. Somebody has said this just to upset you. Be there for him. This is just one more episode in this whole disgusting smear campaign to destroy Bill's chances for the appointment. Don't fall for it."

Tears started to fill Carol's eyes. "I'm sorry. You're both right. It was Paula Pendleton. I never should have believed her, let her get to me like that. I was stupid. Jennifer, please forgive me."

"You weren't stupid. You love your husband, and you're willing to fight for him. Hopefully, one day I'll have someone I want to do that for."

❦   ❦   ❦

Christmas fell on a Saturday, so Jennifer flew to Detroit to spend the Christmas weekend with her family. For Christmas, David gave Jennifer an exquisite pair of diamond-and-pearl earrings. She wore them on the flight to Detroit, knowing her mother would notice them immediately.

❦   ❦   ❦

The Madisons still got up at the crack of dawn to open their Christmas presents. By nine o'clock, all of the gifts had been opened, and the family sat at the table enjoying a big breakfast topped off with homemade fruitcake that had been soaking in wine since Thanksgiving. Gloria Madison answered the telephone. "Merry Christmas."

"Merry Christmas, Mrs. Madison. I'm David Walker. We haven't met, but I feel as if I know you. I've heard so much about you from Jennifer."

"David, Merry Christmas. I've heard so much about you too. My husband and I have been looking forward to meeting you. Whenever you're in Detroit, please come by to see us."

"I'm looking forward to it."

"And, David, those earrings you gave Jennifer are just lovely. You have wonderful taste."

"I'm really glad Jennifer liked them."

"David, I know you didn't call here to talk with me. Here's Jennifer."

"I would like to speak with her, but please tell Mr. Madison I said Merry Christmas. I was very sorry I didn't get a chance to meet him when he was in New York." David paused, thinking how wrong it felt to lie on Christmas morning. It felt like a sacrilege, but he wanted to tell Jennifer's mother what he knew she wanted to hear. He certainly couldn't tell her that on the evening when he'd claimed he had to work and therefore couldn't have dinner with Jennifer and her father, he'd dropped by the apartment of the receptionist from one of the law firms in his office building. It was a simple physical encounter. He knew he really should have had dinner with Jennifer and her dad rather than playing with this sweet, dumb girl's mind and body. So he lied, "I was tied up in a business meeting and just couldn't get away. I was really disappointed. I hope we'll have a chance to get together soon."

"David, I'm looking forward to it."

Mrs. Madison covered the receiver with her hand and, with eyes bright, whispered to Jennifer, "He sounds charming. I love that deep voice."

Jennifer took the telephone from her mother. "Merry Christmas, David. I can't believe you're up this early."

"Well, I wouldn't be, but I wanted to wish you a merry Christmas. I remembered you told me that your family still gets up early to open presents."

"We were up at seven."

David moaned, "Seven? Well, it's nine now, and I'm going back to bed. I'll get up about noon and head over to my grandparents' house. I'll pick you up at the airport tomorrow night. Have a good time."

"Tell your parents and grandparents merry Christmas for me." Jennifer returned to the breakfast table glowing.

Chapter 56

Leslie

Jason picked up Jennifer and David at the Aspen airport. During the short ride from the airport to the chalet, David and Jason traded stories about their time at Yale.

When they arrived at the chalet, Leslie was sitting by a two-story stone fireplace and drinking hot mulled wine. She looked like a travel poster for après-ski in an Alpine sweater, tight jeans, and fur boots with her frosted blond hair hanging loosely around her shoulders.

"Jennifer, David, so glad you could come. There's a deep base and lots of powder. The skiing is going to be terrific."

Jason chuckled, "And what do you care? You'll punk out after an hour."

❧   ❧   ❧

They hit the slopes first thing in the morning. It was cold, but the sun was bright and strong, making the snow, as yet unmarred by the endless winding tracks of skis, twinkle brilliantly. They took the gondola to the top and skied down the trail at a leisurely pace, enjoying the scenery. David skied with grace and style. On the second run, the masculine need for power and speed prevailed, and Jason and David attacked the mountain, leaving Leslie and Jennifer far behind. When they reached the bottom, Jason and David were impatiently waiting for them so they could try another trail.

Jason suggested that he and David ski a black diamond run and discouraged Leslie and Jennifer from joining them. Leslie and Jennifer made a couple more easy runs and headed for the lodge, found comfortable chairs by the fireplace, and ordered hot buttered rum. By the time David and Jason arrived, they had each finished two mugs and were feeling slightly tipsy as they listened to Jason and David excitedly relive their exploits on the treacherous moguls.

After finishing a bowl of bouillabaisse, Jennifer, leaning on David's shoulder, moaned, "I think I need a nap."

Leslie joined in dreamily, "Me, too. Are you guys going to ski some more this afternoon?"

"Absolutely," David and Jason said in unison.

"Well, you're on your own. I'm with Jennifer. A nap sounds perfect."

Jennifer slept for an hour and a half. When she awakened, Leslie was flipping through *Town and Country*. "Sleep well?"

"I needed that nap. I haven't skied since last year. My thighs were screaming at me. They are very angry at me for doing this to them."

Leslie laughed. "I know what you mean. How's it going with David?"

Sighing and then smiling, Jennifer said, "He's unpredictable. One minute he acts as if his world revolves around me, that I'm the most important thing in his life, and then I won't hear from him for several days."

"Is he dating other women?"

"I don't think so."

"What's he doing?"

"Just getting away from me. I think he's afraid of commitment. That's why I'm so glad you guys invited us. There's nothing better than being around happily married couples to eliminate some commitment anxiety."

Leslie admitted bitterly, "Well, there's no happily married couple here."

"You've wanted to tell me something was wrong for months and never got it out. What is it?"

"I want to have a baby," Leslie declared emphatically.

"So, that's not Jason's fault. It'll happen."

"It can't happen if you don't make love to your husband."

Jennifer's eyes opened wide. "The problem is sex?"

"No, it's lack of sex. I just don't want to make love to Jason anymore. There's no desire there."

"Bored?"

"I'm tired of Jason, the football star, the macho jock celebrity, the groupies." Leslie took a deep breath. "Jason plays around. I never told you that before, but you knew I always worried about it."

"I knew you were concerned."

Leslie was hurt and exasperated. "I feel that other women are watching me when I make love to my own husband. They're right there in bed with us. It's eerie."

"Have you talked to him about it?"

"Yes, and he denies it like a good Jewish husband, but it's true. He gets off on the adoration. I bet he's slept with a cheerleader in every city the Redskins played and then doesn't recognize them the next time the team's in town!"

"He obviously doesn't care for those other women. They're just faceless bodies."

"While I'm confessing, I might as well tell you the rest. You were right. I had an affair—well, not really an affair—with Danny. We slept together once."

"And?"

"It felt good. I wanted to be as free and liberated as Jason."

"Are you?"

"Sort of. Jennifer, what's so frightening is that my relationship with Danny made me feel better about Jason. I don't hate him now. I understand him. He likes adoration; so do I. The problem is I certainly can't risk getting pregnant now. I wouldn't be sure of who the father was, and I'm not *that* liberated."

"Thank God. Maybe now isn't the time for a baby."

"I think you're right. Something inside says that's what I want, though. Maybe Jason shouldn't be the father."

Jennifer wondered if now was the right time to confess that Jason had once made a pass at her. She didn't say anything, though, believing that there was never a good time to tell a friend something like that.

Looking out at the gently falling snow, Jennifer asked, "Are you still seeing Danny?"

Leslie sighed heavily. "No. I admit that I'm no real swinger, because I didn't want you or anybody to know it. I wanted you to see me as happily married Leslie. What did you used to call us? The golden couple? I liked that."

❦   ❦   ❦

After dinner, the four of them sat in the hot tub, drank champagne, and told dirty jokes. Jason asked, "What do you get if you cross a donkey with an onion? A piece of ass so good it makes you want to cry." After their skin had become wrinkly and they were very drunk and in danger of drowning, they crawled out and went to bed.

❧   ❧   ❧

On the flight back to New York, David said, "I really like Jason and Leslie. They're fun people and really care about you. It's nice to have old friends like that."

"Yes, it is. We go way back."

"Does she know how much he plays around?"

"Yes, she knows. How do you know?"

"We stopped at a couple of bars in Aspen. The ladies just descended on Jason. He's a celebrity. It happens, and Jason doesn't discourage it. I got the impression they have a so-called open marriage."

"I guess you could say that."

"Why be married?"

"Leslie is asking herself that question right now."

Chapter 57

Paige

Paige entered the Waldorf-Astoria and quickly climbed the steep steps to the lobby in three-inch heels and a dark blue maternity suit. She refused to give up the heels, although her OB kept telling her that as she put on more weight, her balance would be affected and the heels should go. She saw David seated in the lobby and walked over to say hello.

David removed the papers from his lap as he stood and greeted Paige. "What brings you to the Waldorf?"

"I'm meeting with an alcoholic author who's already spent his hefty advance for an article for *Superwoman* but hasn't yet delivered. I'm going to encourage him to get it done ASAP. Graciously, of course. The guy's brilliant but a drunk. Probably hooked on cocaine, as well. He's slowly killing himself. It's too bad. He's a gifted writer. How about you?"

Placing the documents he'd been reading when Paige approached into his briefcase, David said, "Meeting a client."

"David, I'm really happy that you and Jennifer have found each other. She's the right one for you."

"Think so?"

"Yes!" Paige placed her hand on David's arm. "I can remember the two of us, sitting on my patio in California, drinking jug wine, and talking about love: who to love, when to love, why to love, what love is."

David grimaced. "Did we cover all those topics?"

Paige laughed. "Maybe not. In our California jug wine-induced fog, maybe I just imagined we did."

"How's the pregnancy going? You look great."

"I feel wonderful, and my doctor says I'm fine."

"Well, you look fine."

"Thanks. What are you up to? Doing any traveling?"

David said, "As a matter of fact, I'm leaving for Paris in a few days. The client I'm meeting is part of the Paris trip."

"We're two lucky people. We get to go to Paris on business. I was there a little while ago for a fashion show. Is Jennifer going to be able to join you in Paris?"

"Don't know."

Paige sighed, "That would be so romantic: you and Jennifer strolling along the Left Bank. I've always admired Jennifer. We weren't close when we were in college, but I knew, even then, that she was a person of substance. I think she's perfect for you."

"You think so?"

"I do. You two should definitely spend some time together in Paris. It's so romantic. There's nothing like being in love in Paris. Mark and I have been to Paris together a couple of times. To be in love in Paris is perfect." Paige started to bite her thumbnail but jerked her hand away from her mouth. When in deep thought, she sometimes reverted to her childhood habit of nail biting. "Wait a minute. Let me think. One of those times in Paris, Mark and I were definitely not in love. We were not even in like." Paige looked at her watch. "Got to go. Have fun in Paris."

Chapter 58

Jennifer

In the weeks prior to the Foster trial, some of the local newspaper headlines included EMINENT BLACK LAWYER CAUGHT WITH HAND IN THE TILL and BLACK LAWYER INDICTED FOR CONSPIRACY TO DEFRAUD CITY.

Jennifer approached Bill's office. "Lucinda, is he in?"

Lucinda looked up from her typewriter with a worried look on her face. "Yes, let me check if he can see you." She pushed the button for Foster's office, spoke softly, and then motioned Jennifer into the office. Foster was sitting behind his desk with the chair facing the window when Jennifer entered.

"Bill, I just wanted to stop by and wish you well."

Foster turned from the window to look at Jennifer. He looked tired.

"Are there any new developments?"

"If you're asking if the district attorney has dropped the case against me, the answer is no. We go to trial Monday morning. What I haven't told you is that those quiet inquiries I had about becoming attorney general have evaporated. I'm not surprised. I expected it."

Jennifer held back tears. "This is so unfair! What can I do?"

"Nothing." He started shifting papers on his desk and then added, "You know what you can do?"

Jennifer brightened. "What? Name it."

"Continue to work hard and be the best lawyer you can be. Don't give them any excuses. That's what it's all about. When you do that, you're helping yourself and all of us."

"I understand." She added, in a feeble attempt to lighten the mood, "David's in Paris. I know you and Carol love Paris. Before he left, he told me to tell you good luck." Mentioning David forced her to confront the fact that she hadn't spoken with him since she kissed him good-bye at the airport three weeks earlier. She was disappointed that he'd not called or written or even responded to her letters or calls. She tried to convince herself that he was so busy working that he didn't have time to write or call. Before he left, she told him that she would love to come over for a long weekend. He told her then that he didn't think he would have time for her to visit. She continued to hope that he would change his mind.

"Thanks. I can use some good luck." The sound of Bill's voice brought her back from her unsettling thoughts about David. Bill added, "Maybe when this is all over, I'll take Carol to Paris to celebrate." Jennifer prayed that Bill and Carol would be able to celebrate in Paris.

Dozens of television and newspaper reporters were on hand to cover the opening day of the trial. Their presence lent a circus atmosphere to the somber proceedings.

As soon as Jennifer walked into the courtroom, she saw him standing in the well of the court. She hadn't seen him in a long time—not since college. Steven Greenberg looked strikingly handsome in a charcoal gray suit. His hair was shorter than it had been in college, but the thick mustache remained.

As Jennifer walked toward a seat in the front of the courtroom, Steven looked up. Initially his face was an enigma: first expressionless and then quizzical. Steven mouthed her name. She nodded and smiled.

He approached her and with a stern expression, he asked, "What are you doing here?"

Still shocked to see him, Jennifer said, "I'm an associate at Bill Foster's firm." Then she added, "He's my friend."

"Damn." Steven said emphatically, "I've got to see you." Before anything else could be said, they were interrupted by one of the men who had been talking with Steven when Jennifer entered the courtroom. Reporters surrounded Steven and the other man, badgering them about their trial strategy. Jennifer quietly took a seat behind Carol Foster.

Carol turned around to face Jennifer. "Who was that?"

"He's the prosecutor. I dated him in college."

Carol's face registered shock, but she said nothing and just turned around to focus on Bill.

❧   ❧   ❧

Jennifer remained in court throughout the morning session. She couldn't keep her eyes off of Steven.

John Armstrong, Bill's lawyer, made a dignified opening statement in a voice reminiscent of Martin Luther King's. The district attorney, A. T. McDowell, with his pockmarked face and broken nose from his days as a Golden Gloves boxer, was combative in his opening, punctuating the fact that he remained a fighter.

Jennifer returned to the office at the lunch break and immediately telephoned David in Paris. For the first time in three weeks, she reached him. "I know you're busy, but I wanted you to know that Bill's trial started today. The opening went well."

David mumbled, "I'm glad."

Shifting to a more lighthearted voice, she asked, "How are you?"

"Jennifer, I can't talk now. I'm late for an appointment."

"Oh." She paused; the coldness and dismissive tone of his voice and words went right to her heart, and it began to break. "I understand. I just figured you'd want to hear about Bill's trial."

"Got to go." He hung up as she attempted to say good-bye. As she held the telephone in her hand, tears filled her eyes. This brief conversation confirmed what she already knew but didn't like knowing.

❧   ❧   ❧

A little after five, Steven telephoned Jennifer. She composed herself before answering. All afternoon, she periodically fought back tears as she grappled with the reality of the demise of her relationship with David. She hated herself for all of the excuses she'd made for him over the past few hours to combat the reality of his actions and words.

"I just got out of court. I had to reach you before you left the office. I don't know where you live."

Jennifer tried to sound nonchalant despite her rapidly pounding heart. "I wasn't expecting to hear from you. I figured you would be too busy to call until after the trial was over."

Steven said emphatically, "I told you I *had* to see you."

Jennifer's voice expressed her surprise but not the pleasure she felt at his words and the sound of his voice. All she could mutter was, "Oh."

There was a long silence, neither sure how to continue.

"How about a late dinner tonight?" he asked. "I'm swamped with this trial, but I have to eat."

She wavered momentarily as she mulled over her tearful afternoon and what could be the potential ramification of such a meeting; then she said, with a hint of resolve in her voice, "Fine."

As promised, at eight o'clock Steven knocked on Jennifer's apartment door. She opened the door, and immediately it felt right that he should be standing there. He was holding a bouquet of purple irises, white baby's breath, and fragrant purple freesia.

Jennifer reached for the flowers and said, "Thank you. Come in. You look tired. How about a glass of wine?"

"Thanks."

Jennifer went into the kitchen to place the flowers in a vase and get wineglasses. When she returned, she placed the flowers on the table and handed him the wine. "Thank you again for the flowers."

"Do you still love flowers?"

"Very much."

"I like your apartment." Steven glanced around the apartment and then let his eyes rest on her. "You're still amazingly beautiful!"

Laughing nervously, she said, "You know exactly what to say." He stood there smiling at her as she rambled on. "You must be starved. If you'd like, I could fix us a couple of steaks here rather than going out."

Steven, exhausted, said gratefully, "That's the best offer I've had all day."

Jennifer busied herself in the kitchen preparing the meal as Steven stood and watched her. She said, "Look, given my relationship to Bill, I know we can't talk about the trial. So, don't worry. I won't mention it, and I know you won't either. But, you should know that I adore Bill. If he wasn't married, well … Tell me about you."

"We won't talk about the trial." Steven leaned against the refrigerator. "I went to Columbia Law School. Been in the DA's office for a couple of years. Love it. Great job. And you?"

"Went to Harvard Law School and then joined the firm after graduation. Have you kept in touch with Barry?"

"Yeah. Barry got married last year."

"Who did he marry?"

"Nice girl. From Boston. Her name's Martha, but they call her Muffy."

Jennifer laughed out loud. "You've got to be kidding! I imagined Barry would marry somebody called Muffy."

She could see the confusion on his face when he asked, "Why did you imagine that?"

"Muffy is just one of those rich-white-girl nicknames. I bet she can trace her ancestry to some Revolutionary War hero."

"You're right. She's definitely Boston Brahmin. Her mother is a member of the DAR, Daughters of the American Revolution."

"I know what the DAR is," Jennifer retorted. "It's the same group that wouldn't let Marian Anderson sing in DAR Constitution Hall in Washington, DC just because she was black, and then Eleanor Roosevelt arranged for her to sing at the Lincoln Memorial on Easter morning. Oh, I know the group. Four knew his place in the world, and he was going to always stay in it. Dating Susan was a college experience to be chalked up and taken out only as a sentimental memory of 'wild college days.' Enough about Four. Hey, you became Perry Mason just as you'd planned. Are you going to stay? Make it a career?"

"I'm surprised you remember that Perry Mason stuff. I don't know. Probably not forever."

"You must be good if they assigned this case to you."

"So far, I haven't lost a case!"

"This will be your first!"

Softly, he said, "I can't talk about the case."

"I know that!" Jennifer snapped, and then she laughed. "Just couldn't resist. Steaks are ready."

During dinner, they both started to feel relaxed in each other's company, and it was like old times at Princeton when they talked and laughed a lot about anything and everything. Very abruptly, Steven became very serious. "Why did you really break up with me in college? You know we never really talked it out. I want to talk about it now."

Jennifer took a deep breath and released a resigned sigh. "When I saw you today in court, I thought about this conversation, as well as the one about Bill, and how it's inevitable that we talk about them. Both of them are too long and complicated to discuss tonight. Let me just say, for now, that I ran scared."

"What were you afraid of?"

"You were great, but I knew we wouldn't work out. Life's scary, and this trial scares me. I would like to believe that you wouldn't prosecute Bill if you didn't believe he was guilty. I don't want him to be guilty."

Steven got up to leave. "It's late, and these subjects are too complicated for now. We'll talk later."

Jennifer walked Steven to the door and opened it. He shut the door quietly and turned to face her. "I'm glad I've found you again." She could tell that he'd wanted desperately to kiss her as soon as he walked into the apartment. Now, just before leaving, he kissed her softly on the cheek and then embraced her tenderly. For a few moments she let him hold her. It felt good to be in his arms again, but then she squirmed away and said accusingly, "You're going to lose, and I'm going to be glad. I wish this wasn't your case."

On Sunday, before the start of the second week of the trial, Jennifer joined the Fosters' friends for brunch. There was a forced sense of gaiety. Everyone talked about the trial preliminarily, and then Carol gracefully switched the conversation to a discussion of everyone's summer vacation plans. "We're going to spend the summer at the Vineyard. For the last several years, Bill hasn't gotten up there very much. This summer, we're definitely going to spend some more time there."

Bill said solemnly, "Carol, we'll see."

"No, Bill," Carol insisted. "This year, you're definitely going to get some much-needed rest."

Bill looked at his wife. "Sweetie, if I'm found guilty, I may be going to jail."

"Bill, don't say that," Carol said sharply. "I can't think about that."

Jennifer helped Carol clear the dishes. When they were alone in the kitchen, Carol's serene exterior broke, and she started to weep. Each day she had been in the courtroom sitting behind her husband, a poignant portrait of the ever faithful wife. Their three children sat by her side, lending their support. This family group had to make an impression on the jury. They represented all the strength, fortitude, and courage of the American black family. They made the perfect cover for *Ebony* magazine.

Carol pleaded, "Jennifer, how's it going? Tell me, please. Bill tells me it's going fine, but I know he says that because he doesn't want me to worry. You're a lawyer. Tell me what you think."

"Carol, no one can predict what a jury will do. Bill didn't steal anything. The prosecutor has only circumstantial evidence provided by one sleazy guy's accusations. That guy has convictions for passing bad checks and drug possession. He's a Harlem numbers runner, for God's sake! Bill takes the stand tomorrow. I'm sure that once the jury gets a chance to listen to Bill, he will be able to persuade them of his innocence. Who will the jury believe, Bill or Mr. Sleaze? My vote is with your husband."

Jennifer's words had their intended soothing effect. Carol's spirit was markedly lifted and her resolve sufficiently fortified to get her through the next few days. Carol, having recovered her composure, inquired, "By the way, why didn't David join us today?"

"David's been in Paris for the last several weeks on business."

"Oh, how wonderful! I adore Paris!"

Jennifer added sullenly, "He must adore it too, because I haven't heard from him. I've written; he hasn't. I called, and he said he was too busy to talk. I've tried to tell myself that he's just busy and distracted. But I'm not a complete fool. He's in Paris, not the Amazon rain forest. There are telephones! If he cared about me, he would have invited me over for a romantic weekend. My mother has always said, 'Don't love nobody who don't love you.' Well, I have to face it. David is not in love with me."

"I'm so sorry. David seems like such a terrific guy. I guess, like most young men today, he's just afraid of commitment. There's so much out there to choose from that some men can't decide."

"My heart wants him, but my brain says, 'Don't be no fool.' I would prefer for him to tell me that we're over, but I think he's sending me a message through his silence. You know, in the law, silence can be interpreted to mean something. David's silence means he's backing away from me."

"I'm sorry it's not working out." As Carol cut slices of homemade sweet potato pie, she asked Jennifer casually, "Have you had a chance to talk with Steven Greenberg yet?"

Jennifer responded sadly, "Yes, just once."

"Jennifer, I'm not prying. You don't have to talk about it."

"There's nothing to talk about. Well, maybe there is. I thought I was falling in love with him once, but I didn't want to be, so I ran away instead of dealing with it."

"Dealing with the color problem?"

"Yes. Anyway, now he appears, and he's prosecuting my friend on charges fabricated by white men to keep a black man down. It's really fucking upsetting. Excuse me."

Carol laughed. "I'm not so old that you have to say, 'Excuse me' when you say ... uh ... that word."

"Oh, you're not, huh? How come you didn't say 'fucking' just now?"

"All right, all right. It's just so crude. Back to Steven Greenberg. Even I understand that he's just doing his job, that it's not personal. He's awakened in you some old feelings though, hasn't he? And it doesn't help that David is so far away both physically and emotionally, does it?"

"No, that doesn't help. And he has awakened in me some old memories. It doesn't help that I'm so fucking—excuse me—miserable and vulnerable. Even when David's here, he's always coming close and then backing off. I don't want to talk about this anymore. I'd much rather have a piece of sweet potato pie."

As she was leaving, trying to be lighthearted, Jennifer said in a serious yet playful voice, "Bill, you'll win the case tomorrow. No jury has ever been able to resist you." Although she presented a positive face to Carol and Bill, she knew that it was possible that he'd be found guilty. She also regretted that she and all black people would be devastated by a guilty verdict.

Chapter 59

Leslie

Jennifer returned to her apartment and sat down to read the *New York Times*. She replayed in her mind the one brief and disappointing telephone conversation she'd had with David. She hadn't spoken to Steven since the night he stopped by for dinner, although she had seen him in court. The phone rang. Jennifer ran to grab it. She didn't attempt to hide the disappointment when she heard Leslie's voice.

"Well, I'm glad you're so happy to hear from me," Leslie said sarcastically. "Who were you expecting?"

"I was hoping you were David. I called him to tell him about the trial, and he rushed me off the phone. I thought he'd want to know how the trial was going."

"How is it going?"

"Who can tell with juries? I had dinner with Steven."

"Steven Greenberg? Really? What did he say? What did you do? What did you say? How did that happen?"

"He's the prosecutor in the Foster trial."

"You're kidding."

"No. I wish I was. We didn't talk about the trial, naturally." Then Jennifer added dryly, "He kissed me."

"And?"

"That's all."

"How did you feel?"

"Damn it, I liked it."

"Are you going to run away again?" Leslie probed. "You shouldn't. Steven loved you. I could tell that you really cared for him, too."

"We'll see. Are you dealing with your problems?"

"I'm trying to. I've certainly done a lot of thinking about it. I'm trying to step back and see what, if anything, I can salvage, or want to salvage, of my marriage. I look at Jason and see the golden hunk in tennis shorts and mirrored aviator sunglasses at the Scarsdale Country Club. I see a nice Jewish boy who I thought would always make me happy."

"Is Jason still a nice Jewish boy, or was he ever?"

"Wow," Leslie said with a laugh. "Jennifer, you ask hard questions."

"Yeah. Unfortunately, I don't have any answers for you or for me at the moment."

Leslie's eyes focused on a photo taken at her wedding; it brought a smile to her face. "You know, when you're falling in love, you see what you want to see rather than what's actually there. Love really does wear blinders. I anticipated some of the very problems I'm having right now, but I was so much in love that I convinced myself that they weren't real problems. I thought that because what Jason and I had was so special, bad stuff couldn't happen to us. I guess that's what everyone does when they're falling in love. We refuse to say, or even think, some of the stuff that we know in our hearts to be true. We figure if we don't acknowledge it, it'll go away."

Chapter 60

Paige

Paige rushed into the hospital and quickly took the elevator to the third floor, where her weekly Lamaze class was already in session. The room was full of young couples, who were seated on the floor and learning how to pant. She hung up her coat and took a seat on the floor next to her mother, who had thoughtfully brought the pillow; last time Paige had forgotten it.

Mrs. Wyatt whispered, "Darling, remember: you're the one having the baby. I'm merely the coach." Mrs. Wyatt looked around the room and noted, "I feel strange enough being here when you're here, but alone, I cannot ignore the questioning looks of our classmates. I'm sure they're thinking, *This old woman cannot be having a baby.*"

Paige hugged her mother quickly. "Thanks for doing this with me. I know this whole thing is weird for you. I love you. I appreciate it."

Mrs. Wyatt smiled at Paige's profession of love, which had become a common occurrence during Paige's pregnancy, and said, "When I had you, your father took me to the hospital, he immediately disappeared, my doctor administered lots of drugs, and then you were born. That's it."

Giggling quietly so as not to disrupt the class, Paige whispered, "New day, Mother. All the research shows natural childbirth is much better for the baby. Maybe that's why I'm all screwed up. It was the drugs at birth. Your fault."

"Please, stop blaming me for your life. Just start panting while I rub your back." Mrs. Wyatt rubbed her daughter's back as the instructor directed, but she whispered into Paige's ear, "Are young people so stupid now that they don't know how to breathe or rub a back? You need classes for this?"

"Shh. Keep rubbing. Feels good."

Chapter 61

Jennifer

The judge asked, "Ladies and gentlemen of the jury, have you reached a verdict?"

The foreman, a slightly overweight white man with a mixed-gray crew cut, stood and said, "Yes, your honor, we have."

Bill's lawyer felt the knot in his stomach tighten when the foreman stood up. The fact that this man had been chosen by the other jurors did not bode well for him.

The judge said, "Will the defendant please rise?"

Bill stood up with his lawyer by his side. Although he'd stood in response to a question that referred to him as the defendant, he radiated a quiet dignity, dispelling any association with that pejorative term.

The foreman's face and the faces of the other jurors provided no clue as to the outcome. Bill boldly looked into the eyes of the foreman and waited. He thought, once again, *Some white man is announcing my fate.* He wondered, as he had hundreds of times before throughout his life, when, if ever, he would be in control of his life. Although he had reached a level of financial independence that gave him a freedom few people, black or white, would ever experience, he sometimes felt subjugated by the color of his skin. He believed that his skin color blinded some to his intelligence, knowledge, fortitude, courage, and spirit.

The jury foreman looked Bill in the eye and announced, "We find the defendant not guilty on all counts."

Bill turned immediately to Carol, who was weeping silent tears of joy, smiled, and said, "I love you."

Jennifer was in her apartment listening to the radio when the music stopped abruptly, and the announcer said, "I've just received a special bulletin from the newsroom. William Foster, the eminent black civil rights lawyer, has been found not guilty."

❧   ❧   ❧

Jennifer peered through the peephole and saw Steven. She swung open the door and said triumphantly, "I told you that you would lose."

She was surprised that Steven didn't look depressed, although he had just lost his first case. He said dryly, "I lost because the evidence was insufficient. If it had been up to me, we'd never have gone for an indictment."

Jennifer handed Steven a glass of wine and then positioned herself at the other end of the sofa so that she was facing him but not touching him. She'd rehearsed this speech in her head several times in the past week and prayed she'd be able to deliver it with clarity despite her passionate feelings.

"From the moment Bill's name was being talked about as the next attorney general, there were rumors that America was just not ready for a black person in that powerful position. The funny thing was that his credentials were incontestable by everyone, even white folks: Dartmouth College, Harvard Law School, years as a litigator with important wins to his credit, a former prosecutor, a stint at the Justice Department in Washington, arguments before the Supreme Court, partnership in a prestigious Wall Street firm, on the boards of several major corporations. But Bill is black. Too many people see the color of his skin before they see the quality of the man. Too many others can only see the color of his skin.

"Unlike Jews, who've changed your names from Rosenberg to Rose and had your noses fixed and then disappeared into white America, black folks cannot change the color of our skin. The first thing people see is the skin color. And Bill is very dark. There's no mistaking him. If given a chance, we can prove ourselves to be intelligent, charming, hardworking, resourceful people. But the first thing people see is the color, and unfortunately their initial reaction is negative."

Over the rumbling sound of a fire truck racing down the street and the blaring sound of the siren, Jennifer continued, "So, what did they do? They couldn't attack his legal ability or experience. His credentials were impeccable. A racist frontal attack was clearly out of the question. This isn't the 1950s! Instead, they attempted to discredit the man. Thank God, it didn't work!

ment now."

Steven looked at Jennifer incredulously. "Who's the *they*?"

Jennifer matched his look of incredulity. "White people, of course."

"All white people?"

Jennifer's voice reflected her frustration that Steven didn't just automatically understand this. "The white powers that be."

"You believe I was a willing accomplice to this alleged conspiracy, don't you?"

Jennifer said deliberately, "If I thought that, you wouldn't be sitting here right now. And I heard that patronizing tone of skepticism in your voice when you said 'alleged conspiracy.' You think I'm crazy. That I'm paranoid. But you're wrong. You don't get it. It's a black thing. We get it. Anyway, I don't believe you were a willing or knowing accomplice, and neither was your black co-counsel. What's his name?"

"Jimmy Harris."

"Right. Harris was on the team just to show his black face. I'm not saying he's not a good lawyer, because he proved that. Bill and Armstrong were quite impressed with him, as they were with you, I might add."

"That's good to hear."

"But Harris's purpose on the prosecution team was to counter any suspicions that this case looked like whites prosecuting a black. See, no racist frontal attacks. The DA was saying to the jury, 'Look. Even this distinguished young black lawyer believes Foster is guilty.'" Jennifer took a deep breath. "I believe neither of you were willing accomplices. It's just a tough game out here, and we're all called from time to time to play, although we may not like it."

Steven finished his wine and leaned his head against the back of the sofa, attempting to digest all that Jennifer explained. "I advised against prosecuting. I was even instructed not to plea-bargain. The DA wanted to try the case."

"Of course he did. The trial brought publicity. The trial was one way of letting America know that Foster was not the man to be attorney general. The DA wanted to win, but not getting a guilty verdict does not equate to a loss. After all, we've had several weeks of pretrial discussion of the allegations of stealing in the newspapers and on TV. Then there was the daily coverage of the trial. The word on the street is that Foster's tainted and couldn't possibly be the next attorney general. Win or lose, they got what they really wanted: Bill will not be the first black attorney general of the United States. America's not ready for that yet."

Steven continued, "I have to admit, I was suspicious about the motivation behind this case." He stroked his mustache thoughtfully. "You know, I can't believe I'm saying this, but I'm glad we lost. Unfortunately, I was able to push back my suspicions and try to win."

Jennifer waited several moments before responding. Then she finally said what was in her heart. "That's the difference between you and me."

"I want to talk about you and me. Why did you break up with me like that in college?"

"Because we're different."

"The black-and-white thing?"

Jennifer looked at Steven, and just like old times, his blue eyes mesmerized her. In the last week, she had pulled out old photos and letters, and as she brooded about David, thoughts of Steven comforted her funky mood. "I know I owe you a real explanation. Believe me ... the actual breakup was impulsive. Phillip saw us together at the Simon and Garfunkel concert, called me the next week, and asked me out. He provided an easy way to back away. By the way, Phillip and I spent most of the weekend talking about you and how and why interracial relationships were difficult—the whole black power thing. Phillip really liked and most of all respected you. We were never a couple. Just friends."

"Really?"

"Do you remember when the black students took over Nassau Hall? The South African antiapartheid protest?"

Chuckling, he said, "Sure, I do."

"Phillip told me that you were outside with the white students leading a support demonstration, and then when some students burned a stuffed Princeton tiger in effigy, you made them put out the fire and kept them from getting out of control."

Steven stroked his mustache. "I haven't thought about that demonstration in a long time. And, unfortunately, things are still the same in South Africa. Back to you and me."

Jennifer took a deep breath and then continued her explanation. "I was already angry about Four and Susan."

"What did Barry and Susan have to do with it? By the way, why do you always call him 'Four'?"

Jennifer laughed. "His name. Barton Winston Pennington the *Fourth*! Such an old-money name. My own little joke. Anyway, just before the Simon and Garfunkel concert, Susan and Four broke up, remember?"

"Yeah, so?"

"Well, I thought that Four didn't marry Susan because she's Chinese. I even predicted that he would marry someone named Muffy. I knew Four had made the safe choice, and I condemned him for it. Do you know that Four's parents never met Susan? I wish I could have been a fly on the wall when Four's parents were discussing Susan. Bet they even threatened to cut him off financially if he continued the relationship."

Steven responded accusingly, "But so did you. You did exactly what you say Barry did." Steven corrected himself. "Four did."

"I know."

"Well, why is it OK for you to do it and not OK for Barry?"

"Did I say that it was OK? I just admitted to you that I did it. I didn't say it was OK. At the time, it felt like the right thing for me to do. It was the sixties; we'd gone beyond 'black and white together, we shall overcome' to 'black is beautiful.'"

Once again Steven interjected, "It still is."

"I didn't want to be a pioneer. It's too hard. You just don't get it."

"Explain it to me."

She knew that having to explain it to him was the problem. She wanted someone who just naturally got it without a lot of explanation. She said, "I tried to explain it then. I remember talking about weddings and everybody supporting the marriage. Back then, I wasn't ready, so I split." Jennifer's thoughts returned to her college years, that four-year hiatus when all things were theoretically possible within the cloistered sanctuary of the ivory tower campus, and then asked, "Why did you ask me to dance that first night we met?"

Steven stood, flexing his fingers, and moved closer to Jennifer. "I've been completely engaged in this trial for weeks. But as soon as I saw you in court, I tried to remember every detail of our time together. I remembered playing 'Rhapsody in Blue' the first night we met." With a sly grin he admitted, "I was trying to impress you."

"You did."

"I remember our first kiss under Blair Arch. Why did I ask you to dance? That's easy. I saw you dancing, and I wanted to dance with you. You were pretty."

She thought his answer was too simple and queried, with no attempt to disguise her consternation, "Did you really think I was pretty?" She still found it hard to believe that this handsome Ivy League white boy thought she was pretty.

Steven laughed. "Yes, I thought you were pretty." He stopped laughing and said, "And now you're beautiful."

"I like the sound of that." She bit her lip and added, "Did you feel sorry for me because I was the only black girl at the party?"

"Were you the only black girl there?"

"Yes, I was. See, that's one of the differences between you and me. I *always* notice when I'm the only black person. Always! You didn't think about it, because you didn't have to."

Shrugging his shoulders, he said simply, "You were pretty, without a date, and therefore available. I wouldn't be snaking a friend's date. Pretty. That's it. No big deal."

"I remember thinking that people were looking at us while we danced. I was sure that your eating club buddies were not used to seeing someone like me at their party. I was uncomfortable, but I fought the feeling."

Jennifer was envious that he was oblivious to the fact that she had been the only black girl there, while it loomed large in her memory. She was still attracted to his white American handsomeness, that look she had been acculturated to admire while flipping the pages of *Seventeen* magazine; she had fantasized about it but simultaneously accepted that the look could never be hers. Needing to fill the space while she wrestled with her memories, she rose to refill their wineglasses. She yelled from the kitchen, "Can you believe that Leslie told me that Princeton had lots of black students, and I believed her? That's the reason I came up for the weekend. Did Tower have any black members then?"

"No, it didn't. In fact, it was one of the few clubs that had Jews."

Jennifer handed the wineglass to Steven. As she started to sit on the far end of the sofa, Steven took her hand and pulled her down beside him. With his hands tenderly stroking her cheeks and his fingertips barely touching her lips, he asked, "Are you ready to make another choice?"

Before she could answer, he was smothering her lips with his own. Jennifer wanted to say she was ready, but in fact she was unsure. Steven gently pushed her back onto the sofa. She thought she should tell him to stop. But then she thought that she must be crazy for allowing such a ridiculous idea to cross her mind. Then the little voice inside her admitted that his kiss felt great. The same little voice reminded her that she hadn't been kissed since David left for Paris. The little voice started telling her, "David doesn't love you. He's in Paris but hasn't called or written to you." Then her mother's voice interrupted her thoughts and said, "Don't love nobody who don't love you." Jennifer lay back on the sofa as Steven crawled on top of her. His tongue moved gently to push her lips open. She readily succumbed to the pressure of his tongue. The old doubts and concerns persisted, aggravated by the little voice in her head, so she said nothing and merely enjoyed the moment. When her body screamed for more, trying to drown out the little voice inside her head, she rolled to the side. "Steven, I think you'd better go."

Steven sighed and then caressed her cheek. "I don't want to."

Jennifer wiggled to her feet and adjusted her shirt. "Please."

"OK, but can we see each other tomorrow?"

"I'd like that."

❦   ❦   ❦

The following morning, the *New York Times* ran an editorial expressing its support of Foster for appointment as attorney general of the United States. The editorial recounted Foster's impressive credentials and stated it appeared that the charges had been fabricated to discredit a noble man. The last line of the editorial said, "Fortunately, that did not happen. To the contrary, Mr. Foster's integrity has been tested, and he has prevailed."

Steven called. "Did you see the editorial in the *Times* this morning?"

Jennifer squealed, "Yes, I can't believe it. It's truly a progressive position for the *Times* to take. I think it's great."

"This crisis is over. May I take you out to dinner and dancing?"

Jennifer and Steven had dinner at a small bistro on the West Side; then, they went to a discotheque. Just like the first time, they danced together in perfect rhythm as if they had been dancing together for years. This time it was the Hustle. They moved easily around the crowded dance floor, the huge glass disco ball above their heads refracting the colored lights. They executed a perfect turn, and the couples near them clapped. She noted that they were the only interracial couple in the disco.

❧   ❧   ❧

Jennifer and Steven saw each other constantly. Just as she'd anticipated, he was still the intelligent, affable, sensitive, caring man she'd known in college. It was very easy to fall in love with him. He made it easy. He sent flowers to her office, called in the middle of the day to say he was thinking about her, and constantly told her she was the most beautiful and desirable woman in the world until she believed it.

After a wonderful two weeks together, Jennifer decided it was time to tell Steven about David. "You should know that I was seeing someone just before I saw you in court, but it's over. He's been in Paris for the last several weeks. I haven't heard from him."

"Tell me about him."

"His name's David Walker. He's a lawyer. Does international trade. That's why he's in Paris."

"Is he black?"

"Yes."

"I'm glad he's in Paris. I hope he stays there."

❧   ❧   ❧

On the following evening, Steven invited Jennifer to his apartment for dinner. He lived in a modern co-op on the Upper West Side decorated in tones of gray, beige, and white. It was definitely a man's apartment, full of large, functional furnishings. His baby grand piano dominated the living room. On top was a photograph of his parents and siblings on the beach in Jamaica.

When Jennifer arrived, wonderful aromas permeated the apartment. Steven was smoking a chicken over tea leaves in a wok. Jennifer followed Steven into the minuscule kitchen. With two people in the kitchen, cooking became an intimate affair. Steven proudly showed off the chicken with its crispy, golden brown skin. He replaced the lid on the wok and in the close confines of the kitchen brushed against Jennifer's breast as he turned to reach into a cabinet for the sake. He stopped and placed his hand gently on her breast. She didn't move as he slowly unbuttoned her blouse, revealing dark chocolate brown nipples that became erect at his touch.

He took her hand and led her from the kitchen to his king-size bed, where they made love, both eagerly trying to recover those years of separation. At midnight, they got out of bed, ate the smoked chicken, drank sake, and watched the late movie, *Casablanca*, reciting lines from the movie along with the actors.

❦   ❦   ❦

In the morning, Jennifer was awakened by Steven's hand gently rubbing the inside of her thigh. She closed her eyes again so she could savor the sensations. Before she opened her eyes, she thought of David. She pushed his face out of her brain. "Mmm … what a wonderful way to wake up."

"Jennifer, I love you. I've never stopped. That's crazy, isn't it? You walked away and never looked back, and I kept on loving you."

"Steven, I loved you when we were in college, but …" Jennifer's voice trailed off.

"What's the but? Never mind. I know the answer to that. The but is I'm white. You're the racist. You're holding my color against me."

"I'm not racist. I'm just a realist," she murmured, trying to address his words while his hands explored her body.

"I love you. Doesn't that matter?"

"Of course it matters. That's the very reason we're together now. You make it very easy to love you. There's still a but. I didn't put the but there."

Chapter 62

David and Mark

David had been working nonstop ever since he arrived in Paris. He was at his client's office all day and most of the evening or grabbing a few hours of sleep at his hotel. He enjoyed his work. Most of all, he loved Paris, with its broad boulevards and crazy traffic patterns.

After finishing earlier than he'd expected, David decided to walk back to the hotel. The city appeared even more beautiful than usual. In the distance, he could see the Arc de Triomphe rising majestically above the Champs-Élysées. He decided to stop at a sidewalk café for dinner. As he strolled along, he thought about Jennifer and remembered that she also loved Paris.

David had often thought of Jennifer while in Paris and intentionally hadn't called her. He needed this time alone to assess his life and his future. He wondered what Jennifer's reaction had been to the Foster verdict. He had read about the verdict in the *New York Times* and saw the editorial. The verdict made him feel better about life for some reason. David ordered a glass of wine, sat back, and people watched. Parisian women were probably the best dressed in the world, in David's opinion. He pondered, as he sipped his wine, whether they were the best dressed or merely the sexiest. Whatever it was, he liked it a lot and wasn't ready to give it up.

As David sat under the brown-and-white-striped umbrella, he watched two women in very tight jeans and high-heeled shoes walk down the avenue. He was fascinated by the gentle yet erotic sway of their hips. Although he was concentrating on the provocative side-to-side movement of their hips, out of the corner of his eye he saw a tall, slender man approaching wearing a Burberry raincoat. "Mark!"

"David! What are you doing in Paris?"

"Business. What about you? I saw you on television a few weeks ago reporting from some place in South America."

Mark sat down at the table with David, motioned to the waiter, ordered an espresso, and said, "I came here to get an interview with an exiled Guatemalan revolutionary leader, but it's rumored he's planning to return and take control of the guerrilla forces." Mark sipped his espresso. "So far, I've been twiddling my thumbs for three days, waiting for my contact to set up the interview. The guy's a real clever character but paranoid. He's afraid that the CIA has infiltrated his organization. He probably believes I'm CIA, so I'm sure they're checking me out to make sure I'm not before they let me see him."

"Sounds fascinating and a little dangerous. What's his name?"

"No, it's not dangerous. No American has actually seen this guy in the last year since he went underground. As far as I know, the guy could be a figment of everyone's imagination, but I don't think so. My sources are good, and they say he's about to make a major move. So, I'm going to try to talk with him. His name is Jose Luis Mendez. Ever heard of him?"

"Of course. I even know him. He was at Yale with me. He was kind of an ex officio member of the black student organization. I wasn't surprised when he returned to Guatemala and got involved in the revolution. He was always talking revolution and liberation. I believe his father's a college professor who also went to Yale. But Jose liked to consider himself part of the oppressed masses. He liked to talk Marxism. Brilliant guy. Tell him I said hello if you catch up with him."

"I will. Have you seen Paige lately? I haven't spoken to her in a while. This is the first time I've been out of South America in a couple of months. Things are really hot down there."

"Yeah, I saw Paige just before I came to Paris. Do you know she's pregnant?"

Mark's nostrils flared as he bellowed, "Pregnant? Paige? You've got to be kidding."

David shook his head. "No. I'm not kidding. The baby's due very soon. Couple of months or so, maybe more. I'm not sure."

"When did she get married?" Mark slammed his fist on the table, causing David's wineglass to teeter. "Damn! I figured she'd at least tell me if she got married, after all ..."

"She's not married."

David could see Mark's eyes brighten as he said, "Oh. Who's the father? Is she getting married?"

"I don't know who the father is. Paige's not saying. Basically, Mark, Paige decided she wanted to have a child. So she did. She plans on raising the baby alone, without a father."

"I see. Sounds like Paige. I always admired her strong, independent spirit. She's a woman unfettered by the traditional female role, and I've always loved that in her, but she's also so assertively independent that it's hard to be close to her. I remember when we first met; I thought it was someone else that prevented me from getting close to her. By the time we got divorced, I finally realized that it was Paige."

Taking a deep breath and nodding in agreement, David said, "I know. Paige and I are good friends and have been for a long time, but I'm never quite sure which personality she's going to show me or how close she wants me to get."

"She's complicated, and I still love her."

"She knows that."

Mark silently calculated when Paige's baby was due and then asked, "How's Jennifer?"

David looked embarrassed. "Actually, I don't know. I haven't been in contact with her since I came to Paris."

"Why not?"

"Hey, you know. This relationship stuff is difficult. Complicated. I'm still figuring out who I am. What I want. Who I want. If I want anyone at this point in my life."

Rubbing his hands together, Mark agreed, "You're right. It's complicated."

✿   ✿   ✿

At midnight, Mark was picked up, searched for weapons, and then blindfolded and driven to meet with Mendez. The driver drove in a circuitous route for over an hour before reaching the exiled leader's headquarters in a working-class Parisian neighborhood. The men escorted Mark into the small stone house before the blindfold was removed. His eyes smarted from the light in the room. Jose Luis Mendez greeted him warmly and offered him a cup of coffee, which Mark gratefully accepted.

Mendez was short and dark with slick black hair, wearing a yellow Lacoste polo shirt, jeans, and Nike tennis shoes. He spoke with an American accent. But for the fact that he had an international reputation as a revolutionary, he looked and sounded like a Yale preppie.

Mendez said, "I'm sorry for the delay in our meeting, but we had to check you out. I didn't realize we had a mutual friend, David Walker."

Mark was not surprised by the reference to David. "Yes, I told him that I was hoping to meet with you. He asked me to send you his regards."

Mendez laughed menacingly. "I had almost decided not to meet with you, but when my people saw you drinking with David, I figured you had to be OK. David's a good man. I've always admired and respected him, even when we differed on tactics. He's more conservative than I am, but that's a function of his situation. The United States is not Guatemala. However, we share a deep-seated philosophy about the roles of our people in the world. They're both oppressed. I understand David. We were never buddies, but we are kindred spirits. We partied together. We both love beautiful women. Well, tell David I would love to see him again, but I wouldn't want to jeopardize my friend in any way by having your CIA see him with me; please tell him I wish him well. Maybe we'll party together again."

Mendez discarded his friendly conversational tone and assumed the voice of the intellectual and fierce revolutionary strategist. "Now, I want to send a message to the world. I intend to return to Guatemala and personally lead my people in this war we're forced to wage against our oppressors."

Mark asked, "How do you define your oppressors?"

"Our oppressors are those imperialists who have concentrated the wealth in a select few and kept my people as ignorant and starving peasants. Hopefully, my people will gain their freedom, unlike the blacks in the United States. I sincerely believe we will, because our fight is not burdened by the additional factor of race. It only has to do with money."

Mark and Mendez discussed his political and economic philosophies until just before dawn, when Mark was again blindfolded and returned to his hotel by a different circuitous route.

That afternoon, Mark reached David at his client's office. "I'm flying to Mexico City today, but I wanted to say thanks."

"Thanks for what?"

"Two things. One, apparently Mendez had me followed and only decided on the interview when he saw me with you. He figured I had to be OK if you were a friend of mine. He sends his regards."

"Glad I could help. What's the second thing?"
"Thanks for telling me about Paige."

Chapter 63

Paige

Instead of flying directly to Mexico City from Paris, Mark flew to New York and went to see Paige at her office. Mrs. Callahan greeted him with surprise. "Mark, I didn't know you were in New York."

"Just got in today. Is Paige in?"

"Yes, she is."

"Don't buzz her. I know my way in."

The two exchanged a conspiratorial look when Mrs. Callahan said, "You know that Paige doesn't like unannounced interruptions."

"I know." He confidently walked passed Mrs. Callahan into Paige's office. She was sitting behind her rosewood desk going over some copy.

She looked up angrily.

"How are you?"

Without getting up, she said, "I'm fine."

"I know you're pregnant."

Paige laughed and got up. "I wasn't trying to hide. In my condition, it's not possible."

"Motherhood becomes you."

"So far, pregnancy seems to agree with me. No morning sickness or anything."

"Who's the lucky man?"

Looking confused, Paige asked, "What do you mean?"

Rolling his eyes, Mark said, "Who's the father? That's what I mean."

"Oh, that? Uh, no one you know."

"Are you going to marry him?"

"I don't know."

"What about the baby?"

Paige looked perplexed. "What about the baby?"

"Doesn't the child need a father?"

"Not necessarily. No relationship is probably better than a bad relationship. Look at me and my father."

Leaning over the desk, Mark countered, "The relationship doesn't have to be bad. It could be great. Look at me and my father."

She adored Mark's dad, and it brought a warm smile to her face. "Yeah, I've always liked your dad."

"He likes you. It's almost dinnertime, and I know pregnant women must eat nutritious meals. Can we have dinner together?"

They went to their favorite restaurant. Since getting pregnant, Paige had stopped drinking, so she ordered a glass of skim milk over ice as Mark drank a vodka martini before dinner.

After dinner, they went back to Paige's new apartment. She had moved to a larger apartment overlooking Central Park so that there would be room for the baby and the live-in nanny.

She showed Mark the nursery, decorated in strong colors of red, white, and black, which she'd read were much better for a baby's development than traditional sexist pink or blue. "The crib hasn't arrived yet, but it's going right there where you're standing."

Mark had been holding back all evening. "Paige, is this my baby?"

Shaking her head, she replied, "No."

"Don't lie to me. I love you, and you have always loved me. We had a tough time living together, but it was not because we didn't love each other. It was because each of us is too damn independent. At the time, we each had too much to do, and we were going in different directions. You and I, we need a lot of space, and we never seemed to work that out between us, but we could. Please, tell me if the baby is mine. I know you. I'm sure this baby is mine. I want to share this child with you. Most of all, I want us to share our lives. In a sense, we have since the moment we met. For a short time, we called it a marriage and had papers to prove it, but even after the divorce, what have we done but come in and out of each other's lives?"

"No, Mark. I'm sorry; this is not your child. It's mine."

"Look, I'm leaving for Mexico City in the morning. I'll be there for a little while and then probably Guatemala. Things are going to heat up when Mendez returns, and I have to cover that. But consider my offer."

Paige said, "Stay safe."

Chapter 64

Mark

Mendez and his forces secretly entered Guatemala, and Mendez assumed leadership of the guerrilla army. The peasants and freedom fighters welcomed his return as their conquering hero. In only a few days, the tide was turning in the war. He decided to grant an interview. Mendez sent word to Mark, giving him an exclusive.

This time, meeting with Mendez was dangerous. Mark and his camera crew secured a jeep on the black market and started their trip into the countryside, where he met Mendez. Mendez was dressed in battle fatigues with several days' growth of beard on his angular face; he appeared tired but exhilarated by his recent victories, which kept him going despite the primitive conditions.

"These surroundings are not quite as comfortable as Paris."

Mark, exhausted by the long trip, laughed and said, "I preferred the Paris trip. By the way, David sends his regards."

Mendez said, "Tell David I wish him happiness. Sit. We may not have much time. I want the world to see me and understand that we intend to build farm cooperatives and schools using the Israeli kibbutz as a model. We're going to make education free and mandatory for children until they reach the age of sixteen, and we're going to embark on a program to teach adults to read. Now, friends of the General control most industries. We'll reorganize these companies and reinvest the profits in the companies and the workers rather than siphoning off the profits to indulge their jet-set taste."

The interview with Mendez was cut short. "Government forces are headed in this direction. I have to abandon the camp and move further into the hills. You can't go with us. Too dangerous. Tell my story to America."

Chapter 65

Jennifer and Leslie

The negotiations for the land for a new shopping mall in Los Angeles were extremely complex, resulting in Jennifer staying in L.A. several days longer than she had originally planned. As she dressed for her meeting, she thought that only in California did one have business meetings outside by the pool rather than in stuffy, smoked-filled conference rooms.

Leslie and Jason were also in L.A. for a few days while Jason filmed a commercial for a men's cologne.

Leslie telephoned Jennifer. "There's a party in Malibu. This guy who made a fortune producing daytime game shows is giving it. His shows were dreadful. For morons only. But he gives great parties. Come."

"I'll meet you guys there, OK?"

Having heard stories from Leslie about the Hollywood crowd, she thought she may need her own escape vehicle. She loved driving too fast on endless superhighways. Driving fast was a bad habit she picked up from Bobby. She turned on the radio, and Aretha was singing "Natural Woman." She sang along and thought of Steven, who'd found her when she was feeling rejected and unloved and made her feel beautiful and adored again.

Jennifer parked along the ocean road and then walked down the hill to the house. It was all steel and glass with the Pacific Ocean for a front yard. Before she spotted Leslie, she wove her way through a throng of white people with too much suntanned, exposed skin for her taste; the clearly identifiable aroma of marijuana hung in the air despite the ocean breeze.

Leslie yelled out, "Jennifer, over here!" Leslie's blond hair was pulled back in a sleek ponytail, and she was wearing skintight white jeans and a low-cut white halter top.

Jennifer said, "You look very California."

"Thanks. Wait a minute? Was that a compliment? You know how you New Yorkers are."

"It was a compliment. You look beautiful as always. Where's Jason?"

"Who knows? Let's get you a drink."

A sixtyish man with a silk shirt opened to his navel, with several gold chains hanging amid the profusion of gray hairs on his sagging chest, said, "Leslie, doll, let me get your friend a drink."

Leslie said, "Howard, meet my friend, Jennifer Madison. Jennifer's a lawyer."

Howard grinned. "And a very beautiful lawyer, I must say." Howard took Jennifer by the arm and maneuvered her away from Leslie and over to the bar. "What's your pleasure?"

Jennifer said, "Gin and tonic with a twist of lime sounds good."

As Jennifer sipped her drink, Howard babbled about the TV business. Within minutes, he said, "Why don't you and I go sit in the hot tub? I'll rub your back."

"No back rubs today. Oh, there's Jason. Excuse me."

Howard said, "Oh, you belong to the quarterback."

"Excuse me? Jason is an old friend of mine."

Howard laughed sarcastically. "Honey, believe me, Jason has a lot of old friends, if that's what they're calling it these days."

Jennifer handed her unfinished drink to Howard and walked away. "Jason, how are you?"

Jason got up from the foot of the chaise, on which lay a gorgeous brunette in a very tiny bikini. He pecked Jennifer on the cheek. "Glad you could make it."

"Me, too." Looking around, she added, "Wild party."

Jason displayed his now famous devilish cover-boy grin. "Life's wild."

Jennifer stared at Jason, who was obviously drunk or high or both. The gorgeous brunette on the chaise turned over and purred, "Jason, put some oil on my back."

Jennifer blanched at the bikini's request. "Jason, good to see you as always. I'm going to go." Taking a circuitous route to avoid Howard as she made her way to the door, Jennifer spotted Leslie passing a joint to an older woman with waist-length gray hair. "Leslie, think I'll go."

Leslie pouted, "Don't go. We haven't talked."

Jennifer surveyed the sun-drenched drunken mob scene and said, "This isn't exactly the best place to talk. And Howard wants me to get in the hot tub with him."

Leslie followed Jennifer's gaze. "You're right. You do *not* want to get in the hot tub with Howard. Let's have lunch tomorrow and do some shopping. OK?"

"OK. I'd like that. See you tomorrow."

❦   ❦   ❦

The following day, Jennifer and Leslie had lunch at a Rodeo Drive restaurant. "The spinach salad with toasted sliced almonds, mandarin oranges, and balsamic vinaigrette dressing is divine here," Leslie said.

"Sounds good. I'll have it."

As Leslie picked at her salad, she said, "Sorry about the party."

"Why are you sorry about the party?"

"You know that group isn't really me. All of those lecherous people. The drugs. The tasteless nakedness. Within half an hour of your leaving, Howard convinced some little starlet, still in her teens, to get into the hot tub with him, and the girl took off all of her clothes."

As Jennifer listened, she perused the dessert menu. "Really? But for Howard, I think I might have stayed longer. I knew that hot tub was not going to be a good idea. Shall we have dessert? The cream cheese swirled brownie sundae with vanilla bean ice cream topped with Kahlua whipped cream sounds like just our thing."

"Jennifer, come on. We're recovering chocoholics, remember?"

Jennifer persisted. "But it sounds wonderful. We could share it."

Leslie shook her head. "No, we're being good."

"You're right. I need to show some self-control. That's how you stay so thin and gorgeous. Let's get out of here before I convince you to reconsider."

Laughing, Leslie said, "We've shared many brownies over the years. Let's go."

Their first stop was the Gucci store and then Valentino's. Jennifer followed Leslie into the Yves Saint Laurent shop. "Jen, look at this skirt. This would look great on you."

The two continued to look at the racks of clothing. Jennifer saw the same skirt in purple. "Leslie, look at this. I like it in this color."

"That is a good color for you. Try it on."

Jennifer took the skirt from the rack and proceeded to the counter. Leslie, empty-handed, followed her to the counter. The salesclerk looked up and saw Jennifer holding the skirt and Leslie standing by her side. The clerk turned to Leslie and asked, "May I help you?"

Jennifer responded. "No, you may help *me*!" She thrust the skirt at the salesclerk. "I'd like to try this on."

The salesclerk took the skirt and said, "Please follow me."

Jennifer came out of the dressing room and twirled in front of Leslie. "What do you think?"

"I like it."

Jennifer returned to the dressing room, changed, and then approached the same salesclerk. "I'll take it." The clerk smiled and said, "Lovely choice." Jennifer did not return the smile, handed the clerk her credit card, and turned to chat with Leslie as the clerk completed the sale.

"Did I tell you that Steven had flowers waiting for me when I checked into the hotel?"

"Ah. That is so sweet. He's a really nice guy."

They walked out onto Rodeo Drive. Jennifer said, "We've gotten too close, too fast."

"Too fast? You've known him since college."

"Yes, but we've only been seeing each other a very short time, this time around. I'm on the rebound, and I know it. I care for him, but I think I've let this relationship happen because I was running away from David breaking my heart."

Leslie stopped walking and gathered her thoughts, as the sunshine beamed down on her and highlighted her hair. "Sometimes you have to run away from the bad, and it's really great if you have someplace good to run."

Placing her sunglasses on the top of her head, Jennifer listened carefully to Leslie and said, "You're absolutely right. Friends often tell you what you refuse to tell yourself but need to know."

When Jennifer returned from L.A., she met Steven for lunch. He was seated when she arrived and stood as she crossed the restaurant to join him. He looked handsome in a navy blue double-breasted blazer, gray trousers, and a sky-blue shirt that made his eyes look even bluer.

"You look beautiful." Steven kissed her gently on the lips and then pulled out her chair. He reached across the table and took both of her hands in his. "I missed you while you were away."

The waiter came over to take their orders. Jennifer glanced at the menu and ordered scallops. Steven let go of her hands momentarily so he could concentrate on the menu and ordered the stuffed trout; then, he started playing with Jennifer's fingers.

Enjoying the touch of his hand, she asked, "How did your trial go?"

"I won," Steven responded triumphantly.

Jennifer laughed. "This time I'm glad you won." She placed her fingers to Steven's lips, and he kissed them gently. She said, "Steven, I missed you. I really did."

🍁   🍁   🍁

David was having lunch with some lawyers from his office when Jennifer walked into the restaurant. When he saw her standing in the doorway, he rose to get her attention, but then she walked in the opposite direction from him. He saw the kiss. He sat back down and tried to finish his lunch, but he couldn't. He just sat there, trying to participate in the conversation on recent legislation restricting certain imports from Malaysia. He couldn't concentrate. He couldn't stop watching her or him. Conflicting emotions welled up inside of him, causing him to feel as if he were choking. He couldn't swallow. He pushed the scallops away and drank some water.

Chapter 66

Paige

Throughout her pregnancy, Paige looked elegant and professional; she made pregnancy look chic and sexy. She went into labor in the middle of her weekly story idea conference. That evening, she delivered a seven-pound five-ounce boy, with her mother as her coach during the delivery. The two women experienced that special bond that only a new life can create. The next day, David came to see her in the hospital. Although still exhausted from several hours of labor, Paige looked radiant propped up in bed wearing a teal blue silk dressing gown. Her lustrous dark brown hair was casually pinned on top of her head, with thin tendrils dangling over her face. The whole room smelled of Chanel No. 5. A huge bouquet of her favorite white orchids had been placed in a Lalique crystal vase beside her bed.

"David, did you see him? He's gorgeous."

"I saw him. He's handsome. You look great." He kissed her on the cheek.

"Thanks. I'm tired, but I'm so excited that I don't care."

"What did you name him?"

Paige smiled demurely. "I thought for months about a name, and nothing ever seemed right. The names didn't suit him or me, but as soon as I saw him, I knew what his name had to be. I named him Wyatt Elliott."

David automatically responded politely, "Nice name." A moment later, he asked with a sly look in his eye, "Are you telling me something?"

Paige grinned sheepishly. "Yes, and I'm telling myself something too, and if it's not too late, I'm telling Mark something. The baby's Mark's."

David nodded his head thoughtfully. "I thought so. I'm happy for you, Paige. You and Mark belong together."

"So do you and Jennifer. Hopefully, you won't be as stupid as I've been and take too long to figure that out." She adjusted herself in the bed and added, "Jennifer's dating someone. A guy she dated in college. Really nice guy. It looks serious. You better do something before it's too late."

"What does he look like?"

"Tall, dark brown hair. Mustache. The weird thing is that he was the prosecutor in the Foster trial. That's how they got reacquainted."

David flashed back to his last telephone conversation with Jennifer. It had been the first day of the trial. "Maybe I've already taken too long. You know how it is. Timing's important in relationships. Hey, can I do anything for you? Get you something?"

"As a matter of fact, you can. I tried to call Mark in Mexico City, and I can't seem to reach him. I want to tell him about our son, so I wrote this very long letter. Mr. International Lawyer, will you mail it for me, airmail, special delivery, something? I want him to know about our son as soon as possible."

David took the letter. "Glad to."

As David got off the elevator and headed through the hospital lobby, Jennifer was at the reception desk getting a visitor's pass. As she pinned the pass on her jacket, she saw him. Her heart started to race. She called out, "David."

At the sound of her voice saying his name, he turned in the direction of the sound and saw her as she approached him. He stopped walking, stood perfectly still, and enjoyed looking at her. He took one step toward her and embraced her.

Having imagined this encounter on numerous occasions, she couldn't believe that it was occurring in the starkness of a hospital lobby. "I assume you saw Paige."

He unconsciously patted his coat pocket to be sure the letter was still there. "Yeah."

"Did you see the baby?"

"Yeah. Fat."

Refusing to let this already awkward encounter dwindle into a polite discussion of the weather, she said, "Well, I can't wait to see him." She started to walk away.

"Jennifer, wait. We need to talk."

"Excuse me?"

"About us. We need to talk about us."

Her heart slowed down, and she asked, "What about us?"

"I'm sorry for not contacting you while I was in Paris. I needed to get away." He paused.

She didn't fill the pause; instead, she merely stared at him, adjusted the strap on her shoulder bag, and thought that he was her fantasy BMIS.

"We were getting so close, so fast. I just needed time to think about us. I knew I wasn't ready for a relationship, but there you were. We were having a good time. I needed some time to think and sort things out." He stuffed his hand in his pockets. "I'm rambling here. I don't know what to say."

"I understand." She looked around the bustling hospital lobby and saw an elderly man slowly pushing an elderly woman, probably his wife, in a wheelchair. She saw two women in their thirties hugging each other and crying as a man in a blue plaid shirt raced to the elevator. "You clearly didn't anticipate running into me here."

Scanning the lobby, he said, "You're right. No, I didn't. Let's go someplace where we can talk."

She considered his offer, remembering the various romantic scenarios she had envisioned for this encounter. None of them took place in a hospital lobby. "David, I'm here to see Paige, and then I have plans for the evening. I don't have time to go someplace to talk with you. Whatever you have to say to me, please say it right here." She paused, but he didn't respond. Nor, did he reach out to touch her. The long, soulful embrace that had been a part of her fantasy did not occur. She continued, abandoning her soft manner and turning more confrontational. "If you really wanted to talk with me, you would have called, and I would have met you someplace more conducive to conversation. It's obvious to me that you don't want to have this conversation. But for me accidentally running into you and calling out your name, this conversation would never have happened. You walked away and never looked back. That conduct speaks for itself. So, if you have anything to say, say what you have to say right here."

Knowing she was right, he started, "The Paris trip was a really great assignment for me professionally, and I intentionally used it to test myself to see just how much I would miss you. I wanted to see if I was ready for a relationship with you. I called you as soon as I returned, but you were out of town."

"And? Did you leave a message?"

"No message. I needed to *talk* with you. Leaving a message didn't seem right. Several days later I was having lunch, and I saw you come into the restaurant. I saw this guy kiss you. I knew from that kiss that I'd blown it with you, that you'd moved on. I'd waited too long."

Cocking her head to the side, Jennifer asked, "Waited too long for what?"

Bowing his head, he said, "I've been stupid. I shouldn't have walked away like I did."

"David, you did what you felt was right for *you*—not *us*, but *you*."

"I was wrong. We should be together. We have so much in common. Remember, I said it when we first met: we're from the same place and time. That's why it felt as if we had always known each other. We are mirror images."

"David, we may have many things in common, but that's not enough to make a relationship work. Those common experiences merely gave us an opportunity to have a relationship. The rest was up to us. But obviously we don't want the same things."

"Jennifer, I'm still trying to figure stuff out."

"David, if you had been honest with me and said that *before* you went to Paris, I might have given us time to work it out. But you ran away."

Looking down at his feet, shaking his head, he said, "You're right. I ran away. I'm sorry. You deserved better than that."

"That's right. I do." Jennifer headed for the elevator and didn't look back, because she realized that he never once said he loved her. Never even touched her. She stopped at the nursery and then entered Paige's room. "Paige, I saw him. So cute. What did you name him?"

"Wyatt Elliott."

With a knowing smile, Jennifer said, "That's wonderful."

Paige, laughing, said, "Yes, that's right. Mark's the father."

Leaning forward to embrace Paige, she said, "I'm really happy for you and Mark."

"Mark doesn't know about the baby yet. In fact, David was just here. I wrote a letter to Mark telling him about our son, and David's going to send it for me."

When Jennifer heard David's name, the smile on her face disappeared.

"If you'd come a few minutes earlier, you would have seen him."

"I ran into David downstairs."

"Great! You and David belong together. I told David that, and now I'm telling you: don't make the same mistake I made and take too long to figure that out."

"Thanks for the advice."

The nurse entered the room, cutting off this conversation. "This little man is ready to be fed."

❦   ❦   ❦

Paige and little Wyatt had been home from the hospital for a week without any word from Mark. Paige sat in the antique rocker in Wyatt's room and rocked him to sleep. She thought of the night that Mark had stood in the nursery on the exact spot of Wyatt's crib. She couldn't wait for him to see the baby, who had her gray eyes and a dimple in his chin like Mark's.

The doorbell rang. Paige called out and asked her nanny to answer the door. Mabel Johnson, who was now one of Paige's favorite people, had recommended the nanny, and it had been an immediate match.

The nanny walked into the nursery, where Paige was standing over Wyatt's crib, watching him sleep. "There's someone here to see you."

"Who is it?"

"Mr. Elliott."

Paige ran down the hall into the living room. He was looking out of the French doors that opened onto the terrace.

"Mark!"

He turned around. "Paige, it's good to see you."

Paige squealed with delight.

"Richard, what a wonderful surprise. Mark must have told you about the baby. Come see your grandson."

Richard Elliott was a slightly heavier version of his son. Theirs was a special father-son relationship. He never forgot his role as father; at the same time, he was Mark's best friend.

Paige admired the connection between Mark and his father. Mark's father, just like his son, had been immediately charmed by Paige, and they developed a special relationship of their own.

Richard kissed Paige very gently on the cheek and hugged her. "Paige, Mark told me about the baby, and I can't wait to see him."

"Come on. You must see him right now. He's sleeping, but you can at least take a peek at him."

"In a minute. Before I see my grandson, I have to tell you something." Being a doctor, Richard Elliott had been in this position many times before. It was never easy. There was no right or best way to do it. "Paige, Mark is missing and presumed dead."

Paige heard the words, refusing to comprehend them; she stared blankly at Richard. She needed time for the news to sink in. Finally, the tears silently streamed down her face. "No, no. This can't happen."

Richard sat down beside her. "The network contacted me. Apparently, Mark went into the hills of Guatemala to interview Mendez. On the way back, he and his camera crew were caught in a battle. It's believed government soldiers captured them, but we don't know yet. In his hotel, there was a letter from you. The network shipped everything to me."

"Oh my God."

"Paige, Mark never got your letter, so he never knew about his son. After he came to see you, he called me and told me that you were pregnant and that he truly believed that you were carrying his child, although you denied it. He also told me that it didn't matter to him whether it was his child or not, that it was enough for him that the child was yours, and that, if you let him, he would love that child as his own because he loved you."

"Did he say that even after I told him it wasn't his?"

"Yes, he did. Now, let me see my grandson. The three of us are family. I hope you will let me share this child with you."

"Of course!"

Chapter 67

Jennifer, Leslie, and Paige

Within six weeks of giving birth to Wyatt, Paige was back at *Superwoman*. In fact, she never for a moment relinquished control, although she remained at home so she could breast-feed Wyatt. Paige loved to kiss the little dimple in his chin. Each time she did, she would whisper, "That's just like your daddy's."

Leslie telephoned to announce that she was coming to New York. "I got the picture you sent. He's adorable. I can't wait to see him."

"I'm dying for you to see him, too. He's wonderful. Hey, I'll call Jennifer. The three of us can have dinner at my apartment, and you can see Wyatt."

❧   ❧   ❧

Wyatt allowed himself to be held by the three women—first, Leslie, then Jennifer, then Mommy, and then back to Leslie.

Jennifer demanded, "Give him to me, Leslie. You've held him long enough."

"No, I haven't. You've had a head start on me since you've held him before. This is the first time I've seen this handsome devil," Leslie protested.

Paige laughed. "I love it. My son's going to be a lady-killer. Already women are fighting over him."

Finally, after much cooing and cuddling, the nanny put Wyatt to bed. Over dinner, Leslie said, "Paige, he's a beautiful baby. I have to admit, I never thought you'd be the first one of us to have a baby."

Paige responded with the smile that rarely left her face now. "I need Wyatt. Unfortunately, I didn't realize that what I really wanted was Mark. And now it may be too late."

Jennifer added, "But you have Wyatt."

Paige spoke softly, "And I have not given up hope that Mark will be found alive."

Leslie said, "Of course he will be. He has to be. None of us are giving up hope." Leslie attempted to lighten the mood. "I know you all thought Leslie Cohen Abrams from Scarsdale would be the first mother of the three of us."

"You've got all the makings, kid," Jennifer responded.

Leslie sighed, "Not all. I don't have a nice Jewish husband." She paused, stared at the faces of her two friends, and confessed, "I left Jason."

Instead of questions, there was silence. Jennifer and Paige stared at her, neither really surprised, and their eyes encouraged her to say whatever she wanted and needed to say.

Leslie continued, "I knew it from the very beginning. I was not cut out to be the wife of a professional jock. Jason's the only jock I ever dated. Don't you remember I always hated jocks? Remember that jerk football player from Hopkins who was always following me around?"

"I remember," Jennifer said quietly.

"Anyway, I couldn't maintain the lifestyle. I wanted Jason to be a nice Jewish husband. I should have married Joel. My mother always wanted me to marry a doctor. Jason just happened to be Jewish and from Scarsdale, but he was always a star. I've finally realized that although he had, on the surface, all those qualities nice little Jewish girls like me dream about, he was part of a different world. We wanted different things. I even got caught up in it."

Although Leslie was trying desperately to lighten the moment, it was clear that this was a painful and difficult decision for her. "Jason was screwing around. I started having affairs of my own—first with Danny, who's wonderful to me. I truly cherish him. I'm not sure if I want to marry him, though. He wants to marry me. Maybe I don't want to be married at all." She dabbed her eyes. "I only said that because I'm feeling a little bitter. Then I started just screwing around. Jason and I were playing little mind games with each other. He knew I was screwing around, and I knew he was, but we pretended that we didn't. Stupid. Jennifer, you remember that party in Malibu we dragged you to when you were in L.A.?"

"I remember."

"You were smart to leave early. I was just pretending to like those people. The drugs. The sex. It's not me. I always knew it. But I tried in order to hold on to Jason. Then it hit me. What was I holding on to? A husband who was more a figment of my imagination than anything else. It was a sham. I don't need it anymore."

Jennifer clasped Leslie's hand. "You've got to do what's good for you. I'm glad you've made a decision about this. I know it's hard. You deserve to be happy, and if being married to Jason is not making you happy, you shouldn't be there."

"Leslie, I also know it's hard," Paige added. "Relationships are very difficult. You've got to find someone who complements you and supports you. I'm not talking money. I'm talking about making room for the other person in your life and being their biggest cheerleader."

Screaming and laughing, Leslie said, "Please don't talk to me about cheerleaders. Those girls have wrecked too many marriages."

"OK, no cheerleaders." Paige paused as she thought of another way to express her thoughts. "The bottom line is about a shared lifestyle. If you want to be a married lady with a five-bedroom house in Scarsdale and two perfect children and a husband who only sleeps with you, that's what you should have. I don't mean that disparagingly. Don't get caught up in today's free love and free sex. If it's not for you, don't buy into it."

Leslie smiled. "It's not me. I'm a Scarsdale Princess and proud of it."

"You should be, because you're a wonderful person," Jennifer added. "What we all want in a relationship, just like Paige said, is someone who complements us, who wants what we want, who wants to help us get what we want, who respects us, who makes living easier, not harder."

Leslie asked, "Does Steven do that for you?"

Jennifer sat back in her chair before speaking. "He does in so many ways. He's so kind to me, loving, gentle, caring. When we're alone, just the two of us, it feels right. But it's not just the two of us. We don't live in the world alone."

Leslie interjected, "His family likes you. Your parents like him, don't they?"

"Yes, they like him," Jennifer admitted. "My father really respects him. My mother? Well, he's not her fantasy, but she likes the way he makes me feel."

"What's the problem?" Leslie asked.

Before Jennifer could answer, Paige said, "David. David's the problem. Admit it. You still love David, don't you?"

Jennifer said, "There's no question that, at one time, I was in love with David, but he made it impossible. Besides, it doesn't do you any good to love someone who doesn't love you back, does it? I can't love someone who doesn't love me back."

"Jennifer, he does love you," Paige said.

Jennifer asked, "Did he tell you that?"

Paige admitted reluctantly, "No, he didn't tell me that." She quickly added, "But that's because David wouldn't tell me something like that. He's a very private person, and though I consider him a friend, I know he doesn't really confide in me. However, I know enough about him to know that he loves you. He wants to love you. He should love you. You two are perfect for each other. Jennifer, don't be like me and discover too late what's really right for you."

"Paige, remember. I ran into David at the hospital when you had Wyatt. He had a chance to tell me that he loved me, but he still couldn't get it out. He said he still had stuff to figure out. He walked away because he wasn't sure what he felt for me. And he's not sure now. Steven walked in at the right moment and made me feel loved and valued. That's what I want." Jennifer turned to Leslie. "Do you remember when you were dating Joel in college?" Leslie nodded. "You said he had great credentials. He had the right résumé. You thought you *should* love him, but you didn't. David's résumé was perfect for me. I should love him, and he should love me. But a relationship is about more than the right résumé. Both people have got to want it."

Wyatt started to cry, so Paige got up from the dining room table and went into the nursery to breast-feed him. Leslie and Jennifer followed and watched incredulously as Wyatt sucked vigorously on Paige's breast. Paige seemed at peace. Wyatt fell back to sleep while Paige held him. When she placed him in the crib, his little mouth continued to make a sucking motion although his eyes were tightly shut and he was asleep. Jennifer and Leslie watched in awe.

Paige walked Leslie and Jennifer to the foyer as they prepared to leave.

"Well, this has been some evening. I'm glad I had a chance to talk to you two," Leslie said. "You know, I haven't had my anxiety dream, the one where I'm standing naked in a public place waiting for someone to see me and frantically trying to hide. That one. I haven't had it since I made the decision to divorce Jason. That's a good sign."

Jennifer smiled. "That is a good sign."

"Leslie, you'll be fine," Paige said. "You've never been just a pretty face, although I admit I thought that when we first met." All three of them laughed, remembering when they first met as college students. "I've learned over the years that you're also a strong and good person."

Leslie said, "Well, thanks. See, when you get to know people, you learn they may not be what they appear to be. I'm off with Mabel. We start her two-week, eight-city tour tomorrow: speeches, workshops on Social Security and fringe benefits, and some TV appearances. It's going to be hectic, but Mabel's ready. She's raring to go, and traveling with Mabel for the next two weeks will help keep my mind off of Jason. I still love him. Don't like him much. And I know I can't spend the rest of my life with him."

"Mabel will keep you busy. The woman seems to have boundless energy," Jennifer said.

"Mabel's a great lady," Paige said. "And so are we."

The telephone rang as Paige started to walk her two friends to the door. "Hold on. Let me get that." Jennifer and Leslie continued to chat as Paige grabbed the phone in her office. "Hello?"

The line was full of static. Paige could barely hear the voice on the line. She repeated her hello several times and finally said, "Who is it?"

Through the static, she heard, "Paige, it's Mark!"

Paige started to scream, "Mark! Mark!" Leslie and Jennifer, hearing her screams, ran into the office.

Mark continued, although the static made his voice difficult to comprehend. "Paige, I'm OK. I'm still in Guatemala. I love you, and I can't wait to see our son!"

Paige slumped into the chair behind her desk. "Mark, come home. Marry me!"

The telephone line finally cleared. Mark said, "Say that again."

Paige, with Leslie and Jennifer as witnesses, repeated her earlier words, this time slowly and solemnly. "Mark. I love you. Will you marry me?"

Although exhausted, Mark felt completely at peace. "I can't wait to marry you, again!"

Chapter 68

Jennifer

Steven dialed Jennifer's office. "Can you meet me for a quick lunch?"

"Of course. Love to."

Steven and Jennifer arrived at Gold's Deli at the same time. Together, they approached the hostess stand; an elderly white woman with mixed-gray hair sprayed into a stiff 1950s-style bouffant returned to the station. She looked at Steven and Jennifer and then spoke directly to Steven. "Table for one?"

Steven looked momentarily confused, as Jennifer was standing beside him. "No! Table for two."

The hostess replied, "You're meeting someone?"

He put his hand on Jennifer's back. "No, we're together."

The hostess looked at Jennifer, said nothing, and then proceeded to lead the way to a table by the door to the kitchen. "Here you go."

Steven said, "We'd rather have that table by the window."

The elderly hostess snatched up the menus from the table and led the way to the table by the window.

Jennifer placed the menu to the side, because she already knew what she wanted to eat. She inquired, "What did you want to talk about that couldn't wait until this evening?"

Steven looked at his menu, intently trying to buy time to curb his anger. "I don't know what I want to eat. Uh, maybe I'll have a Reuben." He got the waitress's attention.

The waitress inquired, "What'll you have?" looking right at Steven.

Steven turned to Jennifer. "What would you like?"

"I'll have the number four on rye bread with a Coke."

"Pepsi, OK?" the waitress asked.

"Fine."

Steven ordered. "I'll have a Reuben and a draft."

As soon as the waitress walked away, Jennifer asked Steven, "Well, what is it? Is something wrong? You look uptight."

"I'm not going with you to the reception for Bill Foster tonight. I don't deserve to be there. I don't want to ruin it for you or Bill."

Jennifer smiled tenderly into those blue eyes, which always mesmerized her. "That's just like you. Always thinking of others. That's very kind of you, but don't feel that way. Bill doesn't hold a grudge against you. He completely understands your role in the prosecution."

Steven looked uncertain. "That may be. I'd certainly like to believe that." He paused and grasped Jennifer's hand. "Most of all, I believe that you understand my role and have forgiven me."

Jennifer cut him off. "You're right; I did have to forgive you. But I got past that, because I understand that you were part of a larger system not of your making. Steven, I know that if you'd been the DA, you wouldn't have brought those specious charges based on the allegations of such a disreputable character. The guy was a Harlem numbers runner! You would have shown some deference to Bill's sterling reputation. You would have viewed him as a man of proven integrity and would have factored that into the equation. You would have given Bill the benefit of the doubt regardless of the fact that he's black. You would have insisted upon an investigation that would have uncovered the frame-up and never prosecuted!"

In her heart, Jennifer believed what she had just said to Steven. However, her heart ached because she believed white men like Steven were rare. Too many would have assumed the worst about Bill just because he's black, just like the DA did. Others would have been happy to think he was guilty.

Steven slid his hand from under Jennifer's gentle touch and squeezed her hand. "Thanks for believing in me. But I'd rather not go. My presence would bring back the specter of the trial, and I would hate that to ruin this big night for Bill."

"That's sweet of you. Overcoming adversity is what Bill is all about. He's done it all of his life. Being born a black man in America, he had no other choice but to gain strength from challenges, because that's mostly what he was offered. He always knew that he was going to have to fight and scratch his way to the top. He always knew he had to be better than everybody else in order to do as well. We all know that. He made his success. It was never given to him.

The beauty of the man is that he always kept his eye on his goal, worked hard, and didn't give up."

Glancing around the deli and then back at Jennifer before speaking, he said, "I know you understand him. I know you have also felt some of the same burdens that Foster has had to face."

Seeing the sad look on Steven's face, she asked, "What are you thinking?"

Steven rubbed his thick mustache. "I'm thinking about how my white skin insulates me from the pressures you and Bill face daily and separates me from you. As you said, if Foster hadn't been married, you would have been in love with him. He has all the characteristics you want: strength, intelligence, shared race, shared struggle."

Embarrassed at hearing those words coming from Steven, she said, "Gee, I forgot that I told you that I could have been in love with Bill."

"You said it the first night I came to your apartment."

"Steven, you don't let your white skin separate you from me. I love that about you."

"I know that, and for me it never has separated us. But I can't forget that just because I'm white, you ran away from me in college."

In frustration, Jennifer threw her head back and stared at the ceiling before responding. "Remember, I was a twenty-year-old cocky college student who ran scared. I wasn't ready to truly confront hard issues. I didn't really understand why I acted the way I did back then. It was an impulsive action. All I felt was that being involved with you was too hard for me then. I didn't like being looked at all the time when we were together."

Steven shook his head slowly and stroked his mustache. "Tonight is another example of how being with me is too hard, isn't it?"

"No, it is not! Now let's eat. I've got to get back to the office. I really want you to come with me tonight."

"No, you don't. Part of you wants me to come, and another part of you doesn't. Part of you is embarrassed that I was on the Foster prosecution team." Steven took a long sip of his beer and then wiped the foam off his mustache. "Couples have all kinds of issues that stymie relationships. I now understand what you told me on the telephone that night you broke up with me when we were in college. You talked about weddings."

Laughing, Jennifer said, "Weddings! That was presumptuous of me!"

"You said there usually was a part in the ceremony when the minister, priest, or rabbi turns to the guests and asks them to support the newlyweds in building their married lives together. Usually, the crowd smiles and murmurs their support, all of the people promising to support the marriage. But for us, you said that wouldn't happen. You're right. There's a whole world out there that questions our being together. Just now, that old lady didn't think we were together, even though we were standing side by side. She even tried to give us a bad table to punish us. How often have we seen people staring at us! Even you admit that when you see an interracial couple, you take a quick furtive glance. Even you!"

"Steven, this time you're making too much out of a little incident. I saw the old lady, but I can't react to every look, every slight. I'd be forever angry if I did. Instead, I focus on you, how good you are, how much you care about me. So people look. Big deal. We have each other."

"Jennifer, we don't live in this world alone. You said that back in college, too. You said I was naive if I thought we could live alone. I'd be happy living with you in a little box, but that's not fair to you."

"I was wrong." Jennifer took Steven's hand. "I've grown up since then. What we have *is* special. Please come with me tonight. I *have* to go to the reception. I want to go, and I want you to go with me."

"I know you have to go, and I want you to be there and really savor the moment and not have it tarnished by my presence. I'll meet you after the reception."

"Look, when I get back to the office, I'll speak to Bill about this. I'm sure he'll say he wants you to come."

Jennifer started to get up, but something told her that this conversation was not really over. "This is about more than attending the reception, isn't it? You're trying to tell me something."

With his head bowed and his hand rubbing his mustache, Steven said, "You're right. It's just starting to hit me. This little deli is a microcosm of America. The only black person in here besides you is the busboy sweeping the floor. America is so white. Because I'm white, I never think about it or notice it. You must feel like a stranger most places you go. It's not easy loving me, is it? Is what we have special enough? Do I insulate you from the harsh realities of today's world? Do I provide enough or the right kind of comfort from the storms, or are you always compromising, making excuses, looking the other way, ignoring the dirty looks, explaining stuff to me?"

Jennifer looked intently into Steven's blue eyes. "It is very easy loving you. It's harder loving you in the middle of all this." Jennifer glanced around the deli, and her eyes settled on the 1950s-style bouffant. Steven followed her gaze.

"I'm not going to let the likes of someone like her keep us apart. You're always considering my needs, my wants. I need that. You love me, and I love you."

"I want to make life easier for you, Jennifer."

Jennifer grabbed both of his hands. "Steven, I'm old enough to know now that life can be hard. But you try to make it easier. I know you've got my back. I love that about you."

❦   ❦   ❦

Jennifer raced to Bill's office. "Lucinda, does he have a couple of minutes to see me?" Lucinda stuck her head into Bill's office and then motioned to Jennifer to come in.

"Bill, I just need a couple of minutes of your time."

"Sure, Jennifer. What is it?"

"It's about tonight's reception. Steven doesn't want to come, because he feels his presence will bring back the ugly specter of the trial and he doesn't want to tarnish your big night."

Bill help up his hand, indicating that Jennifer should stop talking. "Jennifer, tell Steven I'm going to be pissed off if he doesn't show up."

"Thanks, Bill. I thought that's what you would say. I'll tell him."

❦   ❦   ❦

Approximately four months earlier, Bill Foster had stood ramrod straight in a courtroom and awaited the verdict, which could have sent him to prison. Today, he was again standing with classical military bearing but in a receiving line at the Plaza Hotel. This time, he was not awaiting a verdict but was receiving the congratulations of the members of the New York City bar association, because the president of the United States had nominated him to be the attorney general. He would be the first black person to ever hold this esteemed position. All of the partners and many of the associates from his law firm were present. The most important and influential lawyers in New York were all assembled to congratulate him on this significant achievement. This was indeed a moment of accomplishment and ultimate triumph for Foster. His supporters were proud, and his detractors were temporarily silenced.

Carol stood proudly by her husband's side, endlessly shaking the hands of the well-wishers and the hushed enemies. In the midst of all the celebration, their eyes met; they exchanged a silent look that said they each knew they had trod a long and often challenging road to reach this point. What their exchanged look acknowledged was the fact that they had come this far because they had each other's love, a love they defined as unyielding support and respect for each other mixed with a large dose of old-fashioned kindness. They both understood that his success was not just his alone, because blacks everywhere would take pride in and garner hope from his position. America was changing, and they were part of that change.

Jennifer and Steven worked their way through the crowd of well-wishers to Bill and Carol. Jennifer caught their reflection as they passed the gilt-edged mirror on the ballroom wall. She thought that Steven looked very handsome in his navy blue suit and white shirt, and she was happy and proud to have him by her side. As she reached Bill, she said, "Bill … I'm sorry … Attorney General Foster …"

Bill laughed with that big bass laugh he was known for. "Sounds good."

"Attorney General Foster, congratulations! It's been a pleasure working with you. Thank you for all of your guidance."

"Jennifer, thank you!"

Steven extended his hand and shook Bill's hand. "Congratulations, sir. The country is going to be in a better place with you at the Justice Department."

"Thank you, Steven. Did Jennifer tell you that I was going to be pissed off if you didn't come?"

With a humble smile, Steven said, "Yes, she did. I hope you know that I'm honored to be here. I was reluctant to come, because I didn't want anything to tarnish in any way this special event for you and for Jennifer."

"Steven, I respect our legal system. You're a good lawyer. Remember, I had a front-row seat and had a chance to see you in action." With that comment, they both laughed. Bill patted him on the back and then said, "You did your job, and the jury did its job! Justice was done."

Bill then grabbed both of Jennifer's hands. "Jennifer, remember, you're also a good lawyer; don't let anyone try to tell you differently. I know the firm can be a tough place. Understand?"

"I understand. I'm really going to miss you."

Placing one hand on Steven's shoulder and the other on Jennifer's shoulder, Bill said, "Maybe I can convince you two to come to Washington with me. You two would be perfect!" Their conversation was interrupted by others wanting to congratulate Bill, so Jennifer and Steven moved away, got a drink, and mingled with the other guests.

One of Steven's law school classmates joined them. Others joined the group, and they discussed what a great appointment this was. Jennifer whispered in Steven's ear, "I'm going to the ladies' room. I'll be right back."

Steven pecked her on the cheek. "I'll be right here waiting for you. Love you."

Jennifer maneuvered her way across the ballroom, stopping briefly to speak to colleagues. When she exited the ladies' room and headed back toward the ballroom, she saw David. She was surprised that her only thought was that she liked the way he looked. He was her fantasy BMIS.

David took a sip from his drink, and when he raised his head, he saw her.

"Jennifer." He turned to the man standing with him. "Jennifer Madison … Sidney Stein."

As she extended her hand to shake Stein's, she said, "Professor Stein, it's a pleasure to *finally* meet you. I've heard a lot about you from David and from Bill. I'm with Bill's firm. They both spoke very highly of you."

"Well, that's good to hear, because I think very highly of them."

Jennifer started to move away. "Well, nice to meet you."

"Jennifer, wait." David turned to Stein. "Sid, excuse me. I'll be right back." Jennifer didn't wait, and David started to walk in step with her. "Jennifer, I've been looking for you all evening. I knew you would be here."

"Of course I'd be here. I'd never miss an opportunity to support Bill."

Taking another quick sip of his drink and then staring down at the floor, he mumbled, "I miss you."

Jennifer looked at David and thought carefully about how she would respond. "I want and deserve more than merely being missed."

At that very moment, she felt a hand on her back. Steven was by her side. "Steven, I'd like you to meet David Walker. David, this is Steven Greenberg."

Steven placed his arm around Jennifer's shoulder and then extended his hand to shake David's. "Nice to meet you."

Recognizing him immediately, David said softly, "Yeah, you too."

Steven turned to Jennifer and said, "I just saw Carol, and she and Bill want us to join them in their suite after the reception for dinner with a few friends. I told her we would."

"Sounds great. David, excuse us."

Jennifer, with Steven's hand firmly on her back, walked back into the ballroom and smiled at their reflection in the ballroom's mirrored walls.

978-0-595-41773-5
0-595-41773-6

Printed in the United States
72762LV00004B/100-249

9 780595 417735